AGAINST YOUR WILL

THE DCI PETER MOONE THRILLERS BOOK 5

MARK YARWOOD

This novel is entirely a work of fiction. The names, characters and incidents portrayed in it are the work of the author's imagination. Any resemblance to actual persons, living or dead, events or localities is entirely coincidental.

BiscuitBooksPublishers © Mark Yarwood 2025

The author asserts the moral right to be identified as the author of this work Published by Amazon Kindle All rights reserved. No part of this publication may be reproduced, stored, or transmitted in any form or by means, electronic, mechanical, photocopying, recording or otherwise, without the prior permission of the publishers.

ISBN: 9798262216123

Cover design

by

Nick Castle

Respectfully dedicated to
the victims of the Plymouth Keyham
shootings, and their families.
May we never forget.

EXCLUSIVE OFFER

Look out for the link at the end of this book or visit my website at www.markyarwood.co.uk to sign up to my no-spam Monthly Murder Club and receive
two FREE and exclusive crime thrillers plus news and previews of forthcoming works.

Never miss out on a release.

No spam. You can unsubscribe at any time.

PROLOGUE

The suspect was sitting opposite Moone and Butler in the interview room, his wrists chained to the metal desk. An armed officer was standing in the corner, another one was posted just outside the door. No one was taking any chances.

The suspect had hardly moved since they brought him in. He remained sitting upright, his eyes fixed dead ahead. Moone couldn't tell if he was looking at him or through him, maybe at the wall behind him. Whichever it was, the look in his dark grey eyes gave him the creeps. Moone looked down at the file in front of him, suddenly aware of the silence expanding in the room.

'What's your name, for the recording?' Moone asked, pretending to examine his notes.

'You know my name,' the man said, his voice calm, deep and harsh.

Moone looked up and engaged those dark eyes again. There was a smirk too, an expression that seemed to say I know it all, I've won.

'Abel?' Moone said, sitting back, trying to look calm and not at all shaken by recent events. 'We know that's not your real name. None of the names you've used are yours, are they? Come on, we've got you now. We caught you. Why not tell us who you really are?'

The light flickered above them, the room going dark momentarily before it lit up again.

'Did you feel that?' their suspect asked, looking between them.

'The light?' Moone asked.

The man nodded. 'Can you feel it? The change in the air?'

'It was just a power interruption or something. Now, your name? You were going to tell us who you are and why you've done what you've done.'

The man stared at Moone for a moment, the eyes burning out to him again for a few seconds before he burst into a deep grinding laugh.

'Is something funny?' Butler snapped. 'All those dead people? All those victims of yours? Are they funny to you?'

The man turned his head slowly and took

her in as he stopped laughing. He lost any signs of amusement. 'No. They're not funny. Nothing about their deaths was funny.'

'Then why laugh?' Moone asked, the irritation starting to dig into his back and spine, bringing his muscles crashing together.

Abel leaned forward, staring. 'Because I know what's coming.'

CHAPTER 1

FOUR DAYS EARLIER

Peter Moone let out a contented sigh and leaned back against the rocks as he looked out across Firestone Bay, over the view of the kids splashing in the concrete pond and out to the sea where some swimmers were going further out. Even though it was a hot summer's day, he knew only too well the water would still be icy cold, and he shivered at the thought of it. Seagulls squawked overhead, gliding on the thermals. Beyond the bay was the dark craggy shape of Drake's Island and, for the millionth time since he'd moved to Plymouth, he wondered what it was like there. Then he stopped wondering as he felt something cold and wet trickling down his hand. He looked to see ice cream dripping down the cone Mandy Butler had just handed him and gave it a lick. He'd never been the biggest fan of ice cream but it was a scorching day and it was a refreshing change after the several hot cups of coffee he'd had that morning.

'Eat it before the seagulls come for it, Moone,' she said, then gave him the side eye that he could just see behind her sunglasses. 'Faffer.'

He smiled and tried not to think about how close he had come to telling her how he felt about her almost ten months ago. He tucked it all back into its box and breathed deeply as he licked his ice cream. They had no murders to contend with and hadn't for several months. It was a relief to deal with only minor cases of violence and some robberies. But he could already see one particular black cloud moving in, threatening to block out the summer sun.

As if she had read his mind, Butler said, 'Are you worried about the trial?'

He let out a sigh. 'Yes, I am a bit. I don't like giving evidence at the best of times but this…'

Butler took off her sunglasses as she looked at him. 'What do the prosecution think?'

'It's mostly circumstantial evidence. We're lucky we found the flat where Carthew had been staying.'

'Not luck. It's door-to-door. The owners had been away at the time, and one of the neighbours identified Carthew. Then when the SOCOs examined it, they found the blood.'

Moone nodded. 'I know. Rivers' DNA, but not a lot of it. It's all going to come down to clever argument.'

Butler licked her ice cream. 'It always does.'

'She's got Hannah Marvin KC defending her. She's very good.'

'She certainly is. But we've got Jason Harris, the star witness.'

Moone licked the sides of his cone as he saw a seagull hopping over the rocks towards him. 'If he doesn't bottle it. Or someone shives him in prison.'

'I thought your mate's mate was looking after him inside?'

'He is. Well, turns out my mate's really hard-nut mate got out a couple of months ago. But Terry promised me he's still got a couple of mates inside to protect Harris, but they're not as tasty, he said. And obviously Harris doesn't want to go to the secure wing…'

'Because that's where the nonces live.' She rolled her eyes. 'Problem is, what's that psycho cow going to say about us?'

Moone felt his chest and shoulders tighten and bunch up at the prospect of her giving evidence. He flashed back to Carthew in his bed before all the bad things had happened. 'There's a lot she could say. She could stitch us up over Parry's death.'

'No, she's got nothing there. She's got no

proof. It's your relationship with her that'll mess it up.'

Moone shook his head as he cringed. 'Please don't.'

'Well, I did try and warn you. You men, I don't know.'

'I'd like to go and sit in the public gallery tomorrow and see what each side says…'

'But you can't because you're giving evidence in the trial in a couple of days. Anyway, at least she won't be our boss. She's off the force. Here's to that.'

Butler raised her ice cream in a toast, so Moone tapped his melting ice cream against hers.

'And no murders to contend with,' he said and froze when he saw the thunder rumble over Butler's face.

'Why the bloody hell did you say that?'

'What?'

'Tempting bloody fate. You're a wally, Moone.'

He shrugged and smiled. 'It'll be fine.'

She huffed. Then she looked at him again. 'Oh, I forgot to say, we got a call from Dartmoor prison. Apparently, Paul Fabre passed away two days ago.'

Moone let out a sigh. 'Sounds awful, but thank God. He was the only one left who knew the truth about Parry.'

'We're in the clear.' Butler put her shades

back on.

Moone looked at her and felt the invisible fingers tighten around his heart. 'Are you going to the pub tonight with the team?'

'No, can't make it tonight.' She didn't look at him, just finished her ice cream.

'Oh, right. Got something on?'

'Sort of.' Her dark glasses turned to him. 'Snout out, trout.'

'Alice will be home all alone.'

She lowered her glasses and glared at him. 'She's a big girl, Pete. She can take care of herself.'

'I know. I know.' Then ringing came from Moone's pocket and they both looked at it as if it was screaming blue murder.

'You had to tempt fate, didn't you?' Butler huffed again.

Moone took out his phone and saw it was Molly calling. 'Hi, Molly. Everything OK?'

'Sort of. Are you two at Firestone Bay still?'

'We are, why?'

'It's nothing really,' she said, but not sounding convinced. 'Just a few hundred yards from you, back up Durnford Street is the Bethlehem House Care Home. Apparently one of the old dears started screaming saying there's been a murder. The person in charge said there hasn't, but apparently the old dear doesn't usually kick up a fuss. I've just got a funny feeling we should…'

Moone stood up. 'Don't worry, Molly, we'll check it out. What's the woman's name?'

'Joy Morten,' Molly said. 'Sorry again.'

'It's OK, Molly. Thanks.' He ended the call and looked at Butler who was shaking her head.

'I told you.' She stood up, giving him the evil eye.

'It's not a body or anything. We've just got a report of a resident at Bethlehem House saying there's been a murder.'

'Bethlehem House?' Butler pointed upwards, somewhere behind him. 'That's it there.'

Moone turned and saw the large brown brick building sitting on the edge of the cliff that looked quite eerie and forbidding to him. As they went up the steep steps, heading back to their car that was parked in Devil's Point car park, Butler said, 'So someone in the care home has reported a murder?'

He shrugged and puffed his way up the steps, feeling the sun roasting the back of his neck. 'One of the residents. Joy Morten.'

Butler stopped dead and looked at him, her eyes wide.

'What?' he asked.

'Joy Morten? Morten? Morte?'

He shrugged so she huffed and pulled out her phone. 'Doesn't that mean death or something? I'll Google it.'

Moone continued walking as the heat

swamped him, making him feel tired all over. He tried not to think of the trial, to put it back in its box but before he knew it, the whole affair was already playing on a big screen in his head.

'I told you!' Butler called out from behind him, but he kept walking to their car. 'Morte. Means death. Bloody hell. We're about to meet a woman who's basically called Joy Death.'

Moone unlocked the car, opened the driver's door and felt the thick wave of heat radiate out and hit him.

'I'll drive,' Butler said and took the keys off him. 'You'll get us killed the way you drive.'

Butler drove them the short way down to Bethlehem House and took them around to the rear of the building which was the side that had a stunning view of the sea. The old building featured large arched windows designed in an ecclesiastical style, similar to a church. Moone noticed the small camera above the glass entrance doors as they approached.

'This place used to be run by nuns,' Butler said as she pressed the intercom. 'Still might be for all I know.'

'As long as they don't start singing about rainbows on kittens and parcels and stuff.'

'What the hell're you talking about?'

The intercom buzzed and saved Moone from explaining his badly worded joke.

'Bethlehem House Care Home,' a woman's

voice said loudly. 'How can I help you?'

Moone held up his ID to the camera as he said, 'DCI Peter Moone and DI Mandy Butler. We've come to talk to Joy Morten.'

The door made a loud buzzing sound and then clicked open. Moone grabbed the door and held it open for Butler.

'You're such a gentleman, I don't think.' Butler walked across the wide-open wood-effect flooring towards a white reception desk that was surrounded by potted plants. There were doors off to different sections which looked like they belonged in a hospital. In fact, Moone thought the whole place looked as if it could have been a nice new large wing snapped off of Derriford Hospital.

'Mrs Morten is in the chapel at the moment,' the receptionist said. She was a woman in her forties, with greying brown hair and a round, friendly face.

'Where's the chapel?' Butler asked.

The receptionist looked beyond them and towards the other side of the room where a younger woman, decked out in a green nurse's tunic, her blonde hair tied back, was looking in some medicine cupboards.

'Yaz,' the receptionist called out. 'Can you show these detectives to the chapel? They want Joy.'

Butler looked at the young nurse coming towards her as she said, 'We could definitely do with some joy.'

'Chapel's at the end of this corridor,' Yaz said, smiling and pointing to another set of brown hospital-style doors opposite the reception. 'Follow me.'

'So this Joy just started screaming murder?' Butler said as they went down a long corridor, past a large lounge area and a breakfast room.

'That's right,' Yaz said. 'You could hear her all over the place. It's not like her at all. Usually, she's either sat in her room or the lounge just staring into space. I mean, she's sometimes a bit more lively, but today she was screaming and hollering.'

'And now?' Moone asked.

Yaz stopped as they came to a set of large arched wooden doors marked "Chapel" and faced Moone and Butler, arms folded. 'She's back to nothing now. Just staring.'

'And no murders?' Butler said.

Yaz shrugged. 'Not that I've seen. Perhaps she was watching repeats of Midsomer Murders and got confused.'

'A not very realistic TV show,' Butler said as she pushed through the doors and entered the hexagonal-shaped room with a domed roof. At the far end was the altar and neat rows of pews faced it. The sunlight beamed in through a window that had a large wooden crucifix running through its centre. Another nurse, this one in her fifties by the look, with a sour face and short greying dark hair, was sitting with an elderly lady on the front row of the pews.

Moone followed Butler as she walked and stood by the elderly lady and the older care assistant.

'Joy?' Butler said and the carer looked up at her with a nod.

'That's right,' the carer said and smiled at the old lady who seemed to be staring into space.

'We're from the police,' Moone said and showed his ID. 'Apparently, Joy was screaming about a murder?'

The carer let out a deep sigh. 'She was, bless her. Weren't you, my luvva? Not now though. She has moments when she's lucid, but then she'll go back to this. Poor girl.'

'Alzheimer's?' Butler said.

'Yeah, such a shame,' the carer said and patted Joy's leg. 'Nature is cruel.'

'It is.'

Moone came around to get a better look at the old dear and crouched down to see into her grey, watery eyes. He flinched when those eyes jumped to him, her pale, wrinkled face turning to take him in.

'Peter?' the old lady croaked.

Moone stood up straight and looked at Butler who had her eyebrows practically jumping off her face.

'Do you know her?' Butler asked.

'No, I don't think so.'

'Oh, Peter, look at you, all grown up and off to school,' Joy said, smiling. 'Is it school photo day?'

Moone didn't know what to say so looked at the carer and Butler and saw they were both waiting for him to reply. He sighed, crouched down and said, 'That's right. School photo day. Do I look OK?'

'You look helluva 'ansome,' she said. 'Would you be a luv, and pop to c'wop for me? Get me some of those custard creams.'

Moone smiled. 'Of course. Joy, why did you say they'd been a murder?'

He noticed the smile seemed to wash away from her face, her eyes lowering. 'You're too young to be talking 'bout such things.'

'Did you see someone get hurt?'

She looked at him. 'A long time ago.'

'You saw someone get hurt a long time ago?' Butler asked. 'Was someone murdered, Joy?'

The woman turned her watery eyes to Butler, her mouth opening and closing for a while before she said, 'Is this real?'

'Is this real? What do you mean?'

'Is this real?' Joy put her head down and started babbling quietly to herself so Moone straightened up and looked at the carer.

'It doesn't look like there's been a murder,' Moone said. 'At least not lately. Thank you.'

'No, thank you for coming to see her. You enjoyed it, didn't you, Joy?'

The old woman kept on babbling, so Moone took out his card and handed it to the carer. 'If anything occurs or if she becomes more lucid, give me a call.'

'I will,' the carer said and smiled.

Moone signalled for Butler to follow him out and they headed through the chapel and back towards Yaz who was waiting by the door for them.

'I thought you'd want to know her nephew's here,' Yaz said as she opened the chapel doors for them. 'He's the only one who visits her really.'

'That's a shame,' Butler said as they headed through to the reception area again. 'Was she married, do you know, or have any children?'

Yaz shrugged. 'I think she was married. Not sure.'

'I wonder if she had a kid called Peter,' Moone said but Yaz just shrugged again. Moone looked at the reception desk and saw a tall man standing there dressed in black. He was of average build and probably in his late forties with greying short brown hair brushed forward.

Moone took out his ID and showed it to

the man. 'I'm DCI Peter Moone. Are you Joy Morten's nephew?'

The man nodded. 'I am. Everything all right?'

'Apparently she was screaming there's been a murder,' Butler said.

The man looked surprised. 'A murder? That's a new one. I'm afraid my aunt is a little... well, her mind isn't quite there.'

'Does she have any children?' Moone asked.

'No, no children.'

Moone nodded. 'Does she know a Peter?'

The man smiled. 'My middle name's Peter. Adam Peter Morten. She used to call me Peter, actually.'

Moone let out a laugh. 'Ah, I see. Now it makes sense. OK. That's fine. Right then, we'll leave you to your visit.'

Moone walked away with Butler behind him and went through the exit and back out into the hot day. The heat rushed at him again and dampened his back and sides.

'That was strange,' Butler said as they headed to their car and climbed in.

Moone stared at the wide stretch of building with its massive arched windows. 'It was, wasn't it? That was a coincidence with the whole Peter business, wasn't it?'

Butler started the engine. 'It was. You should've seen your face when she said your name.'

He laughed but there was a strange feeling that had settled into his chest. Since he had seen the old lady and looked into her grey eyes, he almost had the sense that he'd seen her before somewhere. It was a strange sensation, as if the memory might develop and pop into his brain, but nothing came.

'What is it?' Butler asked as she reversed and then turned them back around to face the exit. 'You've got a weird look on your face like someone not only walked on your grave but took a piss on it.'

'Funny. I feel like I've seen her before.'

'How could you? Unless you met her in the last three years, I suppose. Or you've been to Plymouth before...'

He looked at her. 'I have.'

'You have? When?'

'When I was a kid. My mum and dad brought us here when we were young. We did tours of the coast. I'd practically forgotten all about that.'

Butler laughed. 'Little Moone on the Plymouth beaches. Oh my God, what if we met when we were younger? I mean you would've been a teenager and I would've been a toddler.'

'Very bloody funny.' Moone looked at the building in the rear-view mirror and felt his former strange sensation change to an echo of the past almost. Had he met the old lady before? He decided he would have to look into it.

'You said we. Who's we?'

'What?' Moone looked at her.

Butler side eyed him again. 'You said your mum and dad brought us to Plymouth. Who's us?'

'Oh, yeah, my sister.'

Butler stared at him, looking flabbergasted. 'You've got a bloody sister? Since when?'

'Since always. She's three years older. Haven't seen her for a long time.'

'A sister?' Butler shook her head. 'Just when you think you know Peter Moone, sisters start coming out of the woodwork. What's she called, this sister?'

'Kelly.'

'Kelly Moone,' Butler said and let out a laugh. 'Turns out Peter Moone still has some mysteries. How many other secrets are you keeping?'

He smiled then looked towards the road as they passed the Hoe and the untidy trail of humans, young and old that flickered past. There was only one secret he could think of, and it was one he could never tell her about. The moment seemed to have passed and was probably best forgotten.

It was hours later that the man in the black

baseball cap and sunglasses opened the garage door and slipped under it. He switched on the lights as they flickered above, illuminating the long narrow space that had once been filled with all kinds of junk, dust and cobwebs. It had taken a week to clear it out, and now the whitewashed brick walls had boards screwed to them. The boards had photos of the city and maps pinned to them. His notes were printed on the maps and the sheets of A4 he had stapled alongside everything else. He stood there for a while, looking it over, reading everything. He stared at the photo he'd pinned at the centre of it all. Then he turned away and moved to the small shelving unit he'd put up and filled with his notebooks. Under that was the medium-sized safe he had bought second hand. He patted it with his gloved hand and then looked at the notebooks and removed one and stared at the cover.

'Abel's book one,' he read to himself and opened it up and started to pore over the words written in his own small, neat handwriting. It was all there. The truth. The truth that only he could see among all the things that had happened, the moments that raced past, seemingly not connected. No one else could see it.

He closed the book and held it to his chest and closed his eyes. Even through his closed eyes, he felt it and saw it too, like a hum of electricity passing through everything. He opened his eyes as the light above him flickered and went out, leaving him in the warm darkness for a moment. Then the lights came back on and he nodded, sure that he was reading the signs. He put the book back with a trembling hand and then crouched down by the safe. He pressed the keys on the pad and then opened the metal door and looked inside at the wires and electronic equipment he had gathered together. He reached in and took out the knife and slipped it into his black hoodie as he stood up. He looked at his watch. It was almost time, so he opened up the garage door and slipped out. He looked around the quiet street and the other detached houses. Coach houses, they called them, with their little garages attached. Sherford seemed like the perfect place to set up his base of operations, far enough away from the city centre and prying eyes.

He walked to the old banger he'd bought cheap and climbed in. He started it up, letting it turn over, hearing it grumble. He drove away and took the narrow roads towards Plymouth, avoiding the traffic cameras as best he could. His biggest risk would be the Tamar Bridge. But it didn't really matter as long as he got to where he was going. Nothing really mattered but what happened next.

He took the roads through Plymouth

then over the bridge and turned off towards Waitrose. He turned again, heading for the Tamar View industrial estate. Beyond the line of shop units and the large kitchen outlet, there was a strip of littered grass and old thick trees. Behind that was a battered fence that lined mostly empty fields. He could see the blue van parked up close to the entrance to the field. He pulled in close to the van, then climbed out. He saw the thick-set man look at him in the rearview mirror then hesitate before he climbed out. He was a short muscular man squeezed into a tight black t-shirt. He pulled his NY baseball cap down over his face as he walked over to Abel with a nod.

'Bit reckless this, mate,' the man said, looking around the estate. 'I couldn't see any cameras though.'

'There aren't any,' Abel said and pointed to the van. 'Did you bring what I wanted?'

The man chewed the inside of his mouth as he looked at his van, then nodded and opened up the back doors. There were some plumbing supplies on one side, next to a large metal box that the muscle man opened. He pulled on some blue surgical gloves then took out a semi-automatic Glock and briefly showed it to Abel before putting it back in its case.

'That and the ammunition are a grand,' the man said.

'The assault rifle?'

'It's here,' the man patted a bag next to the metal box. 'Three grand all together. You got it?'

Abel looked in at the bag, nodded and faced the man. 'Yes, I've got it. The cash is in my car.'

'Mate, what do you want all this for? Don't seem like home defence.'

'These are dangerous times. We can't even trust our own governments. Can we?'

The arms dealer gave him a strange look. 'You ain't gonna start going after people, are you? I can't sell all this to a nutter who's gonna... I don't know...'

Abel stepped closer and smiled as he slipped his hand into his pocket. 'You've got nothing to worry about. The police won't bother you.'

'I hope not, mate.'

Abel lurched at him and wrapped his arm around his neck as he brought up his knife and stuck it into his side. The man grunted and tried to break free, but he held him tight as he jabbed it in several more times. He looked over his shoulder as he let the man fall back against the vehicle. Then he lifted the dead man's legs and swung him round and stuffed him into the back of the van. He grabbed the weapons and put them into the boot of his car. After he made sure the arms dealer was fully in the back of the van, he shut the doors and went back to his car and started the engine. He looked around and saw no one nearby, no one looking his way. It was all playing out as it should. He started to drive, thinking about the night to come and the mayhem he would unleash.

CHAPTER 2

When Moone entered the incident room, he saw Molly Chambers at her desk, typing away and busy as always. He started to clap loudly, making the rest of the team look round at him as he walked towards her desk.

'There she is,' Moone said, smiling at her and still clapping. Much to Molly's embarrassment, the rest of the team was standing up and applauding. 'Detective Sergeant Molly Chambers. Well done. See, I told you you'd ace the sergeant exam, didn't I?'

She blushed as she nodded and looked around the room awkwardly. 'Yeah, you did. I still can't believe it.'

'Well done, you,' DI Anna Jones said as she came over from her desk, which had previously been Carthew's desk. She was a welcome recruit to the team as she had a much sunnier outlook than Carthew and was definitely less of a sociopath.

'Don't forget drinks down the Dolphin tonight,' Butler said, appearing next to Moone.

'Oh yeah,' Molly said, still blushing. 'Can you make it now?'

'No, sorry, Molly, I can't,' Butler said. 'But I'll try and pop in later if I can.'

'I'll be there for a bit,' Harding said, poking his head over his monitor. 'Only for a while though. If I'm not home early to help get Ava to sleep there'll be hell to pay.'

Moone walked over to his desk and could already see the dark circles under Harding's eyes. It had been a long time since he'd had to change a nappy or try and calm a screaming baby who was teething, but he still felt his pain. 'How's life as a father going?'

Harding shrugged. 'You know, OK, usual. Not enough sleep... and, well...'

'What?'

'I just don't feel like we've bonded yet. It's all time spent with Mummy. I don't get a look in.'

Moone smiled. 'Yep, I remember those days. But it'll come. It won't be long before she's a daddy's girl and you'll be moaning you don't get time to yourself. Just you wait.'

Harding was about to say something else, but the incident room door opened and

Inspector Kevin Pinder came hurrying in.

'Sorry to break up the party,' Pinder said, looking at Moone, 'but looks like we've got a DB. Looks like a stabbing in Saltash.'

Moone automatically looked towards Butler and saw that she was giving him the evil eye already.

'I told you, didn't I?' Butler said. 'You and your big mouth, Peter Moone. When will you learn? Come on, stop faffing.'

When Butler had disappeared through the incident room doors, Pinder gave him his knowing look as his eyebrows raised.

'Don't,' Moone said. 'Don't say a word.'

'I wasn't going to say anything, boss,' Pinder said, following him out into the corridor. Then Moone heard him singing, *'Love is in the air...'*

The uniforms from Saltash Police Station had already done an exceptional job of sealing off the area and creating a cordon. There was a SOCO tent already set up by the bank of grass and the cluster of trees. Moone recognised one of the uniforms as PC Pippa Cummings, a ruddy-faced and stocky police officer who certainly knew how to do her job. As Butler parked up on the edge of the industrial estate, close to the kitchen outlet, PC Cummings came over, her hands resting on her stab vest.

'Afternoon, Pippa,' Moone said. 'I see

you've got things in hand. Great job.'

'Don't take any notice,' Butler said as she stood behind him. 'He's just a natural sycophant. Do you know who the victim is?'

Pippa smiled and then pointed to the tent where the SOCOs were entering. 'In that tent is a van that belongs to Ryan Preston. Mr Preston is a plumber by trade.'

Moone scratched his head. 'Someone stabbed a plumber? Maybe a rival plumber?'

Butler sighed. 'What? Are you thinking this is a plumbers' turf war? Come off it. What about drugs? Maybe he had a sideline.'

'Oh, I think he had a sideline all right,' PC Cummings said. 'We found a metal box in the back of his van with some ammunition inside.'

'Selling weapons?' Moone said and looked around the estate. 'No CCTV around here. Perfect place to meet and hand over the merchandise.'

'So rather than pay,' Butler said, 'the buyer stabs him to death. Nice.'

'Means there's someone out there who just bought a gun or guns,' Moone said. 'Firearm offences are up,' Butler said. 'Record high for Devon and Cornwall. Could be a drug dealer arming up, or someone planning a robbery.'

Moone nodded. 'Could be. Probably is. Well, let's check all the ANPR and CCTV nearby and see if we can spot how our killer and our victim got here. Let's look into the victim's life, see if he had any rivals in the arms dealing world, or anything else that turns up. Get your people knocking on the businesses around here, see what they know. Thank you, Pippa.'

Butler and Moone turned away and started towards their car where Inspector Pinder was waiting, leaning on their vehicle.

'I hope you're not scratching the paintwork, Kev,' Butler said, tutting.

Kev stood up, rolling his eyes at Moone. 'No, I was careful, Mand. Just wanted a word with DCI Moone.'

Butler looked between them both, suspiciously. 'All right, I can see I'm not wanted. There's a lovely bakery down the road, think I'll get myself a pink iced finger. Anyone else fancy a finger?'

Butler walked off laughing to herself, so Moone faced Pinder who he couldn't help but notice had a worried expression dug into his usual jovial face. 'You OK, Kev? You look worried.'

Pinder nodded. 'I am a bit. It's the trial. I've got to give evidence relating to the search of her car and God knows what else.'

'Just tell them what happened. I put the search team together because you had intel that the Dark Horses were going to move their drugs and then you spotted Carthew hanging around with them. Hence why I decided to send that undercover officer to Harris' place to check out what was going on. He ends up getting assaulted by Carthew and we arrest her and search her car. Which we were legally within our rights to do. Job done. It's down to me, not you.'

Pinder didn't look convinced. 'What about all the other stuff she's done? It's not just Redrobe and Rivers, is it? It's Armstrong and the rest. And our boss and his wife.'

Moone sighed. 'I know. But we've got nothing tying her to that, and we can't just bring it up at the trial. It's the two murders. That's what she's going down for. For a long time, I hope.'

Pinder nodded. 'I hope you're right. It's just that she's clever and she's got a very good, very clever barrister.'

'Hannah Marvin, KC. I know. It's going to be OK. Just give your evidence and that's all. Let me worry about the rest.'

Pinder managed a smile. 'OK, I'll try.'

'Right,' Moone said, rubbing his hands together and trying not to let on how worried he was too. 'Let's find out who murdered our plumber.'

There was the thunderous noise from below, the laughing and shouting travelling through the entire wing. Jason Harris was sitting on his bunk looking towards the open door of his cell, listening to the usual prison life below.

Occasionally another prisoner would walk past, sometimes laughing about something or maybe shouting or moaning, He couldn't get used to it, just couldn't make it sit right in his head. They had fucked him over. No. She had fucked him over, that bitch. He leaned over, grasped his head and closed his eyes.

'Hey, you fuckin' coming or what?'

Harris sat up and saw Wes leaning against the door frame, looking at him like he was wearing a dress.

'What the fuck's wrong with you?' Wes said and came in. He was a big lad, arms as thick as tree trunks. He'd told Jason that he used to be a champion bodybuilder, but he said the steroids fucked with his head. That's why he stabbed his girlfriend and her dad. Yeah right, Jason thought, but didn't suggest it was less to do with steroids and more the fact that he was a big nutter with a short fuse. But he was protecting Jason from being stabbed to death, so he had to be diplomatic.

'Who's out there?' Jason asked.

Wes shrugged. 'Every fucker. Come on, you big jessie, get out here. You can't hide in 'ere or they'll know you're scared.'

'I'm not scared.' Jason stood up. 'I just don't trust the bastards. You don't know the bastards who're after me.'

'Na, but you got me now, ain't yer?' Wes flexed his massive bicep and grinned. 'I told

Terry I'd look after yer and that's what I plan to do.'

'What're you two up to?' a familiar scouse voice said behind the massive mountain that was Wes. 'Out the way, Batley, you lard arse.'

Wes stepped back, revealing the short and stocky screw, Mr Loughty. He was shaking his head and smiling. His eyes, which were buried deep in his pasty skin, jumped to Harris.

'Youse alright, son?' the screw asked. 'This lard arse not giving you any trouble, is he?'

'You know me, Mr Loughty,' Wes said. 'Gentle giant I am.'

'Gentle giant?' Loughty rolled his eyes at Harris. 'Nothin' gentle 'bout you, lad. Now, clear off, would ya? Give us some privacy.'

Wes looked a little pissed off as he stared at Harris. Jason nodded, so the big man turned and sloped out of the cell.

When they were alone, Loughty reached into his pocket, took out some tinfoil and unwrapped it to reveal six cigarettes. 'Here, thought you could do with these, lad.'

Harris looked at the fags being held out to him, then up at the screw.

'Now don't look at me like that, lad,' the screw said. 'Look, I like to look after the fellas on my wing. Especially the ones finding themselves serving time for the first time. I treat youse right and youse don't give me no bother. Right? Go on, take 'em, don't be daft.'

Harris weighed it up and, even though he still harboured his suspicions, he decided not taking them might cause offence. 'Thanks.'

'You're welcome.' Loughty sat down on the bunk opposite and looked around the cell. 'I know it's hard, lad. Finding yourself locked up in here... but yous got to find the strength inside yourself to get through each day. And youse got to walk out there and face the other inmates. Youse can't stay in here, 'cause they'll notice and they'll think to themselves, what's he scared of? It'll be a target on ya back that fear. I know, I know, youse were one of the Dark Horses and they've got people in here looking for you. Well, they're on another wing, lad, so youse ain't got nothin' to worry 'bout. I'm keeping an eye out for ya, so is big Wes by the look.'

Loughty stood up, stretched and stifled a yawn. 'So, youse get yourself out there, even if ya stand on the landing and have a look round. Show them youse not scared. Got it?'

Harris nodded.

The screw smiled. 'Good lad. Enjoy the fags. I'll see youse around. I'm never far away.'

Loughty strolled out the door, whistling to himself. Harris stared towards the open door, listening to the constant clatter of prison life, the shouts and swearing. He looked at his hands and saw they were shaking while his heart thumped. He took a deep breath and pushed himself to his feet and took a few steps towards the cell door. He paused then went out and stood on the landing. He moved out of the way when some of the inmates barged past, chatting. He leaned against the railing and looked down at the crowds of his fellow inmates. He looked across the way and saw more of them standing near their open cells. A couple turned his way, eyeing him, so he made sure he stared them down. With Wes and Loughty looking after him, it would be all right, and he'd give his evidence in court and then he'd do his best to forget all about the Dark Horses and that bitch. He would make it to the trial and stare that bitch right in the eyes.

Moone looked down at the paper bag he was holding as Butler took them towards North Prospect, or Swilly as people still liked to call it. He wasn't quite sure why it was called Swilly, but he thought he'd heard it had to do with pigs or pig farming. The pasty he was holding was warming his hands, making them even sweatier.

'Do you want to stop and eat this?' Moone asked and Butler glared at him.

'Not in the car, wally,' she said. 'I don't want crumbs everywhere and the whole interior stinking like sweat. Here we go.'

Butler turned off North Prospect Road and parked up. The house they wanted was one of the new builds that had been constructed a few years back when they knocked down most of the old houses that lined North Prospect. This had taken place not long after Moone arrived. The place had changed a lot in that time, but there was much of the same vibe he felt as they climbed out. The people were the same, far friendlier than the London crowd. Yes, there were troublemakers like there are in any major city, but on the whole, he found he liked the locals. In fact, wasn't he one of the locals now?

'When do I get my Plymouth passport?' Moone asked as they walked up the short concrete path to the third box-like new build set on the opposite side to the row of shops and the library.

'Never,' Butler snorted. 'You'll never be a true Plymothian. Definitely never a Janner. You have to be born and bred here. Like me.'

Butler rang the bell of the house and Moone thought he could hear the cries and the familiar raucous noise of family life. A life he seemed too far from now. 'I don't think I'd fit in back in the smoke any more.'

Butler looked him over, seeming to scrutinise him. 'No, I'm not sure where you'd fit in. Hang on, isn't the pace of life a helluva lot faster in London?'

'Yes, it is. Everyone rushing everywhere. I don't miss that.'

'How did you survive with all your

faffing? I'm surprised you weren't trampled underfoot.'

'Very funny.'

The door opened and a dark-haired young woman, probably in her late twenties, appeared looking a little flustered. She was made up the way a lot of women were these days, he noticed, with all the thick brown makeup carefully put on to make them look pretty much identical to the next young woman. She wore a low-cut top that her large breasts were trying to squeeze out of. Moone made sure he kept his eyes up as he showed his ID and said, 'I'm DCI Peter Moone. This is DI Mandy Butler. We're sorry to disturb you, but we'd like to talk to you about Ryan Preston. You are Danni James?'

The young woman straightened up and pulled some of her jet-black hair from her face as she looked at them with suspicion. 'What about Ryan? What's he gone and done now?'

'Can we come in?' Moone asked, gesturing to the narrow, white-painted hallway behind her. The sound of kids shouting and playing echoed out to them.

'Hang on a minute,' Danni said, putting her hands on her hips. 'Why're you here harassing me? Me and Ryan ain't together no more. I've still got to look after his daughter, but me and him are done with.'

Moone looked in the hallway, thinking of

the daughter about to lose a father. His heart clenched as he imagined someone knocking on Alice's door with bad news. 'I think we'd better come in.'

She must have sensed something bad coming, and so Danni James let them in and told them to go into the small kitchen on the right, while she shouted at the kids in the front room.

'You lot keep quiet!'

'Try and keep your eyes off her boobs, Moone,' Butler whispered. 'I saw you looking.'

'I wasn't looking...' Moone stopped speaking when the young woman came into the kitchen, arms folded across her chest.

'Go on then, tell me,' she said and there was a tremor to her voice. 'Hurry up. Something bad's happened, hasn't it?'

Moone took a breath. He hated this bit. 'I'm sorry, but Ryan was found dead a few hours ago.'

The woman stared for a moment, then she shuddered as the tears came. Surprisingly it was Butler who went over and put a supportive hand on her shoulder as Danni James sobbed. She said all the right things, it seemed to Moone, all the things he could never seem to find to say. He found himself watching Butler, seeing the kindness and even the soft side coming out from under her gruff facade. His heart thumped faster, the old yearning reaching out, the way it had in previous months before he had managed to get a hold of it. Back to square one, he said to himself and sighed.

'Don't just stand there looking gormless,' Butler said. 'Make a cup of tea. Come on, Danni, sit down.'

Moone put on the kettle while Butler sat the poor woman at the small round kitchen table then sat down opposite her.

'What happened to him?' Danni asked, the tears still pouring.

'I'm afraid he was stabbed,' Butler said.

'Stabbed? Ryan? Oh God. What am I going to tell Daisy?' Danni asked through her tears and streaked mascara.

'Is that his daughter?' Butler asked.

Danni sniffed and nodded. 'Yeah, oh God, she worships him… she's gonna be heartbroken.'

'Is there anyone we can call?' Moone asked.

'I'll get my mum round,' the young woman said.

'We can get a family liaison officer for you,' Butler said, then after a pause, said, 'Ryan was a plumber, was he?'

She nodded, still wiping her face. 'Yeah, but he didn't like it. He was always looking to make more cash.'

'Did he have any sidelines, Danni?'

She looked at her, narrowing her eyes.

'What do you mean, sidelines?'

Moone finished making her tea and put it in front of her. 'We're just trying to find out why someone might want to kill Ryan. Did he mix in any dangerous circles?'

She shrugged, but Moone could see there was something there, something in her eyes that she didn't know how, or didn't want to communicate.

'You can talk to us,' Butler said. 'We want to find out who might want to kill Ryan. You see, Danni, we found bullets in the back of his van. Do you know why he would have anything like that in his van?'

She looked down. 'I don't know really. But I know... one time he came here and asked me if he could leave a bag here for the afternoon. This was a couple of months ago. It was heavy so when he was gone, I took a look. He had some tools in there, but there was a gun too. I couldn't believe he'd brought a fucking gun into our home. His daughter lives here and he brings a bloody gun here. I gave him an earful. I didn't want to know why he had a gun. I just told him to take the bag and never to bring anything like that here again.'

Moone nodded and looked up as he heard a young girl's voice calling out for her mum. Danni burst into tears again then breathed it all back down and wiped her eyes. She got up and went to the doorway and shouted that she'd be there in a moment. The poor young woman turned and looked at them both, the same question in her eyes. Moone didn't know what to say as usual so let Butler do her thing. He went back to thinking, running it all through his empty skull, wondering why a plumber might have bullets in his van, and a gun. He was starting to believe their first conclusion that Ryan had been selling guns on the side. But where would a Plymouth plumber get hold of guns to sell? Moone cleared his throat. 'I'm sorry, Danni, but do you know of anyone who might know something about why Ryan would have a gun, or bullets in his van?'

She shrugged, her eyes red and puffy. 'I don't know. Maybe one of his mates. I never got on with them, a couple of 'em tried it on with me. I told him but he just laughed it off like it was a joke. But come to think of it, there is one of his mates who's a right dodgy character. He's been in trouble with your lot a few times.'

'Can you give us a name?' Butler asked, taking out her notebook and pen.

'Stuart…', she started to say, then stopped as a worried expression came over her face. 'I don't want to start any trouble.'

'This Stuart, whoever he is,' Butler said, 'isn't going to find out you gave us his name. And you have my word, I'm not going to let him hurt you or your family. All right?'

Danni nodded, seeming to swallow down

more tears. 'Stuart Pusey.'

Butler nodded and put her notebook away. 'I know Stuart Pusey.'

'Who is he?' Moone asked.

'Right lowlife,' she said and stood up. 'Right, Danni, I'm going to get our family liaison officer to call in on you. I know you'll have your mum here, but I just want to make sure you're OK and safe. All right?'

Danni nodded then stood up but Butler held up her hand. 'You stay there, we'll see ourselves out.'

When they were outside on the street, as the late afternoon gave a last blast of heat, Moone said, 'You were great in there.'

Butler shot him one of her Medusa looks. 'Why do you sound so surprised? I'm a lovely caring person. That poor cow in there and her little girl. Some bastard's taken away her father and I'm going to find out who. Let's go and talk to Stuart Pusey.'

As they walked back to their car and climbed in, Moone said, 'So how do you know this Stuart Pusey?'

'I was at school with his older brother, Scott,' she said with a huff as she started the engine and drove them off.

'Is there anyone in Plymouth you didn't go to school with?'

'Be thankful I did,' she said with a tut. 'Stuart was always in trouble, right from being a nipper. Theft. Drugs. You name it. Oh, and I hope you've got your running shoes on.'

Moone sighed. 'He's not a runner, is he?'

'Oh yeah, little scrawny bastard who's fast on his feet. And seeing as you're about the slowest man on his feet, we might be in trouble.'

'Thanks for that. Where are we heading?'

'St Budeaux, Berthon Road. That's where his aunt lives and last thing I heard he was staying with her. Get ready, Moone, 'cause you're about to meet a right pair.'

CHAPTER 3

Butler parked a little way from the box-like house that looked to Moone as if it had been painted white at one time but was now grey and stained by the rain.

Beside the green front door, a block-like extension jutted out from the house, resembling a shed.

'Let me handle this,' Butler said, while Moone looked over the rest of the street, the other houses, the thick line of trees and the football pitch in the distance.

'It's all yours.'

Butler rang the doorbell and rattled the letterbox, then stood back so she could be seen through the front windows. It was a couple of minutes later that a squat, elderly lady with short grey hair, dressed in a heavy metal T-shirt and jeans, answered the door. Her face was set in a narrow-eyed stare as she looked them both over.

'What do you lot want?' she asked, a cigarette coming from around her back and into her wrinkled lips.

'Is Stuart here?' Butler asked, folding her arms over her chest.

'What, have you come to ask him out to play, Mandy?' the woman said with a smirk and sucked at her cigarette. 'Yeah, I recognise you, Mandy Butler. I 'eard you was a rozza, but didn't 'ardly believe it.'

'Where is he, Pat? We just want a word with him.'

'Not 'ere, is he?' Pat said and rolled her eyes up and down Moone. 'Who's this when he's at 'ome?'

Moone showed his ID. 'DCI Peter Moone.'

'DCI?' Pat snorted out a laugh. 'We are 'onoured. How's your old man, Mand?'

Butler huffed. 'He's dead. And you know that, Pat. Now where is he? His mate, Ryan, was murdered today.'

The old lady flinched to life, the anger flicking in her eyes as she poked the fag in Butler's direction. 'Oi, you ain't fitting him up with that. Stuart don't go round murdering his mates. And you're cakey if you thinks he did!'

'Then he should talk to us,' Butler said, then her head turned at the same time that

Moone thought he heard something being knocked over round the back of the house. Something smashed, and then there were shoes slapping at the ground.

'He's making a run for it!' Butler shouted at Moone. As she tried to give chase, Pusey's Aunty Pat grabbed hold of Butler by her jacket.

'Get off, you stupid mare!' Butler growled and then stared at Moone. 'Get him!'

Moone didn't hesitate and ran round the back of the houses where there was a high stone wall. Each property had its own back gate. One of them was swinging open, and when Moone spun around he saw a skinny figure running full pelt across the path and towards the football pitch where some kids were having a kick around. Moone took a breath and started running again, pumping his arms and moving his legs as fast as he could. Pusey was skinny like a greyhound and fast like one too and was making his way across the football pitch at speed. There seemed no way Moone could catch up with him until the skinny man started to cough and splutter halfway across the pitch. He had stopped and was bent over, throwing up on the ground. Moone started to slow down as he approached Pusey and watched as he spat on the ground, the kids looking on in a disgusted kind of amusement.

'Stuart Pusey,' Moone started to say

between pants as he took out his ID.

He didn't see the bony fist coming, just the skinny man spinning around, his wild eyes flashing. The knuckles hit his nose, sending a spike of pain through his skull and tears to his eyes as he stumbled backwards.

Pusey had started running again, but then a dark shape came gliding through the air and hit him and knocked him rolling to the grass. Butler jumped up, huffing and puffing as she grabbed the skinny man, yanked his hands behind his back and cuffed him.

'Stuart Pusey,' she said, as she yanked him to his feet. 'I'm arresting you for assaulting a police officer. You do not have to say anything, but it may harm your defence if you do not mention when questioned something which you later rely on in court. Anything you do say may be given in evidence. Have you got that, Stuart?'

'Oh fuck off!' he shouted, then stared at the kids. 'What you little shits lookin' at?'

'A paedo!' one of the kids laughed, then they all joined in as they chanted 'paedo' over and over as Moone and Butler marched Pusey back to their car.

It was getting towards evening by the time Stuart Pusey was booked in down at the custody suite, where the sergeant in charge talked to the skinny habitual criminal like they were old mates. He was put in a cell for a while and then checked over to make sure he was well enough to be interviewed. His clothes were taken for forensic examination and he was given a hoodie and jogging bottoms from lost property to wear. They were far too big and made him look like a kid playing dress-up.

Moone's nose still stung but had stopped bleeding at least. He had to stop himself from laughing as Pusey was delivered to the interview room in his oversized clothes where he and Butler were waiting. It wasn't long after Pusey arrived, giving them both the dead stare, that the duty solicitor came rushing in panting and sweating. He was a tall, lanky Indian man in a pinstripe suit who sat down and then smiled at everyone in turn as he said, 'Sorry, my car wouldn't start. I haven't had a chance to talk to my client.'

'Fuck that,' Pusey said and snorted, still staring at them both in turn. 'I've played this game before.'

Butler sighed and shook her head as she announced that she was recording the interview and read out who was present.

'So, Stuart,' Butler said when all the formalities were out of the way, 'you're still living with your Aunty Pat? Patricia Pusey of Eleven Berthon Road, St Budeaux? That right?'

'It's temporary.' Pusey leaned back in his seat and looked over at the wall.

Butler laughed. 'Temporary? To my understanding, it's been about ten years now.'

He sent daggers her way as he said, 'Well, it's hard to get on the fuckin' property ladder these days, or don't you pay fuckin' attention?'

'Oh yeah, it's hard if you're a thieving, drug dealing so and so.'

'I don't think we're here to discuss my client's history,' the solicitor said as he leaned forward.

'Recent history,' Butler said. 'I've got some bad news for you, Stuart.'

Pusey eyed her suspiciously. 'What?'

'You remember your old friend, Ryan Preston?'

'What of him?'

'When was the last time you saw him?' Moone asked.

Pusey looked at his solicitor, then at Moone again as his eyes narrowed. 'Don't think I should answer that, so no comment.'

'He's dead, Stuart,' Butler said.

Pusey sat up, staring at her. 'So? What's that got to do with me?'

'We've got you for assaulting a police officer, Stuart,' Butler said. 'Aggravated assault. The minimum sentence is a low-level community order, maximum is two years inside. Now, you've got form, haven't you? Plenty of form. Do you want to go inside again, Stu?'

Pusey just kept staring at her.

She huffed and then said, 'OK, give me the silent treatment, but it's your clothes that'll do the talking. You don't kill someone without getting trace evidence on you or, more importantly, leaving some behind. Like hair or DNA.'

'I ain't fucking killed anyone.'

'Where were you this afternoon?' Moone asked. 'Between one and three?'

'No comment,' Pusey said, shaking his head.

'That tells us something,' Butler said.

'What? Tells you fuck all.'

'Tells us you must have a guilty conscience. Just tell us where you were, if you weren't killing your friend.'

Moone thought for a moment, returning his mind to his younger days with the Met, watching his more experienced superior officers. 'Tell us why you shot him. Why did you do it?'

Butler flashed her eyes at Moone, then looked at Stuart. 'Yeah, why did you shoot him? Did you fall out over drugs or something?'

The habitual criminal sat up, his face changing, now not looking so relaxed. 'I didn't shoot him. I've never handled a gun in my fucking life. What the fuck's going on? What is this? You're going to stitch me up for shooting someone?'

'I don't think you should say any more,' the solicitor said as he made some notes.

'What was Ryan involved in?' Moone asked. 'Why would someone want to kill him?'

'No comment.'

'We found ammunition in the back of his van. What was he doing with bullets? We know he had possession of a gun at one time.'

'What has this to do with the assault?' the solicitor asked.

Moone kept staring at Pusey, watching him squirm, his few brain cells trying to compute it all. 'I don't think you killed Ryan. But I think you might know who did.'

'If I did know, I couldn't say, could I?' Pusey looked away, chewing his lip and scratching at his head.

'Was he dealing guns?' Moone asked.

Stuart shrugged.

'I'm guessing they're dangerous people,' Butler said.

There was a knock on the door and when Moone called out for them to enter, DS Chambers put her head round the doorway.

'Sorry, sir,' she said, looking sheepish. 'But there's been a development in the Ryan Preston murder.'

'Thanks, Molly,' he said, then looked at Pusey. 'I think we'll pause the interview there and you, Stuart, can go back to your cell.'

'But I haven't done anything,' Pusey

moaned.

'You assaulted a police officer,' Butler said as she followed Moone out of the interview room and out into the corridor. Molly was already heading back towards the incident room so Moone hurried to catch up with her.

'What's happened?' Moone asked.

'ANPR and the traffic camera on the Tamar Bridge,' Molly said, and went through the incident room door and towards her desk where she brought up the images she had been going through.

'This van travelled across the Tamar Bridge not long before Ryan was murdered,' Molly said, freezing the image of a dark blue van. 'It also returns across the bridge just after he's murdered. I checked the plates and guess what?'

'The van's stolen?' Moone said as Butler came over and stood behind them.

'No, but the plates are,' Molly said. 'They belong to a van stolen two days ago in Bristol.'

Moone straightened up. 'So, our killer steals the plates two days ago before meeting Ryan and killing him. He planned to kill him. Why?'

'Must be to do with the bullets we found,' Butler said. 'I'm thinking maybe Ryan sold a gun to the killer, and then the killer decided he didn't want any witnesses to it.'

Moone looked at her, nodded, and then

turned to Molly. 'Did you get any good images of the driver?'

Molly tapped at her keyboard again and brought up more traffic camera images from the bridge. 'These were taken at the toll.'

Moone leaned in at the shots of the front of the vehicle. There was the driver, but he had a baseball cap and dark glasses on and his head down. It looked like a man, but other than that it could have been anyone. He let out a sigh. 'He knew what he was doing. It'll be almost impossible to identify him from that. Keep going through CCTV and ANPR and see what you come up with.'

Molly nodded. 'I will.'

Moone walked away with Butler following. He went over to the whiteboard, found the photos of the victim that had been selected and started taping them to the board. He made some notes too, then stood back.

'What're we thinking, then?' Butler asked. 'It wasn't Stuart Pusey who stabbed him, we know that because of his reaction when you said his friend was shot.'

'But he definitely knows something about the guns, I could smell it on him.'

'That's just Pusey's natural rancid odour. So, was Ryan selling guns?'

'I don't know for sure, but looks like it. We need to get hold of the intelligence department and find out what they know about guns being brought into Plymouth. But what worries me, is why Ryan's killer needs a gun. What's he planning on doing?'

'Armed robbery?' Butler shrugged.

'Why did he kill Ryan?'

'Why leave a living witness?'

Moone nodded. 'He didn't hesitate. Just did it. He's cold, calculating and prepared.'

'You might be reading too much into this,' Butler said.

'Maybe, but I've got this strange feeling in my gut that I'm not. I've got this other feeling too, like déjà vu. Know what I mean?'

'I don't think I do. It's just another senseless murder and we'll find the nutter in the end. By the way, I'm going to the opening of the trial tomorrow.'

Moone turned to face her, a little surprised and quite relieved. 'You are? Why?'

'Well, you can't go, and I know how much you'll worry yourself about it. So, I thought I'd see how it goes.'

He smiled. 'Thanks. I appreciate that.'

'Yeah, well, don't make a big deal out of it.' Butler headed to her desk. 'I'd do it for anyone. You're nothing special, Peter Moone.'

He saw her give him a subtle smile before she grabbed her notebook and phone and said, 'I'm going to head to Crownhill and see the intelligence department. Maybe I'll get you a coffee on the way back if you're lucky.'

'Thanks.' He watched her walk out with the same old urge to say something hanging around his head and his heart. When she was gone, he let out a breath and went back to his desk to try and figure out what was going on with their murder investigation. He still couldn't get rid of the sensation that there was something familiar about everything that was happening, almost as if he had been through every step of it before. No, it was ridiculous. Then his mind returned to the old lady from the old people's home who had cried murder. That was another situation that wouldn't let go of him. Why was the old lady so familiar? He made a note in his notebook to look in on her and ask her some questions if she ever got lucid again.

Then finally his stomach sank, as if weighed down with lead. The thought of the trial had entered his mind.

He could already see Carthew sitting across the courtroom with a smug smile on her face. He just hoped it would get wiped right off this time.

Several hours later, when it was growing dark, Abel screwed the new plate onto the scooter he'd stolen and then stood up. He wiped everything over again, just to make sure, then took off his surgical gloves, discarded them in the bin and put new ones on. He put on his black coat and opened the safe. There it was, the Glock handgun with the ammunition next to it. He took it out and put one of the magazines in, pulled back the slide, and slipped it into his jacket. He was just about ready.

He took a few deep breaths and looked around the garage. He nodded to himself, thinking over what he was about to do. The mayhem was about to begin. Chaos would ensue, death and destruction would follow, but it was the only way forward. He took out the latest book he had started and wrote down what had occurred up until that moment. He carefully put the book back and then walked to the scooter and wheeled it towards the garage door. Once outside, he locked up the garage, got on the bike and started it up. It rumbled to life and he raced out of the street and into the country roads, heading towards Plymouth. He kept his head down as he zipped in and out of the traffic. He sped along, his mind racing forward, seeing the pattern in everything as it played out. Nothing would ever change, not until he changed it.

It wasn't long before he was buzzing along Durnford Street, passing by the barracks, and then heading towards the sea. He raced the bike around the bend and then slowed as he reached Devil's Point car park. He pulled in, parked the bike and climbed off. There were a few cars scattered around. He observed them all and then looked around at the dark, calm sea and black outline of Drake's Island. He slipped his left hand into his jacket, pulled out the handgun and held it behind his back as he headed for a car near the back where he had seen movement inside. He had gambled that some couple would be here for a summer's night fondle and it had paid off. As he got closer, he could see a man and woman embraced and kissing, too blind to notice him.

He took out the thin but bright torch he'd brought along and pointed it at the steamed-up windows. The lovers shielded their eyes and moved about in panic. He flashed the torch at them some more, watched them blink and listened to them complain. It was like a film playing and he was watching in his living room, staring at the TV. He knew what to do next, he had no choice but to tap on the window.

The glass came down and there was a young woman with dirty blonde hair staring up at him, looking horrified, her cheeks red. The young, bulky man, probably in his early twenties, looked angry. He shone the torch at him which made him cover his eyes again.

'Fuck off,' the young man snapped. 'What the fuck do you think you're doing?'

He didn't say anything. He wasn't supposed to say anything, just raise the gun and point it at their faces. The horror burned in their eyes. The girl started to open her mouth to scream, so he turned the gun slightly towards her and squeezed the trigger. She slumped sideways as her face was coated in dark red. The young man started to grasp at the door handle to get away. He fired again, hitting him in the chest, making the young man suck in a rasping breath. The next shot hit him in the head, and a star-like wound opened up on his brow.

He looked around but no one had appeared, so he hurried back to his bike and climbed on. He started it up and roared his way back the way he had come.

He knew tomorrow the mayhem would begin.

Moone had been awoken in his caravan by his phone ringing, then was given the bad news. He'd had a quick cigarette before he got dressed, knowing that Butler would accuse him of tempting fate again. He got dressed quickly and drove to Devil's Point. The blue lights were flashing into the night and uniforms were already setting up a cordon. The SOCOs were going to work, examining a car at the back of the car park. Moone watched it all from his vehicle after he parked up along the road before he climbed out. The clouds had gathered in, advertising the possibility of summer rain coming.

The police tape was lifted for him by the male uniform who had the crime scene log. He signed it, then walked towards all the action at the very back of the car park. He stopped halfway there, a strange feeling crawling over him again, that weird sensation that this had happened before. He looked around, then shook his head. No, he'd never been to a murder scene like this before, he was certain of that. He started walking again and sped up as he saw DS Molly Chambers already standing by the grey Peugeot.

'Molly,' he said. 'What is it?'

She let out a sigh, her eyes still on the car and the SOCOs taking photos. 'Two DBs. A young man and a young woman. They both have ID. The girl is Charlie Ridgley, the lad is Adam Spinney. Looks as if they might have parked here... and then someone shot them both.'

Moone stared at her as a cold hand ran its fingers down his spine. 'Shot? Jesus Christ.'

'I know.' She nodded as she looked at him. 'First the stabbing and the bullets. Now a shooting. It could be related.'

Moone stepped closer and his eyes caught sight of the woman slumped towards the gear stick. Her blonde hair was matted with blood, her face... He turned away, his heart beginning to race, his hands trembling.

'You OK?' Molly asked as he faced Drake's

Island and tried to control his breathing. He didn't want to say what it was, couldn't communicate what he had seen when he looked at the female victim. He tried to push away the memory, to tell himself it was only a flashback.

'Was she shot in the face?' he asked.

'Yes, point blank range,' a familiar Welsh voice said.

Moone turned to see Dr Jenkins appear from behind the car, dressed in a green forensic outfit. She came over, her shoe coverings scraping against the tarmac.

'You don't look so hot,' Dr Jenkins said as she reached him.

'I'm OK,' he said. 'Point blank range, you said?'

'Yes, there's definite tattooing around the wound. That's where some of the gunpowder that hasn't fully burned peppers the skin around the wound. I think I'll probably find a fracturing of the bone. I'd say the wound is probably from a nine-millimetre handgun, but I'll verify that tomorrow.'

'The young man?'

Jenkins looked over towards the car. 'Gunshot wound to his chest and head. They would have died instantly, with very little suffering if that helps?'

'Not really. We attended the scene of a stabbing earlier today.'

'So I hear. Crime is certainly getting more violent in Plymouth. It's not often I have to deal with the victims of shootings.'

Moone looked over at the car. 'Thing is, I think they may be connected.'

'How so?'

'We found ammunition in the back of the victim's van yesterday. Nine-millimetre, I'm told. And we know the victim was in possession of a firearm in the recent past.'

Jenkins faced him. 'So you're thinking he had his gun stolen yesterday after he was stabbed?'

'Or he was selling guns and whoever he was planning on selling a gun to didn't want to pay or have any witnesses. Now this. This looks random, doesn't it? A couple come here to... whatever, and the shooter just walks up to the door and starts shooting.'

'Oh, he didn't just start shooting,' a voice came from one of the crowd of SOCOs. One of them got to their feet with a grunt and turned around. Moone recognised Nathan Colman's craggy face and grey hair poking out of his white hood as he stepped closer.

'Hello, Nathan,' Moone said. 'What were you saying?'

'Your killer didn't just start shooting,' Nathan said. 'Did you notice the window on the passenger side is down?'

Moone leaned over and looked at the open

window. 'Oh yeah. So what, he taps on the glass?'

'Probably,' the SOCO said as he walked to the car and started to act it out, pretending to tap on the glass and raise a gun. 'He taps on the glass, they, probably in a panic, lower the window… they may have thought the killer was a police officer, but then he fires at the girl first. Bang. Point blank range. Then the young man. There is something interesting though.'

'What?' Moone asked.

'The angle of the shots. I'd say, the shooter is left-handed.'

Moone nodded. 'Thank you, Nathan. That might make life easier.'

Moone turned to see Molly taking notes. 'You getting all of this, Detective Sergeant?'

She nodded and smiled. 'Yes, boss. This is the beginning of something, isn't it?'

'Feels like it, doesn't it? He steals a gun and randomly shoots two innocent people in a car. Why?'

'You know what this reminds me of?' Nathan said, dragging all eyes on him again.

'What?' Moone asked.

'The summer of Sam case in the States,' the SOCO said. 'It's a bit like the Zodiac murders too. I think the first persons he killed were in a parked car.'

'You think he might be re-enacting the Zodiac murders?' Moone asked.

Nathan shrugged. 'I don't know. Just reminded me of it. Just giving my opinion.'

Moone watched the SOCO go back to work and then looked at Molly and Jenkins who he could see were just as perturbed as him. It was not a good scenario whichever way he looked at it. There was a sociopath out there with a gun and he had no idea where he might strike next.

CHAPTER 4

Just after 9 a.m., DI Mandy Butler had followed the rest of the people into the public gallery, had taken a seat and looked down on Courtroom 3, where the murder trial of Faith Carthew was about to begin. Her stomach was in knots as she watched the judge, HHJ Robert Bowes from the Western Circuit, seat himself under the huge Royal Court of Arms on the wall behind him.

The barrister for the prosecution, Simon Bray KC was sitting at the first bench, while Hannah Marvin KC who was acting for the defence, was sitting on the other side of the court. Butler's gut twisted and her heart raced a little when she saw Carthew, decked out in a dark trouser suit, being escorted to the glass box they called the dock. Her face was straight, no smirking; she knew how to play the game, and so did Hannah Marvin KC, and that's what had put Butler on edge already. When Moone mentioned the trial the day before as they had sunned themselves and enjoyed their ice creams, a horde of doubts had manifested in her chest. She didn't dare say them aloud as she knew that Moone would only start to worry. The fact that Carthew was off the force was what was keeping her spirits up. She just hoped Bray was as good a barrister as Marvin. Then she looked over at the jury, the ordinary men and women of Plymouth, who she prayed would see beyond Carthew's lies and Marvin's clever arguments.

'Good morning, everyone,' the judge said, looking over the courtroom and giving a brief smile. 'Before proceedings begin in this trial, can I ask you to look towards the dock where you'll see the defendant, former Detective Sergeant Faith Carthew. She is the woman whose case you will be trying. The defendant stands charged on this indictment of murder, and of conspiracy to commit murder. The defendant has pleaded not guilty to this indictment. It is your job, as jury, after hearing all the evidence put before you, to decide if she is guilty or not.'

There was mostly silence in the courtroom when the judge paused. Butler's sight jumped to Carthew whose eyes were scanning the jury. She looked a little fearful, Butler thought, and a little meek. It was all pretence. She was playing a game, getting ready to fool the jury just like she had fooled most in her life.

'Are the defence and prosecution ready for their opening statements?' the judge asked. They both replied that they were and bowed their heads to the judge.

'Then I'll let you begin, Mr Bray,' the judge said.

'Thank you, Your Honour,' Simon Bray KC said as he stood up and looked towards the jury with a brief smile. 'If it pleases Your Honour, and ladies and gentlemen of the jury, we are here today to embark on the trial of Faith Carthew, a woman who once stood as a sworn protector of the law. As a Detective Sergeant in the Devon and Cornwall Police, she was entrusted with the duty of bringing justice. But as you will hear throughout this trial, the evidence will show that she grossly betrayed that trust over a long period.'

Butler watched as Carthew lowered her head as if guilt had overcome her. She wanted to burst out laughing.

'The defendant stands accused of two counts of murder,' Bray KC continued. 'The first is the suspected murder of Detective Inspector Maxine Rivers, who was the defendant's former lover. Now, as the defence will no doubt point out, there is a lack of a body in this case. But the significant forensic evidence I lay before you will show clearly that Maxine Rivers was murdered in the flat where Faith Carthew, the defendant was staying at the time. The second count of murder is, in fact, an indictment of conspiracy to commit the brutal killing of her half-brother, Lloyd Redrobe. The evidence of a star witness, Jason Harris, who carried out the murder, will illustrate and confirm that the defendant did indeed plan the brutal and tragic murder of her half-brother. Lloyd Redrobe was killed in an incident that can only be described as premeditated and callous. He was riding his scooter when he was struck and fatally injured by a vehicle driven by Jason Harris, an associate and former lover of the accused. The defence will try and persuade you that Redrobe's death was a tragic accident, but we will show you that it was nothing of the kind. The evidence will make it clear that Faith Carthew orchestrated this fatal attack on her half-brother, motivated by malice and greed.'

Butler had been listening to the prosecution, and then staring over at the jury. But then she had the strange feeling she was being observed and looked over automatically towards the dock. Carthew's eyes, now burning, were on Butler, the hate and repulsion glistening in them. Butler huffed and shook her head. Carthew looked away, putting the look of innocence and worry back on her face.

'As I have said already,' Bray continued. 'DNA traces were discovered in the flat where Faith Carthew was staying, traces belonging to DI Maxine Rivers in quantities and locations that cannot be explained by any innocent interaction. DI Rivers' mobile phone was discovered under the driver's seat in the defendant's car. It is the prosecution's case that Faith Carthew murdered Maxine Rivers, disposed of her body, and sought to cover her tracks. Faith Carthew was a former officer of the law, a fast-tracked Detective Sergeant with Devon and Cornwall Police, and therefore she knew its workings intimately. She used her knowledge, her training, and her connections to evade suspicion for as long as possible. But, as the evidence will show, she underestimated the very system she once served.'

The prosecution barrister looked around the room, making sure to make eye contact with the jurors as he said, 'Ladies and gentlemen, this case is built on the careful, meticulous piecing together of evidence. It is a case about betrayal of family, of trust, and of professional integrity. Over the course of this trial, you will hear testimony from witnesses, you will be asked to examine forensic evidence, and you will see how these two murders are intertwined by a web of deceit spun by the accused. At the conclusion of this trial, you will be asked to deliver the only verdict that the evidence supports, and that is that Faith Carthew is guilty of both these heinous crimes. Thank you.'

Butler stared at Carthew, willing her to look her way, but the bitch kept her poker face on, her eyes averted. The game had begun.

Moone tried to clear his mind of the trial and bring his thoughts back to the three murders he had on his plate. One had been bad enough, and now he had the two young people, shot randomly for all he knew. He was sitting in the car, which DI Anna Jones was driving fast but extremely carefully. There were a couple of uniforms following as they drove to Maker View, close to Pennycomequick where the parents of Charlie Ridgley lived. As DI Jones parked up near the gated end of the narrow road of terrace houses, Moone's whole body tensed up like it always did in these moments.

'You don't have to do this, boss,' Anna Jones said, taking off her seatbelt. 'I'm OK to do it by myself.'

Moone looked towards the house a few feet away and saw that it was the right one. There was a white-painted porch at the top of a short flight of red steps. A driveway was set next to the steps and a dark blue Renault Megane was parked there. 'It's OK, I'm in charge, it's my responsibility.'

'But you've got a lot on your plate,' she said. 'What with the trial and everything. And please notice, I didn't blare out Celine on the way here.'

He dredged up a smile. 'I do appreciate that, DI Jones. Right, let's go.'

Moone climbed out and started towards the house, his legs turning to jelly with every step. He wondered if they could see them coming through the windows as he travelled up the steps. Before he had time to reach the front door, it opened, and a distraught-looking, slender blonde woman stood at the top of the steps, her large eyes burning into Moone. Her hands went up and covered her mouth for a moment as a beefy-looking, dark-haired man came and stood in the doorway.

'Oh no,' the woman said, then made a strange high-pitched noise before she said it again. 'Oh no. Oh no, no, no.'

Moone as usual didn't know what to say so he took out his warrant card and held it up. Then a blur rushed past him and he saw DI Anna Jones take hold of the sobbing woman and direct her through the door and into the house. He was left facing the man who was staring at him, his mouth open.

'Mr Ridgley?' Moone asked.

The man nodded, then seemed to blink himself back to some kind of consciousness. 'Is she? I mean, has something...'

'Let's go inside,' Moone said and thankfully the father turned and walked through the narrow hallway and led the way into a large lounge where Jones was already comforting Mrs Ridgley on a brown leather sofa. The poor mother was sobbing, a tissue now clenched in her right hand.

Eventually, after they were all silent, apart from a sobbing Mrs Ridgley, the mother wiped her eyes and looked up at Moone. 'What happened? All we know...'

'She didn't come home,' Mr Ridgley said, his voice breaking.

Then the mother turned to look at Jones. 'No, it can't be right, she was out with Adam. He's a good lad. There's been some mistake...'

Moone closed his eyes momentarily, ready to give the rest of the bad news, but then he heard DI Jones say, 'I'm afraid a young lad was found with her. His ID said he was Adam Spinney...'

The mother started her sobbing again, words coming out between pants of breath. In between it all, Moone thought he heard the woman saying something about Adam's poor father.

'They were found?' the father said quietly to Moone.

There came a knock on the door, so Moone hurried and answered it and found a WPC on the doorstep. She had dark hair piled on her head and a ruddy face.

'PC Freya Taberer, sir,' she said and he let her in.

'Couldn't make a cup of tea first, could you?' he asked, and then looked back into the living room and saw the dad watching.

'Yeah, no problem,' Taberer said and headed along the hall to the kitchen at the back of the house. Moone went towards the father who was now standing in the hallway, looking completely lost.

'You said they were found?' the dad said, his voice low. The wife was still crying and trying to speak between sobs in the background.

'Yes, they were found in a car in a car park,' Moone said, suddenly aware of the delicate nature of the situation. 'We think they must have stopped for some reason. That's when... that's when they were attacked.'

The dad's eyes widened. 'Attacked? Jesus... attacked?'

'I'm so sorry. But they were shot.'

The father kept staring at him, his head shaking. 'Shot? Someone shot them? What? I don't... with a gun?'

Moone nodded. 'We're obviously still looking into it. Thing is, Mr Ridgley, we need to ask you a few questions, like if you know anyone who might have wanted to harm Charlie or Adam?'

'What, shoot them?' He shook his head again, the flicker of anger starting in his eyes. 'No, no one would want to shoot them or anything... it makes no bloody sense. Why would someone shoot my... oh God...'

PC Taberer appeared with a flowery tray of teas, so Moone grabbed it from her and nodded for her to take care of the father. Then he went through to the living room where DI Jones was still comforting the mum. Jones looked up at Moone and mouthed, 'I've got this, you go.'

Moone managed a smile and then hurried out of the house, the sickness and guilt heavy in his chest and stomach as he went down the steps. He was trembling as well, his breath coming much faster than he'd like.

'Are you all right, sir?'

Moone looked up and saw a male uniform climbing out of a response car and staring at him with concern.

'Yes, I'm fine. You couldn't give me a lift back to Charles Cross, could you?'

'Good morning,' Hannah Marvin KC said as she stood up from her bench. 'Ladies and gentlemen of the jury, today you have the weighty responsibility of examining the many pieces of evidence that will be presented by myself and the prosecution in this trial and deciding whether my client, former Detective Sergeant Faith Carthew, is guilty of the most serious charges brought against her, that of murder and conspiracy to commit murder. I encourage you all to approach this task with the utmost care and impartiality and to keep at the forefront of your minds the principle that underpins our justice system. Please remember at all times that Faith Carthew is presumed innocent unless the prosecution can prove her guilt beyond any reasonable doubt.'

Butler watched on as the defence barrister looked around the room, gazing sternly at the jury before she continued. 'As I said, Faith Carthew was once a well-respected Detective Sergeant in the Devon and Cornwall Police, but now finds herself in the traumatic situation of being accused of being involved in two murders. The first, the alleged murder of her former colleague and lover, Detective Inspector Maxine Rivers, a charge brought even though no body has ever been found. The second indictment is that she conspired with Jason Harris, a member of the Dark Horse motorcycle gang, to have her half-brother, Lloyd Redrobe, killed when the scooter he was riding was struck by an oncoming van. Let me address these charges one by one, beginning with the alleged murder of Detective Inspector Maxine Rivers. The evidence the prosecution will put before you is mostly circumstantial and riddled with uncertainty. The prosecution has no body. They have very little evidence of a murder at all. What they do have is a small amount of blood found in a flat that they claim was used by Faith Carthew, although again there is no evidence she was ever there apart from the testimony of one eyewitness. Another piece of evidence they will put before you as proof of the accused's guilt is the fact that a search team found Rivers' mobile phone in my client's car. Well, given the nature of the defendant's and the victim's relationship, that is hardly surprising. But the police search itself warrants careful examination, which I will urge you to do later on.'

Butler looked towards Carthew in the dock and thought she saw a flicker of a smile. So that was it, the defence was trying to discredit the search of her car. Butler huffed to herself, knowing they had brought in a separate search team from Bristol in case there was any question of evidence tampering.

'Ladies and gentlemen,' Marvin KC said, 'I urge you to keep fresh in your minds the fact that DI Rivers' disappearance remains just that, a disappearance. The prosecution's case is built on speculation, trying to fill the gaps in their investigation with theories rather than hard facts. They will suggest a sinister narrative, but narratives are not evidence, and conjecture is not proof. When it comes to the charge of conspiracy to murder Lloyd Redrobe, the prosecution will seek to paint a picture of premeditation and malice, but again, the evidence they will lay before you is far from conclusive. We will show that Jason Harris acted independently and without her knowledge or instruction, and did in fact murder Mr Redrobe because of a dispute between him and the Dark Horses, a gang that both Mr Harris and Redrobe have deep connections with. The prosecution's case will rely on supposition and inference, not solid evidence, when trying to link my client to this event. Faith Carthew's exemplary career as a police officer has taught her many things, including the importance of the truth, and of searching out the truth. The truth in this case is that she did not murder her former lover, DI Maxine Rivers, nor did she murder her half-brother.'

The defence barrister paused again, casting her eyes over her audience. 'As this trial unfolds, I implore you to carefully scrutinise the evidence, to question the motives behind these most serious of accusations, and to evaluate whether the prosecution has met the high standard of proof required to convict my client. I am confident that by the end of this trial, you will find that the prosecution's argument, their evidence and their whole case simply does not hold water, and that you will do the sensible thing and return a verdict of not guilty. Thank you for listening.'

He pulled his baseball cap on tighter to his head as he looked towards the skeletal remains of the church that sat between Charles Cross Police Station and Drake Circus. The sun blazed behind it, the heat radiating down on him and the black coat he wore. Abel was sweating under his layers of clothing, but it was important he dressed uniformly. He pulled up the face mask he'd put on and readjusted the rucksack on his back before he walked towards the police station and then in the direction of Drake Circus. The people who passed by him were dressed for the summer; there were women and men wearing shorts and sandals, some chatting and laughing, all unaware of what was coming to break open their world. He carried on and stood at the pedestrian crossing with all the so-called people surrounding him, jostling and making noises with their mouths that sounded a little like conversation. The beeping noise started and everyone obeyed its call and started to cross. There it was, Drake Circus, the monstrous temple where the people of Plymouth all went to bow down and worship their new consumer God. He found the echoing chatter of people and distant music attacking his ears as he walked in and hurried across the concourse and past the shops on either side. The crowds swarmed around him, the people manning the stalls at the centre of the corridor occasionally trying to stop him for a chat. The sweet scent of perfumes changed to the pungent aroma of fried fish. He turned as he saw the escalators, travelled up to the next floor and kept on walking. He kept his head down as the hordes of shoppers scurried around him. When he reached one of the shop fronts, he stopped and stood back against it and observed everyone going past on a kind of loop. The same faces, the same soundtrack of chatter. He took the rucksack off of his back and set it down beside him as he waited. Everything was about to change.

The team were gathered around the whiteboard where DCI Moone was still staring at the new photos that had been taped up. Now there were the photographs of Charlie Ridgeley and Adam Spinney. He took a deep, sad breath and let it out as he shook his head. Both of them had been barely into their twenties and now their lives had been snuffed out in a matter of seconds and randomly, it seemed. But was it a random crime? So far they had found no reason that anyone would want to harm either of them. His mind rewound to Ryan Preston, the plumber who was potentially also an arms dealer. The intelligence department had thrown up a couple of names linked to the selling of guns in Devon and Cornwall and he was preparing to question them. Someone out there had a gun or more than one gun.

He was about to turn and start his briefing to the team, but then he saw DSU Jake Boulton step into the room, squeezed into his usual expensive-looking suit, his hair slicked back. He folded his arms and leaned on the wall and nodded to Moone to carry on.

Moone smiled politely at him, then turned to the team who were chatting among themselves until most noticed him waiting to begin.

'Right,' he said, giving them a brief smile and then quickly clearing his face. 'As most of you know, for the last few months we haven't had any murders to investigate, not since the John Michael King case anyway. Now we've got three in one day.'

There was a lot of head-shaking and sighs from his team, but he could also see a lot of enthusiasm from them. Except for DC Harding who looked as if he was half asleep, but Moone knew that's what came with being a dad for the first time.

'Yesterday afternoon,' Moone said and turned to look at the whiteboard and the photos of the recent victims. 'Ryan Preston, a plumber from Efford, was found stabbed to death in his van. There were bullets found in that van, and we know from his ex-girlfriend that he was at one time in possession of a handgun. The theory is that maybe Ryan was selling guns on the side, but we're waiting for intelligence to come back with some leads. Now, here comes the interesting part, as if that wasn't enough. Last night, two young people, boyfriend and girlfriend were shot in the boyfriend's car. At point blank range...'

More chatter and head-shaking came from the team, so he held up his hands. 'Now, listen, we know firearm offences have been going steadily up in Plymouth and the country in general, but this to me smells of something different. This seems on the face of it to be random. Usually, we're looking at offenders simply being in the possession of illegal weapons, reactivated weapons or even some shootings, but they are usually drug or gang-related. This was someone walking up to a car and callously, cold-bloodedly shooting the people inside. Charlie Ridgely and Adam Spinney. The girl was shot first, then the lad. Look at their photos. These were ordinary, happy young people, not gang members, not drug dealers... why did someone target them? DI Jones?'

'We think there's a connection between Ryan Preston's murder and this,' DI Jones said, standing up and looking everyone over. 'We haven't got anything concrete to support that, but we're going with our gut on this. The killer drove in a van with stolen plates, wearing a baseball cap, a face mask and shades to where he met Ryan. He was preparing to kill him. We think he took a gun or guns from Ryan after stabbing him and then perhaps last night he used the same gun to kill two random victims. But why?'

'Probably just a coincidence,' Harding said, stifling a yawn.

'Maybe,' Moone said. 'But the guns were both nine-millimetres, and I've just been told a little while ago that the ammunition used on the two victims last night match the bullets found in Ryan's van. We need to trawl through CCTV and ANPR and see if we can get a better look at our suspect and spot how he got to the crime scene last night. You've got your actions on the board, so let's get to work.'

Moone watched everyone start to chat as they all got up and headed back to their desks.

'Good work so far, DCI Moone,' DSU Boulton said behind him.

Moone turned and faced him. 'Well, there's not much to go on so far, sir.'

'No, but you'll get there. You proved yourself on the last case. That's why you're SIO on this. The team respond well to you. You're a natural leader.'

Moone smiled. He didn't feel like a leader. 'Thank you, sir.'

'The trial started today.'

'Yes.' Moone sighed.

'When do you give evidence?'

'Tomorrow.'

Boulton stared at him and nodded, then lowered his voice. 'You'll be fine. Just get up there and tell them what happened. That's all you can do. The defence will try and trip you up so go through everything they might ask you.'

'Sir.'

'She had most of us fooled. But not you and Butler. Well done. Now...'

There came a rumble, then a distant boom. The sound of car alarms screaming out filled the silence as they all stared towards the windows. His team were rushing to the windows suddenly, so Moone followed and looked out. Right above Drake Circus was a cloud of black smoke.

What the hell was happening now?

CHAPTER 5

Moone was standing by the cordon that had been set up all around the main entrance to Drake Circus. Between the shopping mall and the tape that had been tied between lampposts to keep back the onlookers, there was very little going on. There were the vans of the army bomb disposal unit parked close by and the fire engines close to them, but on the surface not much else seemed to be happening. All the action was happening inside the mall itself; somewhere deep inside the building, a few heavily armed, incredibly brave individuals had gone in to see if there were any more devices. Moone couldn't take it any more and started to pull out his cigarettes with his trembling hand.

'There wasn't even any warning,' DS

Chambers said as she came and stood next to him. Moone turned and saw the team of uniforms keeping back the hordes of shoppers that had been evacuated from the building. Moone saw the ambulances still parked down the street. He felt sick as he recalled seeing two of them leaving not long after the explosion. He looked at Molly. 'How many dead?'

She sighed deeply as she said, 'Three at the moment. Several injured. One is critical and on the way to Derriford.'

Moone took out a cigarette and poked it into his mouth.

'You're not going to smoke that,' DSU Boulton said, appearing from nowhere. 'The public are watching, Moone.'

He put the cigarette back. 'There wasn't any warning, was there?'

Boulton shook his head. 'No. No messages or calls were received. Who the bloody hell has done this? Could be anyone these days. The Russians, the extremists. Too many to even think about.'

'Boss,' Molly said and nudged Moone.

Moone looked over at the entrance of the mall and saw the armoured figures coming out carrying heavy-looking cases. They returned to their vans and started taking off their helmets and body armour. Then one of the team, a tall and grey-haired man who had a thick matching moustache came towards them.

'Captain Grant. Who's in charge?' the man asked in a northern accent as he looked them all over.

Boulton took out his ID and showed it. 'DSU Boulton. What's it like in there?'

'A bit of a mess,' Grant said and scratched his head. 'No structural damage that I can see. And it looks like there was one IED left in a rucksack on the second floor of the building. Looks crude but effective. I think it was made to create a small but quite deadly explosion. They certainly knew what they were doing. We're going to analyse the device a bit more and see what we can report back.'

'Do you think the person who made it might have had military training?' Boulton asked.

Grant shrugged. 'It's hard to tell until we get a good look at it. Possibly, but there's a lot of bomb-making information out there on the dark web, anyone with an ounce of intelligence can make a device like this. And that's the worry. We'll let you know what we come up with.'

Then the Captain turned and walked back towards his team, leaving Moone and the rest to stare at each other and look lost.

'You know who'll be turning up soon, don't you?' Boulton said.

'Who?' Moone stared at him, the urge for a ciggy biting at the back of his throat.

'Anti-terrorism, MI5, all that lot. They'll be crawling all over this.'

Moone put his hands over his face, enclosing his eyes in darkness for a moment as the realisation hit him. Shit. The anti-terrorism unit. They were always a pain in his backside. He took his hands away and looked at Boulton. 'They're not going to come and take over the station, are they?'

Boulton had his phone out and seemed to be checking for messages. 'I don't know. We'll have to make room if they do or try and send them to Crownhill. Don't worry, Moone, you've got your investigation and now they've got theirs. It'll be fine. Come on, let's get back to work.'

By the time Moone reached the incident room, Butler had already turned up and was sitting at her desk typing something up. He went and stood by her and waited for her to look at him. Eventually, she turned and gave him the once-over and said, 'I hear someone just tried to blow up Drake Circus.'

'They did, or at least part of it.'

She huffed. 'A terrorist attack. Great. That means anti-terror will be on their way.'

'Three people are dead.'

She nodded. 'Sorry. That's awful. I wonder who the bastards are.'

'The bomb disposal people are going to

examine the device and see what they come up with. How's the trial going?'

She started typing again. 'Opening statements have been read out. That Hannah Martin knows what she's doing.'

'She's Plymouth's best, apparently.'

'Makes you wonder who's paying her. My money's on the Dark Horses.'

'Mine too. Do you think she stands a chance of getting off?'

'Let's keep everything crossed. Right, I've had some intelligence back on arms dealing in Plymouth. Apparently, there's a man called Frank Gage who's been in and out of prison for firearm offences. He's made a career out of reactivating deactivated weapons. My friend in the Intelligence department says if anyone knows anything, Frank Gage will.'

'Where does he live?'

'He lives on an old farm near Saltash.' Butler stood up. 'Shall we go?'

Harris unwrapped the silver foil and looked at the fags that Loughty had given him. He sat back on his bunk, looked towards his open cell door and let himself take in the noises of the prison. His body was tight, his chest and shoulders tense with anxiety. He was going to take a walk, but he was waiting for Wes to come back from his workout, as if the big fucker could get any bigger. He wrapped the cigarettes up again and hid them in the little cranny in the metal frame of his bed that Wes had shown him.

He then walked out onto the landing, leaned over the railing and watched everyone going past, careful not to make eye contact. The last thing he needed was trouble, he just wanted to keep his head down and do his twelve years without anyone sticking a shiv into him. Twelve bloody years. He could still hear the old fucking judge handing down the sentences for manslaughter. He let out a harsh breath and lowered his head. When he looked up his eyes jumped to two thick-set, shaven-headed inmates standing down below. Both had tattoos around their necks and poking out of the arms of their prison sweatshirts. They kept looking up at him, giving him the dead-eye stare and saying something to each other. Then one of them stared at him intently before he spat on the floor and they both walked off.

'Alright, mate?'

Harris was still staring at the spot where the two bastards had been standing when Wes strolled up and stood next to him.

'What you looking at?' Wes asked, staring at the same spot.

'Two hard-looking bastards were staring up at me.'

'Yeah? Who were they? Did they say anything?'

Harris shook his head and straightened up. 'Nah, just gave me the evil eye and spat. They had shaved heads and tattoos all over them.'

'So do most of the wankers in here.' Wes laughed and patted him on the back. 'Don't worry, mate, I've got your back. Let's go to the day room and watch a bit of the old gogglebox.'

Harris looked down at the chaos below him where the other inmates laughed, joked or argued. He tried to spot the two fuckers who had been glaring up at him, but there was no sign of them. He straightened, telling himself he couldn't show fear and keep hiding in his cell for the next twelve years, or maybe seven if he kept his nose clean.

'What yous lads doing?'

Harris turned and saw Loughty swaggering along the landing towards them, a big grin on his face. He stopped in front of Wes and nudged the big man as he said, 'Do us a favour, big lad, get Harris out and about, would yer?'

Wes nodded. 'I'm trying my best, Mr Loughty. I'm trying to get him to go to the day room to watch some TV.'

Loughty moved round him and faced Harris. 'That's a good idea, Harris, that's just what yous need to be seen doing, lad and not just when yous getting your grub. Wes here'll keep an eye on yous. Won't yer, big lad?'

'Yes, Mr Loughty.' Wes said.

'Go on, lad,' Loughty said and elbowed Harris.

The next thing he knew, they were walking along the landing and towards the stairs to the ground floor of their wing. Harris kept an eye out for the two tattooed thugs, but as they reached the end of the stairs, he realised there were hundreds of white guys with shaved heads and tattoos. *Shit.* They could've been there among the people sitting at the tables playing chess or dominoes or cards. As they walked through the middle of it all, he noticed a few of them eyeing him.

'Here she comes,' he heard someone say. 'The princess has come down from her castle.'

Harris kept moving, ignoring the wolf whistles and Wes telling some of them to fuck off. He could feel the icy sweat coating his sides and his back. Don't show any fear, he'd been told by his mates before he went inside. It was tougher than they made it sound, because inside he was shitting it. He remembered being the new kid at school, scared of the older boys who would stick out their legs and trip him up in the corridors. He'd been terrified back then, but right at that moment, he realised there had been nothing to be scared of. If he fell, then he might graze his knees, but in prison, someone might stick a blade in him.

'Here we go,' Wes said and pushed him

along a corridor to their right, and then into a long, lime green-painted room that had a few untidy rows of chairs at one end in front of a large TV on the wall. A couple of inmates, one black, one white, were sitting lazily in a couple of the chairs, their feet resting on the chairs in front. Homes Under The Hammer was on.

'I can't stand this fuckin' show,' Wes said and grabbed the remote from the seat next to one of the inmates.

'Oi, we was watching that,' the white one said, while the black guy kissed his teeth.

'Why don't you two fuck off?' Wes said, staring down at them. 'Before I smash your fucking faces in.'

The two of them slowly got up, and then wandered out, leaving Harris and Wes alone.

'See, that's how it's done, mate,' Wes said, grinning. 'What do you fancy watching? Ain't got much choice though.'

Harris shrugged, half watching the door. He didn't really have the head for watching anything. 'I don't mind. You choose.'

Wes started to flick through the few channels there were, while Harris kept watching the open door, his heart pounding.

'This is a good show,' Wes said, but Harris didn't see what it was because he was listening to the footsteps coming closer. His whole body had tensed, the beat of his heart deafening him to everything else going on. The footsteps kept coming.

The thick-set white inmate stepped into the day room and stood blocking the door. He had a shaved head and tattoos covering his thick, muscular arms. There was a swastika on his neck, Harris noticed. He stared at Harris, so he looked at the TV. Out of the corner of his eye, he saw the Nazi inmate sit down on one of the chairs at the back, but he didn't dare turn round to take a look.

Butler turned off the main road that cut through Saltash, then took them onto the narrower lanes until they were heading out into the sticks and were surrounded by patchwork fields dotted with sheep and cows. Eventually, they were driving down a lane with a crumbling stone wall on their left and an old church on their right. Butler slowed and steered into a road that had a newly built brick entrance. A few houses lined the short road and they all looked as if they had been converted from old farmhouses and stone barns. Butler kept driving slowly and took them to the end of the new road and onto an old lane that was full of potholes that made the whole car vibrate. Beyond the trees that lined the lane, Moone could make out the ragged metal shapes of rusted farm sheds and buildings. An old tractor sat rusting away near one of the larger metal sheds. The typical stench of a farm still hung in the air even though there didn't seem to be any livestock left.

Butler parked close to a small farmhouse at the centre of it all and turned off the engine. Moone heard an engine behind them and looked in the rear-view mirror to see a response car with two uniforms in the front seats.

'This is where Frank Gage lives,' Butler said and pushed open her door and climbed out.

Moone followed and stood looking the place over and noticing the eerie quiet that surrounded the whole farm. Then he got that feeling again, the sense of having been here before or in a similar situation. He racked his brain to understand why he kept getting the feeling of déjà vu, but once again he couldn't put his finger on it. All he knew was that he had a growing feeling of dread slowly rising through him, making his pulse speed up.

'Hello,' Butler said, waving at him. 'Earth to Major Moone. Wake your ideas up.'

Moone nodded, then followed Butler as she huffed and walked towards the farmhouse.

'You looked like you'd seen a ghost,' Butler said.

'I don't know what it is,' he said, still looking around. 'I keep feeling like I've been here before or... I don't know.'

'Don't worry, I'll protect you.'

'Scout's honour?' Moone said and Butler

sighed and then turned to face the farmhouse. The uniforms were a hundred yards behind them, Moone noticed and recognised the female PC as Pippa Cummings who'd been on the scene of Ryan Preston's murder.

Butler knocked loudly on the farmhouse door.

'It feels like we're being watched,' Moone said.

'That's because we probably are.' She knocked again, louder this time. 'Frank Gage!' Butler shouted and took out her ID. 'We're the police. We need to ask you a few questions.'

Moone flinched when he heard the bang but didn't realise what had happened until he heard a scream behind him. He spun around and saw PC Cummings lying on the ground, crying out as she gripped her chest. The other constable was keeping low to the ground and crawling towards her.

'Get down, for fuck's sake!' Butler shouted at Moone.

He ducked down and saw Butler had hidden herself behind their car. He started to crawl over to her but another shot rang out, rattling into their vehicle.

Shotgun, Moone thought. Not a good way to go.

'Don't move!' Butler shouted. 'Just keep down!'

His eyes jumped to the uniforms.

Cummings was lying on the ground on the other side of the car where the other uniform had dragged her.

'Call it in!' Moone shouted at the uniform as he held a bloody hand on Cummings' chest. He looked at Moone almost blankly as he said, 'I don't think she's breathing.'

'Call for armed response! And an ambulance!' Butler barked. 'Now!'

Moone's heart was pulsating erratically, his whole body shaking. He didn't know what to do and scrambled around in his empty head for some kind of solution. Only one presented itself.

'Mr Gage!' Moone shouted.

'What the bloody hell're you doing?' Butler growled at him.

'Maybe I can come in and talk to you?'

'Don't you bloody dare, Moone!'

He turned himself around and leant against the low wall that surrounded the farmhouse. 'Mr Gage? Frank?'

'Fuck off!' a voice echoed back. 'You come anywhere near and I'll blow your fucking heads off.'

'I'm going to stand up!' Moone got ready to stand up, but his legs refused to move.

'Don't you bloody dare, Peter Moone!' Butler was staring daggers at him, her eyes burning. He could see tears in them too. His mouth opened, ready to tell her, to say what he'd wanted to say months ago.

Butler's face had changed, the fury fading away, sinking as it was replaced by terror. Her skin became milk-white. Moone didn't understand until he saw the shadow fall over him and he looked up to see a grey-bearded man with wild peppery hair and a leathery face staring down at him. He had a pump action shotgun in his hands and it was pointed at his face.

'Don't shoot,' Moone said, showing his hands. 'You don't want to make matters worse.'

'Why did you fuckers have to come here?' Gage growled, spit flying from his snarling mouth. 'Why can't you let me alone?'

'I'm going to stand up,' Moone said.

'Pete...'

'Get up then, shithead.' Gage jabbed the shotgun towards him.

Moone managed to get to his feet, even though his legs were shaking and threatening to give way. He lifted his hands as he faced the wild-eyed man pointing the gun at him.

'Frank!' Butler said, trying to sound calm. 'Why don't you stop pointing that gun at my colleague?'

Gage swung round and aimed the shotgun at Butler, his eyes narrowing. 'Don't fucking tell me what to do, bitch!'

'It's OK,' Moone said. 'You can point it back at me. It's OK. Come on, Mr Gage, please. Point it at me.'

'Pete!'

He ignored her as he stared at the crazy man with the gun. 'Just turn it to me. That's it.'

Frank Gage turned the shotgun back on him, the dark barrel now barely a foot from him. He tried not to think of what would happen if it went off, but little flashes and terrible images entered his brain before he could stop them.

'Our colleague is hurt,' Moone said.

'I think she's dying,' the uniform said behind him.

'Please let us get her out of here.' Moone looked into his eyes and saw his pupils jump to the two uniforms.

'Too late for her, I reckon,' Gage said and looked at Moone. 'Why'd you have to come here?'

'There was a shooting last night,' he said. 'Two young people. Shot at point-blank range...'

'That wasn't me. I don't go shooting people, not unless you come looking for trouble. I'm defending myself!'

'I understand that. Look, just let us get our colleague out of here and to a hospital.'

Moone heard the sirens in the distance and saw Gage's eyes jump as he must have heard them too.

'More of you fuckers?' The shotgun lifted,

aimed at Moone's face.

'You need to put that down or they'll kill you, Frank.'

The gunman kept staring at him, occasionally his eyes dropping to the gun.

'They'll throw away the key this time.'

'Not necessarily. I'll say...'

'What the fuck can you say? I've just killed one of you lot?'

'She's shot, she's not dead.'

Frank was looking beyond him, staring at Cummings. Moone was willing him to lower the gun. The sound of cars roaring towards them came from the lane behind them.

'Frank, please put it down,' Butler said.

There came footsteps behind them, boots hitting the path as the shouting started.

'Put the weapon down!' one of the armed officers shouted.

Gage was weighing it up for a moment, then he lowered the shotgun, placed it on the wall and raised his hands. One of the armed team rushed in and grabbed the shotgun, while more stormed in, pointing their MP5 submachine guns at the suspect as they shouted commands at him.

Moone, still trembling all over, turned to look at Butler but she was already up and rushing towards him. Her arms wrapped around him and she held him tight.

He held his arms out, not knowing what

to do.

'Don't you ever do that again, you bloody idiot!' she growled into his ear.

'I won't. It's OK. I promise.' He patted her back.

She moved back and stared at him, tears welling in her eyes. 'I know what you were doing. You were stopping him from shooting me. You bloody idiot. You could've been killed. Moron.'

He looked down, his heart racing. 'I couldn't let him shoot you, could I? What would I do without you?'

'You two!' someone shouted at them.

They both looked around and saw one of the armed response team staring at them and looking pissed off.

'You need to get out of here, now!' the officer barked.

'Come on,' Butler said and dragged Moone back along the path. The uniforms were gone and Moone had a sudden rush of panic as he wondered what had happened to PC Cummings. Then he heard the unmistakable sound of a chopper and saw the red Devon Air Ambulance was lowering to the ground in the field over the other side of the road. The paramedics had Cummings on a gurney and were carrying her towards the helicopter.

'Did they say how she is?' Butler asked as she saw the other uniform standing watching it all happen.

The uniform turned and looked at them both, his skin practically translucent. He was trembling as he said, 'She was still breathing, but she's lost a lot of blood. I don't know if she'll be all right. All I could do was...'

Butler patted his back. 'You did amazing. You kept her alive. Come on, follow us back.'

'Hang on,' Moone said and looked back towards the farmhouse and the tumbledown farm buildings.

'What is it?' Butler asked.

'I want to see what he was so desperate to keep us from seeing.' He set off walking towards the old farm, the same emotional echo sounding in his mind, as if he had taken each step before this day. But he couldn't have, he told himself as he watched more uniforms taking possession of Frank Gage who was now restrained. As he moved towards the largest of the metal sheds, he took out a pair of forensic gloves from his pocket and pulled them on. When he reached the large set of rusty doors, he saw the bolt and huge padlock that had been put there to keep people out. He turned and saw the armed response officers getting ready to leave, so he called out to them, 'Have you got anything to get this padlock off?'

A few minutes later, with the help of Butler, he pulled the doors open and a wall of heat burst forth, almost pushing him back out.

'Why's it so bloody hot in here?' Butler asked, but she and Moone learnt the answer after a few more steps when their eyes fell on the neat rows of young cannabis plants that filled most of the huge shed. Heat lamps were hanging down from the metal ceiling, blazing down on the plants. Moone looked at Butler and she stared back at him.

'Now we know why the bastard didn't want us getting in here,' Butler said. 'Jesus bloody hell. You can bet your bottom dollar this isn't just Frank Gage's work.'

Moone walked on, moving down the narrow pathway at the centre of the many rows of plants. 'You're right, this is a major operation. What's in there?'

Butler followed him to the tall and wide metal cabinets at the very end of the shed. Each cabinet was latched and padlocked.

'This might help,' she said, retrieving a gardening fork that was lying on the ground.

She jammed the two prongs of the fork between the latch and the padlock, and with help from Moone, they soon had the latch twisted enough to tug it free.

Butler opened the cabinet with Moone looking over her shoulder.

'Shit,' he said as he saw the shelves full of rifles, submachine guns and handguns. 'There's enough weapons here to fight a small war.'

Butler looked at him. 'But a war against who?'

CHAPTER 6

'Your Honour, I next propose to call as a witness, Mrs Rowe,' the prosecution barrister said as he nodded towards the judge. The judge nodded back.

DS Molly Chambers watched from the public gallery as a grey-haired, middle-aged woman who wore large square glasses and an ill-fitting pink and purple dress was escorted to the witness stand. Neither DCI Moone nor DI Butler were able to come along to the trial, so she thought she would pop in and see the progress. Her stomach had churned when she had seen Carthew in the dock.

'I do solemnly, sincerely and truly declare and affirm that the evidence I shall give shall be the truth, the whole truth, and nothing but the truth,' Mrs Rowe said as her eyes jumped nervously around the courtroom.

'Mrs Rowe,' Bray KC said, looking at his notes as he went and stood by the witness stand. 'You live at flat number 4 Plymview Terrace, Greenbank Road. Is that correct?'

She nodded. 'That's right. Lived there for five years thereabouts.'

'Thank you. In your witness statement, you said that you saw the defendant, Faith Carthew, going to and from flat 6 in your building. Is that correct?'

She swallowed, looking around again. 'That's correct. I didn't know who she was then, but yes, I recognised her when they showed me some photos.'

'You picked her out of several photographs you were shown the day you visited the police station and gave your account to a uniformed officer. Is that correct?'

'It is. I remembered her because of the way she carried herself...'

'And what do you mean by that?'

She raised her shoulders. 'Well, she had this air about her, like she was important or something. Anyway, that's why I noticed her. I thought she must be looking after the flat for the couple who live there. I didn't even think to ask her, because she gave off this air, like I said, that she belonged.'

Bray nodded. 'And can you see the person who you saw coming and going from the flat in question in court today?'

Mrs Rowe looked over at Faith Carthew, then she lifted her hand to point her out. 'That's the woman... the defendant.'

Bray turned to the judge. 'Let it be noted that the witness identified the defendant, former Detective Sergeant Faith Carthew. Thank you, Mrs Rowe. I have no more questions but I believe my learned colleague has some questions for you.'

Chambers watched as the prosecution barrister returned to his bench while Hanna Martin KC stood up and approached the witness stand and said, 'Mrs Rowe, I just have a few questions for you.'

Mrs Rowe nodded and gave an awkward smile that quickly crumbled as her cheeks and neck reddened.

'Mrs Rowe,' Martin began, 'you say you saw the defendant coming and going from flat 6 on numerous occasions. Is that correct?'

'Yes, I'm not sure exactly how many times, but it was more than ten, I'd say.'

'What time of day were these sightings? Do you remember?'

'Well, all times really.'

'All times of the day?'

'Yes.'

Martin KC looked down at her notes, then back at the witness. 'Around the period you say you saw her entering and leaving the flat, which was around the beginning of September that year, former DS Faith Carthew was still employed by Devon and Cornwall Police. Now, I've been through the times she was working around that period and found that she was starting work very early and leaving quite late. Sometimes after ten in the evening. What time do you usually go to bed, Mrs Rowe?'

'Well, I like to be in bed by nine.' Her face became even more red.

'Is that your normal routine? In bed by nine?'

'Normally. Yes.'

'And was it the same last September, do you recall?'

Mrs Rowe hesitated, looked around again and said, 'Yes, it was no different. Nine at night.'

'So, if Faith Carthew was getting home late, sometimes after ten at night on occasion, then it seems unlikely that you saw her coming and going quite as often as you say you did, doesn't it?'

'Well... I definitely saw her a few times.'

'A few times?' Martin KC nodded. 'Now, I'd like to show you a photograph, if I may?'

The witness was handed a photograph which she examined.

'Do you recognise the person in that photograph?' the defence barrister asked.

'Well, yes, but I think I saw her photo in the Herald.'

'That is a photo of Detective Inspector Maxine Rivers, the woman who the prosecution would have you believe Faith Carthew murdered sometime in September and disposed of her body. Can you remember if you ever saw that woman in or in the vicinity of flat 6 in your building?'

The witness looked at the photograph and shook her head. 'No, I don't think so. I only recognise her from her photo being in the Herald.'

'I see you wear glasses, Mrs Rowe.'

'Yes, they're for distance.'

'Now, in your statement, you admitted that your glasses at that time had been broken. Is that correct?'

Mrs Rowe's face became a deep red. 'Well, yes, I'd accidentally sat on them. One of the arms snapped off.'

'So you weren't able to use them very much, is that right?' Martin KC stared at her.

'Not really. I mean, I used them, but only in the house and I carried them around with me…'

'So, the times you say you saw the defendant coming and going from flat 6, you must have hunted out your broken glasses to put them on so you could see her entering or leaving the flat. Is that right?'

'I suppose.'

'One more question, Mrs Rowe. Around

the time when you said you saw Faith Carthew coming and going from flat 6, do you recall ever hearing any loud noises coming from that apartment? Any cries for help or sounds that might make you think a violent struggle or argument was going on?'

Mrs Rowe hesitated, then shook her head. 'No, I never heard anything like that.'

Hanna Martin KC looked towards the judge. 'No more questions, Your Honour.'

Harding saw both of them coming up the stairwell towards the incident room and stood at the top, shaking his head. Moone was still trembling all over as he reached Harding, his heart still pounding in his chest. His mind kept filling up with images of Frank Gage pointing a gun at him, the sound of the gunshots blasting inside his skull, but he couldn't make them stop.

'It always happens to you two, doesn't it?' Harding said and patted Moone on his back.

'It always happens to Moone, you mean?' Butler huffed. 'Next time you can go on one of his little jaunts.'

'Yeah, no thanks.' Harding laughed, then looked towards the incident room as he lost any sign of mirth.

'What's wrong?' Moone asked.

'You're not going to like this,' Harding said. 'But guess who's turned up.'

Moone looked at Butler and she mirrored his look of displeasure. He took a deep breath and headed into the incident room to find a group of suits standing at the centre of it, all chatting away. There she was, Moone said to himself as he spotted Commander Sally Richer standing at the centre of the group of people, talking about terrorism and the way to tackle it. It wasn't only the sight of Richer that upset him, but also the fact that Chief Superintendent Kate Hellewell was there too, nodding and taking in what the self-important woman was saying.

'There's DCI Moone,' Hellewell said as she spotted him. Moone put on a smile and headed over.

'I believe you've worked with Commander Richer before, Moone?' Hellewell said, looking between them.

Moone faced Richer, who was now wearing a smirk. 'Yes, I did. It was a few years back now.'

'Four, I believe,' Richer said and put out her hand. 'You haven't changed a bit, Moone.'

'Neither have you.' He smiled as they briefly shook hands.

'Commander Richer is here to supervise your investigation into the explosion that happened earlier today,' the Chief Super said. 'This is almost certainly a terrorist attack.'

'It is, without a doubt,' Richer said.

Then Hellewell turned to Moone as she said, 'I heard one of our uniforms was shot earlier. Do we think it's the same offender?'

Moone shrugged. 'I'm not sure, ma'am. When we turned up to talk to him, he started firing at us, and that's when he shot PC Cummings. She's being operated on at Derriford. The thing is, when we searched his farm, we found a lot of cannabis plants and a load of guns. I think that's what he was trying to stop us seeing.'

'Any bomb-making equipment?' Richer asked, folding her arms.

'No, not that we could see.'

'I'd better send my team there,' Richer said, looking at the Chief Super. 'My experts will go through the place and tell you whether or not there's any bomb-making equipment. Where are the remains of the IED?'

'With the bomb disposal team,' Moone said. 'We're waiting for their report. They said it was an effective device and whoever made it knew what they were doing. I'm going to interview Frank Gage in a moment.'

'I'd better sit in on it.' Richer looked at the Chief Super.

'Agreed,' Hellewell said, then looked at Moone. 'Richer will sit in on the interview. Are you and Butler OK to carry on? I know you must have been through hell today.'

'We're OK, ma'am.' Moone said the words,

even though he kept hearing the gunshots and seeing PC Cummings and the blood oozing out of her wounds. He put his trembling hands into his pockets. 'I'd like to get on and interview Gage.'

'Good,' Hellewell said and patted his shoulder.

Frank Gage was dressed in a forensic outfit, his face still red and his eyes still full of menace as Moone and Richer went in and sat down. A middle-aged, dark-haired solicitor was sitting next to him.

Moone hadn't said much to the Counter-Terrorism Unit Commander as they had headed to the interview room. He was having a hard time keeping his eye on the ball with the horror of the day flooding his mind, so he thought it best to say little. He'd apologised to Butler about Richer taking her place, but she admitted she didn't want to face the old bastard anyway and she looked like she meant it.

'We'll be recording this interview,' Moone said, then he turned on the recording equipment and read out the necessary information. He sat back and looked at Gage, who had his arms folded and was staring back at him.

'You live at Church Street Farm, Saltash, is that correct?' Moone asked.

'No comment,' Gage said and looked away.

'That's the address we were at when you discharged a shotgun,' Moone said. 'You shot a police officer. That police officer is currently in surgery. Do you recall shooting a police officer?'

The solicitor leaned forward. 'My client admits to illegally carrying a firearm and discharging it. He suffers from paranoia and believed you were there to do him harm.'

'You're trying to get away with manslaughter?' Commander Richer said and laughed. 'What about the cannabis you're growing and all those other weapons you've got stored on your farm?'

'No comment,' Gage said, staring at her.

'I'm from the counter-terrorism unit,' Richer said. 'We're going over your farm, looking for a bomb-making factory. We're searching for anything that could be used to make an IED like the one that was set off in Drake Circus today.'

Gage's expression changed, a look of surprise taking over his face. 'Bombs? What? What're you trying to pull?'

'Two young people were shot in their car last night,' Moone said. 'Point blank range. Both dead. Where were you last night?'

Gage stared at him. 'At fucking home. Jesus Christ, it's happening already...'

'What's happening already?' Moone asked.

'You lot, policing everything, even our

thoughts, everything we post online.'

Richer shook her head. 'So, this is what it's all about? I thought so. I've been in this game a long time, Mr Gage and I can see what's happening here.'

Gage huffed out a laugh. 'Can you really?'

'Yes, I can. Growing cannabis is how you raise the money for all those guns. But why so many guns? Why would a man need so many guns to defend a little farm? Unless they are for a small army?'

Their suspect folded his arms. 'No comment.'

Richer looked at Moone as she said, 'I think we're done for now. Mr Gage can go back to his cell and think about the twenty years he'll be serving in prison.'

Harris had been watching the two tattoo-covered inmates out the corner of his eye while trying to look like he was staring at the TV. Wes was sitting at the front, staring up at the TV, laughing at whatever was now playing. Harris couldn't concentrate as his heart was pounding, half expecting the two prisoners to get up and produce a blade.

'Oi, Bately!' Harris jumped a little but tried to hide it as he turned and saw one of the other screws standing in the doorway looking impatient. 'Bately, you lump, get over here.'

Wes sighed, then looked around at the

screw and took his time getting to his feet.

'What have I done, Mr Vincent?' Wes asked as he lumbered towards the door.

Harris' eyes jumped to the two inmates who were sitting at the back. Both of them seemed to be looking up at the TV. Then the one on his right looked down at him, his dead eyes falling on him.

'You coming, mate?' Wes called out, but the screw held up a hand.

'Nah, he's not wanted,' the screw said and Harris thought he gave him a strange look. 'Harris, you stay here.'

Wes looked back at Jason before his eyes jumped to the two tattooed inmates as he frowned. 'Can't you let Harris go back to his cell, Mr Vincent?'

The screw looked at Harris for a moment, but shook his head as he looked away. 'Stay here, Harris. Do as you're told. Bateley, come with me.'

Wes looked at Harris again and the two inmates, before he was dragged away with a shrug.

Both the tattooed inmates looked at Harris, smirks appearing on their faces. It was the one on Harris' right that said, 'Aww, your boyfriend left you all alone, princess?'

Harris' heart started to thump as he balled his fists, ready to fight for his life.

'No one to protect you now, is there,

princess?' the other one said, laughed and then stood up.

This was it. Harris looked towards the door, wondering if he could make it if he made a run for it. But as if they knew what he was thinking, the one on the right got up, stood by the door and checked the coast was clear.

'What the fuck is going on here, lads?' Mr Loughty's voice echoed down the corridor and Jason let out a breath.

The familiar stocky shape of the screw came into the doorway as he folded his arms and looked them all over.

'What're yous two doing?' Loughty asked them.

'Nothin', Mr Loughty,' they both said, one after the other. 'Just watching TV.'

Loughty nodded and looked at Harris. 'Best yous move on then, Hughes,' the screw said, staring at Harris. 'You too, Duff. Go on, get out of my sight.'

The two inmates started to dawdle out, one of them, either Hughes or Duff, shot him a dead-eye stare before they both left.

'Where's Wes?' Loughty asked.

Harris felt himself still trembling all over. 'Got called away by one of the other guards.'

Loughty nodded then looked Harris over. 'Get up, lad. Come here.'

Harris got up and walked over to the screw.

'It's a dangerous place in here, Harris,' Loughty said, his face tight. So far he'd never seen the guard without some kind of smile on his face, but now it looked as if he was struggling with something. 'You can't trust anyone. Not anyone.'

Harris nodded. He was slowly learning the truth of what the screw was saying.

Loughty nodded and looked down as he put his hand behind his back.

It happened in a blur. The guard lunged, wrapping an arm around Harris's neck and yanking him close. Harris clawed at his arm, struggling to break free, but the man was too strong. His face was close, his eyes looking into his as he said, 'Sorry, mate. I'm so sorry.'

He felt a burn, that was all. The second time he felt an icy burn of pain. He looked down and saw the blood pumping out of the wound to his stomach. He was trembling and cold. The blade punctured him again, but he couldn't move. It went into him again and then he was let go and he stumbled backwards to the wall.

Loughty was stepping backwards, wiping the blade with a cloth before he dropped it on the floor. Harris slipped down the wall, his hands covering the wound as the warmth poured through his fingers. He looked up at the guard, asking for help.

Loughty stood in the doorway, his face

pale. 'Sorry, lad. I'm so sorry but you fucked up.'

'So, looks like we're dealing with some kind of anti-authoritarian, terrorist group,' Richer said as she walked into the incident room and stood in front of the whiteboard.

Moone had followed her as he thought it all over. Some of it, well, a lot of it didn't make sense to him, so he sat at his desk and said, 'Why shoot two kids in their car? If they're all about fighting the police and any kind of authority, then why target two innocent young people?'

'Because these people are about chaos.' She let out a deep sigh. 'They want death and destruction, DCI Moone. They may say they want the government and the police to have less draconian powers or want them to stop harassing them, or whatever they're obsessed with this week, but really, it's all about the mayhem. Trust me, I know these people.'

Butler looked up at her from her typing. 'So, did he admit to being part of a terrorist group?'

'No,' Richer said. 'Of course he didn't. But he's got a massive shed full of drugs they're selling to raise money for their cause. There's a whole arsenal of weapons stored at that farm… we need to find his comrades. We'll let him sweat for a bit, then we'll go back in…'

'Have your search team found any bomb-making stuff?' Butler asked, and Moone almost smiled when Richer's face turned thunderous.

'No, not yet, but they will.' Richer turned and looked at Moone. 'Have the bomb disposal team come back with a report on the device?'

Moone checked his emails. 'Not yet. But they said whoever made it, knew what they were doing.'

Before Richer had a chance to speak, Commander Hellewell came into the incident room looking fed up. She folded her arms and looked them all over.

'We've got the press clambering for information,' she said. 'They want to know if extremists are targeting the city, or if the Russians decided to start World War Three. We're going to need to set up a press conference for tomorrow, so if you, Commander, and DCI Moone could take care of it, then we can reassure the public that we have everything in hand.'

'Do we?' Butler asked.

The Chief Superintendent looked at Butler, then back at Moone and Richer. 'You have a suspect in custody, don't you, Commander?'

'Yes, Frank Gage,' Richer said, stepping up to her. 'We believe Gage and some yet-to-be-identified accomplices, are in the midst of a terror campaign in Plymouth.'

'Do we know why?' the Chief Super asked.

'I believe they are a group of anti-authoritarian terrorists trying to cause chaos and a massive strain on our resources. We can expect more attacks across the city.'

'Moone and Butler,' the Chief Super said but looked at the whole team. 'From now on, your team will be working under Commander Richer and her team as you all try and find the rest of Gage's terrorist cell. This is our priority at the moment, to make the city safe again. Moone, press conference first thing. I'll get our PR team working on a script. Right, everyone, excellent work. Commander Richer, can you give me a full debrief, please?'

After Richer and Hellewell left the incident room, Moone turned to Butler and saw she was already staring at him, the thundercloud hovering over her head.

'I don't believe it,' Butler said and sat back with a huff. 'Are we really working under that cow now?'

Moone nodded. 'Looks like it. But I'm not convinced this has anything to do with Gage, do you? I mean, we've got a murdered plumber who sold guns on the side and two dead kids in a car. Then a bomb goes off. We still don't know if it's all connected.'

'Boss,' DI Jones said and came over. 'The ballistics report has come in and it says the same bullets found in the plumber's van were used in the shooting of the young couple.'

'There you go,' Butler said, rolling her eyes. 'Someone stabs Ryan Preston, steals his gun or guns and then for some crazy reason shoots those poor kids.'

'But did he blow up Drake Circus?' Jones said, looking between them.

'Any more sightings on CCTV?' Moone asked and turned round to Harding. 'Keith?'

Harding peered over his monitor, looking tired. 'Sorry, boss?'

'CCTV around Drake Circus?'

'Oh, yeah, there's a lot to go through but I think I've got one suspicious-looking individual. Take a look.'

Moone, Butler and Jones went to his desk while Harding brought up the images. He ran through a few images before a freeze-frame shot of the ground floor of the mall filled the screen. He played it and people started to stream slowly through the building, some turning into the shops along the way. Harding tapped the screen where a darkly dressed individual was passing through the crowd. He wore a dark top and a black baseball cap, and had a small rucksack on his back.

'Look at everyone else,' Moone said. 'Relaxed, chatting, dawdling along.'

'Oh, we're dreadfully sorry,' Butler said. 'We don't all walk like the maniacs in London.'

'No,' he said. 'Look. Look at the way he's moving, the way he's looking around.'

'He's walking with purpose,' Jones said, nodding. 'And he's got a rucksack. Any more shots of him?'

Harding brought up more images and played some footage showing the same suspect going up the stairs to the next level as he said, 'This is a better shot of him, but then he enters a blind spot close to where the bomb went off.'

'Of course, he does,' Butler sighed.

Moone stared at the suspect on the screen. 'Can't see his face. He's made sure he's kept his cap pulled down. Who is this bastard?'

'Is he part of a terrorist cell operating in Plymouth?' Jones asked. 'And if he is, why haven't they claimed responsibility?'

The phones had been ringing non-stop since the device had been detonated, but Moone noticed one of the female civvies, Paula, taking a call and then staring right at him after she'd put the phone down.

'Was that for me, Paula?' Moone asked.

'Yes, it was,' the middle-aged woman with the browned bobbed hair said, looking serious. 'That was Exeter Prison.'

Moone immediately got a stomach full of crazed bats at the mention of the prison where Harris was locked up. 'What's happened?'

Paula looked around at the team looking at her. 'Jason Harris was found stabbed, they said.'

'Is he alive?' Butler asked.

Paula let out a breath, then shook her head. 'They said he died on the way to the hospital. I'm so sorry.'

Moone looked round at Butler and once again she was returning his look with angry eyes.

'That bloody cow has done it again,' Butler said.

CHAPTER 7

Detective Sergeant David Haines adjusted his uniform a little as he sat in the witness box after swearing to tell the truth and nothing but the truth. His eyes skirted over the jury and the crowded public gallery as his heart beat a little faster. Haines watched the barrister for the prosecution, Simon Bray KC, stand up from his bench and approach with his notes in his hands, his eyes fixed on him.

'Detective, can you be so kind as to state your full name and rank for the record?' Bray said with a slow nod.

'David Edward Haines,' he said, leaning forward a little. 'Detective Sergeant, Devon and Cornwall Police.'

'And where exactly were you stationed during the investigation into the suspected murder of Detective Inspector Maxine Rivers?'

'Exeter Police Station, Sidmouth Road. I've been there for the last seven years.'

'Thank you, Detective Sergeant.' Bray gave another nod. 'Is it true that you were part of the search team assigned to examine the car and property of the defendant, former Detective Sergeant Faith Carthew?'

'Yes, I was. I headed the search team.'

'And for the court, can you explain how this search was authorised?'

Haines sat up a little. 'Yes, the search was carried out after we received the warrant issued by Magistrate Julia Castle. The warrant was specifically for the suspect's vehicle and any property owned or leased to her.'

Bray stepped closer. 'So, for clarification, Detective Sergeant Haines, was the search carried out by any officers who were posted at Charles Cross where the accused was stationed at the time?'

'No, none of the search team were posted at Charles Cross. The reason being that we didn't want any accusations of bias or any conflicts of interest. It's standard procedure.'

'Thank you. Before the search, were you aware of Detective Sergeant Faith Carthew or had you heard any rumours about her?'

'No, I'd never heard of her, I wasn't even aware of her existence.'

'And during the search of the vehicle in question, what, if anything, did you find?'

'We found several large packages of drugs and we also found the victim's personal mobile phone under the driver's seat.'

'How was it determined that the mobile phone did indeed belong to the victim, DS Maxine Rivers?'

'The phone was sent to the digital forensics unit for analysis. The SIM card and the phone's internal data were all examined, and any messages, call logs, and photographs were examined and it was confirmed that it was the victim's phone.'

Bray turned and faced the judge and jury. 'So, to summarise, the search of the defendant's car was carried out after her arrest, under a lawful search warrant legally obtained from a serving magistrate and the search was executed by an impartial search team from Exeter Police Station, which resulted in the discovery of drugs and the victim's mobile phone. Is that correct, Detective Sergeant Haines?'

'Yes, it is.'

Bray KC looked again at the judge. 'I have no further questions for this witness, Your Honour.'

'Thank you,' the judge said and turned to face Hanna Martin KC. 'I believe the defence has some questions for this witness.'

There was a shift in the atmosphere of the courtroom as Martin KC stood up, dressed immaculately as always, Haines noticed. She was very good at what she did and that was why he was starting to feel a lot more nervous. She approached and stared at him intently and then down at her notebook that she held in both hands.

'Detective Sergeant Haines,' she began, her voice firm. 'You have told the courtroom that you were stationed at Exeter Police Station during the investigation into the suspected murder of Detective Inspector Maxine Rivers. Is that correct?'

'Yes, that's correct,' Haines said, his body stiffening as he wondered where she was going with her line of questioning.

'And you have said that police officers from Exeter Police Station were recruited to the search team to ensure impartiality, given that the suspect, DS Faith Carthew had previously worked at Charles Cross Police Station in Plymouth? Is that correct?'

'Yes, that's correct.'

Hanna Martin KC nodded a little as she looked at her notes. Her eyes rose again and fixed on Haines. 'DS Haines, are you familiar with an investigation into a series of suspicious suicides that was undertaken by detectives from Charles Cross approximately two years ago?'

Haines opened his mouth, taken a little by surprise. His back tensed as he realised where she was heading. 'Yes, I remember the investigation.'

'In fact, you assisted the Charles Cross murder team during that investigation, didn't you?'

'That's right, but –'

Martin held up her hand, cutting him off. 'Thank you. During that investigation, is it true that you worked closely with several officers from Charles Cross?'

'Yes, I've worked with some of the –'

'And you've remained in contact with some of those officers, isn't that correct, DS Haines?' She raised her eyebrows.

'Yes, I'm friends with some of them, but only on a personal level. We don't…'

'You're a member of a Facebook group called Charles Cross Police Station, are you not?'

'I am. But it's for socialising.'

'So, DS Haines you are good friends with several officers from Charles Cross Police Station, the same station that former DS Faith Carthew, the defendant, was stationed at? Is that correct?'

He sighed. 'Yes, that's right.'

'Thank you.' The defence barrister let the answer linger in the air as she turned and looked over to the jury briefly before facing Haines again. 'Now, Detective Sergeant Haines, let's go back to the search warrant that was used to search the defendant's vehicle. You mentioned earlier that the search was conducted under the authority of a search warrant obtained by a magistrate. You are, of course, familiar with the Police and Criminal Evidence Act 1984, commonly referred to as PACE?'

'I am.'

'And in PACE, what does it say is required for a warrant to be issued to search a suspect's property after their arrest?'

Haines hesitated, picking his words carefully. 'It says that there needs to be reasonable suspicion that the search will uncover evidence relating to the crime that is under investigation.'

Martin KC looked around the courtroom once more as she said, 'Reasonable suspicion.'

She faced Haines again as she stepped closer and engaged his eyes. 'What was the reasonable suspicion that justified the warrant that was issued after her arrest?'

Haines cleared his throat. 'I believe that the SIO of the investigation, who instigated the arrest and search, was sure that a search of the suspect's vehicle would turn up the mobile phone. The defendant and the victim had been in a relationship and her mobile phone was tracked to Plymouth shortly before her disappearance.'

'So, as the leader of the search team,

all you were aware of was that the Senior Investigating Officer, DCI Peter Moone was convinced that a search of Faith Carthew's vehicle would magically turn up the victim's phone?'

'Well, we had a warrant, and the suspect was in custody...'

'But it was DCI Peter Moone who came up with the reasonable suspicion that led to the arrest and the search?'

'Yes, it was, but...'

Hannah Martin KC raised a silencing hand. 'Thank you, no more questions for this witness.'

The hour-long journey from Plymouth to Exeter city centre where Exeter Prison is located was made in almost silence. Moone knew the Exeter Major Crime Investigation Team would already be at the prison along with their forensic unit. It wasn't their place to solve the murder, Moone knew that and he already suspected who was behind it anyway.

'That cow's done it again,' Butler whispered to him as they walked past tables, chairs and ping pong tables that were at the centre of the wide prison corridor. They followed the governor of the prison, Terence Maitland, as he took them to the wing where Harris had been housed. Moone looked up and saw a crowd of prisoners looking down on them from the landings, their insults and wolf whistles echoing around the hollow building. He shuddered a little at the thought of being locked up with the kind of offenders he knew were contained there. Murderers and rapists aplenty were housed in the prison and he knew there were inmates there who they had put away.

'More than likely it was the Dark Horses that carried it out,' Moone whispered back.

'Yeah, but on her say so. She would've been stuffed if he'd testified.' Butler stopped dead at the same time as Moone when they saw the crime scene tape sealing off a section of the prison. It was quiet there, the prisoners having been taken outside into the exercise yard. There were uniforms guarding the area and SOCOs coming and going.

'This is a rare event these days since the prison was revamped,' Maitland said as he adjusted his tie.

Moone pointed to the sign warning of CCTV coverage in the area. 'I take it you've got plenty of footage?'

Maitland looked over at the sign, then pulled an uncomfortable face as he looked back at Moone. 'Well, the incident took place in the day room on this block, but we've had problems with the system there.'

Butler huffed and folded her arms as she stepped up to him. 'Problems with the system?

What does that mean?'

'It means the camera in the day room hasn't been working for a couple of weeks.'

Butler turned and looked at Moone as she shook her head. 'Are you hearing this?'

'So, the prisoners would've known this?' Moone asked.

'We don't let them know things like that in case...'

Butler huffed. 'In case they want to stab someone?'

'What about this corridor that leads to the day room?' Moone asked, gesturing behind Maitland.

The Governor looked down the corridor where the SOCOs were still at work. 'I'm afraid the camera doesn't work there either. I've given orders that guards patrol regularly along here to prevent any incidents.'

'Who's in charge of this wing?' Butler asked.

'That would be Jim Loughty,' the governor said. 'He also found the prisoner and tried to administer first aid. Unfortunately, it was too late. I've put him in the visiting room. I believe the forensic team have processed him.'

'Then we better go and have a word with him,' Butler said and raised her eyebrows at Moone.

The visiting area was a rectangular room filled

with tables and plastic chairs. It was identical to all the others Moone had seen. It had the same sort of sweaty scent as a gym, Moone noticed, with an extra hint of desperation and loneliness. Across the room a figure was sitting at one of the desks, wearing a white forensic outfit.

'He found him,' Butler said as they crossed the room, their footsteps echoing around the room. 'Had blood all over his uniform when he tried to help Harris.'

'I wonder if anyone else got blood on them.'

'I wonder. Not many places to hide bloody clothing.'

Moone took out his ID and showed the prison guard as he reached the table. 'DCI Peter Moone,' he said and gestured to Butler. 'This is DI Mandy Butler. You know why we're here, Mr Loughty?'

The prison guard nodded as he put his hand around the mug of tea in front of him. 'The name's Jim,' Loughty said. 'Yeah, I know why yous are here. Like I told the other lot, I found him in the day room. He was just lying there. I tried to help the lad, but it was no good. I feel awful. I should've been looking out for him.'

'Yeah, you should've been.' Butler folded her arms and remained standing while Moone took a seat opposite the guard.

'The cameras weren't working in the corridor or the day room,' Moone said. 'Would any of the prisoners know that?'

Loughty shrugged. 'They're not supposed to know, but yous would be surprised what the scum in here find out.'

'How do they find out?' Butler asked.

Loughty looked up at her. 'They have their ways.'

'I bet.'

'Have you heard of the Dark Horses?' Moone asked as he watched for the prison guard's reaction. He thought he saw a flicker of something as he said, 'Course I have. Plenty of 'em have ended up in here.'

'Are there any now?'

'A couple. He was gonna give evidence against them, that right?'

Moone nodded. 'That's right. That's the motive. So, are any of the Dark Horses on this wing?'

'There's two. Duff and Hughes. Right couple of thugs. They were seen hanging round the day room not long before it happened.'

'Who saw them?' Butler asked.

'Danny Vincent. He's another of the guards. He came by to take Wes Bateley to an appointment.'

Moone nodded, recognising the name Bateley. His old mate Terry had promised him that Wes, along with a few other like-minded inmates, would take care of Harris. The other inmates had been moved to different wings or released, leaving Wes to stand guard all by himself. 'So, Bateley gets taken off and that's when the sharks start circling?'

Loughty lifted his tea with a shrug. 'It's a dangerous place in here. Especially when you're going to give evidence against the likes of the Dark Horses.'

'If it was one of the inmates,' Butler said and leaned over the table, staring at the guard, 'they'd have blood all over their prison uniform.'

'Probably,' Loughty said. 'Unless they found something to cover themselves with...'

'But they'd still have to get rid of it.' Butler kept staring at him. 'Unless someone helped them get rid of it.'

The guard widened his eyes as he sat back, the flicker of anger tightening his face. 'Hang on, are yous trying to say I had something to do with this? I found him. Harris was on my wing, I was responsible for the lad. I don't appreciate what yous lot are insinuating.'

Butler straightened up. 'Well, we'll have Duff and Hughes' cells searched and see what turns up. Maybe a shiv, if we're lucky. But the way it stands, you're the only one with blood on your uniform... and your hands.'

Loughty shook his head. 'That's fucking great, that is. They've probably got rid of whatever they stabbed him with by now.'

Moone stood up. 'We'll see. The Exeter major crime team are in charge of this, but we'll be looking into it. Come on, let's go.'

They both turned away, ready to head out of the visiting area, but Moone considered something and turned back to look at the prison guard. 'Have you ever met a police sergeant called Faith Carthew?'

'No, but I know who she is. She's the one up for murder. The one Harris was going to give evidence against. But no, I've never met her.'

Moone saw nothing to tell him anything he had said was a lie. If he was guilty of being involved in Harris' murder, or of actually committing the act himself, then the man was a stone-cold killer, a particularly callous fox guarding the henhouse.

Abel knelt on the ground, his hands covered in grease and oil as he checked over the scooter. He tightened and cleaned the vehicle and made sure it was fuelled up. Then he changed the plate to the latest he had stolen. After he went to the sink in the kitchen and washed the oil off of his hands, he went back to the garage, took out his latest notebook and started writing down what he had done so far.

As he wrote in his neat, bunched writing, the lights flickered above him. He paused and stared up at the bulb that flashed on and off for a while. It was another sign that he was getting closer. It was working, he was on the right path.

He put the notebook back on the shelf and then picked up and read the other book, the one he had put together himself from bits and pieces he had read in other books, TV programmes or from the information he had gained from talking to the people he'd met on his journey. He smoothed his hand over the pages. It was all there, all the knowledge. He put the book away and walked through the house until he was standing in the empty lounge, staring out of the window. Not much happened outside that window, only the occasional car passing or a postman delivering letters or parcels. People went to work, then they came home looking like their spirit had been sucked out. When he looked at himself in the mirror, he saw the burn of light in his eyes, the glow of knowledge because only he and a few others knew the truth. Everything seemed to be normal, though he knew it was anything but. He could read the signs. He had learned over the last few years to read the signs well.

He went back to the garage and approached the safe. He opened it and looked at the rest of the weapons he had taken from the arms dealer. There was the assault rifle with the sight attached. He took it out and lifted it, tucking it tight against his body as he closed one eye. He moved the rifle around the room as he turned, taking aim. He lowered it, then took out the ammunition and put it in his rucksack. He looked at his watch and saw that the time was approaching.

He slipped the assault rifle into the bag he'd bought and put that and the rucksack on his back. He put on his face mask and baseball cap, then opened the garage door before wheeling the scooter outside and locking the door.

The road flashed under him, the white broken line becoming one long one as he zipped towards the city. The petrol cars rumbled around him while the electric ones gave their strange high-pitched hum. Every object, every vehicle was part of everything else around it. He was focused, ignoring the thud of his heart as he got closer to his destination.

He followed the traffic around the city centre, along Royal Parade and then parked the scooter close to where he was headed. This was the risky part. If he hesitated, he would be caught or gunned down by the police. Then what would happen? he wondered as he walked with certainty towards the door that was wedged between two shops. He knew the door led to a concrete staircase and up to some flats. There was an intercom, so he buzzed some of the numbers until someone asked who was there. He told them he was there to read the electric meter for one of the other flats. The door buzzed and clicked open like he knew it would. It was that simple. He went up the stairs without hesitating, turned right and followed the short corridor towards the next door. He took out the blackjack from his coat as he pressed the doorbell. He heard noise from inside, but no one came to the door, so he pressed it again.

This time footsteps were coming from inside, and the cough of someone clearing their throat. He raised the blackjack and waited. The door was opened by the young, untidy and skinny man he'd seen enter there on many occasions. He brought the cosh down hard, smashing him in the face and breaking his nose. The man stumbled backwards. He looked up at Abel just before he slammed the cosh against the side of his head. He collapsed and lay almost still apart from his shallow breaths. Then he brought the cosh down again and again until his breathing ceased.

He stood up straight and looked towards the windows on the other side of the small flat. He closed the door, took off his rucksack and the bag with the assault rifle inside it and put it on the floor. He took out the weapon, went to the window and opened it. When he was knelt down, he raised the assault rifle and rested it on the window ledge as he stared out over the street below where the shoppers were coming and going, criss-crossing the street. He closed one eye as he looked through the sight, following the figures down below.

'None of it mattered,' he whispered to himself as he put his finger around the trigger. He looked at his watch. He wouldn't have long before they responded.

Then it happened, right before his eyes. Everything stopped. The people on the street froze, glued to the spot. There was quiet. Peace. He aimed.

Joshua Hartwell stepped out of the retro sweet shop on the corner and stifled a yawn, then looked back at the shop. His girlfriend, Andrea, was still in the shop with his little sister, Ruby. They were buying a big selection for when they went to the cinema later. The film was on at the Barcode and the Vue, but Ruby reckoned the Barcode had a better selection of sweets. He stretched, thinking about work as he looked up at the shop sign and remembered it used to be Game. Tomorrow, he had a game of footie to play with some of his mates, as long as Andrea didn't mind him slipping out for a couple of hours. He poked his head back into the shop and saw the two of them were getting closer to the till. Thank God, he thought and turned round to look towards the sundial where there was a scattering of people sitting all around it. Pigeons pecked at the ground, while seagulls squawked and came in to push them out of the way. They were the bullies of the bird world, Joshua decided and felt like running over and kicking them.

But then he saw the old man walking towards him, tapping his metal stick as he tried to adjust his flat cap.

His head sprung up and looked towards the blue sky as he heard the cracking sound that seemed to come from all around. For a moment he thought it was thunder, then he looked down and saw the old man lying on the ground a few feet from him.

'You all right, mate?' Joshua asked, then saw a woman coming towards him, looking concerned.

'You OK, my luvva?' the woman said and crouched down.

There was another cracking sound. No, it was more like fireworks popping. The woman fell on top of the man, her eyes staring at Joshua. Then he saw it and he shuddered. There was blood in her hair and on the old man's shirt. He heard the sound again, the echoing crack as several pigeons took flight.

He cried out as a red-hot poker of pain tore into his arm. He fell to his knees as he gripped his arm and felt the warmth between his fingers. He looked around, trying to make sense of what was happening and saw people running and screaming in all directions.

'Josh?'

He turned around, looking back at Andrea and Ruby as they came out of the shop. They were both looking at him with confusion stamped on their faces.

The cracking sound came again and someone cried out across the way.

'What the fuck's going on?!' Andrea shouted as she grabbed hold of Ruby and pulled her close.

'Get back!' Joshua shouted and tried to get up. His arm throbbed as more blood oozed between his fingers.

'Josh!' Andrea was white, her eyes full of tears.

The pain tore through him before he heard the sound echo all around the shops. He trembled as he looked down. His leg was red and hot. He let out a grunt as tears filled his eyes.

'Get in the shop!' he managed to call out. 'Get Ruby inside!'

CHAPTER 8

Butler raced them both back towards Plymouth when they got the call from DS Chambers about the shooting. Moone's head was spinning all the way back to everything that had occurred, trying to fathom it all. His body stayed in a state of rigidness as his heart went into jackhammer mode.

'The Rattery,' Butler said, nodding to a sign on their left that headed off to another junction on the A38.

Moone snapped out of his half-dream, half-nightmare. 'Sorry, what?'

'The Rattery. When I see that, I know I'm ten miles from Plymouth.'

He nodded. 'What the hell's going on? First, a plumber gets stabbed, and then two kids get shot in a car. Then a bomb goes off in Drake Circus, and now we've got another shooting.'

'Another bloody nutter who wants to cause as much destruction as possible. Same shit, different loony.'

Moone looked at her. 'Maybe she's right this time.'

Butler flashed her eyes over to him before putting them firmly back on the road. 'Who? That cow from counter-terrorism? Richer the bitcher? She's here to poke her nose in and take over because that's how she gets her kicks.'

'But this is terrorism, isn't it? He's terrorising Plymouth.'

'They all terrorise in their own way, Moone. When that last psycho was strangling and beating women in their own homes, plenty of people were terrorised...'

'Shootings and bombs?' He stared at her, his stomach filling with lead.

'What?'

'This isn't us, is it? Not on our own anyway.'

Moone saw the strange sails that looked as if they were always fluttering over the Sainsbury's at Marsh Mills. It had always been the first landmark he'd seen when he reached Plymouth by car. The city he had come to love but now couldn't help.

'Why hasn't he made contact?' Butler asked, swinging the car around and heading for the city centre, her words cutting through his thoughts.

'What do you mean?'

'Terrorists, they plant bombs and kill people for attention, to highlight a cause, don't they? What's the cause?'

Moone shrugged. 'I don't know.'

'No called-in warnings. That's what the IRA used to do. Even the extremist groups claim their part, hold up their hands and say that was us, because they want us to know. Why isn't this bastard?'

'Maybe he's waiting…'

Butler put her foot down and roared on. 'Waiting for what? No, he's not a fucking terrorist. Not in the way they think.'

'Then what?'

Butler let out a harsh breath. 'I don't know. But I am going to find out why he's targeting my bloody city and I'm going to stop him.'

Moone stared at her and the grim look of determination stamped into her face. He wanted to feel as determined as her, but that strange sensation crawled up from the dark inside him again as his body trembled. He'd been here before, had been through all this before somehow. He just didn't understand how.

They couldn't get close to the centre of the city and had to park a few streets away and walk the rest of the way. The military and Navy had been mobilised. There were soldiers on the streets, guarding the cordons that had been set up all around the town. It was eerie to see so many armed military and naval personnel standing on the streets and no actual civilians. There were army trucks and police vans dotted everywhere and two police helicopters circling overhead.

Moone approached a line of uniforms who were guarding the cordon that cut off a part of Royal Parade opposite the pedestrian crossing. There were three armed police officers too, each of them cradling their MP5s.

He showed his ID to one of the uniforms, a grey-haired Inspector who he didn't recognise. 'DCI Peter Moone. Who's in charge?'

The Inspector looked round and then shrugged. 'That's tough to say, sir. Counter-terrorism has been crawling all over everything for hours.'

'Richer?' Butler asked with one of her louder huffs.

'Yeah, Commander Richer.' The Inspector nodded. 'She's here somewhere.'

Moone noticed a muscular, shaven-headed man walking towards the cordon. He was wearing a green army T-shirt and camouflage trousers. He also noticed the scars on his neck and chin, as if something very sharp had cut deep into his flesh.

The man came over and eyed them with

cold grey eyes as he said, 'Who're you? Police?'

'That's right,' Moone said as he took out his ID and tried to say his name again, but one of the helicopters came in low and drowned him out.

'Major Nick Lacroix,' the man said and folded his arms over his solid chest. 'You're not needed here. This is now officially a Counter-Terrorism investigation.'

'Oh bloody hell,' Butler groaned and turned away.

Moone kept his eyes on the man who was staring at him with his dead expression.

'Is Commander Richer here?'

'She's busy,' Lacroix said and nodded in the direction of the station. 'I think you're needed back at the station to help out. Better run along.'

Moone tried to keep looking at him, but it was like gazing into a void that stared back at him, reflecting all the bad things he'd ever witnessed on the battlefield. He turned away and found Butler on her mobile.

'Yeah, I'll tell him,' she said into her phone. 'We'll be back soon.'

When Butler put her phone away, she sighed and looked at Moone. 'That was Chambers. The Counter-Terrorism lot has taken over the incident room. It's their base of operations now.'

Moone enclosed his face in his hands and

breathed out before he looked at her again. 'Did you see that guy?'

Butler smirked and looked towards the cordon. 'What, the muscular army guy with the dead soul? How could I miss him? I didn't know if I wanted to slap him or rip his clothes off.'

'Really?'

'I'm a copper, but I'm also a woman, Moone.' She stepped closer to him as another helicopter roared overhead and an army truck went rumbling past, heading for Derry's Cross. 'Listen, there's five dead, two seriously injured.'

'Jesus. Who is this bastard?'

'From what Chambers says, he was using some kind of assault rifle and firing at anyone walking past. A young lad is critical and on his way to Derriford. His girlfriend was shot trying to get him to safety. His eight-year-old sister was with them, but luckily, she's OK.'

Moone nodded as his stomach sank again. 'Come on, let's head back to the station.'

As DS Chambers had said, the incident room was filled to the brim with the Counter Terrorism team. Most of the desks had been pushed out of the way and more whiteboards had been moved in and covered in maps of Devon and Cornwall. Moone was standing at the top of the stairwell for a while, looking through the glass doors at the military personnel who raced around and shouted orders at each other. He turned and headed down to the floor below, where the small incident room was. Butler and DI Jones had already set up their desks at either end of the table sitting at the centre of the room. All their crime scene photos were missing, but Moone assumed that Richer's people had staked a claim on them.

He stood by the door, his hands in his pockets, wondering what to do now.

'Welcome to the B-team,' Jones said when she saw him, then pressed something on her phone. Music started playing and then Celine Dion's singing came out of a speaker by the empty whiteboard.

Butler sighed as she looked at Moone. 'So, what do we do now?'

Moone shrugged. 'I don't know. There's plenty of robberies and drug offences to look into.'

'Is that it?' Jones asked, turning down the music. 'They've taken the case away from us and we take the scraps?'

Moone nodded. 'I guess so.'

'Ah, DCI Moone, there you are,' the Chief Super's voice called out behind him. He turned to face her and saw she was wearing a look of both sympathy and sadness.

'This is an awful day for Plymouth,' the Chief Super said in a solemn tone as she stepped into the room and looked them all over. 'Five dead. Two seriously injured. This terrorist group needs to be stopped.'

'Terrorist group?' Butler said.

The Chief Super nodded. 'That's what Counter-Terrorism believe. They're interrogating Frank Gage again to see if they can get any more information from him. Maybe he'll give up some of the group.'

'Did they find a bomb-making factory on his farm?' Butler asked.

'No, but the bomb-makers might be situated elsewhere.' The Chief Super looked at Moone. 'Peter, you've had a trying few days. You too, Butler. I suggest you two take the rest of the day off. That's my order. And don't forget, Peter, you've got evidence to give first thing in the morning.'

He had forgotten, what with everything going on, but now he had been reminded, his whole body revolted at the thought of seeing Carthew across the courtroom. Then there was the whole deal of being cross-examined. He wanted to throw up.

'And the prosecution barrister will want to go over things with you beforehand,' the Chief Super added. 'So you'd better get there early. Right, I'll see you tomorrow.'

Before she could turn away, Moone said, 'Are we sure this is a terrorist attack committed by Gage and whoever he's running with?'

The Chief Super looked at him from the door, then came over, her face set into serious business mode.

'Listen to me, DCI Moone,' she said, looking him straight in the eye. 'We've got shootings and bombs going off all over the city. Frank Gage has a tonne of cannabis that he and his cohorts have been growing and selling to fund some kind of war they're now waging. I won't pretend to know why they're doing this, but Richer and her team seem to have a handle on things. They're getting ready to transport Gage to a special facility for further interrogation.'

'A special facility?' Butler said, her voice thick with exasperation. 'You mean they're taking him somewhere to torture him until he spills the beans?'

The Chief Super's eyes blazed a little as she looked over at Butler. 'Interrogate him, DI Butler. We don't go in for torture. They have their techniques.'

'Oh, yes, they have their techniques all right.'

'Go home, DI Butler,' Hellewell said, a darker tone entering her voice. 'And you, Moone. Bright and early tomorrow.'

When she had gone, Moone faced Butler and Jones with a shrug. 'So, that's it then. Over to Counter-Terrorism.'

'They couldn't find a pair of tits on a

nudist beach!' Butler huffed.

Jones nearly spat out her coffee as she was mid-drink. She wiped her mouth as she laughed and snorted. 'That's hilarious. I've got to remember that one.'

'Don't forget our other problem,' Butler said, raising her eyebrows at Moone.

'What?'

'The fact that our star witness in the murder trial is now dead, remember?'

'How could I forget? They've still got his witness statement. That's got to count for something.'

Butler gave a deep sigh as she collected her things together. 'Unfortunately, a witness statement read out in court doesn't have the same weight as the witness giving actual evidence. And she knows that.'

Moone nodded. 'Well, it's my turn tomorrow.'

Butler walked up to him and lowered her voice. 'That's what worries me. You and the bitch have history. You can bet your last fiver that they'll use that against you.'

'It'll be fine.' In no part of his brain did he think it would be fine. He felt like throwing up when he pictured himself in court, facing Carthew and being cross-examined by the defence. He tried to put it out of his mind as he said, 'Are you still going out tonight?'

'Too bloody right I am. I need something

to take my mind off all this.'

He wanted to ask her again where she was going but he didn't want to be barked at again. 'Have a nice time.'

'I will. See you in the morning. You too, Jones.'

Where was she going that night and why was she keeping it such a big secret, he wondered. Then he had a terrible thought. *What if she was going on a date?* His stomach jumped in a lift and hit the ground floor while his heart imploded. He was brought out of nightmarish visions by his phone ringing. He'd had other missed calls from the same number he hadn't noticed until that moment. He answered the unrecognised number and said, 'DCI Peter Moone.'

'Oh, hello, this is Sandra Philips. I'm one of the carers who looks after Joy. Joy Morten?'

'Right, yes. Is she OK?'

'Oh, yes, she's fine. It's just that she's having one of her lucid days. I was going to ask her about the whole murder business, but I thought I'd better leave it to the police.'

'Yes, that's probably a good idea. You know what, I've got some time to spare now. I could pop in and see her.'

'That would be great. I'll sit her in the chapel. She likes it in there.'

'Good. I'll see you soon.'

When he was off the phone, DI Jones said,

'You'd better go, boss, before they get security to remove you from the building.'

Moone nodded and headed for the door. 'Bye, Jones.'

'Oh, don't forget, boss, you still owe me Celine Dion tickets.'

He smiled. 'I haven't forgotten.'

Moone went into the Bethlehem House Care Home with the same sense of déjà vu he'd been carrying with him for the last couple of days. He couldn't quite put his finger on when the feeling had been given birth, but now it was there most of the time, sometimes a faint echo in the back of his mind, other times a full-blown scream. But what the hell was it all about? The sensation was in a medium setting when he showed his warrant card to the young man at the reception and was then directed to the chapel.

He walked once more into the hexagonal room and saw the two figures sitting at the far end of the pews under the large cross. The room was duller now that the charcoal clouds had come in and were trying to hide the bright sun. He walked over and saw Sandra Philips, the care worker smiling at him and the little withered shape of Joy Morten. He walked round so the old lady could see him and said, 'Hello, Joy. Do you remember me?'

The old lady looked up, blinking at his

face, a smile breaking out. 'Do I remember you? Have I met this young man before?'

Sandra patted Joy's hand as she said, 'He came to visit you the other day. He wanted to ask you some questions, Joy.'

Moone crouched down. 'I'm from the police, Mrs Morten.'

'The police?' the old lady's eyes glistened as they widened. 'I'm not in trouble, am I?'

Moone laughed. 'No, you're not. It's just that apparently you got upset the other day and said they'd been a murder.'

'A murder? Did he say murder?' The old lady looked horrified as she stared at the care worker.

'It's all right, my luvva,' Sandra said, gripping her liver-spotted hand. 'No one's been murdered. Everything's all right.'

'Has Brian come to see me?' the old lady asked.

The care worker looked at Moone. 'That's her husband. No, sorry, Joy, Brian can't come now.'

Moone smiled, realising that he probably wasn't going to get any answers from the poor old lady. But there was that sense again, the suddenly overwhelming feeling that he'd met the old lady before. He crouched down again as he said, 'I'm sorry, Mrs Morten, but have you ever lived in London?'

The old dear fluttered her bloodshot eyes

as she stared at him. 'London? Did he say London? Ever lived in London? No, my dear, I've been there a long time ago, probably before you were born. No, I lived in Plymouth all my life. Went to Montpellier Primary School when I was a girl. Honicknowle County after that. Happy days they was.'

Moone nodded as the old lady stared off into a dream. 'That's nice. I used to come and stay in Plymouth when I was a kid. We'd come in the summer holidays and go to the beach.'

'Joy used to run a bed and breakfast, didn't you?' Philips said, patting Joy's hand.

'Really?' Moone asked. 'Where was your bed and breakfast? We used to stay in one, but not sure where it was.'

'Oh, that was a long time ago,' Joy said. 'I used to love that place. Right down by the Hoe, it was. Near the citadel. That's brought back memories.'

As Moone stood up, the strange familiar feeling hung about his brain again but now he could almost see the old woman back then, when his family would be sitting around one of the tables in the dining area of the bed and breakfast place. There she was, much younger, serving them their cereal or fry-ups. He nodded to himself, somehow sure that that was how he knew the old woman. He smiled at her and said, 'Thank you, Mrs Morten, it's been lovely meeting you.'

But the old lady was now chattering away about the old days, so he decided it was time to make his exit and smiled apologetically at the care worker before he started to leave. He thought of his family back then, of him and his sister always bickering in the back of the car and his mum and dad doing pretty much the same in the front over the A to Z. Melancholy overtook him as he headed to his car and he made a mental note to go and see Alice tomorrow after he'd been in court. He felt sick at the thought of the whole procedure and tried to get it out of his mind as he drove towards home. He looked out at the coast as he raced past, the bright sun glinting off the sea, the silhouettes of tankers and smaller boats out on the horizon. Thin strips of cloud cut into the cornflower blue sky. He let out a deep breath and tried to relax. He would go home, try not to think about the case or court and crack open a bottle of wine. Also, he would try not to obsess over Butler's date, if it was, in fact, a date.

He parked up next to his mobile home, then climbed out, unlocked the door and went in. It was warm and smelt a little stale inside, so he opened a few windows and loosened his tie. He sat down at the breakfast table, found his cigarettes and lit one. His hand trembled as he brought it to his lips and took a deep drag as he leaned back. Relax, he told himself and closed his eyes, listening to the squawk of the seagulls outside and the sound of someone cutting grass somewhere. It was fine. Everything was fine. Then why was his heart racing?

He sat up, grabbed the remote and put the TV on. He found the news and watched with ice in his stomach as the BBC Spotlight news showed live images of the cordon around Royal Parade and the police and counter-terrorism personnel standing guard.

'We're pursuing several lines of enquiry at this very moment,' Chief Superintendent Hellewell said as she was being interviewed outside Crownhill Police Station. 'What happened today in our wonderful city is not acceptable. We are working closely with the Counter-Terrorism unit to find the culprits of this heartless attack. My heart goes out to the victims and their families at this time...'

Moone turned off the TV and let out a ragged breath before he took another drag of his cigarette. He got up and went to the door and stood there smoking for a while as he looked out at the other mobile homes and the families that had arrived for the holidays.

Relax, he told himself and closed his eyes. He opened them again, his mind sucking him back to the farm, the shotgun pointing at his head, the mad eyes of Gage behind it. Butler's horrified face, PC Cummings lying bloody and pale. She was still in a critical state in hospital, but hanging on. His whole body was trembling, the cigarette shaking between his fingers. He threw it out onto the grass, then locked the door and went to his car. He started the engine and drove towards the exit of the park, where he pulled up and watched the traffic roaring past in both directions. He sat there, thinking it all through, then grabbed his phone and called DS Chambers.

'Hello, boss,' she said and he could hear Celine Dion belting out a song in the background. 'I thought you were having the rest of the day off?'

'I am,' he said. 'Has the CCTV and ANPR been checked yet?'

'We're going through it and then we're supposed to present our findings to the Counter-Terrorism team.'

'I know. Anything interesting?'

'There's a masked figure on a scooter that comes into the city,' Chambers said. 'Looks like he's got a large backpack on his back.'

'Big enough to hold an assault rifle?' Moone asked as he saw a car coming up behind in the rear-view mirror.

'Big enough, I think. I expanded the search area to the Tamar Bridge, but I didn't pick him up there. So it looks like he was already in Plymouth before the attack.'

'He went out of Plymouth to meet and kill the plumber, didn't he?'

'Yes, we picked him up coming and going. So he lives in Plymouth somewhere.'

There came a toot from the car behind, so Moone started driving as he put the phone on speaker and placed it on the passenger seat. 'He's targeting Plymouth, so in terms of crime and geography, I'd say it's likely he lives close to Plymouth. But he's trying to lose us on the B-roads and he'll need somewhere quiet to prepare for all this. Say he wants to do some target practice? He'll need somewhere further out.'

'But not Cornwall?'

'I don't think so. Check to see if there are any cameras in between Plymouth and any of the smaller villages or estates.'

'There's a few newly built estates. Shall I check there?'

'Anywhere. Let me know.' Moone ended the call and kept driving, his mind now up to speed as the grey of the road dashed underneath him and the green fields zipped past on either side. He didn't know where he was heading, so he kept moving up and down the A38, running everything through his brain as he gripped the wheel, his heart still pumping fast.

He saw Butler on a date somewhere with some good-looking guy. He shook his head and brought his mind back to the terrorist attacks. Why is he targeting Plymouth? Is it just one guy or a group?

Then his phone was ringing again, so he reached over and put the phone on speaker.

'Molly?' Moone called out.

'I've got something,' she said and he heard the note of excitement in her voice.

'What is it?'

'I found a traffic camera on the way to Sherford,' she said and he could hear her typing. 'The camera is slightly hidden on that route, so I don't think people notice it and get caught out. Looks like a scooter coming and going down Billacombe Road. I've tried to capture the image but can't make much out.'

'Any more from there? Any more cameras?'

'No, sorry.'

'It's OK. So Billacombe Road?'

'Yes, close to the turning for Elburton.'

'Thanks, Molly.'

'What shall I do with this? Pass it on to Counter-Terrorism? That's what we've been told to do.'

'Can you sit on it for a bit?'

He could hear the hesitation, then Molly said, 'OK. Do you want me to send some uniforms to meet you?'

'No, don't worry, I'm just going to take a look. I'll call in a bit.'

Moone ended the call before Molly had anything else to say or tried to talk him out of driving the route. There was no harm in it and it was only fifteen minutes away along the B-roads. He put his foot down but cursed his luck when he had to slow to a crawl for a tractor. Eventually, it turned off, so he raced again as signs for Sherford appeared. He glanced around him for a while, looking at the houses on the way, and the other cars and bikes that flashed past, but soon realised he was getting distracted by thoughts of déjà vu, by bombs and shootings, by the nightmare that would be tomorrow's grilling in court, and by Mandy's imagined date. He needed a break, a cig.

Up ahead was another road that had a gate at the entrance of it. It was a private road, but there was room for him to tuck his car in. He pulled in and turned off the engine, took out his cigarettes, then lit one and sat back as he took a long drag, listening to the traffic zipping past.

He tried to clear his mind, thinking of a smiling Alice. Memories of the sun-filled B&B came floating back, sitting at the dining table as kids, laughing and fooling about. Now he was smiling, feeling calmer.

He was about to take another drag when he heard the buzzing sound. It was getting louder – the engine of a scooter or small motorbike.

The black shape raced past. They were wearing a black jacket. He dropped his cig out of the open window, started the engine and said thanks that the road was clear and he could pull straight out. The scooter was ahead of him, a few hundred yards. It kept on down the road at a steady pace, but he saw the rider's head turning to get a look at what was behind him.

Then the engine was gunned and the scooter roared on. Moone sped up, his heart punching against his ribcage as he stared at the black figure tearing off and turning right. He put his foot down, getting ready to make the turn. He slowed, watching for traffic, his heart pounding in his ears. It was him, it was him, a voice kept whispering in his ear. He turned into the road but he couldn't see the scooter. The narrow road was clear. He carried on driving down it but there was no sign of anyone. Shit. He braked and then looked around at the bushes and fields. The sun was starting to bleed out into the horizon.

He turned and looked back, then decided to reverse a hundred yards. He stopped and climbed out, looking around at the fields and the empty road. Nothing.

There was a clicking sound close behind him that made him jump. His heart pounded again as he turned his head and saw the dark shape of someone standing a few feet back. They were holding something in their hand that looked very much like a gun.

CHAPTER 9

'Turn around very slowly,' the deep, muffled voice said.

Moone was shaking as he raised his hands and turned to face the man dressed in dark clothing. There was the gun, wavering a little as it was pointed at Moone's head. There was a rattling beat of blood in his chest. He heard the echo of a gunshot and flinched. But it was quiet, apart from the sound of birds in the trees and his pulse thudding in his ears.

The man with the gun wore a dark baseball cap, sunglasses and a face mask. He was white, taller than Moone and of average build. He made mental notes in case he survived this moment. An image burned into his mind; Butler going into the morgue to identify his body.

'How did you find me?' the man asked, almost matter-of-factly.

Moone shrugged. 'Luck, I suppose.'

'Luck?' The man gave a strange, dry laugh. 'No such thing as luck. You found me because you had no choice.'

'I don't understand.'

'No, you don't understand. But you will one day.'

'Will I? Why will I?'

Those dark glasses stayed fixed on him, but he didn't say anything for a while. But Moone could feel his eyes on him, and all the dark thoughts behind them.

'Why did you do it?' Moone asked, trying to keep his voice steady.

'Why?'

'The couple in the car, the bomb, and the shooting today? That was you, wasn't it?'

There was a nod. 'Because I have no choice.'

'Everyone has a choice. Like now. You can lower that gun, put it away.'

'Then what? Hand myself over to you?'

'Why not? Otherwise...'

'What?' The man stepped nearer, the gun getting so close to Moone that he flinched. 'Otherwise what? Your armed response team or the counter-terrorism lot will shoot and kill me?'

'Something like that.' Moone thought

about psychology as he dug around in his dusty mind to find a way to survive. He had shot two young people in a car, point-blank, and randomly gunned down a passer-by in the street. He knew he wouldn't hesitate to shoot a policeman because they were just part of the machinery of the law, of the government. They weren't real people.

'My name's Peter Moone,' he said quickly.

'I know.'

'You knew my name already? Have we met?'

The man took another pause before he said, 'Abel.'

'I'm sorry, what did you say?'

'My name is Abel. At least that's what I'm called now.'

'What were you called?'

There came the dark and troubled laugh again. 'Just Abel. Everything else is gone.'

'They think you're a terrorist.'

'Of course they do. That's all they understand. They can't see beyond the facade, they can't see the intricate patterns.'

'So… you're not a terrorist?'

'No.'

'Then why…?'

The man lowered the gun a little, the light shining on his dark glasses. 'You wouldn't understand. Actually, that's not true. You wouldn't believe me. But you'll understand.'

'How will I?'

'When the time comes. Tell me, Peter, do you get the feeling you've done all this before? People call it déjà vu, but that's just their tiny minds trying to make sense of things. It's more than that. Can you feel it?'

Moone nodded because he didn't know what else to do.

'No, you don't get it. I hoped you would.' The gun rose again, trembling in his gloved hand. 'Now, turn around and get on your knees.'

'Abel,' he said as the thunderous beat of his heart started again. 'You don't have to do this.'

'Yes, I do. That's the point. I have no choice. This is fate and it will always overpower my will. Now, turn around and get on your knees. Now!'

His body violently trembled as he managed to shuffle his feet and turn around. He saw Alice, crying when she found out what had happened. Then Butler, who he never got to tell how he felt. What an idiot he had been.

'Now, on your knees and put your hands behind your back.'

He crouched down and rested his knees on the hard road, then put his hands behind his back, locked his fingers together and dug them into his palms. This was it. The end.

He saw the figure grow larger behind him, his cool shadow blanketing him. The gun was close, he could sense it almost touching his scalp. He closed his eyes. Alice. Tears welled in his eyes.

His heart pounded, pounded, pounded.

He jerked and let out a cry when the engine roared behind him. The man sped past on the scooter, racing off down the road, leaving Moone still on his knees as he watched him growing smaller and wavering in the heat of the road.

He stayed there for a moment, the tears still in his eyes, his whole body trembling. It was a few minutes before he managed to climb up on his unsteady feet. He took a few shaky breaths and then pulled out his phone to call the station.

The car shook as the door slammed shut. Moone looked up and saw DSU Boulton had climbed in behind the wheel and was adjusting the mirror so he could look at him. Moone caught sight of himself dressed in a forensic outfit. The SOCOs had taken his clothes for analysis, even though he had protested that the suspect hadn't touched him.

'What the fuck were you thinking, Moone?' Boulton said, his eyes burning in the mirror.

'I just...'

'You didn't think, did you? You could have been killed, you bloody idiot. You do understand that, don't you?'

Moone nodded. 'I know. It's just that Richer and the Counter-Terrorism…'

Boulton turned in his seat to look at him. 'What, you think you know better than them? I suppose your time in the Met has taught you how to track down terrorists, has it?'

'No.'

'No. It hasn't, Moone. Fucking hell.' Boulton turned round and faced the road as the sound of another car engine came from behind. A Range Rover pulled up beside them with Commander Richer in the back. Moone sighed when he saw her face was red and tight as she climbed out and slammed the door behind her.

'Wait here,' Boulton said, then climbed out and cut her off.

'I want to talk to DCI Moone,' she said, her eyes jumping to him as he watched the confrontation from the back seat.

'I'm dealing with it, Commander,' Boulton said.

Richer came over to the car and stared icily at Moone. 'You realise he's going to run, don't you, Moone? We might have had a chance to track him down but now you've royally fucked that up.'

Moone nodded. 'He calls himself Abel.'

Richer raised her eyebrows, still looking pissed off. 'What was that? I didn't quite hear.'

Moone started opening the door, so Richer

and Boulton stood back as he climbed out. He looked between them, his stomach sinking even further, trying to crawl into a ditch. 'He's white, between five feet nine and six feet. He doesn't have much of an accent. He calls himself Abel. That's what he said.'

Richer folded her arms. 'Abel? As in Cain and Abel?'

'Yes, I think so.'

'What else? What do they want? What are their demands?'

Moone let out a ragged breath. 'I don't think it's a group, I think it's just him.'

'Bollocks,' Richer said. 'What about Gage and the farm? No, he's messing with you, trying to put us off the scent…'

'I don't think so…'

Richer huffed. 'You don't know anything, Moone. You know exactly fuck all. Do you know what you need? You need putting in your place. I'm going to do my utmost to get you demoted back to a detective inspector. Believe me, I can do it. I know a lot of people above your pay grade. Now, I suggest you fuck off out of my sight.'

'Come on,' Boulton said. 'I'll drive you home. One of the uniforms can drive your car.'

Moone climbed back in and put his seat belt back on, still aware of Richer standing by the car and throwing dark looks his way. Boulton started the engine and then slowly drove them up the road, steering around the SOCOs and the horde of armed officers that had turned up.

'Armed units and uniforms will be crawling all over the local housing estates and farms, and everywhere else,' Boulton said as he took them into a narrow lane and turned the car around. 'Chances are he'll be gone, though. Might just do a runner now and we'll never see him again.'

'He won't stop,' Moone said.

Boulton eyed him in the mirror. 'Why do you say that?'

'What he said. He said he was doing this because he had to.' Moone picked up his phone which the SOCOs had left for him along with his keys and wallet. He looked up Abel and then read out what he found: 'Abel is the second son of Adam and Eve, brother of Cain. He appears in the book of Genesis. He is righteous and faithful and made a pleasing offering to God. Cain killed Abel in a fit of jealousy and he became the first murder victim in recorded biblical history.'

'So, he's committing acts of terrorism because of religion,' Boulton said, letting out a tired breath. 'Just like so many others.'

'I don't think so. It's more than that.'

'Then what?'

Moone shrugged. 'I don't know but I don't think this is about a religious cause...'

'Well, you don't have to worry about it now. Let Richer and her lot deal with it. I'm taking you home. You've got evidence to give tomorrow morning so you need to rest up.'

For the rest of the journey, Moone looked out of the window and contemplated his fate, cringing when he thought of the bollocking he would face at some point tomorrow. But there was the trial to contend with first and again fear gripped him at the thought of giving his evidence. There was so much that could go wrong.

He saw the gun wavering close to his face, the blurry face of Abel behind it.

The gunshot rang out, the high-pitched whine remaining after it. Moone jumped, convinced he had been shot.

'You all right?' Boulton was staring at him in the rear-view mirror again. 'You're shaking and you look like death.'

Moone picked up his phone and his other possessions when he realised they were parked close to his caravan. 'I'm fine.'

He opened the door and climbed out.

'Get some sleep, Pete,' Boulton said through his window. 'Just tell the truth tomorrow. It's all you can do.'

Where the night went to, Moone wasn't sure, but he woke up on his mobile home's built-in sofa with a crick in his neck. He remembered a female uniform, PC Natalie Naylor, had brought his car to him. He had still been wearing the forensic suit when she'd handed the keys over with a smile, and he'd felt like a total idiot as he stammered his thanks.

He made a coffee and stood at the door with a smoke, watching two seagulls fighting over a few discarded scraps that one of the holidaying families had thrown onto the grass. He took a deep drag and tried to imagine what he might be asked during the trial, but he couldn't concentrate because he kept seeing Abel pointing the gun at his head.

He showered and dressed in a daze, forced a slice of toast down, and more coffee, before he found himself driving to Plymouth and parking close to the Combined Courts. He had another cigarette before he went inside.

'Take your time and be precise,' Simon Bray KC said as they sat opposite each other across the highly polished table in the court's consultation room. Bray was already dressed in his stark black robe and wig, his eyes sharp and serious. The overhead light hummed away.

'The defence will go hammer and tongs at the legality of the search of her vehicle. They will claim it was personal and more than likely, bring up your past with the defendant. Don't let them make this about you.'

Moone sat up, his jaw and his shoulder muscles tight. 'I won't. We searched her car because we had reasonable suspicion to believe she was the last person to see DI Rivers alive.'

'Good. Stick with that. You had reasonable suspicion and not only that, remember we have the blood found in the flat that DS Carthew was staying at. Anything else is irrelevant. The jury won't care about your previous relationship with the defendant unless the defence makes them care. We cannot let them.'

Moone nodded. 'I'll do my best.'

Moone followed the bailiff into the courtroom. He heard hushed voices but didn't look towards the jury as he was directed to the witness stand.

He swore to tell the truth, then waited for Simon Bray, the prosecution barrister to come towards him, his presence commanding as his eyes fell on Moone.

'Can you please tell the court who you are,' Bray said.

'My name is Peter Moone,' he said after he cleared his throat. 'I'm a DCI, Detective Chief Inspector, with Devon and Cornwall Police.'

'Thank you, DCI Moone,' Bray said, looking at his notes. 'It was you that ordered a search of the defendant's car after her arrest for murder, was it not?'

'It was.'

'You had a search warrant, signed by a magistrate. Is that right?'

'Yes, that's correct.'

'And during the search, what did the search team find?'

Moone gave a quick look towards the jury and saw them all staring towards him. Out of the corner of his eye, he could see the shape of Carthew and felt her eyes radiating out to him, calling him to look at her.

'The team found the victim's mobile phone,' Moone said and cleared his throat again. 'Her phone had been tracked to Plymouth.'

'And you can tell the court why you believed the defendant might have a reason for murdering DS Maxine Rivers?'

Moone prepared himself for the lie he had to tell, that he and Butler had agreed on. 'I had previously talked to Maxine Rivers when she visited Plymouth and she admitted that she was in a relationship with Faith Carthew.'

Bray looked towards the jury. 'The victim told you that she was in a relationship with the defendant?'

'Yes.'

The defence barrister stood up. 'Objection, Your Honour. Hearsay.'

'I'd like to hear where this is going,' the judge said. 'Objection overruled. Please get to the point, Mr Bray.'

'Yes, Your Honour, thank you.' Bray looked at Moone. 'When you spoke to DI Rivers, did she give any indication that she was in fear for her life?'

'Yes. Because Rivers had previously been investigating a case where the defendant was a suspect, she came to believe that the defendant had only entered a relationship with her to keep her quiet. She told me she feared that she wanted to permanently keep her quiet.'

Murmurs came from the public gallery until the judge called the court to order.

'So, when Maxine Rivers disappeared, you came to believe that Faith Carthew had done away with her?'

'Yes, I did. I consulted with my team and they agreed and so we issued a warrant for her arrest.'

'So, to summarise, because of Maxine Rivers' fears and her admission that she was in a relationship with the defendant, you and your team decided that Faith Carthew's car should be searched for evidence that would prove her guilt in the suspected murder of Maxine Rivers, where the search team found the victim's phone. Is that correct?'

'Yes, that's correct.'

'Thank you, no more questions, Your Honour.'

Moone let out a shaky breath as the judge said, 'I believe the prosecution has some questions for this witness. Mrs Martin?'

Moone watched Hanna Martin KC stand

up from her bench, and then approach carrying her notes. His chest throbbed as she looked at him with an intense stare before she said, 'DCI Moone, you have been a police officer for how long?'

Moone swallowed. 'Nearly twenty years. I was originally stationed in London...'

'Thank you. You are now stationed at Charles Cross Police Station in Plymouth, are you not?'

'I am.'

'The same station in fact that the defendant was stationed at before she was accused of murder. Is that correct?'

'Yes.'

'Yes.' Martin KC looked round and made eye contact with the jury before she turned her intense stare back on him. 'Now, DCI Moone, I'd like to discuss the legality of the search that was carried out on the defendant's car after her arrest. Was the search conducted under the authority of a warrant? You are, of course, familiar with the Police and Criminal Evidence Act 1984, commonly referred to as PACE?'

Moone adjusted his seating position as he felt the beads of cold sweat drip down his sides. 'Yes, I am.'

Hanna KC returned to her bench and looked at him as she said, 'I have discussed this issue with your colleague who conducted the search of Ms Carthew's vehicle and now I'll ask you. What does PACE say is required for a warrant to be issued by a magistrate to legally search a suspect's property after their arrest?'

'It's required for the police officer who asked for the search to have reasonable suspicion that evidence will be found relating to the crime they've been arrested for.'

Again, Martin KC looked round at the jury. 'Reasonable suspicion, relating to the crime they have been arrested for. In this case, suspicion of murder. So, I ask you, DCI Moone, what was the reasonable suspicion that led you to believe that a search of former DS Faith Carthew's vehicle would magically produce the victim's mobile phone?'

'Well, DI Rivers' mobile phone had been tracked to Plymouth, and as I said before, I had been informed by her that she and DS Carthew –'

'Were in a relationship. Yes, you've told us as much. Now the problem is, as we know they were in a relationship, and I'm not disputing that fact, then isn't it quite plausible that the victim's mobile phone might have dropped out of her pocket or bag and ended up in her girlfriend's car?'

'Objection, Your Honour,' Bray said as he stood up. 'My colleague is leading my witness.'

'Overruled,' the judge said. 'The witness will answer the question.'

Moone put his hands on his legs and

gripped them. Shit. 'I suppose it's possible, but by that point, DI Rivers had been missing for several days...'

'But you agree it's entirely plausible that her phone fell from her person and ended up under the driver's seat where the search team discovered it?'

'Yes, it's plausible.'

'Thank you, DCI Moone. Now we return to the reasonable suspicion that you say you had when you obtained the warrant you used to search the defendant's vehicle. From where I'm standing, it doesn't look very much like reasonable suspicion, but an unreasonable leap to conclude that her lover would have murdered her and kept her mobile in her car as some kind of trophy, I suppose.'

'Well, as I said, DI Rivers had already told me that she feared...'

'That she feared for her life? Are there any witnesses to this convenient conversation you had with the victim?'

Moone let out a sigh. 'No. There was only the two of us.'

'No. So, it seems to me that your reasonable suspicion for the search warrant fell far below the legal requirements needed to justify the search itself. Wouldn't you agree?'

'No, because –'

'No, you wouldn't agree, because it puts you in a bad light.' Martin began flipping through her notes. 'DCI Moone, we've heard a great deal about the arrest that led to a search of my client's vehicle. But I'd like to explore something the jury hasn't yet heard. Your history with Ms Carthew. You do have a history with Faith Carthew, do you not?'

Moone tried to keep his composure but he was shaking and images kept flashing before his eyes. He kept seeing the wavering gun so close to his face as Frank Gage and Abel somehow combined together. The gunshot boomed and Moone shuddered.

'DCI Moone?'

He shook himself out of it and looked at the defence barrister who was staring at him, her eyes narrowed. 'I'm sorry?'

'Are you still with us, DCI Moone?'

Moone nodded and took a deep breath as his heart raced. 'Yes, sorry, I'm OK.'

'Please answer the question. Do you have a history with the defendant?'

'We've worked together for nearly four years, I think –'

'I'm not referring to your working relationship. I'm referring to the fact that you and the defendant were in a relationship. Is that true?'

Moone's eyes jumped to the dock. There she was, Carthew staring back at him. The subtle smile of victory appeared on her lips for a split second, not long enough for anyone on the jury to see it. He looked away. The truth was all there was left.

'Yes, we were involved in a brief relationship.'

Murmurs and chatter ran through the courtroom again until the judge quietened the room down.

'You were a detective inspector at the time, and the defendant a police constable. Is that correct?' The barrister raised her eyebrows.

'Yes, I saw that she was clever and resourceful during my first investigation and tried to nurture that...'

Martin KC laughed dryly. 'You tried to nurture her. But when she ended the affair...'

'No, she didn't...'

'When the affair ended and the defendant was put on the fast-track programme, you found yourself resenting her, didn't you?'

'Objection!' Simon Bray stood up. 'Your Honour, my colleague is badgering the witness...'

Martin turned to the judge. 'Your Honour, I'm merely illustrating that there was little legal ground for the client's arrest, and therefore I believe there must be another reason why DCI Moone would try and pin the alleged murder of DI Maxine Rivers on my client.'

The judge sighed heavily. 'I'll allow you to

continue, but please hurry up.'

Martin KC looked at Moone and he saw in her eyes almost the same hunger and victorious look in them. His heart sank as he realised he had messed everything up.

'DCI Moone,' the defence barrister continued. 'There was no reasonable suspicion that led to the arrest of my client and for the subsequent search of her vehicle, was there?'

'I believed –'

'You made a massive leap when you decided that the defendant had murdered Maxine Rivers, even though as we know there is no body to prove she was murdered. The DNA evidence in the flat where the defendant was staying, which can be argued is quite insignificant, was found after her arrest. As was the victim's phone which, as I've shown, could have easily fallen out of her pocket. I put it to you that instead of having reasonable suspicion, DCI Moone, what you had was bias, resentment, and jealousy, and you concocted the whole murder charge to destroy the career of the once-promising DS Faith Carthew. Isn't that what happened?'

'No, that's not true.'

'No more questions, Your Honour.'

The defence barrister turned away and left Moone sitting in the witness box, still trembling. He looked at the jury and saw only doubt in their eyes, and when he turned to see Carthew, there was the slow-burning smile, and like him, she knew it was all but over.

CHAPTER 10

Moone barely got a foot into the smaller incident room, carrying his morning coffee, when he was swarmed by the team, all hurling questions at him. The only person who wasn't in his face as he tried to put his coffee on his desk, was Butler. She wasn't there, which made him think again of her imagined date – maybe she's still curled up in bed…

'Did you really come face to face with him, boss?' Harding asked.

Moone managed to put his coffee down and looked the hungry pack of dogs over. 'I did. I drove out to where he was last spotted and… somehow, I bumped into him. Next thing I know, he's shoving a gun in my face.'

'Oh my God,' DI Jones said, a hand over her mouth. 'You must have been terrified.'

Moone nodded and took the lid off his coffee. 'I was. I had to go home and change my pants.'

They all laughed at his bravado, but inside Moone kept seeing the gun in front of his face, and hearing the imagined gunshot echoing in his skull. But it wasn't the only horrific moment that kept playing on loop in his mind; the whole debacle in the courtroom, how Hanna Martin KC had torn him to shreds was also playing non-stop.

'Oh, here he is,' Butler said, waltzing into the incident room. 'The hero of the day.'

'You've heard too, have you?' Moone asked.

'Word gets around,' she said, shaking her head. 'You could've been killed, you idiot. You should've called me!'

'You were busy... doing whatever you were doing.'

She huffed as the team dispersed and went back to their new desks, all crammed around the room. 'How did your giving evidence go?'

Moone let out the sigh that had been building all morning.

'That good, eh?' Butler raised her eyebrows. 'Let me guess, the defence tore you to pieces?'

Moone nodded and came over, not wanting the team to overhear what he was about to say. 'I think... Carthew's going to get off.'

Butler stared at him for a moment. 'I think so too. But, the good news is, she's off the force. She'll never be our boss.'

He smiled. 'There is that. Jason Harris' witness statement will be read out in court today, but with him gone, I don't think it'll stand up to much scrutiny.'

Butler set up a desk near the door, then sat down and looked at him. 'Let's just face facts, that she's not going to prison. Not for very long anyway, even if she does. There's the possession charges, but I don't think they hold water. She might get a few months, if we're lucky.'

'I fucked it all up.' Moone buried his face in his hands, rubbed his eyes and then looked at her again. 'I thought I was being clever. Thought I'd finally got her, but I just ballsed it all up.'

Butler's face turned thunderous as she pointed a finger at him. 'Don't you dare put yourself down, Peter Moone. You did what none of us could've done. You stopped her becoming our boss. You did that.'

He dragged a smile, kicking and screaming to his face. 'Thanks. How did your evening go?'

She narrowed her eyes at him. 'Snout out, trout. So, what are we looking into, now we're not chasing this nutter?'

'Abel,' Moone said.

Butler frowned. 'Who's able?'

'That's what he calls himself,' Moone said and noticed the small team were listening. 'Abel, from the bible, as in Cain and Abel.'

'Why Abel?' DI Jones said as she picked up a marker and wrote the name at the centre of the whiteboard with a question mark next to it. Then she faced them all. 'Didn't Cain murder Abel?'

'Yes,' Moone said. 'Abel was the first murder victim in biblical history.'

'Maybe that's relevant,' Harding said with a shrug.

'Did he say anything to you?' Butler asked Moone.

'He said he couldn't stop even if he wanted to, like he was doing it all against his will.'

Butler huffed. 'Typical nutter, always blames someone else.'

'He said I'd understand what it was all about one day.' Moone walked to the whiteboard and stared at the name. 'But this isn't our case.'

'DCI Moone, a word, please.'

He froze when he recognised the well-spoken voice of the Chief Superintendent and turned and gave her a solemn look. He followed her into the corridor and then up the stairs to his office. His name was no longer on the door, which he was quite pleased about. The Chief Superintendent sat down behind the desk and gestured for him to take a seat.

'Well, you've had a few bad days, haven't you, Moone?' the Chief Superintendent said as she leaned back.

'Yes, ma'am. I'm sorry about…'

'About the court case or yesterday's mess?' She dug her eyes into him as she raised her eyebrows. 'I heard about what happened in court. Basically, it's a complete nightmare. It's not looking good for the prosecution. Frankly I'm surprised the judge hasn't thrown out the case. Basically, you messed up the arrest and the warrant. You ignored procedure. That can't be overlooked and there'll have to be an investigation. Do you understand?'

He nodded as the horror of it all landed on his shoulders. Shit. 'Yes, ma'am. I'm sorry, ma'am.'

'I get it, Moone. I understand that you were desperate to bring down DS Carthew, but you should've gone about it another way, brought it to me or…'

'There was no other way, ma'am. She's too clever. We had no other proof, and no one else believed us that she was corrupt.'

The Chief Super nodded. 'Well, for what it's worth, I believe you. So, there'll be a formal investigation and you'll face a disciplinary board. It might mean a demotion, but that'll be the worst of it. I don't think you'll lose your job, not if I can help it.'

'Thank you, ma'am.'

She nodded. 'Of course, there's also last night's fuck up, pardon my French. I don't often swear, but you were a bloody idiot to go it alone. Who do you think you are, Dirty Harry?'

'Sorry, ma'am, but I didn't honestly think I would run into our killer.'

'Well, he's not our killer any more. Counter-Terrorism are now tracking him and his group down...'

'That's the thing, ma'am, I don't think he is part of a group. From talking to him, I got the sense he's doing this by himself. He told me that he couldn't stop even if he wanted to...'

'Perhaps because other people in his terrorist group would kill him?'

'It's possible, ma'am.'

'Anyway, I think there's some robberies your team can look into. You should get back to work.'

Moone stood up and nodded. 'Thank you, ma'am.'

When Moone went back to the smaller incident room, DI Jones came striding up to him, a smile on her lips. 'Guess what?'

'Celine Dion's performing at Argyle?'

She laughed. 'I wish. No, I've just had word that the counter-terrorism lot have just found the house Abel's been using.'

'Really? How?'

'Some clever sod checked the area near

where you ran into Abel for any reports of anything suspicious, and apparently one of the neighbours had called us a few times complaining about a noisy scooter coming and going. Lucky, eh?'

'Where's the house?'

'Have a look,' Jones said as she directed to him to the whiteboard where she had taped a large black and white map of Plymouth. She pointed to Sherford with her pen.

'Sherford?' Moone said and took a closer look. 'That was only a mile from where I saw him.'

'That's right. He was staying in a house owned by a couple called Sara and Lee Danton.'

'Where are they?'

Jones raised her shoulders. 'No one knows. No sign of them. From what I hear, all their stuff is gone. He got rid of it all.'

Moone let out a harsh breath. 'Jesus. Just wiped away their lives. Who is this bastard? Why's he doing this?'

'Because he's a nutter,' Butler said from her desk.

Moone decided to ignore her input and looked at Jones, his curiosity piqued. 'How do you know all this? I just talked to the Chief Super and she didn't know.'

Jones smiled. 'I know one of the guys who's been seconded to the search team. In fact, he says they're still going over the house now, if we want to take a look.'

Moone flashed back to his conversation with the Chief Superintendent. 'I can't... we can't. This isn't our investigation any more. And it looks as if I might be demoted.'

Butler's head shot up, her eyes full of brimstone. 'What? Why?'

'Because I made a hash of Carthew's arrest and because of last night's cock up. There's going to be a conduct investigation.'

Butler sat back, shaking her head. 'Oh, that's great. So what do we do now? Go and take a look at the series of robberies they've landed us with?'

Moone shrugged, but looked back at the whiteboard and the map, a feeling crawling up his back and a voice telling him to say to hell with it all. 'I don't suppose a quick look would hurt.'

Jones patted his shoulder. 'That's the spirit. I'll drive us.'

'Oh, nice, you two get to swan off while we investigate a break-in.' Butler shook her head.

Moone went over to her. 'It's a quick look and I'll be back. By the way, I popped back in to visit that old dear in the Bethlehem care home. Mrs Morten?'

'Oh, yeah, the bringer of death. How is she?'

'Well, actually she wasn't too bad. It's weird, because I keep getting this sense that

I've met her before somewhere… anyway, when I talked to her, she said she used to run a bed and breakfast near the citadel. Me and my family used to stay in a bed and breakfast…'

'Oh, wow. She had a B&B, and you stayed in one a million years ago. You must be related.'

Moone shook his head and made a face at her. 'Bloody funny. I need to find out if that's the place we stayed.'

'Why? So what if it was? Why is this bothering you?'

'I don't know. I've just got this feeling it's important somehow.'

'Well, ask your sister. The mysterious Kelly Moone.'

'God, no. No way.'

'Why not?'

'For one thing, I have no idea where she is. I haven't seen her for years.'

'Come on, boss!' Jones said as she strode past and out into the corridor.

'Don't worry, I'll hold the fort here,' Butler said. 'And don't go chatting up DI Jones, she's out of your league.'

'Don't get jealous.' He regretted saying it as soon as the words fell from his mouth.

'Yeah, right. As if I'd be jealous of one of your many conquests.'

He was about to leave, but stopped. 'Many? Have you met me?'

'Oh, I'm aware of your nature, Moone. It's a

good job I'm not your type.'

His mouth opened as he saw her turn and go back to what she was typing at her desk. His heart thudded. He remembered the gun wavering inches from his face. The gunshot echoing. Tell her, you idiot.

'What?' Butler was staring at him. 'What're you staring at?'

'Nothing.' He hurried out to find Jones.

The house was in a close on the outskirts of Sherford. It was one of the newbuild estates that had been constructed a few years ago as the town slowly expanded. 'Once it had been another lush part of the green and wild of Devon, land where horse owners kept their animals in the fields,' Jones told him as she drove them towards the house. One of her friends, a uniformed officer called Faye, kept her horse, Meg, nearby and had been horrified when the plans to develop the land had appeared.

Moone saw a response car parked at the edge of the turning and a couple of uniforms stood chatting. DI Jones slowed the car as one of the uniforms, a dark-haired, goatee wearing police sergeant came towards the car as he held up his palm.

'Oh, it's you, DI Jones,' the sergeant said as he looked in her window. His eyes jumped to Moone. 'Sir?'

'We just want a quick look, Sye,' she said and Moone watched as the sergeant flicked his eyes back and forth nervously.

'You'd better be quick,' he said, his voice low. 'We've got orders that no one but the counter-terrorism lot go in. They've been here and taken everything away, so there's not much to see.'

'We'll be quick, I promise,' Jones said and started taking the car to the turning and then went left and towards the wide semi-circle of neat, yellow brick houses. Each one had a large garage, Moone noticed as Jones pulled up outside the house and parked.

Moone climbed out at the same time as Jones and followed her to the door where the police tape had been tied across it. She put on some forensic gloves, then pulled the tape away and went into the hallway. Moone snapped on his gloves and looked at the shiny wood flooring that stretched far into the house and along to a sunlight kitchen at the back. There were stairs to their left and a door to the right. DI Jones pushed open the door that was slightly ajar, then stepped down into the large garage. There were empty shelves on their left-hand side and a table. On one of the walls were a row of noticeboards that had pins in, but whatever they had been holding had been removed.

'Not much to see here,' Moone said as he stood at the centre of the garage.

Jones nodded and turned round, taking it all in. 'Richer has taken everything. Look over there.'

She was pointing to the concrete floor in the corner, close to the garage door. He crouched down as he saw scrape marks. 'Something large was dragged out of here. Maybe a large container.'

'Where the guns were kept?'

'Probably. I wonder what happened to the people who lived here,' Jones said as Moone straightened up.

'I've got a horrible feeling they might be dead,' he said. 'This bastard doesn't hesitate. Killed the plumber, murdered those two kids, planted the bomb and then shot those people in town as well as the person who owned the flat he did the shooting from. He doesn't care who gets in his way...'

'If that's the case, then why didn't he just shoot you?'

Moone faced Jones. 'I keep asking myself that. If he thought I was after him, then why not kill me and slow the investigation down? I mean, of course I'm glad he didn't but it doesn't make sense, does it?'

'Maybe he's got a list and you're not on it.'

Moone shook his head. 'No, the people in town and the bomb... he killed random people.'

'Perhaps because you came face to face and talked? Maybe he couldn't because there you were, up close. He saw you as human, maybe?'

He nodded. 'It's possible. I did tell him my name in the hopes that it might stop him killing me. It might have worked.'

'Sounds like it did.'

'But somehow I'm not convinced. I feel like there's something else going on here.'

Jones narrowed her eyes. 'Like what?'

'I don't know. But I keep getting this feeling that I've been through all this before. Do you know what I mean?'

Jones smiled. 'Not really. Shall we take a look at the rest of the house?'

Moone smiled and gestured for her to go ahead and waited for her to enter the house. The place was pretty much bare now that Richer and her band of miserable men had removed all the evidence. Jones went up the stairs so Moone followed and found himself standing on a wide, carpeted landing, a few open doors all around him. There was nothing in any of the rooms, no scraps for them to feed on or any scent for them to follow. He went to the back bedroom and saw that it had a single bed, a couple of bedside cabinets and a large window. He went to the window and saw that the garden lay beneath it. What had probably been a nice, picturesque garden, was now a dug-up mess. Counter-Terrorism had been thorough. He sighed and looked up beyond the fence that surrounded the large garden. There were fields beyond the garden, and a scattering of thick and old trees which made him happy to see that the developers hadn't quite gone the full hog and destroyed all the greenery.

'There's nothing here,' Jones said from the doorway. 'Sorry, we've been chasing a ghost. He's probably in the wind by now.'

As she spoke, Moone's eyes travelled over the field and the trees. They stopped on a piece of ground close to the line of trees a few hundred yards from the back fence. He was sure he could make out where the ground had been disturbed. He noticed two large rectangles of earth sat close together, as a cold feeling wrapped itself around his spine.

'Jones,' he said, pointing to the window. 'Look at this.'

She came over and looked out the window. 'What am I looking at?'

'About four hundred yards beyond the garden, right by that line of trees.'

Jones leaned forward, staring. 'Oh… is that? That's two mounds of earth, isn't it? Do you think that's…?'

'Yes, I think that might be the couple who used to live here.'

'Oh, God. But the problem is, we can't find them.'

'No, we can't because we weren't here. But your mate out there can. He'll have to say he came to have a look around and just happened to look out this window.'

Jones nodded. 'OK, I'll tell him. Well spotted, boss.'

Moone smiled as she left the room and went back down the stairs, leaving him to watch the possible graves alone. He started to feel a little spooked as he was standing there, so decided to go back down the stairs and stood at the bottom. He looked towards the garage for a moment and then shrugged and went back in. His steps echoed round the empty room. Counter-Terrorism had left nothing for him, no evidence or clues. He was onto a loser. He stared at the boards that someone, probably Abel, had attached to the walls. He stepped closer, trying to imagine what had been pinned to it, guessing it was maps or photos. He could see the pin marks. His eyes passed over the empty board, then stopped. Something wasn't right, his mind was telling him. His eyes went back over the board. What was it?

He focused on one particular area where there was a cluster of pinholes. They were many tiny pinholes collected in a small rectangular shape, the size of a photograph. Why so many pinholes? his brain asked. Because he took it down and put it up again several times. Why? He didn't know, but he needed to find out.

'Boss?' Jones called out.

He came out of the garage and made her start as she was staring up the stairs.

She held her chest. 'God, you made me jump. Found anything?'

'I'm not sure,' he said and went back to the board. Jones followed and stood shoulder to shoulder with him. 'Look at that cluster of pinholes. It forms a rectangle, like there was a photo pinned there. But why so many holes?'

Jones stepped closer. 'Because he moved it, or took it down a few times?'

'But why?'

She looked at him. 'I don't know, but we need to find out what the photograph was of.'

The courtroom felt stifling and airless to Mike Barker, crime scene manager, as he watched the defence barrister going through her notes before she stood up. The wood-panelled walls seemed to be closing in on him as he loosened his tie a little. His back was damp with sweat. Martin KC came striding towards him with determination in her eyes as she held her notebook open.

'Mr Barker,' she said, her tone conversational. 'I'd like to revisit your testimony from earlier, if we can? You examined the flat in which the police believed that the defendant was staying when the alleged murder of Maxine Rivers took place, and you said you found bloodstains. Is that correct?'

'Yes, I found a few areas where there were definite bloodstains.'

'Where exactly in the flat did you find these bloodstains?'

Barker cleared his throat and loosened his tie again. 'Well, first of all, there were spots of blood close to the bookshelf, and some spatters on the corner of the coffee table. Also, there were traces of blood found on a mop under the sink in the kitchen.'

'A mop?' Martin KC turned and briefly looked at the jury.

'Yes, a mop. Which suggested someone had tried to clean up after the crime.'

'Let's talk quantity. How much blood did you find?'

'Well, a few spots, as I said, by the bookshelf and on the coffee table and on the mop...'

'So, not a great deal of blood?' Martin stared at him. 'Some spots and some smears, would you say?'

'Yes, but someone had tried to clean up the blood...'

'DNA was extracted from the blood, was it not?'

'Yes.'

'And did it match the alleged victim's DNA?' Hanna Martin KC raised her eyebrows.

'It did.'

She nodded. 'Let me ask you another question. The amount of blood you found was small, as you freely admit. Is it possible that the victim had merely had an accident, say she cut herself and that's how the blood ended up on the floor and the coffee table?'

'Objection, Your Honour,' Simon Bray KC said as he stood up. 'My colleague is leading the witness.'

The judge leaned forward. 'I'd very much like to hear where the defence is going with this line of questioning. I will allow it. Please get to the point of your question, Ms Martin.'

'Yes, thank you, Your Honour,' she said and faced Barker. 'So, I ask again, is it possible that DI Maxine Rivers injured herself in some way and that's how the blood ended up in the flat?'

Barker swallowed, then nodded. 'It's possible. Yes.'

'Thank you. Now, we know the police believe that the defendant murdered Maxine Rivers in that flat and then somehow disposed of her body. And you say that you found spots of blood around the flat and on a mop in the kitchen. Is that correct?'

'Yes. And the blood belonged to the victim.'

The barrister nodded. 'The defendant, Faith Carthew, was herself a police detective. A detective who was fast-tracked. A detective by all accounts who is very clever. Now, my question to you, Mr Barker, is why would a clever detective like Faith Carthew murder someone in a flat where she was staying and then fail to clean up properly after herself and leave all that evidence behind? What do you think?'

Barker shrugged. 'I don't know.'

'No, because it doesn't make sense. Does it, Mr Barker? It's possible that Maxine Rivers was staying there and that she cut herself and that's how the blood ended up in the flat before she decided to up and vanish for whatever reason. Isn't that possible?'

'I suppose it's possible…'

Martin KC turned and faced the judge. 'No more questions, Your Honour.'

CHAPTER 11

Moone had his small team gathered around the whiteboard, most of them holding the coffees that he and DI Jones had bought on the way. There weren't many of them as most had been seconded to the Counter-Terrorism team upstairs. There was Harding, Butler, Jones and himself, a ragtag of battle-hardened detectives who were stifling yawns.

'Some crack team of cops, we are,' Moone said and opened his coffee.

'I wouldn't like to be chased by us,' Jones said as she rested her backside on her desk.

Moone looked towards the door. Butler saw where he was staring and said, 'Are you expecting someone else or have you got a thing for open doors?'

'Very funny. No, I asked DS Chambers to

make an appearance.'

'No chance of that,' Harding said, suppressing a yawn as he stretched. 'She's been sucked into the world of covert operations and all that shady business.'

Moone nodded. 'All right. I'll get started. Well, the bad news is, the house where Abel was staying has been emptied by Richer and her lot. They haven't left even a juicy little morsel for us. Well, that's not exactly true. We kind of found something... well, actually it's nothing.'

'Oh, God, stop faffing,' Butler groaned. 'I'd like to catch this sod before I have to collect my pension.'

Moone held up his hands. 'OK. In the garage there were boards on the wall where Abel had pinned stuff. Probably maps of the area or something. Well, we noticed that there was a small rectangular space where something the size of a photo had been pinned. Thing is, whatever it was, had been pinned, taken down and re-pinned a few times by the looks.'

'That's it?' Butler asked. 'All you found was an empty space where there might have been a photograph? Bloody hell. I can't believe we've cracked the case already.'

There came a knock on the door frame. They all turned to see DS Molly Chambers standing there looking a little red-faced.

'Come in, Molly,' Moone said. 'Shut the

door.'

Chambers did as she was asked and then came towards the whiteboard. 'I can't stay long. They're giving a press conference today. Hellewell and Richer are going to give it.'

'Oh, good,' Moone said, glad he'd been overlooked. 'Right, I asked Molly along because… well, Molly, I have a big favour to ask.'

All the team looked at her, making her face burn again.

'What is it?' Chambers asked, eyeing them all.

'You can say no.' Moone smiled as he prayed she wouldn't.

'What do you need?'

Moone cleared his throat. 'When they found Abel's house, Richer and that lot took everything that was there. Well, just about everything that was there.'

Molly nodded. 'Yeah, it's all in the special room they've put aside for it.'

'We need something from there, or at least a photo of it,' Moone said.

Chambers' eyebrows almost lifted from her head as her face went an even deeper shade of red. 'You want me to take a piece of evidence?'

'Not take it, just take a photo of it.'

Chambers shrugged. 'I don't know if I'll be let in there.'

'Maybe you can make up an excuse,' Butler

suggested.

Chambers nodded. 'I suppose.'

Moone noticed the worry in her eyes. 'I know you're worried you'll get in trouble…'

She looked sheepish as she looked at them all. 'You know what Commander Richer's like. She'll throw me off the team if I get caught.'

'I know. I know we're asking a lot…'

'Do they still think Abel's part of a terrorist group?' Butler asked.

'That's the official line,' Chambers said. 'They've got Gage locked up somewhere, but I don't think he's given them anything so far.'

'That's because he doesn't know anything,' Butler said, huffing, and shook her head.

Molly was about to say something else, but then her phone started ringing in her pocket. She gave an apologetic look as she took it out and then went back out of the door, leaving the team to stare after her.

'Maybe we're asking too much,' DI Jones said and sipped her drink.

'Probably isn't anything anyway,' Butler said and went to sit at her desk. Then she looked at Moone again as she said, 'Oh, by the way, I've got a lead on where you might have stayed when you were here as a kid.'

Moone went over. 'Really? How?'

'I found your sister.' She smiled.

'You what? Why? How?'

'Facebook, grandad. It was pretty easy. She was Kelly Moone and now she's called Kelly Barber.'

'So you talked to my sister?'

'I messaged her.'

'What did she say?'

'Said she'd look into it. Thinks she's got photos somewhere. She's pretty sure there's one taken outside the hotel. Anyway, she'll be back in touch.'

Moone nodded, a little taken aback that Butler had communicated with his sister when he hadn't talked to her since... it must have been their dad's funeral. He wondered about her life now. 'Does she have any kids?'

'I think so. I'll ask her. Or you could ask her.' Butler stared at him.

'Maybe. Thanks anyway.'

The door to the incident room opened and Chambers put her head around the door as her eyes found Moone. 'Boss, they're on the move. Apparently two bodies have been found near the house in Sherford. Probably the owners.'

'What a sick bastard,' Butler said.

Moone went over to her. 'Thanks for letting us know. What I asked before...'

'There'll be fewer people around now,' Chambers said. 'What is it you want me to take a photo of?'

Moone explained about the missing photo that would likely have many pin holes. 'Or it might be a postcard, we don't know for sure.'

'Alright,' Chambers said. 'I'll see what I can do.'

'Thanks. Be careful.'

She smiled, then shut the door. He turned and faced the team, but they were back at their makeshift desks, typing or making calls. Moone walked to the whiteboard as he stretched, looking at the large map of Plymouth. He was out there somewhere, hiding out. They thought he would be on the run but he knew that the man he had met, who had stuck a gun in his face, would never stop.

Abel parked in the car park and looked towards the lane that ran through the centre of the park, alongside Argyle Football Ground. There was the statue of Jack Leslie, holding out his fists. His eyes scanned past the coach sat waiting outside the stadium, close to the entrance. He climbed out, locked the car, then started walking towards Argyle as he pulled his baseball cap down. He stopped before he joined the path to let a group of women pass as they pushed prams. He turned as he observed the whole building, then reached into his pocket and brought out his phone. He started to record as he quickly swept over the outside. He was trying to think of the best way inside. Buying a ticket wasn't an option as that would leave a paper trail. He walked around the building, careful not to look too interested in the ground. A group of schoolkids came out of the grounds of the stadium and started lining up to get on the coach as its engine rumbled away.

No one paid him any attention as he stood still for a moment, looking the structure over. Then he saw the large doors open, revealing part of the stadium and seating. A couple of men came out. They had uniforms on. A cleaning company's logo printed on their blue polo shirts. He discreetly lifted his camera and started to film them as they carried cleaning equipment towards the car park. He kept watching as they headed for a white van with the same cleaning company logo on the side. He nodded to himself, then hurried towards his car and got in. He started the engine as he kept watching the two cleaners as they opened up the van and put away their equipment. The two men chatted and laughed as they climbed into the vehicle. Abel started his engine as the van started to move, turning towards the exit.

He followed, keeping back a little as the van turned onto Outland Road and headed in the direction of Derriford and then onto Tavistock Road. The van slowed and signalled to turn right to travel along William Prance Road. It passed the large Realm store, then turned into a small parking area opposite a small group of offices. Abel pulled in and parked up at the far end of the car park and watched the two men head towards the building. It was the cleaning company's headquarters.

He took a few photos and then opened the glove box and took out his notebook. He wrote down everything that had happened up until that moment and then put the book away again. It was all laid before him like a flowing river, and he felt himself gripped by the current and pulled towards his fate.

As she walked along the corridor where the new evidence room was, DS Chambers had a quick look around to see who was about. Just down the hall in one of the smaller offices, sometimes used by the Inspectors to catch up on the morning briefings, was a small group of civvies working on the case. They had all been made to sign the Official Secrets Act, as had Chambers. Her heart fluttered as she thought of it; was taking a cheeky look for a missing photograph going against the Official Secrets Act? Surely if she kept it in house, and didn't share it with the general public, then she wouldn't be breaking any rules.

She stopped by the conference room that was now being used as the evidence room and pretended to look at her phone.

Occasionally some of the Counter Terrorism personnel walked past, hardly looking her way. Then there was no one, just her in the corridor, so she backed up and put out her hand to grab the handle and pulled it down. Shit, it was locked. She let out a sigh of relief. If she couldn't get in the room, then she wasn't letting Moone and the rest of the team down. It was just the luck of the draw.

She was about to hurry away when she heard a man's voice ask what she was doing. She turned around, her face burning as she saw Major Lacroix standing in the doorway of the small kitchen at the far end. She couldn't bring herself to say anything as the muscular and steely eyed Major started heading towards her with a mug of something hot in his hand.

'I asked what you were doing,' Lacroix said, a dark menacing tone to his voice.

'I just needed to…'

'You need to get into the evidence room?' He stared over her shoulder.

'Yes, that's what I was going to take a look at.' She smiled, but she felt it slipping from her face.

He stared deep into her eyes, she could almost feel him looking around her brain. 'OK. Out the way.'

She stepped aside as he took out a key and unlocked the door.

'I'm the gate master,' he said as there was a flicker of a smile that vanished in an instant. 'Don't be too long.'

She smiled as she was about to go in, her

heart still going for a jog around her chest. Something told her she should try and make conversation so she said, 'Major Lacroix?'

He stopped as he was walking away and turned back to her. 'Yes?'

'Any news on the two bodies they found?'

He kept his dead eyes on her for a while, searching around in her head again before he said, 'No. Hurry up.'

She watched his back as he walked away, the way his muscles moved under his tight T-shirt. She could hardly imagine the things he had seen. She knew he'd been in Afghanistan, one of the team had told her that, and he had apparently been blown up by an IED. The lower part of his left leg was missing, she'd also been told, replaced by a metal foot. The horror was in his eyes, buried deep in there somewhere. She shook herself out of her daydream and went into the room and shut the door behind her. There were boxes filled with stuff from Abel's house. No, not his house, the house bought by Lee and Sara Danton.

She let out a sad breath as she looked at all the evidence piled up on several desks around the room, all bagged up and labelled. She kept eyeing the door nervously, her heart on another of its runs around her chest. She hurriedly looked through the boxes until she saw it, all the stuff taken as evidence from the house. She sighed. There wasn't much. A map of Plymouth with some areas marked on it. She put some gloves on, then took the map out and laid it on an empty desk. After taking a few snaps, she put it back, her eyes jumping to the door every time she heard a noise. She couldn't see any photograph or anything the size Moone was talking about, so she realised either Richer's team had it somewhere, or Abel had more than likely gone straight back to the house, grabbed it and then done a runner. Moone would be disappointed, but there was no way they would be able to find out what the photo was of, or if it was a photo at all.

She made sure she put everything back the way it was, then stepped towards the door as she surveyed the room. Satisfied, she opened the door and headed out.

'Find what you were after?'

Chambers held her chest as her heart pounded. Lacroix was staring at her, not blinking, leaning against the wall, a cup in his hand.

'Yes, thanks.'

'It was the couple that owned the house,' he said, matter-of-factly. 'They just called me. He tied them up, shot them in the back of the head and buried them a few hundred yards from their home.'

'That's awful.' She shook her head, the well of sadness opening up in her chest.

'Life is harsh. But we'll find him and his

group.'

She smiled. 'Good. I'd better go.'

He kept staring into her eyes, so she turned and headed back down the corridor.

It was nearly an hour later that Abel followed the same cleaners in their van as they headed towards Plympton on the A38. Soon, as he drove a couple of cars back, they seemed to head for Modbury. No, they kept going. It was Kingsbridge, South Hams, they were heading for. He looked at the estuary as the sun glinted on the water and boats bobbed. It was hard to believe sometimes that life was anything but… well, life. He shook himself out of his thoughts as he followed the van until they headed up the high street, along the narrow roads lined with tourist shops, restaurants and cafes. They turned off and headed towards another road further out of town until the van came to park on the large driveway of a white and grey manor house which was surrounded by trees and the deep green fields all around it.

He parked a little way up the lane from the house where he could observe the two men as they opened the back of the van. One of them took out a pack of cigarettes and lit one while the other vaped. There was some chatter and laughing going on between them. One of them reached into the window of the van and then music started to play, some tinny and irritating dance music that pounded the air.

When the two cleaners retrieved their equipment from the back of the van and went into the house, Abel climbed out, then paused as he looked around at the other homes that were quite far away, at least four hundred yards on either side. The sun was warm on his skin, a slight breeze blowing as his heart kick started. He walked to the boot, opened it and took out the semi-automatic and then shut it again before he walked up to the van, leant in through the window and turned up the volume.

The music beat, beat, beat loudly, thudding, as he walked towards the front door that they had foolishly left open.

He saw the light change inside the house, the silhouette of someone moving before one of the men came strolling towards him, whistling. He stopped when he saw Abel.

'You looking for someone?' the man asked, then his eyes jumped to the gun in his hand as he raised it. The man shook his head as he took a couple of steps backwards, then turned to run.

He fired, hitting him in the shoulder. The man dropped to the floor, grunting as he tried to get up again. Abel fired down at him, hitting him in the chest as he carried on into the house. He followed the sound of a vacuum cleaner buzzing away somewhere deep in the house. A wide hallway, with a few doors on each side of it led to the back of the house. There was a large conservatory that faced the huge garden at the rear of the property. Abel watched the man vacuuming the carpet as he pointed the gun. He stopped and stood in the doorway.

The man must have seen him from the corner of his eye, then turned and widened his eyes, the loud roar of the machine still going.

'What the fuck?' the cleaner said, his words muffled by the noise.

'Turn it off!' Abel shouted.

The cleaner scrambled to turn it off, his eyes trying to remain on the man and the gun. 'You here to rob the place, yeah? I don't know where anything is.'

'Take off your uniform.'

Confusion filled his eyes. 'What?'

'Take off your uniform.'

'Why?'

Abel took a few steps closer. 'Take off the uniform. Now.'

The man did it, visibly shaking as he took off the polo shirt and the trousers. He stood in his boxer shorts, his arms folded over his chest.

'Just take them,' he said.

Abel pulled the trigger. The man slumped to the floor and he watched for a moment for signs of life. There were none, no movement of his chest. The game was over for him. The room became dark, all the light sucked out of it, but only for a moment. He nodded, knowing he was right about it all. He grabbed the uniform and walked fast towards the van and climbed in. He would park the van close by before he drove his car somewhere hidden, out of the way. The keys were in the ignition, so he started the van and drove along the road.

'There's no photos in the boxes of evidence,' Chambers said when she entered the small incident room and shut the door behind her.

Moone stared at her for a moment, absorbing what she had said and feeling the rising tide of disappointment climbing up to his neck. 'No photos?'

'The lady said no photos,' Butler said as she typed up her report.

Molly shook her head. 'Nope, and nothing the size of a photo either.'

'He must've taken everything,' Moone said and faced the whiteboard. 'Which means he's in the wind. Shit, why did I even go looking for him?'

'Because, believe it or not,' Butler said and stood up. 'You're a copper. You were using your instincts and going after the bugger. Hopefully, we'll not hear from him for a while and we'll have time to find him before he strikes again.'

Moone looked over at the vacant desks where DI Jones and Harding had been earlier. 'Where's Harding and Jones?'

Butler gave a strange laugh. 'Jesus, you have got your head up your arse. They went to take a look at those robberies we're meant to be looking into, remember?'

He barely did remember. His mind was so clouded with the case and the replay of the gun being waved in his face, that he could hardly recall his own name. 'Yeah, I remember. So, we've got nothing?'

'Well, there is this,' Chambers said as she took out her phone.

Moone watched as she brought up a photo. It seemed to be a hastily taken snap of a map of Plymouth. 'This was amongst the evidence taken from the house he was staying in?'

'Yes, but there wasn't much else. Looks like he got there and took everything. But I took a few snaps of this map because he'd circled certain areas.'

Moone took the phone and swiped through the images. 'Could these be potential targets?'

'That's what I was wondering,' Chambers said.

'Hang on,' Butler said with a huff. 'Aren't you missing something bloody obvious? If this nutter managed to get to the house and grab his stuff, then why would he leave a map behind that has his targets all over it?'

Moone sighed as he nodded. 'Butler's right. He's not going to leave something so crucial behind. Not unless... he wanted us to find this?'

Chambers' eyes lit up. 'You think this could be some kind of message?'

'I don't know. Let's print these and then mark the areas off on our map. Once we see it properly, we might be able to make sense of it.'

Butler folded her arms and sighed. 'Yeah right. It's probably a dot to dot and when you put them all together, it'll be a picture of him giving us the middle finger.'

Moone laughed. 'Well, let's see.'

As Chambers went over to her desk to print off the photos, she said, 'I nearly forgot, when I went to the evidence room, I bumped into Major Lacroix... I really get nervous around him.'

'Oh, don't get me started,' Butler said. 'I don't think I could talk in front of him without getting all cakey. It's the way he stares right through you.'

Moone loudly cleared his throat until they both looked at him. 'I was going to ask about the two bodies, when you've finished crushing on Lacroix.'

Chambers lost her smile as she blushed. 'Sorry, boss. It was the owners of the house they found buried. He said they were tied up and then... he shot them in the back of their heads. It's awful.'

Moone saw the gun right in front of his

face, the wavering muzzle of it. Then the two people, hazy images of a young couple on their knees out in the garden. Boom. The gun goes off, rattles around his head. The gun barks again as both of them fall to the ground. Two bodies lying next to him. He's next, waiting to be shot in the head, his heart punching its way out of his ribcage.

Then he's in a street. It's quiet as he walks across to the other side where a large red brick police station stands like a fortress. There's no one else around.

A gun booms in the air, echoing around the buildings. Pigeons flutter off in panic. All around him on the street are the bodies of his colleagues, blood escaping from wounds to their heads.

'Moone!' someone's shouting.

Moone flickered out of his catatonic state and saw Chambers and Butler staring at him, their eyes stamped with concern. His back was damp with sweat and he was trembling.

'Moone?' Butler said. 'What the bloody hell happened?'

He blinked and looked at her. 'I know why this is all so familiar.'

'Go on.'

Moone grabbed a chair and sat down, his hands still trembling. 'You remember that stupid medal I got? Well, before I got that medal... some of my team were shot and killed by this man who thought he was some kind of messenger of Armageddon or something. He called himself The Firstcomer. Anyway, I think that's why all this... it's like I've been through it before. Last time it didn't end so well.'

Butler pulled up a chair and faced him, staring intently into his eyes. 'Now, listen, you cakey sod, that ain't going to happen here. We're going to catch him soon. What worries me more, is you zoning out. That can't be good.'

'I'm fine,' he said and looked at Chambers. 'Have you printed out the photos yet?'

Chambers crossed the room quickly, snatching fresh A4 printouts from the corner printer. She moved with purpose, barely glancing at him as she returned to the whiteboard. One by one, she began marking off the same zones Abel had highlighted at some point.

Moone got up and stepped closer, eyes scanning the map. The red marks were scattered across Plymouth with no clear pattern, no obvious link. Just quiet pockets of the city.

He was about to say something to Chambers when the incident room door opened. He looked around to see Harding poking his head in, his eyes wide.

'Boss,' Harding said. 'There's been another shooting. In Kingsbridge. If you go now, you might beat the Counter Terrorism lot there.'

Moone looked at Butler who was already getting up. 'Let's go.'

CHAPTER 12

Moone watched Kevin Pinder stretching the police tape across the front of the long driveway as he sipped the double espresso Americano he bought on the way. Butler was fetching them some forensic outfits so they could go into the house.

Moone almost dropped his coffee when there was a hard knock on the passenger window. He turned, his heart racing a little, and saw the red and squashed face of Mike Barker, SOCO manager, staring at him. He took a breath and lowered the window.

'Sorry, didn't mean to make you jump,' Barker said, giving a cheeky smile which he quickly lost.

'It's fine,' Moone said, then nodded towards the house. 'Quite a mess in there, is it?'

Barker briefly looked over then back at Moone. 'I've seen a lot worse. But I didn't want to talk to you about that. It's the trial.'

Moone nodded as his stomach reached the top diving board, ready to go. 'How was it?'

'Not good, I'm sorry to say. She's good, that defence barrister.'

'Hannah Martin QC.'

Barker nodded. 'Yes. Well, she made mincemeat of me, and the blood and DNA.'

'We always knew it was flimsy. I'm sure you did your best.'

Barker gave a sad smile then said, 'From what I hear, she might get off.'

'Where did you…?' was all Moone managed to ask as Butler appeared decked out in a white forensic outfit, the hood drawn tightly over her face. Moone started to smile, but she raised a warning finger as her eyes blazed.

'Don't you dare, Peter Moone,' she said. 'It's your turn now.'

He opened the car door and climbed out, trying to keep the laugh at bay.

'Maybe we could all meet up tonight and discuss the case over dinner and a few drinks?' Barker called out. 'You too, DI Butler?'

She looked back at him. 'I can't tonight. I'm busy.'

As Moone was handed a forensic outfit and started to put it on, he said, 'You're out again tonight?'

'Yes, is that all right with you, Dad?'

'Yes, of course. Big date?'

'Hurry up and put that on. And stop nosing into my business.'

Moone smiled even though the thought of her having a date was eating him inside out with some rusty cutlery. 'What about Alice?'

'She's a big girl, Moone, she can take care of herself. Why don't you pop around and see her though?'

As Moone zipped up the forensic outfit, he said, 'I might actually. I've hardly seen her lately.'

He wondered if Alice might know something about what Butler was up to these days and decided he definitely would go and see her, which suddenly sounded pretty mercenary in his head. He did want to see her anyway, so he could catch up on her life. With how much he worked these days, he always felt so distant from Alice and the other kids.

His mind was taken away from his thoughts by the sight of the small forensic tent set up over the front of the house. He looked around for Inspector Pinder, but now there was no sign of him, and he really wanted to get his opinion on the trial.

'Come on, stop faffing,' Butler said as she held the tent open for him. 'We've got to get out of here before Richer and her lot turn up.'

'I know.' Moone stepped in and blinked at the light beaming out from the corner. There on the ground was the first victim, a man, probably in his thirties, wearing a uniform. His shoulder was a bloody mess, and there was a hole at the centre of his chest, less blood. Moone felt the tremor climbing up his body again, the sickness filling his gut as always. There were evidence markers on the ground where shell casings had fallen.

'Two shots from less than ten yards away,' Mike Barker's voice said behind Moone. 'Looks like the shooter hit him in the shoulder as he turned to run, then he stumbled in the doorway and ended up on his back. The second shot was taken as the shooter stood over him.'

Moone nodded, then stared at the victim's uniform. 'Well Clean Cleaning Services. Any ID?'

'Patrick Foreman,' Butler said, reading from her notebook. 'Thirty-six. No age at all. Who is this bastard?'

'You're assuming it's the same shooter?' Barker said, and Moone turned to look at him.

'That's what I'm thinking,' Moone said, then looked at Butler. 'I mean, how many shootings happen around here? Too much of a coincidence, isn't it?'

Barker nodded. 'You're probably right. Same shell casings too. The other victim is at the other end of the house.'

Moone let Barker go ahead of him, his ears filled with the scratch of the forensic outfits as they all walked deeper into the large and quite flash house. Moone took it all in. 'Who lives here?'

'Local businessman,' Butler said. 'One of Plymouth's high and mighty. Edward Harrak. He owns lots of restaurants around Plymouth. You think this might be a robbery gone wrong?'

'No. By the looks, he arrived then started shooting straight away.' Moone stopped speaking when they reached the second body. He let out the air from his cheeks as his eyes jumped to an almost naked young man lying close to a vacuum cleaner. There was a bullet wound to his chest.

'He was found like this?' Moone asked. 'No clothes?'

'No clothes.' Barker nodded.

'You didn't find a uniform anywhere?'

'No.'

Moone looked at Butler as she was making notes, his heart starting up. 'The killer took his cleaning uniform. I didn't see their van, did you?'

'No van.' Butler looked up at him. 'Bloody hell. He's taken his uniform and their van. The bastard's going to pretend to be a cleaner.'

Moone rushed back through the house with Butler hurrying after him as he started pulling off the forensic outfit. He took it all off and pulled out his phone to look up the cleaning company. He Googled the company and found them halfway down the page. Well Clean Cleaning Services. He dialled the number as Butler reached him, pulling off her forensic outfit.

'Well Clean Cleaning,' a woman's voice said.

'This is DCI Peter Moone,' he said. 'I haven't got a lot of time. You had two cleaners sent to a house in Kingsbridge today.'

Butler held up her notebook with the names of the victims. 'Patrick Foreman and Dave Reader are the cleaners.'

'I'm sorry, you're from the police?'

'Yes. DCI Peter Moone. I need to know where the two men clean regularly.'

There was a pause on the other end, then he could hear the woman talking to someone else.

'Who is this?' a gruff man's voice came on the line.

Moone sighed. 'DCI Peter Moone. I've got some bad news. Your cleaners, Patrick and Dave, are dead. I'm very sorry, but I need to know where they would be cleaning next or have cleaned today.'

There was a long pause. 'They're dead? Is this a joke?'

'It's not a joke. Is this your business?'

Butler grabbed the phone from him.

'Listen to me. This is DI Mandy Butler, Devon and Cornwall police. You need to listen. Your two cleaners are dead. Now we need to stop more people dying. Where do they usually clean? Where did they clean before Kingsbridge?... Right, yes, but we haven't got time right now. This is extremely important... Yes, check your appointments.' Butler rolled her eyes at Moone. Then there was nothing for a while, the both of them waiting on the drive, the warm sun beating down, the sound of birds in the trees. It was a beautiful part of the world, now broken up, smashed to pieces.

'Hello, yes, I'm still here,' Butler said. 'What? You're sure? OK. Thanks.'

She hung up, staring at Moone as she handed him back his phone. 'The last place they cleaned before here was Plymouth Argyle stadium. This was their last job of the day.'

'Bloody hell. So, what if he followed them from Home Park? What was he doing there?'

Butler shrugged, looking around. 'Scouting the place? He sees them come out and decides to take a uniform?'

'What better way to get inside without anyone giving you a second look? So are we thinking he's planning on shooting people or blowing it up?'

'Could be bloody either, knowing the sick bastard,' Butler said. 'We'd better get moving.'

Moone got in the car, his whole body now

trembling again as adrenaline surged around his system. Butler climbed in and he flinched when she slammed the door shut and started the engine.

'There'll be families at the game tonight,' she said as Moone prepared to call the station.

He saw a flicker of images, kids smiling and enjoying a nice game of footy. His gut started to chase its tail as Butler put her foot down. Moone called it in.

There was the usual heavy build-up of traffic around the stadium at Home Park and Moone could already see the car park in front of it was jam-packed. The roads all around would be filled up with the supporters' cars too.

The two incident response cars, one in front and one behind, had their lights and sirens going but the other cars were slow in responding. It seemed to take them an age to get anywhere close to the stadium and Moone stared as the Green Army fans ambled en masse towards the ground. There were families with young kids among the throng, most decked out in green.

'Right, I'm pulling in here,' Butler said and swung the car into the car park and pulled up in a non-parking area. 'They can give me a ticket if they like.'

As Moone got out, he spotted a black Land Rover and a green truck belonging to Richer's

Counter-Terrorism team. They had called her and given her the heads up on the way.

Richer was standing, arms folded, waiting by the stadium as the crowds started to queue up. She spotted him and stormed across the car park, her face tight as always.

'What the hell do you think you're playing at, DCI Moone?' she demanded as she stood in front of him and Butler, eyebrows raised. 'I've been informed that you've been trampling all over my crime scene.'

'Like you say, it was a crime scene,' Moone said, staring her in the eyes. 'The last time I checked, that's what my team respond to.'

'We'll deal with that later.' Richer pointed to the stadium. 'Why are we here? I take it you've received solid intelligence that this is a definite target?'

'Kind of. We found two dead cleaners at a house in Kingsbridge. They both worked for a cleaning company that helped clean this place. One of their uniforms was taken along with their van. They cleaned here this morning and I'm thinking Abel saw them leaving here and saw an opportunity.'

Richer's face changed, going from looking unimpressed to alert as she swung around and looked over the mass of cars and crowds starting to pour in.

Richer had already started hurrying towards the stadium, pushing past the crowds of supporters, before Moone could say anything.

'He must be bloody here somewhere,' Butler said as she and Moone jogged after Richer and caught up with her as she started barking orders at some of her team to start securing the area and to start the search for the cleaning company's van. The rest she told to arm up and follow her. Moone and Butler watched on as the armed team, all dressed in black combat gear and helmets, grabbed their MP5 submachine guns and followed her towards the building. It didn't take long for the doors to the stadium to be opened for them, and soon Moone found himself entering the building and staring round at grandstands, massive white letters that spelt out Argyle on one side, Home on the other. He looked over the pitch and then up at the seating. Already the stands were filling up with supporters. The yellow vest-wearing security team were spread out throughout the stadium. Music was playing loudly and a rumble of chanting had started.

'Finley Masters, head of security,' a large and bald-headed man, who was squeezed into a grey suit, said as he came towards them, his hand out. He was flanked by two tall and well-built young men.

Richer ignored his outstretched hand as she seemed to scan the stadium. 'Where's your cleaning crew?'

Masters' brow furrowed. 'The cleaners were in earlier, preparing for match day. You're from Counter-Terrorism, that right?'

Richer looked at him. 'Yes. We believe there might be a terrorist group planning to attack this stadium today and one of them is probably dressed as a cleaner.'

'A cleaner came in a while ago, boss,' one of the security men said.

'Where is he now?' Richer asked as she squared up to the security man.

He shrugged. 'Dunno. Probably gone home by now.'

Richer sighed. 'Where do they keep the cleaning stuff? Show us. Now!'

The man snapped to it and hurried towards the end of the away stand and to the doors where the players come out. Moone and Butler followed the crowd into the interior of the building, the armed officers on either side. More security staff stepped aside as they entered the area where the teams had their changing and boot rooms.

Eventually, they reached a large set of doors that had "Cleaning" written across them. The security man grasped the handle and started to open the door.

'Stop!' Richer commanded. 'Get back. My team go in first. Harris, Jakes.'

Two of the armed team went into

the room, sweeping their weapons into the corners. Moone could already see there was no one there but one of the armed team came out and announced, 'It's clear, ma'am.'

'Told you,' the head of security said with a smile.

'So why was someone dressed as a cleaner here?' Richer asked, staring at the man, her eyes trying to peel his skin off.

He shrugged. 'I don't know. You're welcome to look around. I can probably arrange for you to meet the players if you'd like.'

Richer ignored him as she walked away, scanning the staff moving around her. 'We need your team to start checking for any bags or packages left lying around without raising suspicion. We don't want to cause panic.'

She spun around and faced the security man. 'For God's sake, make sure they don't bloody well touch anything. I'll call in bomb disposal. Go on, go!'

The man and his team sprang to life at her words and started heading off down the various corridors. Moone watched them before he turned his eyes on Richer and saw she was now facing him, a stony expression on her face.

'This looks like it's been a huge waste of time, Moone,' she said as she walked up to him. 'He could've taken that van and uniform anywhere in Plymouth or he might have left the city.'

'Surely it's better to be safe than sorry,' Butler said.

Richer's phone rang and she answered it. 'Talk to me... You've found the van?... It's in the car park? OK. Secure it. I'll come out.'

Richer ended the call and turned to Butler. 'This is a waste of time and resources. You've led us up the garden path, Moone. You made a wild assumption without –'

He'd had enough. 'He shot and killed two bloody cleaners. And then he stole their van which is now sitting out there in...'

He stopped talking as a horrific feeling came over him. 'Oh, Jesus Christ.'

'What?' Richer asked.

'He took the uniform and was seen coming in here to confuse us,' Moone said, staring back at her.

'Oh, shit,' Butler said as she came closer.

'What are you on about?' Richer asked, looking between them.

'The van,' Moone said, his voice trembling as adrenalin filled his veins. 'He only wanted the bloody van.'

'Fuck,' Richer said and started running along the corridor as she pulled out her radio. 'This is Richer! It's the van!'

Moone and Butler ran after her, heading at speed towards the doors at the other end and dodging more of the staff coming the other way. Richer pushed the doors open and sprinted out towards the car park. Moone was right behind her, his heart ready to burst as he saw in his rocking vision the police and Richer's people surrounding the van, looking in the windows.

'Get away from the van!' Richer was screaming.

Moone saw it all in slow motion as the uniforms and one of Richer's team turned to look their way, questions in their eyes. Richer was ahead of him, calling out to them. Then the uniforms were moving back. Moone looked around and saw people still coming towards the stadium, ragged lines of supporters coming to see the game. Shit.

'Run!' he shouted. 'Get out of here!'

There was a burn of light, a bright and hot flash as Moone was thrown through the air.

A voice, distant and quiet but somehow full of desperation was calling out above him. There was a whining or ringing sound in his ears. When he blinked his eyes open, all he saw was thick black smoke surrounding him like fog had rolled in, but then there was the horrendous smell that filled his nostrils.

There was the voice again, a muffled shout and he looked up and saw Butler staring down at him, her face pale, and tears in her eyes. She pulled him upright and he raised himself and sat on the asphalt, the smoke clearing enough to see what was left of the van, all blackened twisted metal. The cars around it were scorched, the windows all shattered. Myriad car alarms were screaming out.

'Where's Richer?' he asked and looked around until he saw a pile of clothes lying a hundred yards away from him. No, not a pile of clothes, but a person lying twisted on the ground.

'It's Richer,' Moone said and started to crawl towards her, but Butler grasped hold of him.

'Don't you dare move,' she growled. 'You need to be checked out. Please, just don't move.'

He kept staring at the body, trying to see if there was any movement before his ears took in the sound of groaning. He looked around to see one of the uniforms on the ground a few feet away, his clothes were charred and blood dripped onto the asphalt as he tried to get up. As Moone watched him helplessly, he saw that most of his right forearm was gone. He closed his eyes as tears threatened to pour out.

'Oh, God,' Moone said. 'I brought them here.'

'Don't you dare try and blame yourself,' Butler said behind him as he felt her hands grip his shoulders. 'He did this, this is him. You were trying to stop it.'

He leaned back and looked up at her, her face above him, tears on her cheeks as she stared around her. She was trembling.

His mouth opened. 'I... I love you.'

She blinked and looked down at him. 'What did you just say?'

He was about to repeat himself but he heard a sound to his right and looked to see a couple of paramedics rushing towards them.

He didn't recall getting in the ambulance, but there he was, in just his white shirt that he realised, with a shudder and stomach full of sickness, was now mostly red, spattered with blood and dust. He was lying down as the paramedic was putting a blood pressure cuff around his arm and generally checking him over. He shone a light in Moone's eyes and asked him questions. The siren was going but everything was muffled.

Butler was sitting on the other side, staring at him. She would smile every time he looked at her but he could see the trouble in her eyes.

Then he remembered what he had said. Or did he say it? Perhaps he only imagined saying it.

There was still the ringing in his ears, but it was a little quieter now.

'Richer?' Moone asked, looking at Butler. She shook her head.

He nodded, then sniffed again, the awful stench still in his nostrils. 'What's that smell?'

'Sorry?' the paramedic said.

'I've got this smell in my nose. It won't go.'

The paramedic nodded and looked a little sad. 'Yeah, that happens.'

'What is it?'

The paramedic shrugged.

'Just leave it, Moone,' Butler said.

'But I want to know.' Moone looked at the paramedic and saw him let out a harsh breath.

'It's the smell of burnt flesh, mixed with the chemicals used in the explosives, and burnt plastic too, probably.'

Moone sat up, his body trembling violently, his hand grasping out for something as his stomach rose to his mouth.

The paramedic gave him a disposable vomit bowl, so he threw up into it. He handed it back as he said, 'Sorry.'

'Nothing to be sorry for,' he said.

'How many dead?' Moone asked, sitting up in the cubicle, the green curtain pulled around. Inspector Pinder was sitting by the gurney he was on.

'Seven confirmed,' he said, his voice brittle sounding, none of the usual humour in it at all.

'Butler said Richer is...'

'Yeah, she's gone. You were bloody lucky.'

Moone looked down at himself. 'I don't feel lucky.'

'Well, it could have been worse for you,

mate. One of the uniforms has lost most of his right arm.'

Moone nodded, flooded with guilt. 'I'm sorry. What about the people arriving to go the match?'

'Mostly injured with shrapnel. One's in critical condition…'

'Any kids?'

Pinder sat up and cleared his throat. 'No, thank Christ. They tell me it wasn't a massive explosion. But it did plenty of damage.'

Moone lifted his trembling hands. 'What is this about? What's he trying to do?'

'I don't know. I really don't know.'

'He told me he couldn't stop even if he wanted to. Like he's doing this against his will. Do you think someone could be making him do this? Do you remember that case in America, that pizza delivery guy who walked into a bank with a bomb around his neck?'

'No, I don't think so. He's a sociopath or a psychopath, or whatever you want to label him… he's doing it because he's sick in the head.'

'I need to figure this out before he kills more innocent people.'

Pinder let out a deep sigh as he looked Moone in the eyes and patted his shoulder. 'Mate, I think your chances of that are over. Counter-Terrorism is in charge now. I think that's for the best.'

Moone couldn't find the words or arguments, so he thought he'd change the subject. 'She's going to get off, isn't she?'

'Carthew, you mean?'

'Yep. They tore me apart on the witness stand.'

'Me too. It does look like she's going to walk. But, on the bright side, she isn't going to be a copper anymore.'

He tried to smile. Something else came to mind. 'I told her.'

Pinder's forehead creased up. 'What? You told who what?'

'Butler. I told her.'

'You did?' He sat up. 'What did she say?'

He shrugged. 'It was after the bomb went off. We got interrupted. I don't even know if she realised what I said.'

'Well, you've got time to tell her again. You've got another chance.'

Moone nodded, then flinched as a woman's voice called out, 'Where is he? Is he in here? Moone. Peter Moone. That's who I'm bleeding looking for.'

Then the curtain was yanked back and a woman stepped into the cubicle.

There she was, still with bleached blonde hair, red lips, and wearing a leopard print dress. A right dog's dinner as always.

'Look at the bleedin' state of you, Pete Moone,' she said, tutting and shaking her head.

'You can't leave you alone for ten years, can ya?'

'Who are you?' Pinder asked, standing up.

'This is my sister,' Moone said, then he gave a laugh that almost turned into a sob.

CHAPTER 13

'Kelly Barber,' the woman said, winking at Pinder. 'The artist formerly known as Kelly Moone.'

Pinder laughed. 'I didn't know you had a sister.'

'Well, he bleedin' well does,' she said and hugged Moone. 'And a bloody gorgeous specimen she is. Now, little Pete, I hear you just got blown up.'

Pinder shook his head, waved, and then left the cubicle. Kelly pulled up a chair and sat down.

'So they tell me.' He nodded, but he really didn't want to keep thinking about it. 'It can't be ten years since I saw you.'

'Yeah, it was Mum's funeral.'

'Bloody hell. That was ten years ago? No, it

can't be.'

Kelly crossed her legs. 'It is, I swear on my life. Now, I can see I'm going to have to look after you. You don't look like you've eaten a good meal in a while. You're as skinny as a whippet.'

He laughed then felt sick. 'Don't you start.'

The smoke was all around him, the scent in his nostrils. The police constable was trying to sit up, half his arm gone.

'Pete?'

He flickered out of it, then focused on Kelly as she was staring at him. 'What was that?'

'What?'

'You just stared into space with this awful look on your face, drained of all colour. I couldn't snap you out of it.'

'I'm OK,' he said, trying to raise a smile, but she kept looking at him with disbelief.

Then the curtain opened and Butler came in, her hair tied back with bits of debris and dust caught in it. Her face was pale, her clothes covered in dirt and dust.

'Sorry, didn't realise you had company,' she said, nodding at Kelly.

Kelly jumped up and stuck out her hand to Butler. 'Kelly Barber. Formerly Kelly Moone. Nice to meet yer.'

Butler broke into a smile. 'Oh, you're Kelly. Moone's infamous sister.'

Kelly looked back at Moone. 'Oh, so I'm infamous, am I?'

Moone shrugged. 'Kind of.'

'I think I like that,' Kelly said and faced Butler again. 'You must be Mandy Butler, the one who messaged me.'

'I am.'

'Oh, God, look at the state of you both. What happened?'

'A nutter just blew up a van and killed and injured a load of people,' Butler said and walked over to Moone. 'How're you feeling?'

'I'm fine. They checked me over and it's all superficial. What about you?'

'Not a scratch on me.' She smiled, but it didn't reach her eyes. 'I just can't help thinking about the others. That poor constable and Richer, and her people. I know she was a pain in the arse, but...'

Moone nodded. 'I know. What we need to do is find the bastard before he does this again.'

'You can't go after this bastard,' Kelly said, wide-eyed as she glanced between them. 'You really will get yourselves blown up. Just leave it to the terrorism people, whoever. You, little Pete Moone, need to take some time off.'

Butler gave a dry laugh. 'Little Pete Moone, I like that. Tell me, Kelly, what was he like as a kid? I bet he was a pain in the bum.'

Kelly smiled. 'Was he ever. Always cramping my style.'

Moone groaned.

'Well, you did, Pete. Oh, Mandy, he used to do this thing on the way to school. Mum made me walk him to school every day. He used to do this parrot voice all the way to school. Do you remember, Pete? It was so bleedin' embarrassing.'

'I don't remember that,' he said, but he did remember and inwardly cringed as he saw Butler lapping it up. He was glad to see her smile after what they had been through, although he felt awful to even consider laughing or smiling while their colleagues were either dead or being treated in the Emergency department.

'There you are,' a deep voice said and Moone looked over and saw Major Lacroix standing with the curtain pulled open. His face, usually blank, was now tight with anger. He looked at Kelly as he said, 'Who are you?'

'I'm his sister...'

'Well, you need to fuck off right now.' Lacroix held the curtain open for her.

'Charming.' Kelly looked at Moone. 'I'll see you in a min.'

When she went out, Lacroix came to the side of his bed, looking him and Butler over, the anger still clear in his eyes. 'I see you two have hardly got a nick on you.'

'We were lucky,' Moone said.

'There's several of our people who weren't

so fucking lucky.' The soldier's eyes remained on Moone, digging into him.

'Yeah, and don't forget our people,' Butler said, making Lacroix raise his eyes to her. 'There's a uniform with part of his arm missing.'

'I'm aware of that, thank you. Commander Richer is dead. I'll have to inform her family. Thing is, we were there on your say so.'

Moone felt his muscles stiffen. 'I was just... we attended the shooting earlier...'

'That should've been our crime scene. But you stuck your wooden top head in, and look where it got us.'

Butler let out an empty laugh. 'And if you lot had gone there before us, then you would have found yourself in the same shit.'

Lacroix's jaw ground for a moment. 'Shut up and listen. What do you know about this fucking bastard, Moone?'

Moone sat up. 'He's not a terrorist...'

'You could've fucking fooled me. He just set off a great big fucking bomb.'

'I mean, not like you think. He's not doing it for a political cause, he's not made any demands.'

Lacroix straightened up and folded his arms over his muscular chest. 'Then what is this about?'

Moone shrugged. 'I don't know. He told me he couldn't stop even if he wanted to. It's like something or someone's driving him to do this. There's something else going on here other than just death and destruction. I know that sounds crazy, what with all this… but there's some other reason. We just need to find out what that is and then maybe we can figure out what he'll do next.'

The former soldier stared at him for a moment, seeming to chew it all over, then he looked at Butler. 'What do you think?'

'I'm with Moone. Like he said, why hasn't he claimed responsibility or made any demands? It doesn't make sense if he's meant to be a terrorist. Does it?'

Lacroix breathed in, then let it out. 'I don't know, but we've got lots of dead people and no fucking clue. We've got to start from scratch. Right, I'm in charge now, so I'm setting up a new team. You two are on it. You do what I say, when I say, or you're out on your scrawny arses. Got it?'

They both nodded and then Major Lacroix pointed a meaty finger at Moone. 'If you fuck up again, I'll cut your balls off and hang them off the lighthouse on Plymouth Hoe. Understood?'

Moone didn't dare say anything, so nodded again.

'Go home. Both of you. Get some rest. I'll see you first thing.'

The Major then turned on the spot and made to leave as Moone found words crowding his throat.

'I'm sorry, Major,' he said, his voice breaking up. 'I'm sorry about Richer and all the others. I didn't...'

He held up his hand. 'Save it. You were right before. We would've ended up in the same situation. He was counting on it. He fooled us all. It wasn't your fault. I know you were trying to save innocent people from getting killed. I get that. Now, fuck off home, the both of you.'

They watched him leave, then remained in silence for a moment.

'And I thought he was made iron or something,' Butler said, then looked at Moone. 'What a day, eh?'

Moone nodded, thinking back to what he'd said after the explosion. 'I wanted to say something...'

'Is it about what you said after the bomb went off?' She shook her head. 'It's all right. You must have had a concussion or something. Yeah?'

He stared at her, his heart rippling, the same words on his lips. Say it again, you stupid fool. 'Yep. I must've hit my head.'

Butler lost her smile, then patted him on the shoulder. 'I'll get your sister to take you home. I'll see you in the morning.'

Kelly drove them away from Derriford Hospital as the sun had started to dip. Moone had asked her to pass by Home Park, to which she protested so he came close to begging her. She gave in and tried to get as close to the stadium as possible, which was difficult as the car park and most of the area of Outland Road had been cordoned off with hazard and police tape. Armed police and soldiers were guarding the area, and redirecting the traffic. The car park itself was now sealed off and at the centre where the explosion had happened, was covered by a huge forensic tent. His stomach rolled over and over as the car slowly passed the scene.

The boom of the explosion pounded into his ears, his body punched backwards as the ringing started in his skull.

The gun wavering in his vision. The trigger was pulled, the bark of the gun rattling through him.

He shuddered, and Kelly looked over at him as she drove them away.

'You're shaking all over, Petey,' she said, the concern glistening in her eyes.

'I'm OK.' He looked away from the scene.

'Let's get you home.'

Nearly forty minutes later, Kelly was driving them along the coast, the sun getting lower in the sky, slowly dyeing the sea scarlet and the sky a deeper shade of red. Moone could see boats bobbing out on the water and figures on the sand, their shadows stretching out with the falling sun. Everything looked normal, the world still turning as it always did; but how could it be? How could anything be carrying on when part of it had been torn to shreds, burnt to ashes?

'Where're we going, Pete?' Kelly asked, looking down towards the sea down below, beyond the cliffs. 'We're in the middle of nowhere.'

'Take the next left turn.' Moone leaned his head back, closed his eyes and tried to blot everything out, to calm his still thumping heart.

Richer was lying a few feet from him. The constable was sitting up with half his arm gone. The scent dug deep into his nostrils.

The gun wavered in his face, the masked face behind it, out of focus. Hate rose to his skin and made all his hairs twitch.

He opened his eyes.

'The next turning is a holiday park,' she said, slowing down.

'Turn in here.' He felt suddenly tired, completely drained of all energy.

Kelly signalled and took them through the holiday park as the light began to fade.

'Is this a shortcut?'

'Here we are,' he said and pointed to his mobile home on the right. She slowed, then stopped the car.

'Oh my God,' she said, staring at his home. 'You're telling me you live in a bloody caravan?'

'It's a mobile home.' Moone pushed open the door, climbed out, and then found himself stumbling a little as if his legs weren't quite as solid as they used to be. His head spun as he steadied himself and took out his keys.

Kelly followed him to the door and then inside and stood looking round the place. 'Well, it's cosy, I'll give you that. My little brother, living in a caravan. I can't believe it.'

Moone sat at the kitchen table, opened the window and took out his cigarettes. With a trembling hand, he poked one in his mouth and lit it. Anything to get rid of the taste and smell that lingered.

'You smoke too?' Kelly sat down opposite him, sighing and shaking her head. 'What would Mum and Dad say?'

'Not a lot, seeing as they're long gone.' He blew the smoke out the window.

She nodded. 'So, what was all this business about our holidays we had down here when we were kids?'

Moone shrugged. It all sounded ridiculous to him now, so dull and empty after what had just happened. 'Nothing really. Doesn't matter.'

'It does to me. You wanted to know where we used to stay. Well, if you still want to know, it was in Leigham Street. Wherever the bloody hell that is.'

Moone looked at her, his curiosity managing a yawn. 'How do you remember that?'

'I've got a suitcase full of our old holiday photos... some of them are hilarious. Oh, Pete, do you remember when you used to insist on going everywhere dressed as a cowboy? Oh, my God, poor Mum and Dad. They were so embarrassed. Everywhere, it was. Dad took us to his work do at that posh place near Epping Forest, and there you were dressed up as the Lone Ranger. Do you remember?'

He took a drag. 'No, I don't. So how did you find the address?'

'There's a photo of us all outside. You can see the name of the bed and breakfast place. The Drake Inn. Was run by someone called Morten. It's not there now.'

Moone sat up, unable to believe what she had said. 'Did you say Morten? Are you sure?'

'Yeah. I looked the place up online. Why?'

'It's funny, but we got this call out to an old people's home a few days ago. An old lady called Joy started screaming about murder. Thing is, there was something so familiar about her. She's got dementia, so we couldn't get much sense out of her. But I went back the other day and she told me she used to run a B&B back in the day.'

'Well, that's why she's so familiar. You met her when you was a kid.'

Moone nodded, then stubbed his cigarette out. 'But there's something about it all that's bothering me. Like a memory or something is trying to break into my head. Did anything strange happen back then?'

Kelly frowned. 'Apart from you being a weirdo? Nah, not that I remember. Got any booze?'

'In the cupboard over the sink.'

Kelly got up and took out a bottle of red and found two glasses. She poured them both a drink and sat back down. 'I can't think of anything strange. What sort of thing?'

He shrugged. 'I have no idea. I don't even know why I'm so obsessed with it.'

Kelly sipped her wine. 'I remember you used to have nightmares and get really scared. They'd always put us in a room together and you'd get upset and start trying to find Mum and Dad. One time you managed to get out of the room and went down into the bar.'

'I don't remember. What happened?'

'I told Mum and Dad and they had to go and get you. I remember some fuss and Dad shouting at someone.'

Moone was about to sip his wine, then put it down. 'Dad was shouting at someone? Dad never shouted at anyone. What happened?'

Kelly sat back. 'I don't know. I never found out. I was only young, Pete. It's all in the past. Forget it.'

He smiled and drank some of his wine, but he couldn't forget it, as now some memory was trying to rise from the deep, cavernous recesses of his mind. It was scratching to come in, but he had no way to open the door. He started to see flickers of that night, saw a dark carpeted stairway as he hurried to find Mum and Dad, panic fluttering in his chest.

The memory faded.

'Come on,' Kelly said, smiling as she leaned forward. 'You haven't told me if you've got a woman in your life.'

'No, no woman. My love life has been a bit of a disaster zone. The first woman I had a bit of thing with when I moved down here is now on trial for murder.'

Kelly laughed. 'You're having me on?'

'No, unfortunately, I'm being serious. She murdered some people.'

'What? Jesus, Pete.'

'Looks like she might get off though. I'm in the shit too because of it. But right now I don't give a monkey's.'

'What about Mandy Butler?'

Moone felt the moths gathering in his gut. 'What about her?'

'I like her. She seems like a tell-it-like-it-is, sort of woman.'

'She is and frequently does.'

'Where's she now?'

Moone sipped his wine, wondering the

exact same thing. 'I don't know.'

Mandy was glad Chris had picked the Dolphin Pub on the Barbican rather than the Union Rooms, where they met last time. The Dolphin had a lot more character and was a lot less noisy. She needed peace and quiet after the hell she had been through that day. They had found a quiet corner, away from the older men who were chatting and drinking on the other side of the pub.

He walked back from the bar, carrying her large glass of sauvignon blanc and his pint of ale. He smiled as he reached their table and she looked him over again. He hadn't changed that much since their school days. He was still the cheeky chappie who loved a good game of footy. Back then not much had happened between them, only the occasional snog at school discos. His hair, still short and wavy, was now speckled with grey. He was broad with a little bit of an overhang, but she preferred that.

He put her glass of wine in front of her, a smile on his face. More of a shit-eating grin, she thought. She kept her face straight as she said, 'What?'

Chris sat down with a shrug and sipped his pint. 'Nothing. Just looking.'

'What're you looking at?' Butler made a show of looking behind her before she picked up her drink.

'You.'

'Well, don't.'

'Don't look? Jesus, I'd better go and get my gimp mask out of my van and put it on then.'

She huffed out a laugh. 'Yeah, that sounds about right. I bet you do have a gimp mask in your van.'

'Yeah, I do. I keep it with my trowel and my spirit level.' There was the big grin again and she found herself rewinding back in time to a classroom so many years ago and the stocky young lad sitting in their science class wearing his tie around his head like Rambo. In her head, the lad turns in slow motion and winks at her.

'Didn't think you'd end up as a builder,' she said, sipping her wine.

'Why not? It's a good game to be in, is the building game. People always need houses, that's what my dad always said.'

'Wise words.'

'I never wanted to be a builder though.'

'No?'

'No. I wanted to be a porn star.'

Butler nearly choked and spat out her wine as she laughed. 'What? Shut up…'

'I did. Don't you remember when I got sent out of Mr Davis' class? He was asking everyone what they wanted to be and I stuck my hand up and said porn star, sir.'

'Oh, God. I'd forgotten that. He went so

red! He looked like he was going to have a heart attack.'

'He did, didn't he?' Chris shook his head and sipped his pint. 'You never said what you do now.'

Chris sat back, the grin settling down to a smile.

'No, I didn't.' Butler looked down at her drink, the flashes of the day trying to break into her mind.

'Let me guess.'

'Oh, this should be interesting.'

He looked her over. 'Stripper?'

She tried not to laugh but it burst out of her. 'Stripper? Me? Have you seen me?'

'I meant stripping wallpaper.' He grinned and winked.

'Yeah, right you did.'

'Anyway, I'm sure plenty of men would love to see you strip.'

'Oh, is that compliment?'

'Sort of. I think. Anyway, what do you do?'

She stared at him, weighing it all up, wondering what his reaction would be and realising there was only one way to find out. She huffed and took out her warrant card and pushed it across the table.

He looked up, narrowing his eyes as he slowly opened it. His eyes widened. 'No! You're not a copper?'

'All right, loud mouth, I don't think the

deaf bloke in the corner heard you.' She dragged back her ID and put it away. 'So, are you shocked?'

'A bit. But it doesn't surprise me that much.' He sat back and sipped his pint.

'Why?'

He laughed. 'Cause of the way you used to police the playground.'

'Did I?'

He laughed. 'Don't you remember? You used to protect all the kids that tosser Valance used to try and bully. I think you even punched him once.'

'Oh, God, I'd forgotten about that. He was a right shit.'

'I heard he's in prison now.' Chris sipped his pint.

'Well, I didn't nick him. But it doesn't surprise me. Anyway, that's what I do.' She sighed heavily as the day's events flickered through her mind again.

'What was that?'

'What?'

'That big heavy sigh. Bad day, was it?'

She picked up her wine and stared into it. 'Probably the worst. People died.'

Chris' head popped up, then he leaned forward. 'You didn't have anything to do with what happened today, did you? That bomb and everything?'

She shrugged. 'I can't talk about it.'

She could feel his eyes on her as he said, 'Were they your mates?'

'Colleagues. I don't want to talk about it.'

He nodded. 'Fair enough. Shall we just get drunk?'

She looked at her hands and saw they were trembling. She saw Moone lying on the ground, blood spattered all over him. She remembered standing there, unable to move but wanting to see if he was alive. She was too scared. The blood had pounded in her ears in those seconds. She never believed in God, not really, but she had always wondered. Something had kept her alive through all the horror that she had been part of over the years. Just a couple of days ago, a gun had been fired at her and Moone. Her heart had been in her mouth, but not for herself; she had been scared for the uniforms but mostly Moone. If he had died, she didn't know what she would have done. That's why she knew, as he lay on the ground, probably dead, that she couldn't be with him. Losing him would be more than she could take. In those brief seconds, she had spoken to a God she didn't believe in. We'll never be together, she'd said, but if you can make it so he's alive, that'll be OK. That's enough. Bring him back and I'll stick to being his colleague, his friend and nothing more. For both our sakes.

Then her heart had been squeezed as she saw his right hand twitch, and then his legs move. She had broken out of her frozen state of horror and rushed to him. Then she had heard the words he spoke to her as he looked up at her. Whether he meant it or if he was just concussed, which he probably was, she knew it could never be. She had him back and that would have to be enough.

'Hello, earth to Mandy,' Chris said as he waved his hand. 'You all right?'

She needed a distraction. 'Do you have any booze at your place?'

He raised his eyebrows, then bobbed his head with a big cheesy grin. 'I do. Plenty of booze.'

'Then order us a taxi.'

CHAPTER 14

The morning arrived far too quickly for Moone, especially with a very chatty sister to contend with over breakfast. He tried to eat a bowl of cornflakes and drink a black coffee in peace, but it was as if Kelly was determined to catch up on the last few years before he left for work. They had also necked a bottle of wine each the night before, which didn't help his state of mind. He gave up on the cornflakes, grabbed a quick shower and then drove them both into Plymouth.

'While you're catching this nutter that you're after,' Kelly said as they reached the bombed-out church. 'I'll try and find the place where we used to stay.'

Moone had the memory again, the panic flooding his heart as he saw his own small and bare feet running down the stairs of the hotel. Where were his mum and dad?

Then he was flying backwards, the bright light whitening out everything, that hideous stench in his nostrils. His hands were shaking.

'Did you hear me?' Kelly asked.

'Sorry?' He was back in the car.

'I said I'll try and find anyone who knew Joy Morten or knows anything about the place.'

'I wouldn't worry.'

'Why? Come on, it's obviously bothering you. You kept on about it last night.'

'I'd downed most of a bottle of wine.'

She tutted. 'It's not the only subject you wouldn't shut up about.'

He stared at her. 'What do you mean?'

'Nothing. Just it was Butler this, Butler that. Apparently, the Earth revolves around her backside.'

Kelly raised her eyebrows.

'We work well together. We get on well... Well, sort of.'

'That's what you call it?'

He decided to ignore her and took the car around towards the gates to Charles Cross and pulled in a hundred yards from the entrance to the station.

'Sounds to me like little Petey has a crush on someone,' Kelly said, but was staring towards the tall gates of the car park, where two armed officers were standing dressed in jeans and polo tops with bullet and stab-proof vests and police caps on their heads.

'Jesus,' he said, staring at the armed officers.

'Bloody hell, they're not taking any chances, are they?' Kelly said.

'No, they're not. And I think they're right not to.' He looked at his sister as his stomach filled with lead. 'Maybe you shouldn't be in town today. Not with all this going on.'

'I'll be fine. I'll have a quick look for this place, grab some stuff for dinner and then I'll wait for you.'

'Don't wait for me. Get a taxi. I'll pay.'

'I'll get a taxi, and I'll pay. But message me this afternoon.' She smiled at him. 'Now, get in there and find this sod.'

When she had climbed out and started walking towards the city centre, Moone started the engine and approached the gates. One of the armed officers held up a gloved hand to slow him down.

When Moone stopped, the same officer came to his window and said, 'ID.'

Moone showed his warrant card, which the officer took a snap of. Then he pointed the phone at Moone, then pressed some buttons. Then the officer waved him on as he said, 'Have a good day, DCI Moone.'

The incident room wasn't as busy as he had

expected. What surprised him most was the fact that most of his team, including Butler and Jones, were there, sitting on the chairs placed around the room, while Major Lacroix was standing in front of a whiteboard with something taped to it. Then Moone realised with shock what it was.

'That's right, DCI Moone,' Lacroix said, turning to look at the board, and the map that had been previously pinned up in the smaller incident room downstairs. 'This is a map I found downstairs. With the same markings that were on a map we found in the house our suspect was using. Which, of course, DS Chambers managed to sneak in and take a few photos of.'

Moone looked over at Chambers but she went red and looked down.

'What is it you call him?' Lacroix asked, approaching Moone as he folded his arms.

'Abel,' Moone said, his voice hollow.

'Abel.' The Major nodded. 'Any idea why?'

'No.'

'Maybe we'll find out when we get hold of him. Now, listen up, this map is all we've got to go on. Forensics and the bomb squad have been going over both the Mall bomb and the van bomb. No prints. No DNA so far. They tell me that these bombs are very sophisticated. We've reached out to our friends in MI5 to see if there's anyone on their watch list who can build devices like this. They're also seeing if any of the explosives were purchased on the dark web, but as we know that's a rabbit hole that we could get lost in. So, we're left with this map.'

'A map he left,' Butler said as she leaned against the wall, arms folded, eyebrows raised.

Lacroix looked at her, blank-faced. 'Your point is, Detective?'

She straightened up. 'He manages to get to the house and clear out most of his stuff but leaves a great big map behind? Sounds fishy to me.'

The Major nodded. 'I agree. But if you look at the map, you'll see that Home Park is marked on it. On the original there's something Chambers didn't notice, and that's a tiny number four written next to Home Park. And that was his fourth target. Correct?'

She shrugged. 'If you say so.'

Lacroix raised his eyebrows, staring at her. 'If I say so... what? You do realise I'm in charge here?'

'Sir.'

He turned back to the room. 'Number five is the Royal William Yard, or so the map says. I've already had plain-clothes officers placed there undercover. But there are more places marked off on this map. I've put together teams to take a quiet look at these potential targets. Some of these places are on his map for obvious reasons, like the barracks and the Tamar Bridge, but some of the areas he's marked off are just empty pieces of land as far as we can ascertain. So, you lot will be busying yourselves going to these places. Please try not to look like bloody coppers and do your best to blend in. Right, I've put you in teams, and it's all by the whiteboard. Have a look.'

Moone started to walk towards the whiteboard but Lacroix held up his hand. 'Not you, Moone. Or Butler. He knows your faces by now.'

Butler gave one of her well-timed huffs. 'Oh great, so what do we do? Twiddle our thumbs?'

'No,' he said looking between them. 'You stay here and try and figure this out. Go through everything again, the CCTV footage, the scene of crime photos, everything we have and find me something, anything that helps us find him.'

'We're stuck here?' Butler sighed and sat at a desk. 'Great.'

Moone looked at the board, the map of Plymouth and then at Lacroix. 'What's Counter-Terrorism's take on all this? What's your strategy?'

'Before she died, Richer sent a report to the Home Office detailing everything she knew. Now there's going to be a special Cobra meeting.'

'What?' Moone couldn't believe what he

was hearing. 'Cobra?'

'Whatever way you look at it, Moone, it's terrorism. Richer recommended the city gets locked down.'

'Lockdown?' Butler shot to her feet. 'Not again. What, everyone shut in their homes again? That's great.'

Lacroix looked at her. 'Looks like it. With everyone off the streets, the people will be safe and he'll be easier to spot.'

'Bloody hell.' Butler sat down again. 'Sounds like a cakey plan to me.'

'Cakey?' Lacroix pulled a face and looked at Moone.

'It means stupid. When is this meeting?'

'Tomorrow. I'll let you know how it goes. Get to work.'

Moone watched the Major leave the room then looked over at Butler and saw she had started going over the reports already.

'What did you do last night?' he asked.

She looked up, her face blank. 'Just drank some wine. You?'

'Caught up with my sister.'

'I like her. I notice she moves a little faster than you. Maybe you're the milkman's.' She grinned.

'Nice. Did you stay home or go out?'

Butler stopped what she was doing and glared at him. 'Am I being interrogated?'

'No, I…'

'What? It's none of your business what I get up to out of here. All right, nosey? Snout out, trout. Now, get on with some work.'

He tried to smile and make light of it all, but his stomach was spinning, his heart in flames as it went into a nosedive. He sat down at his desk, feeling lost.

Faith Carthew was sitting in the witness box, back straight, hands folded neatly in her lap. Her expression looked almost as if she was feeling anxious but DS Chambers knew that couldn't be the case. The murder trial was going her way. *But how could it be? After all the terrible things she'd done, how could she be getting away with it again?*

'Ladies and gentlemen, members of the jury,' the judge said, his face morose. 'I appreciate this is a very difficult time, what with the recent bomb explosion. Please do not let yourselves be distracted by outside events. This is a very important case. Thank you. The defence may continue.'

'Thank you, Your Honour,' Hannah Martin KC said and rose from her chair. Measured and composed, Carthew's barrister adjusted her robe slightly before stepping towards the witness stand.

'Ms Carthew,' Martin began, her voice steady but firm. 'Let's not beat about the bush. Let's deal with this matter directly. The prosecution claims you were staying at the flat where Maxine Rivers' blood was found. Were you?'

Carthew didn't hesitate. 'No. I wasn't living there.'

'But you had been there?'

She hesitated for a moment. 'I visited her there once.'

'Only on one occasion?'

'Yes.'

Martin stepped back, putting on a look of surprise. 'Why only the once?'

This should be interesting, Chambers thought.

Carthew paused, then breathed out before she spoke. 'Maxine was using the place, but I wasn't exactly sure why. It wasn't her place, obviously. I asked her why she was staying there but she kind of fobbed me off.'

Martin took a step closer. 'What did you believe was the reason at the time?"

'At the time, I was starting to suspect she might be corrupt.'

A murmur rippled through the public gallery, but Carthew barely reacted.

'Corrupt in what way?' Martin pressed.

Carthew kept her voice steady. 'Something wasn't adding up. Her movements, her access to certain case files… I'd seen her with case files she had nothing to do with. There were signs that she was up to something, I guess.'

'Did you report your suspicions?'

Carthew let out a huff. 'To who? To her partner, DI Crowne? He'd already made it clear he didn't like me. And I couldn't take it to DCI Moone. He's had it in for me since our relationship ended. This...' She gestured at the court. 'This isn't about justice for him.'

Martin KC glanced briefly towards the jury, letting the words settle. Then she asked, 'What is it about, then?'

Carthew's gaze was unwavering. 'It's obviously personal.'

'Do you believe DCI Moone has a vendetta against you?'

'Objection, Your Honour,' Simon Bray said as he stood up. 'My colleague is leading the witness. This is all hearsay.'

Martin KC turned to the judge. 'Your Honour, I believe I've already shown that DCI Peter Moone's arrest of my client and the subsequent search had very little legal backing and was based merely around his own bias against the defendant.'

The judge nodded. 'I'll allow this line of questioning.'

'I'll rephrase the question anyway,' Martin said and faced the witness. 'What do you think is the reason DCI Moone built this whole case around you murdering DI Maxine Rivers?'

Carthew sat forward. 'Because he wanted to get back at me by destroying my career, my reputation.'

Martin took a moment and let the silence stretch. 'Because your relationship ended badly?'

'And because he didn't like my working relationships with senior officers.'

'Meaning?'

'He thought I was getting too close. That I had too much influence. He didn't like that I had the ear of people above him. He saw it as a threat.'

'Are you saying DCI Moone is motivated by jealousy?'

Carthew turned her head slightly, eyes locking onto Chambers. 'Yes, I am.'

Chambers looked away, her stomach flipping over.

Hannah Martin KC took a slow step back, her expression giving nothing away. 'So in your view, this investigation, this case against you, is not about your alleged involvement with Maxine Rivers or her disappearance or suspected murder?'

Carthew's voice was calm, even. 'No. It's about settling scores.'

There was more murmuring across the courtroom until the judge called for order.

Hannah Martin waited for order to be restored then faced her client once more as she said, 'Now, let's turn to the other charge you face, the conspiracy to commit murder.

The prosecution would have us believe you persuaded Jason Harris, a member of the Dark Horses motorcycle gang, to drive a van at your half-brother, Lloyd Redrobe, while he was riding his scooter. Is there any truth to this theory?'

'None whatsoever. Why would I ask someone to kill the only family I had left?'

'The witness statement read out that was signed by the now, sadly deceased, Jason Harris, claims you wanted him out of the way because he knew all about your alleged criminal activities. Is there any truth to that?'

Carthew put on a good show of looking shocked as she said, 'No. I'd only recently got in contact with him because I'd learned that he was mixed up with the Tomahawks. They're the rivals to the Dark Horses. I went to see him to persuade him to walk away from it all. But he wouldn't listen.'

'Then do you know why Harris would have reason to kill your half-brother, Mr Redrobe?'

Carthew took a dramatic pause. 'As far as I understood it, the Dark Horses wanted Lloyd to work for them. But he got caught in the middle of their turf war and... well, they wanted him gone. I just wish I could have persuaded him to walk away.'

Martin nodded. 'So, to summarise, Lloyd Redrobe was caught in the crossfire between two rival motorcycle gangs, both known for their ruthlessness and extreme violence, especially towards anyone who they think has betrayed them. Would you agree?'

'Yes, I would.'

The defence barrister turned to the judge. 'No more questions, Your Honour.'

Chambers let out a harsh breath, then looked around when she noticed one of the people sitting in the public gallery get up to leave. It was DI Victor Crowne, his face set in a look of pure anger. He caught Chambers' eye before he stormed out. It was not a happy look.

It was then the prosecution's turn to cross-examine Faith Carthew, Chambers realised as Simon Bray QC stood up from his bench and approached the witness stand.

'Ms Carthew,' he began, then looked at his notes. 'Let's rewind to a few days before the tragic murder of your half-brother, Lloyd Redrobe, shall we?'

Carthew sat back a little and gave a nod.

Bray said, 'An undercover officer has testified that they saw you in a car with Lloyd Redrobe, Jason Harris, and Jim Nair, the leader of the Dark Horses motorcycle gang. That's quite the gathering, wouldn't you say?'

Carthew met his gaze. 'I imagine it might have looked that way to someone watching.'

Bray let out a sharp breath. 'You were there, were you not?'

'Yes, I was.'

'In a car with a known gang leader, a man with a history of extreme violence, and Jason Harris, a man who, I remind the jury, would go on to kill your half-brother. Quite the coincidence.'

She tilted her head slightly. 'Not a coincidence at all.'

Bray stepped forward, eyebrows raised. 'No?' His voice was calm, coaxing. 'Then perhaps you'd like to explain why you were in that car, Ms Carthew?'

'I was there to get Lloyd out of their clutches.'

Bray's expression barely flickered, but Chambers thought she could see the slight tension in his face as he said, 'That's your explanation?'

'It's the truth.'

Bray turned, glancing at the jury as he spoke. 'The prosecution suggests a different truth. We suggest that you weren't there to rescue Lloyd Redrobe at all. You were there because you were involved with the Dark Horses gang. You were part of their criminal dealings, and when things started to fall apart, you dragged your half-brother into it with you.'

His words hung in the air for a moment before she replied, her voice even, 'You're wrong.'

Bray arched an eyebrow as if amused by

her defiance. 'Am I?'

'Yes,' she said. 'Lloyd was in over his head, and I was just trying to get him out. That's why I was there, and that's the only reason I was there.'

Bray gave a slow, deliberate nod, but Chambers could see the change in him, the shift in his posture. He hadn't expected her to hold her ground quite so firmly. He looked at his notes then seemed to change his tack.

'Let's move on,' he said and cleared his throat. 'Let's talk about your subsequent arrest. You were found and arrested at Jason Harris' home, were you not?'

'Yes.' She held his gaze.

'What were you doing in his house, Ms Carthew, if you were not working with him?'

'It's complicated.'

'Can you please elaborate?'

She let out a breath, her eyes briefly jumping to the jury. How would she get out of this, Chambers wondered?

'I was working on a case,' Carthew said. 'We were after a man who would gain entry to the homes of single women and murder them in their kitchens. I became obsessed with catching him by myself. I know it was wrong, and I'm not proud of myself, and it's the reason I'm no longer a police officer, but I just wanted to stop him from hurting any more women. So when I heard Jason Harris was living at his late nan's house, I thought I could lure the killer there.'

'But Jason Harris claimed in his statement that the two of you had embarked on a sexual relationship and that you used your sexual power over him to persuade him to kill your brother. Isn't that the truth?'

Carthew held his gaze. Chamber's whole body tensed and she could feel the courtroom waiting, listening.

'No,' Carthew said with a trembling voice. 'The only way I could get Harris to help me get Lloyd away from the gang... was...'

Carthew sniffed as she looked down. Chambers let out a harsh breath when she saw her raise her face and there were tears in her eyes.

Carthew cleared her throat as she said, 'I'm sorry, but the only way he would help me was if I slept with him. I'm not proud of what I did but I was desperate.'

A murmur rippled through the courtroom. The judge shifted in his seat. Bray's expression flickered for the briefest moment. Chambers saw it, another break in his demeanour. He hadn't expected that answer.

Bray recovered quickly, but he had been rattled. 'So, you're telling this court that you, a detective sergeant at the time, chose to engage in a sexual relationship with a known criminal to... what? Persuade him to help you?'

'I didn't choose. I was desperate. And I had no other colleagues to turn to for help, as DCI Moone had turned them all against me. So I did what I had to, and I did all the terrible things he wanted me to do. Then he goes and kills my only family anyway. How do you think that makes me feel?'

Bray seemed to study her as her fake tears arrived. 'You expect this jury to believe that you were not involved in gang activity, that you were not complicit in your half-brother's death, and that everything you did, including sleeping with Jason Harris, was all for Lloyd Redrobe's benefit?'

Carthew leaned forward slightly, her voice quiet but unwavering. 'I don't expect them to believe anything. I understand what it sounds like. I'm telling the truth as I know it. But I expect them to at least listen to what I'm saying.'

Bray hesitated. Just for a second. Then he glanced at the judge. 'No further questions.'

Kelly Moone was following her phone's directions from the city centre and towards the Hoe. She stopped at the pedestrian crossing and looked round at the streets and the Tesco Express on her left. She was on Notte Street, her phone told her, so she crossed when everyone else did. She looked up and saw a large hotel on her left. She saw Citadel Road and followed it as it went right. Leigham Street was on her left. Nothing seemed to be familiar, although she did have a vague sense of having been there before. She didn't know what she was doing, but Pete seemed bothered by something to do with that particular holiday, and she didn't want him any more stressed and worried than he already seemed to be. If she could get to the bottom of the mystery then that would be one less thing for him to obsess over.

She stopped, put her phone away and took out the photo of all the family outside the hotel. It had been called Drake Inn back then, she knew from the photo. She kept walking along the street, holding up the photo and looking at the ordinary houses and the occasional one that had been converted into a bed and breakfast. She stopped halfway along the street when she spotted the large, white-washed building with the three white stone steps. The Leigham Hotel, it said in gold writing on a black background. She looked down at the photograph and then up at the hotel. She smiled a little, pleased that she seemed to have found it, although when she walked across the street, she got a deep sense of unease. She tried to shrug it off as she went up the stone steps and towards the glass door of the entrance. She hovered there for a moment, looking in through the glass at the patterned red carpet and the narrow hallway. There was that strange feeling again as she pushed open the door and felt a cool breeze hit her. She looked to her right and saw a large room set out with dining tables. On her left was a lounge area.

'Morning,' a man's voice said as a tall and quite broad figure came out of the darkness at the far end of the hall. He looked to be middle-aged, with a boxer's nose, a ruddy complexion and thinning grey hair. He smiled briefly as he took a couple of plates of food on a tray into the dining area. 'Be with you in a minute.'

She nodded, smiled and waited, trying to get her line of questions in order. She laughed at herself now playing at being a detective while her little brother was out there being the real thing.

The man came back out, rubbing his hands. 'Have you booked? We're very busy.'

'No, I'm not looking to stay here, love,' she said. 'Me and my brother and our family stayed here when we were kids…'

'Only a couple of years ago, then?' the man said, laughed and winked.

'Yeah, right. I just wondered how long you've had this place?'

He straightened up, looking around the hall. 'Oh, we've had the place for nearly ten years, give or take. My wife's round here somewhere. She'd be able to give you a more precise answer. Sorry, what's this about?'

She shrugged as she lifted the photograph. 'To be honest, I'm not sure. Did you know the people who used to run it when it was the Drake Inn?'

'The Drake Inn. Oh yeah, there were loads of photographs all over the walls from those days when we bought it. It was a right wreck, falling apart it was.'

'A woman called Joy Morten used to run the place.'

'Joy Morten? I don't know that name, but my wife might. Hang on.'

The man went striding back into the dark at the end of the hall, leaving Kelly to look down at the photograph. There they were, smiling as they were standing out the front of the hotel. She looked closer, staring at herself and little Pete. He wasn't really smiling, she noticed, and in fact, he looked a little troubled.

'Here she is,' the man said as he was followed by a much smaller woman with greying curly hay-coloured hair and wearing a polo shirt with the hotel's name printed on it.

'Gareth said you wanted to know about the previous owners?' the woman said, folding her arms as her husband disappeared into the dining area.

Kelly smiled, still clutching the photograph. 'Well, I just wondered if you knew the owners. I know the lady who owned it was called Joy Morten.'

'Joy Morten?' the woman laughed.'That's right. I used to live round here before we bought this place. I knew the family. She's in the Bethlehem Home not that far from here if you want to see her. Did you know her?'

'Oh no, but we stayed here when we were kids.' Kelly showed her the photograph.

'Oh, look at the place,' the woman said. 'That takes me back. We used to play here sometimes, running up and down the stairs, making a nuisance of ourselves. Well, we did until…'

The woman seemed to catch herself for a moment.

'Until?' Kelly asked.

She shrugged. 'Well, when we were still kids they closed the place for a while. Several months it was, or seemed like it. After that, it seemed they didn't want us kids there. They were just less welcoming, if you know what I mean?'

'I think so. What happened?'

'I don't know, but I remember hearing that the police came here asking about a missing man or something. It was a long time ago, so it's all a bit blurry. I don't think I can help more than that. Sorry. I've got to get on now.'

'Thanks,' Kelly said, noticing the woman hurried away a little too quickly. She was left in the hallway, the cool breeze coming back again as if a door had been opened somewhere in the dark at the end of the hall. She stared into the house and found that the strange unnerving feeling was rising again, making the hairs stand up on the back of her neck. A shudder ran through her. Something was definitely not right about the place.

CHAPTER 15

'There's nothing here,' Butler said and let out a huge huff as she pushed her chair back from her desk.

Moone looked up as he sipped the coffee he'd made. He was having pretty much the same experience as he went through the witness statements and crime scene reports. Abel knew exactly what he was doing, he had worked everything out. Moone rubbed his temples as he looked up at the map on the whiteboard and the areas that had been marked off. He got up, sipping his coffee and stared at it, trying to spot what no one else had seen. There had to be something there.

'It's not a Magic Eye poster, Moone,' Butler said, picking up her coffee. 'His evil plan isn't going to just pop out. Besides, he left that behind. One of the few things he did leave us. Like I keep saying, why would he leave such an important thing behind?'

Moone shrugged. 'I know. You're right. Unless...'

She stood up. 'Unless what?'

'Unless it's a challenge. You know, try and catch me if you can.'

Butler came over and joined him, staring at the map. 'Home Park, Royal William Yard, Devil's Point, the city centre, Plympton, Derriford, Leigham, Estover, Crownhill, Southway, West Park. Devonport. Random places, all around the city. He's trying to distract us and get us running around so we'll spread ourselves too thinly.'

'They're surrounding the city,' Moone said. 'Look, completely surrounding the city. That's got to mean something, hasn't it?'

'Like I just said, it means he's trying to get us running around distracted while he's putting together his next bomb.'

Moone sighed, thinking maybe she was right. He looked up as the incident room door opened and a glum-faced Chambers came in. She looked between them, failing to raise a convincing smile. He knew what that meant.

'Hi, Molly,' Moone said as she went over to her desk in the corner. 'I take it the trial's not going great?'

Molly sat down and hesitated, looking at

him for a moment.

He went over and said, 'It's OK. You can tell me.'

'She was on the witness stand today,' Molly said.

'The cow?' Butler called out as she sat back at her desk.

Molly nodded. 'She made out like it was DI Rivers that was up to no good and not her.'

Moone looked over at Butler and saw she gave him the same raised eyebrow look. He looked at Molly again. 'What else?'

Chambers let out a long-held breath. 'You were painted as the villain again. Thing is, I think the jury might buy it and they'll let her off.'

Moone nodded. 'But you never know. Let's just hope enough of them see through it and convince the rest.'

Butler gave a loud, unconvinced-grunt, but Moone ignored it.

'But, my dear Chambers, she won't ever be our boss,' he said, putting on the best smile he could in the circumstances. Then he looked over at the board again or at least tried to as his eyes kept jumping to Butler as she worked away. It felt like she was drifting away from him again and he didn't know why. He wondered if it was what he had said after the explosion, thinking maybe it had scared her off. He was an idiot. Why had he blurted it out like that?

He pulled himself back and refocused his eyes on the map. 'What do you make of this map, Molly?'

Chambers came over and joined him. After a few quiet seconds, she said, 'All areas surrounding the city. He could be trying to get us to spread ourselves out and distract us.'

'See!' Butler said, then shook her head and tutted.

'Maybe you're both right,' Moone said. 'He did leave it for us. He numbered each location. Royal William Yard is next. What the hell is he doing?'

'What, apart from terrorising the city and killing innocent people?' Butler stared at her screen, shaking her head. 'My bloody city and there's sod all I can do. We've got him on CCTV coming into the city on a moped before he started shooting people.'

'Any news on the lad and his girlfriend who were in hospital?' Moone asked.

'Joshua Hartwell and Andrea Mitchell,' Chambers said. 'They're on the road to recovery, thank goodness.'

Moone nodded. 'That's one good thing.'

'There's going to be a candlelight vigil tomorrow night,' Chambers said. 'On the Hoe. They're going to light candles for the victims. I was thinking of going.'

'I'm not sure that's a good idea,' Butler

said. 'What if that's what he's waiting for?'

'There's army and navy personnel all around the city centre,' Molly said. 'He wouldn't be able to get close, and they've got sniffer dogs and everything ready. Are you going to come, boss?'

Moone thought about it, not sure it was time to start mourning the victims when there was probably more to come. But he looked at Molly and he could see something in her eyes, a kind of pleading, he thought. 'I'll be there. Butler?'

She sighed. 'OK. Count me in. But if I get blown up, I'm blaming you.'

Harding walked through the main gate of the Royal William Yard, through the large granite archway that had William the Fourth standing on top of it, decked out like a Roman. It was the only land entrance to the yard. The gatehouse was on his left, where the police and the navy used to guard the place to stop anyone coming in to steal the navy's food and other supplies.

DI Anna Jones was striding ahead, so he quickened his pace to keep up. She was decked out in casual clothing, much like he was, both of them trying to look inconspicuous. The place was pretty busy with tourists and locals going in and out of the many bars, restaurants and art galleries. He knew there must be some of the Counter-Terrorism lot around there somewhere, so he kept scanning the crowds walking towards the glistening water all around the yard, or the ones gathered around the food stalls. The sun was out and burning down on the whole stone structure.

'Do you think he's here?' Harding asked as he caught up with Jones.

'I have no idea,' she said, then slowed as they reached the marina. 'We'd better try and not look suspicious. Let's get a cup of coffee or something.'

Harding nodded, so they headed for Seco Lounge which was already bustling with bodies coming and going. All the tables outside were taken, so Harding offered to go in and get the drinks while DI Jones went and looked over the water.

There was quite a queue for the bar and the chatter and noise of the place rattled in his ears. He kept scanning the place in case their mad bomber was already there. They had no idea what he looked like, but he kept his eye out for any lone, suspicious men. No one appeared to be anything other than what they seemed, people out for the day, enjoying the sun or something to eat. Eventually, he got served with their coffees and took them outside.

Jones was resting on the marina wall, staring out towards Princess Yachts.

'Imagine having one of those,' she said as she took her takeaway coffee.

'What?'

'Look at the boats.'

Harding looked out at the huge white speedboats, or whatever they were called, as they bobbed on the water. The ferry was coming in, full of people ready to get off. He looked up at the stone buildings that surrounded them, staring at the roofs and windows. He could see people milling about at just about every building. One of the men he was watching touched his ear, his mouth moving, a definite giveaway that he was part of the Counter-Terrorism team.

'I don't think he's coming here today,' Jones said and sipped her coffee.

Harding blew the air from his cheeks. 'Nah, I think you're right. Waste of time, this.'

'He could be watching us right now.'

Harding looked around at the buildings again, trying to spy anyone in the windows or on the rooftops. Nothing. The ferry came in, docked at the marina and let off a horde of passengers. En masse, like a brightly coloured army, they walked up the ramp. He watched them as he leaned on the wall, sipping his coffee. They were all decked out in their shorts and summer dresses, smiling and laughing. He smiled and decided to bring his missus along one day as it had been ages since they had been out for a meal at the Royal William Yard. Having a newborn never seemed to allow it.

As the crowd dispersed, going in their various directions, Harding's eyes jumped to one of the passengers who got off. He was wearing a black hoodie and had a dark rucksack on his back. He nudged Jones as he turned to watch the person walking away from them and heading in the direction of the gatehouse.

'Careful,' Jones moaned. 'I nearly spilt my coffee.'

'Look.'

Jones turned and looked across the yard. 'Guy in the hoodie?'

'Bit hot for a hoodie, isn't it?'

She shrugged. 'I don't know. My best friend's husband always wears a hoodie in all weather, even when it's boiling out. And loads of other layers. I think he might be a bit weird.'

'Sounds like a weirdo.'

'But is hoodie guy our terrorist?'

Harding looked over at the men and women he'd seen lining the shops and restaurants across the way, the ones he took to be part of the Counter-Terrorism team. They were still in position.

'Do you think the terrorism lot have eyes on him?' Harding asked.

'I don't know, but we'd better follow him. Come on.'

Harding followed her lead as she started casually walking in the same direction. They both dumped their coffees in a bin and followed, but kept far back. Jones got closer to Harding and put her arm through his like they were a couple. He just hoped his missus, or any of her mates, didn't see them.

The hoodie man slowed down as he reached the grassy area, then turned towards the bars and restaurants that sat opposite. He walked across the grass, now walking as if he knew where he was going.

'What the hell is he up to?' Jones whispered.

'I don't know. But the moment he puts that rucksack down... what do we do?'

'Grab him and leave the bag to the bomb squad. They're waiting for our call.'

Hoodie man walked towards the tunnel that led to Firestone Bay. They watched as he walked steadily to the end of it and stood looking out at the sea and Drake's Island.

'We'd better turn around or he'll spot us,' Jones said, and they turned and faced the other way. Harding kept glancing over his shoulder to see what was happening, but the man in the hoodie was still standing there.

'What's he doing?' Jones asked.

'Nothing. He's just standing there. What the hell's he doing? Maybe he's just a bloke in a hoodie who happens to have a rucksack.'

'Let's hope so.'

Harding turned back as he noticed the man start to turn around. 'I think he's heading this way.'

'Let's start walking.'

They started walking casually, still arm in arm, waiting for the hoodie man to pass them by. No one passed by, so Harding turned his head. His heart started to race as he saw the hoodie guy coming up to them.

He pulled Jones close and they both stared at him as he walked up to them and stopped a couple of feet away.

'Excuse me,' he said, slurring his speech. 'You police or something?'

Harding and Jones exchanged looks.

'Who are you?' Jones asked. 'What do you want?'

'Just want to know if you're with the police or what.'

Jones took out her ID and showed it. The hooded man smiled, showing he had a few teeth missing and his gums were almost black. He started to take off his rucksack.

'What're you doing?' Harding asked the man then looked at Jones. 'We'd better call someone.'

But they didn't have to call anyone as several armed figures came rushing across the grass, each of them pointing MP5 submachine guns as they converged on the hooded figure.

'Put the rucksack on the ground!' one of the armed team shouted. 'Get on your knees and put your hands on your head!'

DI Jones pulled Harding back out of the way as the armed team surrounded the man as he put the rucksack on the ground and then slowly knelt. As he raised his hands to his head, his eyes jumped side to side, his mouth chewing away. One of the armed team brought out some cuffs and slapped them on him and read out his rights.

'What's in the rucksack?' a plain-clothed officer asked.

The hoodie shrugged. 'I dunno.'

'We need bomb disposal!' the officer said, then took out his mobile and put it to his ear. 'DI Hudson. We need bomb disposal. Royal William Yard. Now.'

When he was off the phone, he looked at Harding and Jones as he said, 'You two, get the civilians out of this area. Move it! Now!'

Harding and Jones hurried away, heading for the crowds of people who were gathering around the food stalls.

The bomb disposal truck came rumbling through the archway entrance as Harding, Jones and a few of the Counter-Terrorism team shouted for the public to evacuate the area. Crowds of people and the staff from the bars started hurrying down the main strip as they were herded along towards the arched gates.

Two bomb disposal officers, one a thick-set woman with tied-back dark hair, the other a grey-haired man, climbed out of the van and started taking out their equipment. Harding watched on with surprise as he witnessed them flip a coin. The grey-haired man lost, or won, and then put on the protective bomb suit and helmet. He carried a case towards the rucksack as the armed team retreated to safety.

'Let's get back,' Jones said, taking hold of Harding's arm and pulling him backwards.

'I want to see what happens,' he said.

'Do you have a death wish?'

Harding sighed, but they both faced the green again as the bomb disposal officer shouted, 'Clear!'

Moone rushed over to Harding and Jones as they came back into the incident room looking drained.

'You two OK?' he said as they both sat at their separate desks.

Harding shrugged. 'Fine. I just can't believe what just happened. He just walked right up to us and put the rucksack on the ground.'

'But it wasn't a bomb,' Jones added.

Moone pulled up a chair. 'What was it?'

'A letter,' Harding said. 'In an envelope.'

'A letter?' Moone sat back. 'What did it say?'

'I don't know. It's been taken to forensics, but they said they'd copy it and send it over in an email to you.'

'Me?' Moone looked between them. 'Why me?'

'That's the thing,' Harding said. 'It was addressed to you.'

Moone shook his head, taking it all in as Butler came back into the incident room holding two mugs of coffee. She looked them all over, frowning and said, 'What's happened?'

'There wasn't a bomb,' Moone said, looking up at her. 'It was a letter. Addressed to me.'

Butler put Moone's coffee down in front of him as she said, 'Bloody hell. What next? What did it say?'

Moone shrugged. 'Forensics are going to send a copy over. Why the hell is he sending me a letter?'

Butler pointed at him as she sat at her desk. 'Because you caught up with him last time. He probably feels like he's got some kind of connection to you.'

'Really?'

'Yeah,' Butler said. 'In his crazy world, you two are best mates.'

Moone pulled a face at her then looked at Harding. 'What about the man? Who is he?'

'A junkie called Eddie Potter,' Jones said. 'I don't think he's our bomber. He says he was paid to bring us the letter.'

'See,' Butler said. 'That's why he left the map. He knew we'd have people there so he's messing with our heads and trying to waste our resources.'

'Where is he now?' Moone asked.

Jones was about to answer when Major Lacroix pushed through the incident room doors and walked up to Moone's desk.

'Moone, interview room two, now,' he said, as he folded his arms over his chest.

Moone stood up. 'Is this to do with the guy with the rucksack?'

'Just come on.' Lacroix turned and headed out of the incident room.

Moone looked at Chambers and then Butler, but they both shrugged as they stared at him. He sighed and followed the Major out and down the stairs. Lacroix was already waiting at the interview room door, holding it open by the time Moone reached it.

'We're not taping this,' Lacroix said to him quietly.

Moone stopped where he was. 'What?'

'I said we're not taping this. In fact, this isn't even happening.'

'Hang on, what about his rights?'

'He's off his fucking trolley, he doesn't even know he's got rights. Now, get in there.'

Moone walked in and saw that the desk had been moved to the far end of the room. Eddie Potter was sitting in a chair close to the door, his hands still cuffed behind him. The junkie's eyes followed Moone, or at least tried to as he pulled up a chair and sat down.

'Eddie?' Moone said as Lacroix came and stood next to him.

The junkie's eyes jumped up towards Moone but didn't quite fix on him. 'I ain't had me cornflakes.'

'I'm sorry?' Moone sat back, then looked up at Lacroix.

'History of mental illness,' the Major said. 'That's what all the drug-taking does. Even the marijuana that every moron thinks should be legalised. Eats away at your brain.'

'He can't be our killer, because…'

'Because our killer is smart. He knows how to make bombs, how to fire a weapon.'

Moone looked up at him again. 'Do you think he's ex-services?'

'Would make sense. But the thought that the British army, my British army trained him, is abhorrent to me.'

'Me too.' Moone looked at Eddie. 'Who gave you the letter, Eddie?'

His eyes flickered, moving around the room. 'Letter? What fuckin' letter?'

'The letter you had in your rucksack.'

'I don't have a rucksack, bey.'

Moone sighed. 'Who gave you the rucksack?'

'Have you got me cornflakes?'

Lacroix moved in front of Moone, his arm jutting out towards Eddie, seeming to touch his throat. Immediately a choking sound came from their suspect.

'Who gave you the rucksack?' Lacroix asked.

'What the hell're you doing?' Moone got to his feet, unable to believe what he was seeing. The Major had his fingers dug into Eddie's throat.

Lacroix looked at him from the corner of his eye. 'What needs to be done. This is what happens in the real world.'

'Jesus.' Moone turned away, trying not to hear the suspect coughing and choking.

Then Eddie slumped forward as the Major let go and stepped back. He was breathing in sharp breaths, coughing. He looked up at Moone, his eyes appearing more focused.

'Who gave you the rucksack?' Lacroix asked. 'I won't ask you a third time. What you've got to realise, Mr Potter, is that there are no cameras in this room. You're not here. We're not here. This never happened. You understand? I could kill you and tell them you choked on your own vomit. So, it's up to you.'

Eddie looked up at Moone, panic in his eyes. 'He wants to kill me. Help me.'

Moone sat down again. 'I'm not going to let anyone kill you, Eddie. We just need to know who gave you the rucksack. That's all.'

Eddie's eyes kept jumping up to Lacroix as he said, 'He said his name, but I can't think.'

'Long name or short?'

'Short. Weird name it was.' He closed his eyes tight.

'Abel?' Lacroix said, much to Moone's annoyance.

The junkie's eyes popped open as he nodded madly. 'That's it. Abel. Said if I took the rucksack to the two coppers, then he'd give me some cash. I need the cash, you see? I need…'

'More cornflakes?' Lacroix said, but there was no sign of humour on his face.

'I need… a new bike. Going to deliver food for that place, you know, the people that deliver the food. Get meself sorted.'

'Is there anything you can tell us about him?' Moone sat forward, engaging his eyes.

Eddie shrugged. 'I dunno. He wore a face mask and like, shades. Just gave me the bag and that was it.'

'That's it, Moone,' Lacroix said and snapped his fingers.

'What do you mean?'

'You're done, interview over. Now get out.'

Moone stood up. 'What're you going to do?'

'Our friends from MI5 have a facility where they have techniques to help him remember.' Lacroix stared him in the eyes, but there was only a kind of empty blankness there.

'You mean torture him?'

'No. Don't ever repeat that word, not unless you want your career to end very abruptly. Now, please leave.'

Eddie was staring up at him, his head shaking side to side. 'Where you going? You ain't leaving me with him?'

'You'll be OK, Eddie,' he said, trying to smile, but the lie had frozen his face.

'I dunno nothin',' he pleaded. 'I just needed the cash. I didn't think I was doing anything wrong.'

'It's too late for that,' Lacroix said.

'Is there anything you can remember about him?' Moone stared at him, willing the poor man to remember something, anything.

Eddie hung his head, his mouth chewing at itself again, his eyes jumping around the floor. Then his eyes jumped to Moone. 'Tattoo!'

'He's got a tattoo?' Moone asked.

'Yeah, I didn't want to look at his shades, I don't like it when you have to look at people wearing shades. It's not right.'

'The tattoo?' Lacroix said, his voice firm.

'Yeah, it was on his wrist, I saw it when he moved his arm, it sort of poked out.'

'What did it look like?' Moone asked and took out his notebook and pen.

'Sort of round, I think. Sort of like a flower.'

'A flower?'

He shook his head. 'Nah, not a flower,

maybe a sun, with like those flowery bits coming off it, if you know what I mean?'

'No, we don't know,' Lacroix said.

'Can you draw it?' Moone held out the notebook and then looked up at the Major. 'Can you uncuff him?'

Lacroix let out a grunt, then went behind Eddie and let him out of the cuffs. The junkie rubbed his wrists, took the notebook and drew a rough circle and then some strange petal markings all around it. Moone had an inkling of what he was trying to draw, so took the notebook off him and created an image of a sun, with flames encircling it. 'Is this what you mean?'

'Yeah, that's it, bey. But it had something in the middle. Like a shape or something.'

'What shape?' Moone passed him the notebook, but Eddie shrugged.

'I can't really remember. There was a squiggly line too. But that's it. That's all I know. Honest.'

'Square? Triangle?'

'Triangle, I think. Yeah, triangle. That's all I know, I swear.'

The suspect's eyes jumped up to Lacroix who nodded and said, 'OK, Eddie. I believe you. We'll get you out of here soon. Moone, come with me.'

They went out in the corridor where Lacroix faced him, arms folded.

'See, that's how it's done,' he said. 'You just need to scare them a little.'

'Oh, yeah, he was scared all right. It's just not the way we usually go about it.'

'Oh, I realise that, Moone. But you have a rule book to follow, and I don't, and you're playing on my team now. Where's this tattoo?'

Moone showed him the sketch he'd made with the sun shape and the triangle at the centre. 'We need to run this through the system.'

'Could be just something Abel had done on a whim sometime.'

Moone shook his head. 'I don't think Abel does anything on a whim. I'm going to take this to our IT guy and see if he can make sense of it.'

'You do that. I've got to organise more teams to head to the areas on Abel's map. Brief me this afternoon.'

Moone headed to Barry's little broom closet full of computers and energy drinks. There he was as usual, huddled over a desk, staring at a glowing screen in the dark, one hand in a giant pack of Wotsits, cheese dust everywhere.

'Hey, Barry,' he said and stared at the large monitor that had several windows open with lines and lines of code flickering down them.

Barry took his hand out of the bag and licked his fingers clean. Moone was glad when he didn't put his hand out to shake.

'Got a job for me?' Barry asked, sitting back. He looked just as malnourished and pale as ever.

'Looks like you're busy.'

'Nah. This is ongoing. Got anything interesting? I'm bored.'

'Maybe.' Moone opened up his notebook and showed him the drawing.

'What is it?'

'I was hoping you could tell me. It was tattooed on a suspect, and I think it might be significant.'

Barry looked up, his eyes showing something close to stimulation. 'Is this to do with the terrorist case?'

'Yeah, but keep it quiet. Can you check online for this, and find out what it is?'

'Course. I'll just scan it in, reverse image search and see what comes up.'

'Is this going to take a long time? Shall I come back?'

Barry shrugged as Moone watched him get up from his chair and scrape his trainers over to a scanner in the corner. Seconds later, the image was on the screen.

'Could be ages, could be minutes.'

Barry typed something in and the process began as a flicker of various tattoo designs began filling the screen. Then one image jumped up and Barry paused it.

'Is this it?' he asked and Moone stared at

the black and white image on the monitor, a sun with a triangle at the centre. There within the triangle was some kind of squiggly line. Moone nodded. 'It looks like it. Let's see what it is.'

He started reading:

Understanding the Akashic Records: A Spiritual Library of Knowledge.

The Akashic Records are often described as a vast, metaphysical archive that contains information about every event, person and thought throughout history. Believed to be a record of the past, present, and future, these records are considered a source of profound spiritual insight.

The concept of the Akashic Records is rooted in Theosophy, where they are thought to be encoded within the mental plane, a non-physical realm of consciousness. Some interpretations suggest that the records are part of the Divine Mind, serving as a universal source of wisdom. Others view them as a cosmic library that holds the accumulated experiences and knowledge of every soul.

While the existence of the Akashic Records remains a subject of spiritual and philosophical debate, many individuals claim to access them through meditation, intuition, or deep spiritual practice. Whether seen as a metaphor or a literal repository of knowledge, the Akashic

Records continue to captivate those seeking deeper understanding and guidance in their spiritual journey.

Moone stopped reading and looked at Barry. 'What does that mean?'

'I saw a TV programme about this. Certain groups take that to mean everything is predestined, what will happen is already written so you can't do anything about it.'

Moone straightened up. 'But what has this got to do with him killing and blowing people up?'

Barry shrugged. 'There is another interpretation.'

'Go on.'

'Some people take this to mean we're in The Matrix.'

'What?'

'Past, present, future. Think about it, that's what The Matrix is. Everything preprogrammed. Like a computer code.'

'That's crazy.'

Barry nodded. 'But if this guy you're after believes we're in The Matrix, then he believes nothing is real. So it doesn't matter what he does.'

It dawned on Moone then. It fell in place. Abel believed that nothing was real, people were bots or something, so it didn't matter if he killed, maimed or blew everyone up. That was

his psychosis.
    Which meant he wasn't about to stop.

CHAPTER 16

Moone pressed the buzzer next to the front door and waited. He felt a wavering in his chest as well as a swarm of crazed moths knocking around in his gut. He'd come to visit Alice, she was his priority, but he would be lying to himself if he tried to pretend he wasn't hoping to catch Butler in the wild. He wanted a glimpse of her private life, an aspect of herself that she really did keep private, especially from him, and that hurt. He had spilled his guts in a moment of shock and madness, but he was glad he had. The truth was out there, as Fox Mulder used to say. Moone had spent the rest of the day researching the *Akashic Record,* trying to understand how someone could read it and then turn into a psychopathic terrorist. None of it made sense, and he could only guess what traumatic events had happened in Abel's life that had led him to kill a large number of innocent people.

The front door opened and Alice poked her head around, wrapped up in a fluffy pink dressing gown, her hair tied back. 'Dad? You didn't say you were coming.'

'I meant to call you,' he said. 'Is it a bad time?'

'No, course not. Come up. I just had a shower. I'll chuck some clothes on.'

As Alice hammered up the stairs to get dressed, Moone trudged up after and headed into the hallway that led to the kitchen and the living area beyond it. It seemed a long time since he and the team had gathered around the kitchen table with a few bottles of plonk and set the world to rights. Back then he'd felt a lot closer to Butler, so much so that he had become convinced that somehow they would one day be together. They would drive each other mad, he knew that, what with her constant criticism that he did everything slowly. He couldn't think of one thing he disliked about her; he'd even learned to love her huffs.

Alice came out of the smaller bedroom, now dressed in leggings and a long-sleeved top. Butler had, understandably, kept the larger room for herself.

'No Butler?' he asked as casually as he could.

She laughed.

'What?' he asked.

'You're transparent, Dad.' She sat on the sofa and pulled her legs up to her chest.

He sat down. 'Am I?'

'When are you just going to ask her out?'

'I don't know what you mean. Aren't you going to offer your old man some kind of drink?'

She sighed and got up. 'Tea, coffee, wine? I think there's a can of lager.'

'I'll have the can of lager, thanks.'

Alice fetched it and put it on the coffee table, then sat back on the sofa. 'She's out, by the way.'

'Who?'

Alice rolled her eyes. 'Your crush.'

'Oh, right. Where?'

She shrugged. 'I don't know. She tells me to keep my nose out when I ask.'

He nodded, then opened the can. 'I think she's got a fella.'

'What's that on your face?' She leaned forward, staring at him. 'Have you cut yourself?'

'Oh, just an incident at work.'

'Hang on, this isn't to do with the terrorist going around, is it?'

'No, of course not. Counter-Terrorism are dealing with that.'

She didn't look convinced. 'I hope you're

being careful, Dad. I would like you around a bit longer.'

He sipped his drink. 'Trust me, I'm being careful.'

Then the buzzer went and they both stared towards the door.

'You expecting anyone?' Moone asked.

'No. You?' Alice got up.

'Check who it is first.'

Alice went to the intercom and pressed it. 'Hello?'

'Hello, love,' the voice crackled from the speaker.

'It's your aunt,' Moone said. 'Let her in.'

'Aunt Doris?'

Moone laughed. 'I hope not. Aunt Doris died ten years ago. No, it's Kelly, my sister.'

'Bloody hell, I haven't seen her since I was little.' Alice rushed to press the door release.

'I'm glad you're only on the second floor,' Kelly said, coming into the flat. 'Those stairs are steep. Oh my God, look at you, Alice.'

Moone watched as the two of them faced each other, Alice smiling in a state of surprise and embarrassment. Kelly hugged her then came into the living room, plonked herself down on the sofa and scowled at Moone.

'I know, I know,' he said holding up his hand. 'I forgot to message you. Sorry, it's been a crazy day.'

'Well, it's a good job you gave me Alice's

address in case of an emergency.' Kelly tutted and then smiled at Alice as she came and sat down. 'So, my angel, any boyfriend on the scene?'

Alice blushed as Moone said, 'Right, let's not follow through with that line of questioning. Did you find out anything today?'

Kelly wiggled her eyebrows. 'I found the hotel, if that's what you mean.'

'What hotel?' Alice asked.

Kelly looked at her. 'When we were kids, your nan and grandad used to bring us down here in the summer holidays…'

'Really? To Plymouth?'

'To Plymouth. We used to stay at this hotel near the Hoe. Here, have a look.' Kelly brought out the photo and gave it to Alice.

Alice stared at it, laughed and looked up at her dad. 'Oh my God, Dad, look at you. You actually look cute.'

'Doesn't he?' Kelly laughed. 'What happened to him, eh?'

'Very funny,' Moone said. 'What did you find out?'

Kelly smiled. 'I talked to the owners and the wife told me she used to hang around and play there when she was a kid, when Joy Morten ran the place. But then she said it closed for a while. After they opened again, she reckons the owners didn't want them hanging around any more. Then she tells me there was some big to-do when the police turned up looking for some man who'd gone missing.'

Moone sat back as his mind tried to absorb it all. He had that strange feeling again, the sense that a memory was trying to break through. But it wouldn't come. In a way, he was glad, because he also had the feeling that something not very nice might come to light with it.

'What's all this about?' Alice asked, looking at her dad.

Moone shrugged. 'I don't know. Maybe nothing. Me and Butler went to the care home the other day because one of the residents, a Joy Morten, started screaming about a murder. The thing is, she's got dementia, so you can't get much sense from her. But she seemed to recognise me, and since then I've had this strange feeling, or memory or something.'

'Memory of what?' Alice leaned towards him, obviously absorbed by the mystery.

He sighed and sat back. 'I don't know. But I get a sense it's not good.'

'Maybe you need to go and see Joy Morten again,' Kelly said.

'What's the point? Most of the time she doesn't know where she is.'

'Has she got any family?' Alice asked.

Moone shrugged. 'A nephew. Maybe I'll see if I can get hold of him.'

'I would,' Kelly said. 'Otherwise, this'll

drive you crazy. Anyway, where's your girlfriend?'

'Haha. She's my colleague, not my girlfriend.'

Kelly laughed. 'Right, course she is.'

'I knew it,' Alice said, eyes widening as she stared at her father. 'You do like her!'

'Now look what you've done, Kell,' Moone said. 'You've set my daughter off.'

'Do you like her, Dad?'

Moone shrugged, not knowing what to say. 'It doesn't matter if I do or not…'

'Course it matters,' they both said at the same time.

'Jinx!' Kelly said and laughed.

'What're you going to do about her, Dad?'

'Nothing. She's my colleague and she doesn't look at me like that. And I think she might be seeing someone anyway.'

'She is,' Alice said with a frown. 'She got dolled up the other night. Said she was going to the pub and meeting an old friend.'

'So?' Kelly said. 'So she had a date, so what? She's not engaged. Come on, Petey, pull your finger out and tell her how you feel.'

Moone sighed and pushed himself up to his feet. 'I can't. Not right now. We've got too much going on. Maybe when this is over, but not right now. We've got this Abel running around shooting and blowing up innocent people… and I haven't got a clue how to find him and stop him.'

'You'll figure it out, Dad, you always do.'

He looked at Alice who was smiling sympathetically. Then he remembered the email the forensic team were meant to be sending to him with Abel's letter attached. He logged into his work email and there it was. He opened up the attachment. The forensic team had taken a photo of the small piece of white paper that had large, carefully printed writing on it. His eyes jumped to the bottom where he had drawn a sketch of the same symbol Barry had found online. It was all to do with the *Akashic Record*, whatever the hell it really was.

He read the letter to himself:

To DCI Peter Moone,

You believe you are making choices, Peter. That every step you take is your own. But you are mistaken, just as all of them are. You are trapped like a puppet, convinced it controls its own strings. Every thought you have, every move you make, has already been written in the great record of all things. The Akashic Record holds every past, present, and future moment, and you, like the rest, are merely playing your part. You chase me not out of will, but because you must. You investigate because it has already been decided that you will. Even now, reading this, you think you have a choice in what happens next. You do not.

I know you, Peter. More than you think. This is not the first time our paths have crossed. You have hunted me before, in lives long past, under different names and faces. And each time, you have failed to see the truth. But this time, I will help you. Soon, you will understand what I must do. What we must do. When the illusion shatters, and everyone is free from this facade, you will remember me. And then, perhaps, you will finally be free.

Abel.

So he was right, Moone realised. Abel believed nothing was real and that we have no free will.

'What's wrong, Petey?' Kelly asked, looking concerned. 'Bad news?'

'What's wrong, Dad?'

He let out a shaky breath. 'The guy we're after, he sent me a letter…'

'What?' Kelly stood up. 'Why?'

He shrugged. 'I don't know, but he seems to believe in something called the *Akashic Record*. It's some spiritual thing, and people think it has the past, present and future all written down as if everything we've done or are going to do is predetermined. We've got no choice, no free will. What will happen will happen whatever we do. He says about breaking free of this illusion and being free of this fake world or something…'

'Sounds a bit like he's talking about The Matrix,' Alice said.

Moone nodded. 'That's exactly what he thinks. He's convinced we're in a kind of computer program and whatever he does isn't real.'

'The Matrix?' Kelly said, looking between them. 'What, like in that weird film? I never finished watching it. I couldn't keep my eyes open.'

Moone looked at her. 'The point is, if he's convinced none of this is real, like it's a computer game, then he'll just keep killing and killing, with no remorse.'

'Then he's a nutter,' Alice said. 'What're you going to do?'

'I don't know.' Moone slumped into his chair again, his mind desperately searching for an answer and coming up empty. 'I haven't got a clue. I just hope the Counter-Terrorism team might find something.'

'Well, you can't just sit round waiting for something to happen,' Kelly said. 'At least go and see if you can find Joy Morten's nephew. Go on.'

Moone sighed, then pushed himself to his feet again. 'I suppose I could. But I don't know what I'm going to ask him.'

Kelly tutted and looked at Alice. 'And he calls himself a detective. Go and ask him if he knows anything about the hotel and the man who went missing. She might have told him something. Anything. Go on, it'll keep you out of trouble.'

'Aunt Kelly's right, Dad,' Alice said.

'Aww, I like the sound of that,' Kelly said, smiling adoringly at Alice.

Moone sighed. She was right. He needed to take whatever lead he had.

A welcome breeze drifted across the water as Abel stared out from the boat. The outboard motor rumbled as he steered the craft towards the shore. It took a few minutes, but he was soon climbing out of the boat and dragging it up the steep bank. He straightened up and stared over the water, the wavering heat over everything in the city. People were swimming, shouting and laughing in the distance, safe in their ignorance. What he wouldn't give to forget and be one of the automatons once more. He shook his head as he turned and walked along the road and towards the large building that had once been used to store canoes and other equipment. Now it was empty, with cracks in the metal roof where the sunlight swirled through. In each corner, there was a large plastic container. Each one held an IED that had taken days to construct. It had taken him even longer, over two years to gather the explosives necessary. All the containers were covered with tarpaulin. He went over to his safe, opened it up and took out the Glock. He thought of the letter he had written to the policeman. It was so clear now that he was on the right path, otherwise, why would they have been brought back together after all this time? They had shared that moment so long ago, and now here they were, enemies of a kind, or so it would seem. But he knew it was the opposite.

He put the Glock into his jacket and then lifted out the sniper rifle and put it in his holdall. In a few hours, when the sun was up, he had more to do, a few more steps until he could help the glass facade of this world shatter. The equipment was ready for the next stage, but until the day came to an end, he had other places to be.

It was evening when Moone parked up outside the Bethlehem House Care Home, but the sun still warmed the sky as it had only sunk a little way towards the horizon. There were still people on the beaches below, the sound of kids' laughter and splashing reaching his ears. He could see bodyboarders paddling out in the sound. It was hard to believe the city was under attack from some Matrix-obsessed terrorist. He mentally shrugged, trying to cleanse his mind of a case he had little chance of solving now. Counter-Terrorism and MI5 would now take their lead, and he hoped they might find some way of locating Abel before he shot someone else or planted another device.

Moone felt useless as he walked up to the side entrance of the care home and showed his ID to the camera. The doors clicked open and he went into the clinical reception area. There was plenty of noise from the residents, chatter and the sound of cutlery scraping plates. Of course, it was their evening meal time.

The receptionist looked at him with an enigmatic smile and raised eyebrows.

'DCI Peter Moone,' he said and showed his warrant card. 'I was here a couple of days ago to see Joy Morten…'

'Oh, they're having their evening meal now.'

'That's OK. I wondered if you could put me in touch with her nephew, Adam Morten?'

'Oh, OK,' she said and started looking through some paperwork under the desk. 'We have a number for him. Although, he is due to come in and see her shortly. He called earlier and made an appointment.'

'All right, I'll wait outside.' Moone walked back out of the reception area and out through the glass doors. He was glad to get out as the aroma of whatever they were serving up for the evening meal had started to make him feel queasy. He couldn't remember the last time he'd had something proper to eat. He took out a cigarette with shaky fingers and lit it, then took a drag. He looked at what he was doing, smoking again. Again? He hadn't really stopped, and what with all the horrors he had faced lately and the dire situation with Butler, he couldn't face trying to give up again. It was his one comfort.

He stared out across the water at the distant ships that were hazy shapes on the horizon. There were only a few fluffy white clouds scattered about, while the retreating sun made its last effort at warming the earth.

He turned back towards the car park in time to see a tall figure walking through the cars. He wore a dark jacket and dark trousers. Moone took a quick puff and dropped his cigarette when he realised that the person coming towards him was Adam Morten.

'Excuse me,' Moone said, making the man stop and look round at him. He took out his warrant card and showed it to him. 'DCI Peter Moone. Can I have a word?'

Adam Morten looked at his ID, then looked up. 'We've met before.'

'Oh, yeah, the other day. I wanted to talk to you about your aunt, Joy.'

Morten looked towards the home, a little concern seeming to flash in his eyes. 'Is she OK?'

'Yes, sorry. Can we sit down for a moment?' Moone gestured to a stone bench over on the other side of the car park.

Adam looked over at the bench, then

shrugged. 'If you want. Is this to do with the other day when she got upset?'

'Kind of,' Moone said as he led the way to the bench and sat down. He watched Adam Morten seat himself and fold his arms across his chest before he said, 'This is going to sound a bit... weird, but ever since I met your aunt the other day, I had a feeling I'd met her before.'

'Maybe she's got one of those faces.'

Moone nodded. 'Well, the thing is she used to have a hotel round here.'

Adam nodded. 'The Drake Inn. Near the citadel.'

'That's right. Well, when I was a kid, we used to stay there in the summer. But the weird part is, I keep having this memory trying to pop into my head... I know it sounds strange...'

'Not really. If you spent a lot of time here when you were young then there's probably lots you've forgotten. But it'll be in there somewhere.' He smiled, pleasantly enough, but Moone sensed he was just trying to placate him.

'Probably. There's something else. I went to see the new owners and they said the police once came there looking for a missing man. Do you know anything about that?'

'A missing man? When did this happen?'

'A long time ago. I'm not really sure.'

Adam sat back. 'Well, I don't remember my aunt mentioning it, but the police must have a record of it, you know, when he went missing. Sorry, not telling you how to do your job.'

Moone laughed as he stood up. 'No, it's fine. You're right. I should've thought of that.'

Adam Morten stood up. 'Well, I'd better go and see my aunt. Let me know if the memory comes back.'

Moone waved as the man headed off and into the reception of the care home. He was left outside, thinking again, myriad thoughts swimming around in his head as he took out his cigarettes, stuck one between his lips and lit it. He took his phone out and called DS Chambers' desk.

'Hi, boss,' she said, sounding distracted.

'Hope this isn't a bad time?'

'Oh, no, just getting statements written up, collecting the post-mortem results together, etc. I've got to present them to Major Lacroix. Are you OK?'

'Fine. You couldn't do me a favour, could you?'

She gave a short laugh. 'You're the boss. It's not a favour.'

'Well, it's kind of personal. I need to find what we can about a man who went missing about forty years ago, roughly. The police talked to the owners of what was the Drake Inn at the time. It's on Leigham Street. Joy Morten used to run it.'

'OK, tell me again and I'll write that down.'

Moone repeated himself.

'Got it. Is this to do with our case?'

'No, it's not. Just something that's bugging me. Only if you've got time.'

'I've got time.'

'Thanks, Molly.' Moone ended the call and continued smoking as he headed for his car. He climbed in, stubbed his cigarette out, then reversed out of his spot, looking in the rear-view mirror and nearly hitting a car and a scooter. He managed to get out and started back along Durnford Street, turned onto Royal William Yard Road, and then onto Cremyll Street, his mind awash with everything that had happened so far.

His phone rang, so he slowed down at the next traffic light, answered the call and put it on speaker on the passenger seat. 'Hello, Molly. That was quick.'

'Well, obviously there's no sign of it on our system, so I did a search online. There was an article in the Herald about unsolved murders and disappearances a couple of years ago, and they mentioned that case. They also named one of the young coppers working the case at the time. You'll never guess who?'

Moone didn't want to guess who because he already suspected who it might be. 'Please tell me you're not going to say former detective inspector Gary King?'

'Sorry, but yeah, it's DI King. What're you going to do?'

Moone let out a heavy breath. 'Go and see him, I guess. But he's not going to like it.'

CHAPTER 17

'Sorry,' Chambers said. 'I know DI King is the last person you wanted to see.'

'It's fine,' Moone said. 'He must have been young then.'

'Yeah, just a PC at the time. When are you going to go and see him?'

Moone blew out the tense breath filling up his chest. 'To be honest I've been meaning to pay him a visit, to see how he is. No time like the present.'

'Good luck.'

'Thanks, Molly. Good job.'

Moone ended the call and carried on towards Stonehouse where he knew Gary King still resided. He parked up in the narrow street with the pastel-coloured houses and the small pub on the corner. He climbed out, mentally preparing himself, seriously considering having a crafty cigarette before knocking on his door. As it turned out, he didn't even get a chance to take his fags out as King's front door opened and the old man stepped out. He looked at Moone, then did a double take as his face became pinched, his wrinkled eyes sharpening.

'What the bloody hell're you doing here?!' he snapped as he closed the door. He shook his head and started to head down the street towards the pub, muttering to himself.

'I need your help,' Moone called out.

There came a huff followed by a hollow laugh. Then he stopped and swung around and pointed at Moone. 'You want my bloody help? That's a fucking laugh after you stitched up my boy. You couldn't solve it properly so you found someone a little damaged to frame. Nice one. Leave me alone.'

Moone followed, his heart thudding. 'I know you don't want to hear it, but Jonathan confessed. I didn't frame anyone. I'm sorry. I'm really sorry.'

The former police detective had stopped but remained turned away. Moone stepped closer. 'I need your help. I wouldn't bother you but you're the only person who might have some answers for me.'

The old man looked around, his eyes having gone from being on fire to curious. 'Help with what?'

Moone nodded to the pub. 'Why don't I buy you a drink and we can talk?'

King seemed to chew it all over before he swung around and started towards the pub. 'Fine. Mine's a pint of Tribute and a whisky chaser, bey.'

The Artillery Arms was the kind of pub that had seen generations come and go, yet little inside had changed. It had a low-beamed ceiling and worn wooden floors that carried the scent of spilt ale and the faint trace of cigarette and pipe smoke even after all the years had passed since the ban.

The bar stretched along one side, polished dark wood smoothed by the hands of countless regulars. Behind it, rows of spirits gleamed in the dim light. A chalkboard listed the day's offerings.

The walls were a patchwork of dark wood panelling and faded wallpaper, decorated with old regimental photos, naval memorabilia, and the kind of framed newspaper clippings that spoke of local legends, long-dead heroes, and the occasional scandal. A dartboard hung in the corner, its surface pockmarked from decades of friendly games.

As King was greeted by some of the regulars and the bar staff, Moone realised this was his second home. The old copper sat at a table in a far corner near the unlit fireplace.

'Tribute,' King said. 'Whisky chaser. Better make it a double.'

Moone nodded, bought the drinks and delivered them to the table. When he'd sat down, King sipped his pint and looked deep into him.

'I'm not stupid,' King said, his manner softening. 'I know what he did. It's just hard sometimes and I want to blame someone, or find some reason he did all those bloody awful things. But I know, right in my heart, who's to blame.'

The old man turned a withered thumb on himself as he said, 'Me. This fool. I was always working. I loved the job too much, and I wanted to be in the thick of things, not playing house. That's why my marriage failed. But, Jesus... how? How did he get like that? I never hit him. Never. As far as I know, he was never... you know, messed about with. I just can't get me head round it. Now he's stuck in that godforsaken hell hole, Broadmoor. He'll never get out. They've got him on so many drugs, he doesn't know what day of the week it is. I don't mind admitting it, sometimes I leave, and I sit in me car and... I cry.'

Moone stared at the man, his heart being clutched and squeezed. 'I'd be the same. I can't imagine...'

'I hope you never end up like me. I don't really blame you, Moone. I know you was just doing your job. You're a bloody good copper.'

'Am I?'

'You must be. You solved the case that we never could.'

'I had a good team.'

King cleared his throat and gave a shake of his shoulders. 'Anyway, you said you needed my help.'

Moone sipped his ale as he nodded. 'About forty years ago, when you were still in uniform, you took part in the search for a local man who'd gone missing. Some of you talked to the owners of a hotel near the Hoe. The Drake Inn, it was called then.'

King's eyes widened, his breath filling his cheeks until he let out a burst of laughter. 'Bloody hell, bey, you're going back some. I can hardly remember what I had for breakfast, let alone forty years ago.'

'I thought it might be a tough one,' Moone said, feeling a little deflated. 'Never mind.'

'Hang on.' King held up a worn palm. 'I might not remember, but my files will. I told yer, didn't I? My boy... well, he helped me make notes of all my cases...'

'But that was early days before you became a detective.'

'Ah, but I was always a detective, my lad. Even then I wrote everything down, every little detail.' The former copper sat back, sipping his pint, nodding.

Moone could see a change in him suddenly, a glint in his eye now he had a purpose. Good, he thought, even if they draw a blank, at least the old man might find his way again.

'Shall we go back to yours and have a look?' Moone took a big gulp of his pint.

'Hold yer horses. The case is nearly forty years old, I think it can wait until we've sunk a couple more.'

Moone shrugged. 'Why not?'

Harding was driving, taking them into Devonport, along Duke Street before he turned into Ker Street. DI Jones was beside him, studying a copy of the map they had found in the house Abel used as a headquarters. Crazy bastard, Harding thought to himself and caught sight of PC Steve Kenton in the rear-view mirror, sitting in the back, staring out the window. They were all dressed casually again, trying not to stick out, which meant they stuck out like a nun at an orgy.

The evening was drawing in, the sky awash with a splurge of deep orange as Ker Street was bathed in the warm, slanting light of that Plymouth summer evening, the sun sinking low over the rooftops, casting long shadows across the worn paving stones. Devonport Guildhall loomed at the end of the street, glowing an eerie blue, while the column that stood beside it speared the sky. Seagulls bickered as they hopped and danced over the rooftops, perhaps stirred into action by the smell of fish and chips that Harding had also noticed. His stomach rumbled. There were cars parked opposite the Ker Street Social Club with its strange yellow, Egyptian-style exterior. Harding pulled in and parked a couple of hundred yards from the Guildhall and turned off the engine.

'This is number six on the map,' DI Jones said and looked around at the houses, and the blocks of flats.

Harding looked around too and saw the three white tower blocks with their brightly coloured and pointed hats. He sighed. 'Anyone fancy a pint?' he said and heard Kenton laugh.

'Just a quick one,' Kenton said.

'Come on, lads,' Jones said and pushed open the passenger door. 'Let's have a scout around and see what we can see. Then maybe I'll buy you both a drink.'

Harding got out, and felt a welcome breeze coming towards him, bringing with it more of the fish and chip aroma. 'As long as I don't have to listen to Celine Dion again.'

Jones tutted. 'You just don't appreciate good music, Keith,' she said as she walked along the street.

Kenton was stepping towards the Guildhall, hands in his pockets, while Harding stood at the centre of Ker Street, looking around. There was nothing here, he thought, nothing but Devonport Dockyard a few streets away. That was the obvious target.

'It's got to be the dockyard!' he called out.

Jones shook her head, glaring at him as she took long strides to meet him. 'Quiet, loud mouth. The dockyard is locked down tight. He's not getting anywhere near. But you're right, there's nothing here. A social club and the Guildhall, unless he plans to blow that up.'

Kenton came back towards them, hands in pockets, walking with a swagger like he was a member of Oasis.

'Alright, Liam,' Harding said and laughed. 'Good job blending in, our kid.'

The PC shrugged. 'There's no bags or suspicious packages. Nothing. What're we doing here?'

'Search me.' Harding walked back up the street, turning and examining it all. He huffed as he stared at the social club, the houses, the flats. It was a wild goose chase, a waste of resources. What could he be looking to target? He looked up at the three towers that would have a bird's eye view of them down on the empty street. The other flats too, a perfect... He stopped moving, a horrible sense of dread filling him. He turned and saw Jones was near the car, Kenton a few yards from the Guildhall. Panic gripped him, his heart starting to race.

What if he was looking at them?

'Jones!' he called out. 'What if it's…'

The sound rumbled, pounding off the buildings. Like a car backfiring.

Kenton dropped to the ground. Harding stared at him, frozen for a moment. Then a blast of pain tore through his shoulder as he stumbled and fell to his knees. The cracking sound rebounded off the buildings as Harding dragged himself towards the parked cars. Another blast echoed and he heard a cry. Jones. It sounded like Jones, he thought as he kept his head down, his body violently trembling. She was near their car, he thought, breathing hard. He swallowed, trying to organise his thoughts. Call it in. With a shaky hand, he pulled out his phone and almost dropped it. Calm down, he told himself, but his heart kept pounding. He called Chambers and waited.

'Hi, Keith,' she said.

'Molly, get Armed Response here. We're pinned down…'

'What? What do you mean?'

'Someone's shooting at us. Kenton's… he's been hit. I think Jones too. I can't see her. Call someone, please!'

'Oh, God. OK, try and hide. You're at the Guildhall, Devonport? Is that right?'

'Yeah, please get them here. He's in one of the buildings.'

'Just stay where you are. Keep low.'

Harding breathed in, trying to think straight. He closed his eyes as a realisation hit him. 'I can't…'

'Listen to me. I'm alerting the Counter-Terrorism team…'

'Jones. She might be hit.' He ended the call as he huffed. He shuddered when he heard a metallic twang, followed by another. Bullets were hitting their car.

'Jones!' Harding called out. 'Jones!'

'I'm here!' her voice trembled, tears within it. 'I can't move. My leg. I think Kenton's gone.'

Harding tapped the back of his head against the car door, trying to think. He moved his arm and felt the burn of the wound. He gingerly touched it and grunted. It wasn't that bad, he didn't think. The bullet must have just caught him.

He saw his wife. His child. He looked across the street when he heard a door creak open. He poked his head out a little and could see the door of the social club had opened. A man, rotund, balding with glasses was standing in the open doorway. There was a woman behind, middle-aged. Harding's eyes jumped down to a smaller figure by the man's legs, a little girl in a fairy outfit holding a party bag. They were about to walk out into the street.

'Stop!' he shouted. 'Stay there!'

The man turned his head, looking for

whoever had shouted. He looked back and forth, then seemed to shrug as he held the girl's hand and started to step towards the street. *Oh fuck.*

'Stop!' Harding shouted again as he poked his head out. 'Don't move, there's a shooter.'

But the man kept moving, pulling the kid out the doorway and into the open. Harding closed his eyes, his heart being grasped as it throbbed.

His wife flashed into his mind again. Then his daughter. He forced himself up even though his legs didn't seem to want to work. Then he was moving, even though a voice in his head was screaming at him to stay and hide. The man and the child were moving, getting halfway across the street.

Blood exploded from the side of the man's head and he slumped to the ground, pulling the girl with him. She was screaming as Harding ran as fast as he could towards her and swept her into his arms. Another shot slammed into the ground, pieces of tarmac exploding. He moved with the girl in his arms, heading for the doorway. A hot poker speared through his leg as he was feet from the door and he fell forward, the girl under him. Somehow, he pushed her away and she rolled towards the door. The woman grasped the girl and dragged her inside where they both huddled and cried. Harding pressed his hands to the ground, breathing hard, shaking all over.

'Move!' someone shouted. *Jones? Where was she?*

'Keith! Move!'

He managed to push himself up to his knees, the throb of pain surging from his left leg. He couldn't look at it. He started moving, dragging himself towards the doorway. He looked up when he heard a desperate, crying voice.

'Come on, please!' the older woman was pleading for him to come towards her.

A sharp, cold pain ripped through him. He cried out as his back burned. Tears filled his eyes. The woman in the doorway was hysterical, still clutching the girl. Harding kept moving, dragging himself towards cover. The woman had her hands out, beckoning him.

He thought he heard sirens, but then the street became darker, almost thick with clouds. Then nothing.

Moone had managed to avoid drinking too much through the subtle art of drinking much slower and keeping King topped up. The old man could certainly put them away, and when they exited the Artillery Arms to the waves of the barman and the other customers, Moone noticed that King's ability to walk straight had hardly been affected. It was much darker outside, the sun having sunk almost completely behind the rows of houses and flats, the shadows lengthening.

The front door was opened by King as he chatted away about the old days. Moone was just appreciative of the fact that he hadn't said any more about his son being locked up for the rest of his days. He had followed up on Jonathan Michael King's progress and learned that he had been diagnosed with schizophrenia, or a personality disorder of some kind. Since he had been a young man, he'd been hearing the voice of a dark man whispering to him, telling him to do bad things. In his mind it had been an old caretaker in his school who had never actually existed, as far as the doctors could tell.

King walked through the house, still talking, telling him about an old case, stopping only to suggest they order a Chinese takeaway while they searched his files.

'The Royal Chef,' King called from the kitchen. 'That's where I usually order from. What do you fancy, Pete?'

Pete. That's what he was now known as to the man whose son he had put away for ever. He didn't feel hungry, in fact, he felt like throwing up.

'Nothing for me,' he called back as he stood in a small, compact and dusty living room. There were still photos on the walls and the mantelpiece. He noticed there were more now, images of a young Jonathan. School photos. A big smile. There was one where he was older, maybe taken in his last year of secondary school, and King seemed to be distracted, staring off to his left. Moone wondered, with a renewed sickness, what the boy was looking at.

'You don't want a Chinese, bey?' Gary King poked his head in the door.

Moone felt bad. He shrugged. 'Sweet and sour chicken balls. Curry sauce?'

'That's more like it. I've got some ale or even some whisky somewhere. The good stuff.'

'Where's your files?' he called out, but King had disappeared again and he heard him talking somewhere, probably on the phone. Moone sat down on the sofa, wondering if he could get the information and leave before the Chinese arrived. He sighed, knowing he couldn't leave the old man alone now. There was a photo album opened on the coffee table. Moone sat forward and started looking through it. They were black-and-white photos of objects, buildings, and blurry-faced people. The images of someone experimenting.

'Half hour,' King said as he came in and put plates and cutlery on the coffee table. 'Oh, they're Michael's photos. He studied art and photography when he was in the sixth form. He was pretty talented.'

'I can see.' He couldn't say the truth, that

they looked pretty terrible to him.

'I was going through them, trying to find him.'

Moone looked up. 'Find who?'

'The caretaker. The one who he said told him to do it all. Keep up.'

Moone looked down at the photos, not knowing what to say.

'They reckon it was all in his head, that he never existed. But think about it. Why would he make up some bloody caretaker? Don't make sense.'

Moone shrugged. Nothing much ever made sense when it came to murder.

'I keep meaning to ask, bey. What happened to your face? Get in a fight with a lawnmower?'

Moone touched his forehead. 'No. Just… obviously you know about the bomb at Argyll and the shootings?'

King slumped into his armchair, nodding. 'Yeah, that's a terrible business. Wish I could find him. What is he, a terrorist? One of these foreign ones?'

'No, he's local, I think. Thing is… he's not a terrorist, I mean he is, in the sense he's terrorising the city, but…'

The old copper brought out a tobacco pouch and started rolling a cigarette. 'What's he want? What's his demands?'

'Nothing. That's the thing. We don't know

what he wants.'

The old man poked the cigarette between his lips, narrowing his eyes. 'No demands? Strange. Then why do all this? He's not been radicalised, has he? You're sure?'

Moone shrugged. 'The only thing we've found is a tattoo a witness told us he's got on his wrist. It's a sun with a triangle in the middle and a squiggly line. Anyway, I found out it has to do with this ancient thing called the *Akashic Record.* I don't really understand it but it's like a mystic record of all events, past, present and future, like everything has already been mapped out. He sent me a letter too, saying the same thing.'

'He sent you a letter?' King sat up, the fag almost dropping from his mouth. 'So, he's contacted you, specifically? Why?'

'Me, the police, trying to challenge us to catch him.'

The old man looked thoughtful. 'Maybe. Has anyone looked into the possibility that he's had military training?'

'Counter-Terrorism are looking into it. MI5. But you know what they're like. They could've had him on their watch list and they're not telling us.'

King lit his roll-up and took a deep lungful. 'Yeah, they're sneaky bastards.'

'So, these files you've got? You know, the missing man?'

King nodded. 'Yeah, don't wet yourself, Pete, I'll find them in a mo. The food should be here soon…'

Moone realised his phone was ringing and took it out. It was Chambers, he noticed, and looked up at King. 'Sorry, better take this.'

He walked out into the narrow, musty-smelling hallway as he answered the call. 'Hello, Molly. All OK?'

'No, boss,' she said and he heard the strain in her voice. 'There's been another shooting…'

'Oh, God.' His whole body seemed to want to drag him to the floor. 'Where?'

'It's Harding, Jones and PC Kenton. They've taken them to Derriford.'

Moone couldn't take it in for a moment, the world shifting. 'How bad is it?'

'I'm not sure. Harding was hit, and Jones, I think. Kenton's… he was fatally wounded.'

Moone felt like throwing up. 'I'll head straight for Derriford… oh, shit. I've been drinking. I'll have to get a cab.'

'OK, boss, I'll see you there.'

Moone ended the call, then stood in the hallway, shaking a little. Please let them be all right, he said to himself, then went into the living room where King was still smoking.

'Everything all right?' the old copper asked.

'No. There's been another shooting. One of my people is dead, two injured. I need a cab.'

King pulled himself up. 'Jesus. I'll call you one.'

Moone got dropped off by the taxi near the entrance to the Emergency department. He was trembling all over by the time he climbed out of the car. Nothing seemed right; he didn't feel himself at all. It was as if nothing was quite real any more.

'Hey, you OK?' the Polish cabbie had asked him as they had entered the hospital grounds. 'You look like a ghost.'

'I'm fine, thanks,' he had said.

Moone pushed through the doors of Derriford Hospital's Emergency department, the heat of the place hitting him like a wall. The smell of antiseptic and something metallic like blood filled his nostrils. It was chaos as usual inside, patients on trolleys lined the corridors, nurses moving fast, their trainers squeaking on the polished floor. A paramedic brushed past him, muttering something under his breath, and further down, a man was shouting about his mother not being seen fast enough.

Moone didn't care about any of it, he was too busy scanning the scene, searching for any of his team. He caught sight of a young nurse at the triage desk, her face pale and drawn, probably exhaustion, he thought. He rushed over and showed his ID.

'My colleagues have been brought in,' he

said, his chest tight. 'DI Anna Jones and DC Keith Harding. Where are they, please?' His voice came out sharper than he'd intended, but he wasn't in the mood for pleasantries.

She blinked, hesitating for a while as she looked around. 'I don't know. I know they came in.'

'Who are you after?' a man's voice said close to him. He turned and saw a dark-skinned, young man in blue scrubs.

'Jones and Harding, two of my officers that were shot.'

The man turned to a board at the back of the area and Moone followed.

The doctor looked up at the board and said, 'Harding was taken to theatre. When he arrived, he'd lost blood, so that was our priority, to stop the bleeding. Now he's in theatre having one of the bullets removed and repairing any internal damage.'

Moone nodded, feeling sick. 'And Jones?'

'She's in one of the cubicles. Over there.'

Moone didn't stop to thank him, he was already moving, weaving through the crowd, pushing past a man clutching a bloody tea towel to his head. The fluorescent lights hummed brightly overhead. He pulled the cubicle curtain aside and saw Jones sitting up in bed, looking pale and shaken. A full-figured, Indian nurse was taking her blood pressure.

'Boss,' Jones said, her voice trembling.

'Keith?'

He stepped closer as the nurse took off the cuff, then made her notes and left.

'He's in theatre. He's lost blood, and I think they're trying to remove a bullet. He's in good hands.' Moone looked down and noticed the bandages around her thigh. 'How are you?'

'Went right through my leg, they said.' She hung her head for a moment, then looked up, her eyes wet. 'Kenton's dead.'

'I heard. Jesus. What happened?'

Jones swallowed. 'We arrived, we were looking around... we couldn't see anything, there were no devices or anything suspicious we could see. Then Harding called out to me. He'd realised what was happening. He was waiting for us. He must have been sat there, waiting for us to arrive... then Kenton... he just dropped. Gone. It happened so fast. The next thing I know my leg was on fire, but I dragged myself behind our car. Harding was behind another car. I still can't believe what he did...'

'Who? What happened?'

Jones stared up at him. 'Harding. Across from where I was lying, there's the social club. A kids' party must have been going on...'

'Oh, God.'

'This man was coming out, holding a little girl's hand. Harding shouted for him to stop, but he didn't hear him, or ignored him... I couldn't do anything... the man just fell. He'd been shot in the head.'

'And the girl?' Moone's heart throbbed.

'Harding came from nowhere and grabbed her. He managed to get her into the club building and that's when he got shot. He fell and just lay there. Then Armed Response was there. The rest is a blur.'

Moone put his hand on hers. 'I'm sorry I wasn't there.'

'Really? I'm glad you weren't there. I wish none of us had been there. I'll tell you what, Harding deserves a medal.'

Moone managed a smile. 'Sounds like it.'

There came the sound of the curtain being dragged aside, and the cacophony of crying and machinery beeping got louder. Moone turned to see DS Chambers coming in, tears in her eyes.

'What's happened?' Moone asked.

She swallowed a sob and cleared her throat as she looked between him and Jones. 'It's Harding. He's taken a turn for the worse. There's been some internal damage or something. He's in the ICU. I've just seen his wife. I didn't know what to say.'

Moone put out his arms and hugged her. He stared out the parted curtain, the fury pulsing deep inside him. He was going to find Abel and stop him, whatever it took.

CHAPTER 18

There was an obvious chill in the air the next morning as the team gathered in the incident room. Moone stared round the room, his heart running at speed already, his mind wrapped in a layer of cotton wool thanks to the drinks he'd put away with King the night before. The nightmare he had faced in the hospital had sobered him up no end but kept him from a proper sleep. Now he registered the missing team members as he stood in a daze. Jones was resting now, having been discharged from Derriford, while Harding was still in the ICU, his situation touch-and-go. PC Steven Kenton's fiancée had been informed of his death. He closed his eyes, and tried to focus on the matter at hand, the fact that they still had Abel to find.

When Butler came in, her eyes met his,

returning his look of grimness. She came over to where he was standing.

'That sick bastard,' she said, her voice low and tense. 'Do we know how Harding is?'

'Still in the ICU. I'm praying he'll pull through.'

Butler put her face in her hands and let out a ragged breath. 'He's only just had a baby daughter.'

'I know. We need to focus on finding Abel.'

She put her hands down and stared at him. 'You all right?'

'Fine.' His heart had buried itself deep in his stomach as soon as she had come in, but he didn't have time for all that now. 'I just need to get him.'

'We will.'

Major Lacroix entered the room with DS Chambers in tow and a tall, sinewy man in a dark suit. He looked to be in his forties, his dirty blond hair dotted with grey. The Major stood in front of the whiteboard while the few members of the team, now supplemented by detectives from the Counter-Terrorism Unit, sat down at their desks and waited.

'Last night, as you already know,' Lacroix began, 'three of our team came under attack. Unfortunately, PC Steven Kenton was shot and killed at the scene. Detective Constable Keith Harding is in the ICU, and DI Anna Jones suffered a wound to her leg but is now recovering at home. I know you're all going to be upset by the events of last night, but we need to get on and find the perpetrator.'

The Major turned and tapped the map on the board. 'It's obvious now that the map he left behind was a red herring, a way to draw us out…'

'Oh really, I'm shocked,' Butler said with a huff. Moone felt his body tense as Lacroix's cold eyes jumped to her.

'As I said, I understand you're all very upset,' he said, his voice deeper, a ripple of something harsher underneath his words. 'Now, we're going to be examining all the evidence we have…'

'Which is zero,' Butler said. 'I might be stating the bloody obvious, but he's running rings round us. So, why doesn't the man in the suit talk to us? I take it he's from MI5 or some spook outfit?'

'DI Butler,' Lacroix started to say.

'It's fine,' the suited man said and stepped forward. 'I'll take it from here. Yes, you're quite right, DI Butler. My name is Fitzgerald and I'm from MI5. We've been working away in the background, examining the fragments of the bombs with the help of the Bomb Disposal unit, trying to ascertain where this particular terrorist learnt his trade…'

'Is this where you tell us that he was on your radar all along?' Butler asked. 'But you didn't think he was a threat? Is that close?'

Fitzgerald gave a flicker of a smile. 'No, I can guarantee he's never been on our watch list. We're in the dark as much as you are as to why he's carrying out these attacks. The Director General of MI5, Sir Tom Kennedy, sent me here to let you all know that you have our full resources at your disposal. Now, I've been informed that so far he's made no demands. And he hasn't mentioned his manifesto?'

Moone raised his hand.

Fitzgerald looked at him, raising his eyebrows. 'Yes, and who are you?'

'DCI Peter Moone,' he said. 'There is something that's come up that I think might be relevant.'

The MI5 agent folded his arms. 'Moone. Was it you who came face to face with the suspect?'

'Yes, it was me.'

The MI5 man nodded. 'And it was also you who was rewarded a medal a few years ago, was it not?'

Moone sighed. 'He has a tattoo, on his wrist.'

'A tattoo?'

Lacroix turned and picked up a pile of A4 printouts of the design they found online. Fitzgerald was handed one, which he examined for a moment, his brow creased. 'Is this symbol affiliated with some terrorist organisation?'

'I don't think so,' Moone said. 'This is an ancient symbol, related to something called the *Akashic Record*. It's a spiritual thing, some kind of record of everything that has happened or will happen, past, present and future. The thinking is, that everything is predetermined, that there's nothing we can do to escape our fates...'

'What's this got to do with our suspect?' Fitzgerald asked. 'Are you saying he believes in all this rubbish?'

'Yes, I think he does. The fact this *Akashic Record* says that past, present and future are all written down in this spiritual plane, has led a lot of people to believe what it actually represents is a kind of matrix. I think Able believes we're in a simulation.'

Fitzgerald laughed. 'It's an interesting theory, DCI Moone. But how does it help us find him?'

That was the problem. Moone didn't have an answer. Everyone was looking his way. 'Well, we need... maybe look into online groups to do with the *Akashic Record.* Someone might have communicated with him. But what I think we need to figure out is what his aim is...'

'He aims to cause death and destruction,' Lacroix said. 'I thought that much was obvious. Some people want simply to cause chaos.'

'I agree,' Fitzgerald said. 'Our psychological profile suggests we're dealing with a male, aged thirty to fifty. Possibly with a military background. That means discipline, structure, and the ability to plan. He's not acting on impulse, he's methodical, patient, and, crucially, trained. That makes him extremely dangerous.' His gaze swept the room, lingering on Moone before continuing. 'He's carrying deep psychological trauma. Likely from childhood. Sexual abuse is a possibility. Whatever happened to him, it's shaped his worldview. And that worldview is simple, he hates the world, and he wants to see it burn.'

Silence settled over the room. Fitzgerald let his words hang for a moment before driving the point home. 'This isn't just about ideology. It's personal. He's not fighting for a cause, he's lashing out. And he won't stop until we stop him. The orders from the Home Office are shoot to kill.'

Murmurs travelled around the room, and Moone looked to Butler, who rolled her eyes.

Former detective Gary King had spent the morning sitting at his dining table, a constant roll-up smouldering away in an ashtray close by. He'd been going through the stack of old case files that he and Michael had put together so long ago. His heart plummeted again at the thought of his boy locked up in Broadmoor, surrounded by all those crazy, evil bastards. He cleared his thoughts and took a drag of his roll-up.

The house was quiet, save for the occasional creak of the floorboards and the steady tick of the clock on the wall. His hands, still steady despite his years, flipped through the yellowing pages. Then he saw it. The name conjured up a few memories from all those years ago.

Rodney Fox.

Thirty-five years ago, Fox had vanished without a trace. King had been a young PC back then, still green, eager to prove himself. He remembered the search, the enquiry, uniforms doing all the legwork as usual, combing the streets, knocking on doors, chasing down leads that led to nothing. No body. No answers. Just another missing person swallowed by time.

He sat back, running a hand over his stubble-covered jaw, feeling the effects of the booze and the Chinese he'd put away the night before. It was a shame Moone had buggered off in a hurry. He leaned over the files, reading some of the details, how they had found out Fox's wife had kicked him out for some reason that she didn't want to talk about. Probably an extramarital affair, he decided as he read that Fox had been traced to the Drake Inn. But it was a dead end. He'd never booked in.

He looked at the address he had for Mrs Fox. Tamerton Foliot.

King grabbed his coat, stuffing the file into a worn leather satchel, and stepped out into the warm Stonehouse morning. The scent of salt and warm brick filled the air as he made his way to his car, an old Volvo that had seen better days. He started the engine, his mind already firmly in the past as he pulled away from the kerb.

The drive took him north, away from the city's smaller, narrower streets and into the quieter, older parts of Plymouth. Tamerton Foliot still had the feel of a village, tucked between rolling green hills and ancient woodland. The roads narrowed, winding through clusters of stone cottages and houses that had stood for centuries. He passed St Mary's Church, its tower rising against the clear blue sky, a scattering of tumbledown graves surrounding it.

He pulled up outside the local pub, The King's Arms, one of the most prominent features of the area, then killed the engine and sat for a moment, staring out at the village and rolling a cigarette. It was the kind of place where people tended to notice strangers.

Rodney Fox must have walked these streets once, and now it was time to find out what had happened to him. He climbed out of the car and started walking, looking for the address.

He turned off the road as he found the

cul-de-sac where Fox used to live with his wife. Mary Dean Avenue was a quiet residential street, lined with 1950s semi-detached houses, each with small front gardens bordered by low brick walls or hedges. The houses were solid constructions, built to last, with pebble-dashed or red-brick exteriors, and pitched roofs.

The house King was looking for had a faded wooden gate, slightly warped from the rain, that led to a narrow driveway where an ageing Renault was parked. The front door had once been painted blue but now it was discoloured, the paint peeling off.

A curtain twitched in one of the front windows. Someone inside had noticed him as he stopped at the end of the drive and lit his roll-up. He took a drag and stared over at the house.

As he suspected it would, the front door opened, and a middle-aged woman stepped out with a small bag of rubbish that she took to the brown bin at the side of the house. All the time, her eyes jumped to him, full of suspicion. He smiled and nodded.

'Morning,' he said.

'Morning,' she replied and came a little closer, like a scared bird heading to a table of bread. 'Are you looking for someone?'

'I am,' he said, blowing out some smoke. 'I used to know the family who lived here. The Foxes?'

'Oh, right, they haven't lived here for a few years now, my luvver,' she said, stepping even closer. 'We bought this place off their son. That was like ten years ago now, I reckon.'

'Any idea where I might find the son?'

'Oh, I reckon. Did you see the pub up the road?'

'The King's Arms? Yeah, I saw it. That his local, is it?'

She nodded and came closer, looking up and down the street, ready to conspire, it seemed to King. 'Yeah, he's always in there. Had some accident at work a few years back, lost a couple of fingers and got some kind of big payout. Just spends most of his time drinking it away. A fool and their money are soon parted, my nan used to say. But I shouldn't gossip.'

'Nothing wrong with a little bit of gossip,' King said, taking another drag. 'Like when his old man went and vanished.'

'That was a right mystery,' she said. 'They never did know what happened to him, did they?'

'Nah, not as far as I know. You never heard anything?'

'I only know what I was told after I moved in. She, Mrs Fox, kicked him out… apparently, he was up to no good, they reckon. Then he was gone. I reckon he must've left the country or something. I mean, people don't just disappear, do they?'

'I think you'd be surprised. Anyway, you said the King's Arms?'

'Back the way you came, you can't miss it.'

King smiled and waved as he headed back up the street. The King's Arms, he thought and mulled it over. Nothing like the hair of the dog that bit you, he decided.

DCI Moone barely had time to put down the coffee he had made before he spotted a smartly dressed woman standing in the incident room, examining everything with a lot of disdain. She was tall, probably in her early forties, sharp-featured, and dressed in a smart navy suit. She had the look of someone who didn't suffer fools.

Her eyes locked onto him as she strode towards his desk.

'DCI Moone?' she asked as she gave him a once-over.

He forced a smile to his lips. 'That's me. You are?'

'Detective Superintendent Sarah Langley from the Professional Standards Department,' she said, flashing her ID. 'I've been trying to get in touch with you, but you've been... difficult to pin down.'

Moone didn't say anything for a moment but he could feel a few heads turning from nearby desks, particularly Butler's.

'We've been busy,' he said. 'Trying to catch

a terrorist.'

'I'm sure,' she replied, seeming unimpressed. 'We need to talk about your arrest of former Detective Sergeant Faith Carthew and the subsequent search of her car. I need to interview you. Officially.'

Moone let out a sigh. He'd known this was coming, he just hadn't expected it quite so soon and in the middle of their investigation.

'Can't this wait until…'

'No. Police misconduct is taken very seriously.'

'I know. I just… never mind. Let's go to an interview room.' He nodded towards the corridor.

Langley didn't wait for him to lead the way. She turned sharply and walked toward the interview rooms, expecting him to follow.

He looked at Butler and she made a face and mouthed, 'Good luck.'

Moone got ahead of Langley and opened the door for her with a smile. She looked at him briefly, with an expression of derision before she headed into the interview room and took a seat. Moone sat down across from Detective Superintendent Sarah Langley, who was watching him with the detached scrutiny of someone used to picking apart fellow officers. She was here to see if he had broken the rules. His stomach rolled over. Even from prison, Carthew was making his life hell.

'Before we begin,' she said, pressing the record button on the small black recording device in front of her, 'this is a voluntary interview under caution. You are not under arrest, but if you refuse to answer questions, it could be considered during any disciplinary proceedings. Understood?'

Moone gave a slow nod. 'Understood.'

She clicked her pen, glancing at the file in front of her. 'You had a warrant to arrest former DS Faith Carthew and then to search her vehicle.'

Moone nodded. 'That's right.'

She stared deep into him. 'But your reasonable suspicion wasn't sufficient. As it came out in the murder trial, you had no justifiable reason to believe her vehicle contained evidence of a crime, specifically, the murder of DI Maxine Rivers.'

Moone exhaled slowly. 'The circumstances...'

'The law,' Langley interrupted. 'That's what the issue is here. Not circumstances. PACE requires reasonable suspicion, and from where I'm sitting, I see you didn't have it.'

Moone leaned back slightly. 'Maxine Rivers' last known whereabouts was in Plymouth. I believed she was in Plymouth to meet with DS Carthew. Then Rivers went missing...'

'The thing is, DCI Moone, you weren't leading the investigation into the disappearance of DI Maxine Rivers, were you?'

'No, I was heading a murder investigation. But we received intelligence from an informant, Jason Harris, that Carthew planned to trap our killer and kill him. We sent in an undercover officer, who was assaulted by Carthew, by the way…'

'This intelligence came from a member of a criminal gang, did it not? A man who had already murdered Carthew's half-brother. Quite frankly, this whole business is a mess, DCI Moone.'

Langley's expression remained unreadable as she said, 'You had nothing linking her car to the disappearance of Maxine Rivers. No witness reports, no forensic leads, and nothing placing the vehicle at any relevant scene. And yet, you went ahead with the arrest and search.'

Moone didn't answer. He didn't know what to say and had already resigned himself to the fact that he was in big trouble.

'So tell me, DCI Moone, was this about the case? Or was this about Faith Carthew in particular?'

Moone's jaw tightened. 'It was about the case. DS Carthew had been spotted by a fellow officer in the presence of the leader of a motorcycle gang, along with Jason Harris…'

'Yes, I'm aware, and now she is no longer a police officer as a result. But the fact remains that you had no solid reasonable suspicion that led you to believe that DS Carthew had anything to do with DI Maxine Rivers' disappearance, apart from your own suspicions and bias. Have you got any other evidence to back up your reasons for the arrest and search?'

Moone sighed. 'No, I haven't.'

'No. I didn't think so.' Langley put her files back into her folder, collected her recorder and stood up. 'Thank you for your time, DCI Moone. We'll be in touch after further investigation.'

Moone got up and opened the door for her. She said nothing more, just gave a professional smile and then walked away.

Butler was standing by the entrance to the incident room, looking at him as if he'd just stepped out of the headmaster's office.

'Oh, dear, did you get told off?' Butler asked, folding her arms.

'I think I did. I'm being investigated for misconduct or something. It's all to do with the trial. I fucked up. I thought I was being clever, but I was distracted with...'

'What?'

He stopped talking. He meant to say with the fact that Butler had been lying in hospital, hovering by death's door, but he couldn't convince the words to leave his lips. 'You know, the case, trying to find John Michael King. Talking of which, I went to King's last night…'

'He must've been pleased to see you!'

'Well, he wasn't at first but I used the old Moone charm.' He smiled and winked.

'Did he vomit by any chance?'

'Nice. Anyway, turns out King was one of the uniforms that went to the Drake Inn all those years ago to investigate the man who went missing. He was meant to stay there but never showed up.'

Butler held up a hand. 'Hang on. This is because you're obsessed with this whole memory you keep having?'

He shrugged. 'Well, yeah. You encouraged me, you got in touch with my sister.'

Butler sighed and shook her head. 'Yeah, but only because I wanted you to reconnect with your sister, not to go chasing after ghosts. We've got a bloody terrorist to find, remember? A terrorist that's killed and injured our people.'

He nodded. She was right. 'I know. It's just bugging me for some reason. Right, let's go over everything we've got again.'

'Great. We've got more repeats than the BBC.'

Former DI Gary King walked up to The King's Arms, eyeing the building with a mix of familiarity and a little disapproval. The bones of the place were old, centuries old, but the exterior had a fresh coat of white paint and a sleek new sign which made it clear to him that the owners were trying to drag it into the modern age, make it family-friendly and all that rubbish. Not quite how he remembered it from the old days.

As he stepped inside, the scent of polish and fresh paint clashed with the deeper, older smells of beer-soaked carpet and lingering smoke from a time when no one cared that much about breathing in second-hand smoke. The layout hadn't changed, with a low-beamed ceiling, and the same ancient stone fireplace still dominating one wall, but the furniture was new, all matching wood and smart upholstery. The bar gleamed under modern lighting, stripped of the scuffs and dents that once gave it character.

A few locals were sitting nursing their pints, half-watching a muted TV mounted in the corner. A couple of younger families occupied tables near the back, the soft hum of conversation filling the space. It wasn't the rough-and-ready pub he remembered, but the soul of it was still there, just hidden beneath a fresh coat of paint.

King stepped up to the bar, nodding to the bartender. 'Pint of Tribute, mate.'

As the young-looking, tubby barman poured his pint, he cast another glance around the place, noting a couple of men sitting in a far corner nursing their pints. One was dressed in a black hoodie, his back to him, the other one was heavy set, with a dark wiry beard and red, tired skin. He was reading a newspaper and sipping a Guinness.

King looked at the young barman as he put his pint in front of him. 'Thanks. Don't suppose you know if any of these people are called Fox?'

'Nah, mate,' he mumbled. 'That'll be four pound-fifty.'

King sighed and handed over a fiver. Then he faced the room and the scattering of customers, paying particular attention to the two men at the back. He looked around, shrugged, and then called out, 'Fox! Phone call for Fox!'

The heavy-set man's head jumped up, staring suspiciously towards the bar. Eventually, he gathered himself up with a loud grunt and waddled over to the bar. The young barman had wandered off, leaving King alone to observe the rotund man; he looked at one of his hands and noticed three of his fingers were missing. Bingo, he thought.

'Did someone say there was a phone call?' Fox said, leaning over the bar.

'That was me.'

The man swung his head around towards King, his bloodshot eyes staring at him. 'What?'

'I pretended there was a call.' King leaned on the bar. 'Because I wanted to talk to you, Mr Fox.'

The man's face reddened even more as he folded his arms. 'Who're you when you're at home?'

'Someone who wants to ask you a couple of questions.' King took out his wallet and slipped out a twenty quid. 'Why don't I buy you a drink, Mr Fox?'

'You'll need more than a twenty. I'm a thirsty man.'

The barman came back, so King waved the twenty at him as he said, 'A drink for my new friend.'

The barman nodded at Fox.

'Well,' Fox said, rubbing his beard, 'seeing as I've got a Guinness, I'll have a whisky. Make it a double.'

Then Fox turned to face King. 'So, what was these questions you were going to ask?'

King sipped his pint. 'I was going to ask about your old man.'

The man's face changed, a strange, kind of angry look coming into his eyes as he growled, 'Then you can shove your drink where the sun doesn't shine...'

King grabbed him by the elbow as he was striding off. 'Hang on, have a drink. I'm just looking into his disappearance, that's all.'

The man yanked his elbow and gave him a

once-over. 'Why? You from the police?'

King rolled his shoulders and stuck out his chest. 'I was. A long time ago. I'm just looking into this… because, well, I worked this years ago and I'm retired now and I don't like to leave things unsolved.'

The man huffed. 'Well, some things need to be left alone. I don't want to talk about him.'

'Because he upped and left? Any idea why?'

'Hundred quid. No, two hundred.' Fox snapped his fingers and held out his palm.

'Two hundred quid for what? The money for the fingers run out, has it?'

Fox's face reddened even more. 'Oh fuck off then. Just leave us out of it.'

As the man started to walk off, King said, 'Was your mum glad he left?'

Fox turned around, staring at him. 'What does that mean?'

King shrugged. 'It means, was he not the most gentle of men? Did he knock her around?' King took out a couple of twenties and pushed them along the bar.

Fox chewed the corner of his mouth, then walked back to the bar, put his hand on the money, dragged it back towards him and stuck it in his coat pocket. 'Yeah, we was both glad he fucked off. He… he made our lives a misery. And no, I don't know what happened to him and I don't care. Now, I'm going to go and finish my drink in peace.'

It was at that moment that King realised his legendary charm had worn off. But he knew one thing and that was Rodney Fox was not a nice person. As he finished his pint, he wondered if the missing man had abused him or something worse. He would need to look into it further, he decided as he walked out of the pub and headed for his car. He climbed in, put his seat belt on and turned the key. The engine coughed and then died. He turned the key and the engine rumbled and coughed to life. He had a thought then, and put on his hands-free set. He put the car into first, checked the traffic and then pulled out as he pressed the number for DCI Moone. The phone was ringing as he drove back towards Devonport. There was no answer, but he decided he must be busy. An automated message told him Moone wasn't available and to leave a message.

'Hello, hello,' he said and laughed. 'It's me, Gary. Gary King. I've just been talking to your missing man's son. I tracked him down to The King's Arms in Tamerton Foliot. He wasn't too pleased to see me. I didn't get much, but I got the sense that Rodney Fox wasn't a pleasant individual. I wonder if he knocked the mum around or even the son? Who knows? I'll keep digging for you. Tell the truth, I'm enjoying being back on the job.'

There came a buzzing sound and King

looked in the rear-view mirror to see a bloke on a scooter right up his backside. 'Bloody hell. I've got some stupid bastard on a scooter right up my arse. Anyway, call me back.'

King kept watching the scooter in the rear-view mirror. He lowered his window and tried to wave him on, but the scooter stayed right where it was.

He'd had enough, so he indicated and saw a spot to pull over. He checked the road was clear, saw the scooter drop back, then pulled over and stopped. He sighed as the scooter passed by. Then he watched with surprise as the scooter pulled in just a hundred yards ahead. The rider climbed off the bike and faced him, still wearing his helmet.

What the hell? He was just standing there for a moment, staring in his direction. Obviously a road rage nutter, he decided and looked in his glove box for some kind of weapon. There was nothing there but maps and his old sunglasses, so he felt under his seat and found his crook lock. He pushed open the door, climbed out and stood by the car, the crook lock by his side.

'You got a problem, mate?' he shouted, then flinched slightly when the man started striding towards him. 'Stop there! Don't come any closer…'

He started to back away, his heart thundering as the man reached into his pocket and pulled out a gun. He raised it as he hurried towards King.

'What the hell?' he said, dropping the crook lock and holding up his hands. 'Don't do something stupid, mate. I... I'm a police officer. Put that...'

The pain tore through him, then the blast sounded all around. King fell to his knees and looked down to see blood pouring from his stomach. He looked up, a coldness wrapping around him, making him shiver.

The man was standing close to him now, the gun raised, pointing at him.

'Why?' he tried to say. He heard the second blast as he slumped to the ground.

CHAPTER 19

Moone took a sip of his coffee and then carried on watching the grainy CCTV footage that had been pulled from around the Devonport area, particularly anything close to where Kenton had been fatally shot and Harding and Jones were wounded. He'd checked up on Harding and found he was still unconscious after the surgery. It was touch and go. There was always the risk of infection. Jones was at home but she was OK, and trying not to think about what happened. He knew how impossible that was.

Where the hell was Abel? He stood up and looked at the map, at the places marked off. All around Plymouth. Why? None of it made sense, and if it was true that he believed everyone was in some kind of simulation, well… that just meant he was as crazy as they suspected and even more unpredictable.

To him, whatever he did, whoever he killed, it didn't matter.

A phone was ringing near him. He looked over and saw Chambers was answering her phone. Her expression changed, her eyes jumping to him as she listened.

'OK, thanks, I'll tell him.' Chambers ended the call as he stood up and came over.

'What's happened now?' he asked and saw the confusion in her eyes.

'There's been another shooting. One victim, near Tamerton Foliot. It's Gary King, boss.'

Moone stared at her, hearing her words, but unable to register them for a second. 'King? Former DI King? What? Is he hurt?'

'I'm sorry, boss, he's dead.'

Moone shook his head, then looked round and saw Butler coming into the room. She stopped and looked between them as she said, 'What's happened now?'

'Gary King's been shot,' he said. 'He's dead.'

'What? Who shot him?' Butler walked over.

Moone looked up at the map. 'We've only got one shooter at large at the moment.'

'Abel? But why would he target King?' Butler said. 'It doesn't make sense.'

Then it hit Moone like a tonne of bricks. 'I went to see him. What if Abel's been following me and he decides to shoot King to mess with us? Oh, Jesus Christ...'

'It's not your bloody fault!' Butler said. 'It's him, this nutter. Where was he shot? We'd better go and visit the scene.'

'Not far from the King's Arms in Tamerton Foliot,' Chambers said.

'Come on then, Moone.' Butler started to get her stuff together, while Moone still tried to compute it all. He picked up his phone, half a mind to call Alice and Kelly to tell them to stay away until they had found Abel. Then he saw it. He had a missed call from King.

'Hang on,' he said and looked up at Butler. 'I've got a missed call from King.'

'What? Play it.'

Moone found the message, then put it on speaker:

'Hello, hello,' King's gruff, croaky voice said, a laugh in it, and Moone felt a coldness fill his bones. 'It's me, Gary. Gary King. I've just been talking to your missing man's son. I tracked him down to The King's Arms in Tamerton Foliot. He wasn't too pleased to see me. I didn't get much, but I got the sense that Rodney Fox wasn't a pleasant individual. I wonder if he knocked the mum around or even the son? Who knows? I'll keep digging for you. Tell the truth, I'm enjoying being back on the job.'

Then there was a pause, and only the sound of the engine filled the void for a while before King's voice returned. 'Bloody hell. I've got some stupid bastard on a scooter right up my arse. Anyway, call me back.'

Moone's head shot up and he stared at Butler. Her face was rigid, her eyes wide as she said, 'Did he just say a scooter was up his arse?'

'Jesus,' Moone said. 'Abel. Abel uses a scooter. Abel shot him.'

'Come on, let's get to that pub.'

Tamerton Foliot Road was closed off with Incident Response cars and uniforms standing guard and redirecting the traffic, so Butler took them onto Seven Stars Lane and around to the pub. They parked up beside the large, white-painted pub and went in. As they walked to the bar, Moone looked around the place and saw a scattering of customers, some of them families.

There was a young man behind the bar playing on his phone.

'Excuse me,' Butler said, took out her warrant and showed the barman as he came over.

'Do you know this man?' Butler showed him her phone and the image she had found of King on the way.

'Don't know,' the barman said. 'Get lots of people in here.'

'He came in earlier,' she said and Moone could hear the thick layer of annoyance coating her words.

The barman shrugged. 'There was a bloke in here earlier. Could've been him. Was looking for someone.'

'Fox?' Moone said. 'Was he looking for someone called Fox?'

The barman shrugged again. 'He talked to that bloke in the corner, with the beard.'

Moone and Butler turned and saw a bearded, dirty-looking man at a table in the corner. He had a half-drunk glass of Guinness in front of him as he studied a newspaper.

Butler went storming towards the man and stood over him until he looked up. Moone followed her and watched as the man stared up at her, looking a little perturbed.

'Can I help you, luv?' he said, his eyes jumping from Butler to Moone and back again.

'Gary King,' she said. 'He was in here asking you some questions.'

Fox sat back and let out a kind of huff that contained a laugh. Then he tapped his glass of Guinness. 'Get us another pint and I might talk to you about it.'

'Sod that.' She leaned over him. 'King is dead. Shot not long after he left here. So, you better start talking.'

'What? He was shot? Well, I didn't shoot him.'

'We didn't say you did,' Moone said and pulled out a chair and sat down. 'He came here to ask you about your father, Rodney Fox. We're trying to figure out why that got him killed moments after leaving this pub.'

The man's eyes jumped to Moone. 'Search me. How am I supposed to know? He asked about my old man, I told him straight, that he wasn't missed when he fucked off and left us.'

'Why?' Butler asked.

'He was... he was a wanker. We hated him. The day he disappeared, it was a blessed relief. What more do you want me to say? I don't know why your mate was shot. It's got nothing to do with me.'

'Did you see anyone else follow him in the pub?' Moone asked.

'No, 'cause I didn't see him come in. I heard my name being called, someone said there was a call for me, but there wasn't. It was your mate. He asked me some questions and he left. I didn't see him leave either. That's it. Now, can I have my drink in peace?'

Butler huffed. 'You didn't notice anyone come in you hadn't seen before? Nothing unusual happened?'

Fox shrugged. 'Only thing that happened was before your mate came in, so no.'

'What happened?' Moone pressed.

'It was nothing. This is where I usually sit, 'cause there's never anyone around. No one to start chatting. Except today this bloke comes in and sits right there.'

Moone looked over at the table a couple of feet away. 'Right there?'

'Yeah. I get this feeling someone's staring at me, so I look up and this weirdo is staring at me.'

'What did he look like?' Moone asked, his whole body tightening and his heart speeding up.

'Couldn't see his face properly 'cause he had a face mask on. Thought that was weird because no one wears them now. And he had his hood up. Freak.'

Moone stared at Butler. 'He wore a hoodie? What colour?'

'Black,' Fox said. 'Why?'

But Moone was up and heading to the bar without stopping to answer. He stood in front of the barman who was still staring, gormless, at his phone. He waved his hand as he said, 'Hey, remember us? Have you got any cameras in here?'

He looked up, confused. 'Cameras?'

'CCTV? Is there any in here?'

The barman pointed across the room towards the doors, where the large fireplace was. 'There's a camera there, on the ceiling, looks over this side of the bar.'

Moone showed his warrant card again. 'We need to see the footage from today. Now!'

Within five minutes, Moone and Butler were

sitting in a back office, facing a monitor as the CCTV played at speed, the light flickering as bodies came and went, the sunlight moving.

'Wait!' Butler said. 'Go back a bit.'

Moone rewound a little, then leaned in as he saw Gary King entering the pub and heading for the bar. They both watched him in an eerie kind of silence, while Moone's stomach sank at the sight of the former detective who he had probably sent to his death.

'Look where Fox is,' Butler pointed.

In the corner was Fox, and next to him was a hooded man sitting at the next table.

'Jesus. Is that him? Is that Abel?'

'But if he was there when King came in, how could he know he was going to head to this pub?'

Moone sat back, unable to comprehend any of it. 'I don't know. He's always one step ahead…'

'What if he wasn't there for King?'

Moone turned and looked at her as she said, 'Fox said he was staring at him. What if he was there for Fox?'

'Fox? Why would he target him? Anyway, he didn't target Fox, he went after King and shot him dead.'

'Well, let's see what happens when King leaves.'

Moone sped it on until they witnessed Fox and King at the bar. Then King was leaving, striding out of the pub. Moone almost flinched when he saw the hooded man stand up and turn towards the exit, moving with determination towards the door. The camera caught his face, but it was hard to see him with half his face covered by a mask.

Moone sat back. 'He followed him out and shot him. Why? Why the hell would he kill King? I just don't get it.'

'He was here looking into your mystery, wasn't he?'

'I know. I asked him to look at Rodney Fox's disappearance in his old files.'

Butler got to her feet. 'Come on then.'

Moone got up. 'Where're we going?'

'To King's place to have a look at his files. He might've discovered something that got him shot.'

'OK, it's worth a look.'

Butler drove them into King's road in North Stonehouse, found a parking spot over the road from his narrow house and turned off the engine. Moone was staring at the house, trying to get his head around the fact that he was gone, the old copper was dead. Someone would have to tell John Michael King, he thought, but it wouldn't be him. He looked over the street and watched the occasional person pass by, a young woman pushing a pram, a toddler following behind with tears in his eyes. A man with a little furry white dog went past their car. On the corner was King's favourite pub, the Artillery Arms.

'You OK?' Butler asked. 'I mean, I know you're not... did you want me to come in too?'

'You can do.' Moone was about to push the door open when his eyes jumped to the scooter parked outside King's house. 'Hang on. Whose scooter is that?'

Butler looked over. 'Could be anyone's.'

'That looks like the scooter Abel was riding.'

'Really? You think he's still using the same scooter? And why would he come here?'

He looked at her. 'Why not use the same scooter? All he has to do is change the plate. Maybe he's come to find something? Maybe King knew something.'

'What do we do? If he is in there, we can't knock on the door, not if he's armed.'

Moone found his heart racing as he stared at the house, a strange sensation building in his body. He was there, inside. He felt it. That was Abel's scooter, he knew it. 'Run the plate.'

Butler took out her phone. Moone half listened as she called the station and asked Chambers to run the plate on the scooter; his mind was already in the house, trying to put it all together, but he couldn't. His mind ached. Why did he sit in a pub with Fox and why did he kill King? None of it made sense. Were they just the random murders of a madman? No. When he had been face to face with Abel as he held a gun to his head, he had the sense that this was all leading to something.

Butler ended the call. 'That plate's from a stolen scooter. Stolen yesterday. He's in there.'

Moone's chest thumped. 'The bastard's in there. What the hell is he doing?'

'I'm calling for Armed Response.' Butler took out her phone again.

Moone nodded and waited. It couldn't be this simple, could it? He remembered how they had been hunting for John Michael King, desperate to find him before he killed again, but then he just gave himself up. Was this history repeating itself?

The Armed Response van parked up a couple of streets away. Butler got the call from their leader, so she told them to converge on the house. Within a couple of minutes, the team appeared at either end of the quiet street, their boots hammering along the dry pavement. One of them had a mini battering ram. He swung it at the door, knocking it flying into the house on the second hit. As Moone watched them all disappearing into the house, carrying their Heckler and Koch submachine guns, his breath caught in his chest. His ears pounded with hot blood and he felt a cold sweat pouring down his sides.

He pushed open his door and climbed out, staring at the open doorway, the sound of shouting coming from inside. Butler climbed out and followed him to the kerb.

One of the armed team came out and gave them the thumbs up. Behind him came a figure, dressed in a dark hoodie and trousers. The hood was pulled up, his lower face covered by a mask. The armed officer who followed him out had his arms cuffed behind his back as they manhandled him into the street.

As Moone watched, one of the armed team yanked his hood down. Then the mask was pulled down too. Moone stared at the face of the man, a face he recognised. Abel looked back at him, staring into his eyes, his face emotionless, calm, as he nodded. Then the armed team turned him away and pushed him along the street.

'I don't believe it,' Moone said, his mind spinning.

'What?' Butler asked. 'That we got him and it's over?'

He shook his head and turned to her. 'That's the nephew.'

'Whose nephew?'

'Joy Morten's nephew. Adam Morten.'

Butler frowned, then looked up the street where the armed team were helping the suspect up the steps and into a police van.

'Joy Morten's nephew?' She looked at him

again. 'What the hell? He's Abel?'

Moone shrugged. 'I don't know what the hell's going on.'

'That makes two of us. Let's go and talk to him and find out.'

When Moone and Butler walked into the incident room, a cloud of bewilderment still hanging over them both, they came face to face with DI Anna Jones who was standing by Chambers' desk, propped up on crutches, her left leg covered in thick bandages.

'My God, Jones,' Moone said and rushed towards her, looking her over. 'It's great to see you, but what the hell're you doing here?'

'I couldn't stay at home another second,' she said, her face solemn, a darkness deep in her eyes. 'I was going mad, and I can't really sleep properly.'

'Well, we've got him,' Butler said as she came over and stood close by, arms folded.

'What?' Jones said, glancing between them. 'Are you joking?'

Moone shook his head. 'No. We've just seen him marched away. We'll talk to him in a bit when he's been examined and all that business. He shot and killed King.'

'Oh, God,' Jones said and tears welled in her eyes. 'That poor man. I keep seeing...'

'I know. Me too.'

'Is Harding OK?' Jones asked.

'Still in ICU,' Chambers said. 'He's stable. Whatever that means.'

Jones stared at Moone. 'He needs a medal or something…'

'I think he'd appreciate a raise more,' Butler said.

Jones gave the quiver of a smile. 'Seriously though, he does deserve a medal. He just ran and grabbed that girl. He saved her life.'

'We'll get him a medal or something, even if I have to buy it myself.' Moone patted her arm.

'What the bloody hell've you been doing?' a voice called and Moone turned to see Major Lacroix and his MI5 buddy, Fitzgerald, standing in the doorway.

'We caught the bastard,' Butler said, not bothering to curtail her anger. 'What've you lot been doing? Each other's hair?'

Lacroix's face tightened as he stared at Butler. Then he looked at Moone as he came over, arms folded.

'You should've called us,' Lacroix said. 'This is our operation. You could have got people killed. What if he'd had a bomb strapped to him?'

'He didn't,' Butler said. 'It's over. We're going to interview him…'

'No, you're not,' Fitzgerald said.

'Why?' Moone said.

Fitzgerald rested on one of the desks.

'Because he's a terrorist and we need to find out where the rest of his group are.'

'It's not a group, he's one man,' Moone said, feeling the burn of anger rise to his chest.

'I think it's very unlikely that one man did all this.' Fitzgerald wore a condescending smile. 'But thanks for helping. The big boys will take it from here.'

Moone had a sense of something then, a deep suspicion as he stared at the spook. 'I know what this is…'

'What is it?' Fitzgerald gave an empty laugh.

'He was on your radar, wasn't he? Who is Adam Morten? Ex-army or something?'

Fitzgerald stared at him for a moment, the smile gone, then said, 'He's not Adam Morten.'

'Yes, he is… I talked to him…'

'You may well have talked to him, but he isn't Adam Morten because Adam Morten died several years ago.'

Moone scrambled to make sense of it. 'Then who is he?'

'That is need-to-know,' he said. 'By the way, you'll all need to sign the Official Secrets Act.'

'Get stuffed,' Butler snapped. 'So you can sweep this all under the carpet? Bloody hell. You trained him, didn't you? Taught him to shoot and make bombs and here he is doing it. You lot make me want to throw up.'

Fitzgerald sniffed as he straightened up. 'I want you to sign by the end of the day or you're out.'

'No.' Moone stared at him.

Fitzgerald squared up to him. 'No? I'd think about that, DCI Moone, because you're already on incredibly thin ice. You've already fucked up one trial. You're under investigation. Now, if I feel like it, I can use my influence to get you fired. No pension, nothing. Or I can make it all go away. It's up to you.'

Moone stared up into his callous, blank eyes. 'I'm not signing.'

'Fine. Enjoy your last few days as a police officer.'

Fitzgerald walked out, leaving Major Lacroix who was staring at Moone.

'That was stupid, Moone,' he said. 'You've just kissed your career goodbye.'

'I know. But fuck that. They can kiss my arse. MI5 can kiss my arse.'

Lacroix stared at him, blank-faced for a moment. Then he smiled as he said, 'Good for you, Moone. You stupid fool.'

Lacroix left the incident room and Moone let out a ragged breath. 'Did I just end my career?'

Butler patted his shoulder. 'Yes, but what a way to go out. I'm proud of you.'

'Thanks.' Moone enclosed his face in his hands for a moment, took in the fact that his job was all but gone.

'Did you really just do that?' he heard Jones say.

Moone removed his hands and looked at her. 'I think so. To be honest, with the mess I made with the trial, I think it was on the cards. I was on borrowed time anyway.'

'I'm sorry,' Wood said and put her arms out for a hug. He smiled and took the hug as he said, 'I just hope your new boss is as easy-going as me.'

'Let's hope he doesn't faff as much as you,' Butler said.

'Ha ha,' Moone said. 'Very funny.'

'We're all meeting for the memorial service on the Hoe tonight, yeah?' Chambers asked.

Everyone looked at each other and nodded.

'Maybe we could have a drink after?' Jones suggested.

'I think I need one.' Moone thought of something else then, something he needed to do before he finished his time as a police officer. 'I'm going to go and see Gary King.'

'They'll be doing the post-mortem,' Butler said, looking at him strangely.

'I know, but I'd like to pay my respects.'

'Fair enough. Shall I drive you?'

He shook his head. 'It's all right. I'll drive myself. I'll see you in a bit or at the memorial service.'

The drive to Derriford was pretty much a blur as his mind was sprinting in all different directions as the case and everything else scrambled through his brain. Most of all, the whole Butler situation sat heavy like a bowling ball in his chest. Perhaps losing his job wasn't such a bad thing, he thought, seeing as time spent with her would be reduced, the pain lessened. She seemed fine, acting her same old self as if he'd never said those words to her. Now he wished he could take them back. No. No, he didn't. He had the urge to drive back to the station and tell her again, to make sure she knew it wasn't the concussion making him say the words.

He was parked opposite Costa and Subway, which were wedged under the multi-storey car park. He got out, locked his car and headed towards the main building. He lit a cigarette on the way, thinking about his future and wondering what he was going to do for money. There was always security work of some kind. Maybe he could become a private investigator, he considered as he lit his cigarette. He always loved watching Magnum PI when he was younger.

He went into the hospital, took the lift to the basement, and then headed along to the large white door and pressed the buzzer.

One of the technicians answered, so he showed his warrant card and headed through to the post-mortem room. There was a human shape under a green blanket on the metal table at the centre of the room. There was only one living person in the gleaming, brightly lit, white-tiled room. Dr Jenkins was washing her hands at a large stainless-steel sink, dressed in green scrubs, her light brown hair tied back. She looked over and smiled as she said, 'Hello, stranger. It's been a while.'

He nodded. 'It has. Sorry, I've been meaning to come by.'

She smiled. 'It's fine. How've you been? I know you and your team have been through hell lately what with everything.'

He stepped closer to the table. 'We have. We've lost a lot of people.'

'I know. I've had a few of them in here. I still can't believe it. Are you any closer to catching him?'

'We've got him. He's in a cell back at the station, but MI5 and the Counter-Terrorism lot are about to cart him off. There'll be a closed trial and that'll be it.'

She tutted. 'Do you think MI5 knew about him?'

'I do, but they'll cover it up. Is this…?' Moone pointed at the shape under the sheet.

'Oh, yes, this is Gary King,' she said. 'A former detective. Did you know him?'

'I did. This is my fault.'

Jenkins looked up, surprised. 'You didn't shoot him, did you?'

'No.'

'Then it's not your fault.'

'If I hadn't got him involved in our investigation... thing is, he left me a message before... this. He sounded happy that he was investigating again. Like he had a purpose.'

She smiled. 'Then he died doing what he loved.'

'Maybe.'

'There is something else, I should say.'

'What?'

'Two gunshot wounds,' she said, folding down the sheet, revealing King's body. Apart from the Y-shaped sewn-up incision to his chest, he looked the way he had done the last time he saw him.

'Two permanent cavities,' she said. 'Abraded tissue around both wounds. The first was from roughly a hundred yards away. The second close. A close contact wound with muzzle burn and stippling from unburned gunpowder particles. The bullets have been sent away for analysis.'

'The gunshots killed him?'

'Yes, but I also looked at his heart,' she said. 'He smoked a lot, didn't he?'

'He did.'

'I could tell. His heart was in bad shape.

There's extensive damage to the lining of blood vessels.'

'Meaning?'

'He was living on borrowed time.' She raised her eyebrows.

'That makes two of us.'

'You like a cigarette too, don't you?'

'I do. I'm trying to quit. But I made a balls up at the trial, and now they're investigating me. Today I managed to piss off the MI5 agent sent to help us and he says he's going to fix it so I'm no longer a police officer.'

Jenkins widened her eyes. 'Oh, God. You have had a bad day. I'm sorry.'

'It's fine. I'm going to be Magnum PI.'

'That's good. Are you going to grow the moustache?'

'I'm not sure.' He pulled up a smile from somewhere.

She laughed. 'I'm thinking you should give it a miss. So, we won't be working together much longer then?'

'No.'

She nodded. 'OK. So, why don't I take you out for a drink tonight?'

He let out a laugh.

'What?'

He shrugged. 'That would be really nice. The memorial service is tonight but after that?'

'I'll see you there.' She came over, smiling up at him. 'I was thinking perhaps… well, maybe we could try again?'

He smiled, feeling the first rays of sunlight he'd felt in the last few days. Maybe it was time to get on with his life and put away his torch that was getting too heavy to carry. 'I'd like that.'

She smiled. 'Good. Me too. You're one of the good ones, Peter Moone.'

He felt her words squeeze his heart. Tears almost welled in his eyes. He swallowed it down.

'You OK?' she asked.

'Fine. Well, I'd better go and look busy before they kick me out.'

'Oh,' she said, holding up a finger. 'I've passed my findings onto Major Lacroix but I'll tell you too... there was something written on his back in permanent marker. He couldn't have written it himself. I took a photo.'

He followed Jenkins as she retrieved a tablet device and then turned it towards Moone so he could see the enlarged photo. He let out a sharp breath when he read the three words.

'Does that mean something?' she asked.

He said the words aloud. 'The Drake Inn.'

'I looked it up but it doesn't exist any more.'

'No, it doesn't. This is a message.'

'For who?'

He looked into her eyes. 'Me.'

CHAPTER 20

Moone hurried back up the stairs to the incident room, his heart beating just as fast as it had been the moment he realised what was written on King's back. He burst through the incident room doors and everyone stopped and stared at him.

'You all right?' Butler asked.

'Where's Lacroix and Fitzgerald?' he asked.

Butler got up, narrowing her eyes at him. 'Downstairs having some kind of top secret meeting. They're getting ready to take Abel away. Did you go to the morgue?'

'I did. Come on.' Moone went back out of the incident room, down to the next floor and along the corridor. Butler was hot on his heels when he saw Lacroix and Fitzgerald standing in one of the meeting rooms, conspiring over something. He rapped his knuckles on the window and they both stared around at him.

It was Lacroix who opened the door and faced him. 'Yes, Moone?'

'I need to talk to Abel, or whatever he's really called.'

Fitzgerald pushed past the Major and faced Moone in the corridor as he said, 'Why?'

'Because he left me a message on King's body.'

Lacroix and Fitzgerald exchanged a glance that Moone was unable to read.

'What message?' Fitzgerald said, folding his arms.

Moone prepared himself, digging around for the right words. 'It's hard to explain.'

'Try. Come on, I know you've got a modicum of intelligence in that head of yours.'

'After he shot and killed King, he wrote the name of a hotel on his back. The Drake Inn.'

The MI5 agent regarded him, gave him the once-over. 'A possible target?'

'No. I don't think so. This is where it gets strange. I stayed there when I was young. That's what the hotel was called back then, The Drake Inn. A few days ago we got called to an old people's home, one of the residents had been screaming about a murder. Joy Morten. She used to run the Drake Inn. Abel has been pretending to be her nephew. I don't know why, I don't know how, but there's a connection...'

'He found out you were the lead detective,' Lacroix said. 'He found out something about you and he's using it to mess with your head.'

'This Joy Morten business started before the bombings and shootings,' Butler said behind him. 'This isn't him just messing with us. It means something.'

Moone stepped up to Fitzgerald. 'Let me talk to him. What harm can it do?'

Fitzgerald stared back. 'OK.'

'OK? Just like that?'

'Yes. I was going to call you anyway. Abel's asked to talk to you.'

'He has?' Moone looked between the agent and Lacroix.

'Yes,' Fitzgerald said. 'But you go in and you ask him questions we write down for you. We don't want you digging into his background. We'll be watching.'

'I want Butler with me.'

'No. Absolutely not.'

'Then I walk away.'

Fitzgerald laughed. 'You've got no leverage, Moone.'

'Let her go in,' Lacroix said. 'It can't do any harm.'

Fitzgerald looked over at the Major, then back at Moone. 'Fine. We'll write up the questions. You two get ready.'

Moone went in first, and Butler followed

him into the interview room where Abel was sitting. An armed officer had been posted outside. They weren't taking any chances. The prisoner's hands were chained to the desk, his eyes fixed forward. Moone wasn't sure if Abel was staring at him, or trying to stare at the wall behind him, but he found it hard to hold his gaze.

'What's your name, for the recording?' Moone asked, pretending to examine his notes. The questions Fitzgerald had written down were in front of him.

'You know my name,' he said, his voice calm, quite deep and harsh.

Moone looked up and engaged those dark grey eyes again. There was a smile too, an expression that seemed to say I know it all, I've won.

'Abel?' Moone said, sitting back, trying to look calm and not shaken by everything that had happened lately. 'That's not your real name, is it? Come on, we've got you now. We caught you. Why not tell us who you are?'

The light flickered above them, the room going dark momentarily before it was lit up again.

'Did you feel that?' their suspect asked, looking between them.

'The light?' Moone asked.

The man nodded. 'Can you feel it? The change in the air?'

'It was just a power cut or something. Now, your name? You were going to tell us who you are and why you've done what you've done.'

The man stared at Moone, his eyes burning out to him for a few seconds before he burst into a deep, grinding laugh.

'Is something funny?' Butler snapped. 'All those dead people? Our colleagues? All those poor victims of yours? Are they funny to you?'

The man turned his head slowly and took her in as he stopped laughing. He lost any signs of amusement. 'No. They're not funny. Nothing about their deaths is funny.'

'Then why laugh?' Moone asked.

'Because none of it matters,' he said, then he leaned forward. 'Adam Morten. That's my name.'

'No, that's not your name. He died, years ago. You've been visiting Joy Morten, pretending to be her nephew. Why?'

'She's an experiment. But she was like an aunt to me at one time.'

Moone looked at the questions, then up at the camera in the corner. The suspect turned and looked to where Moone was staring before he faced him again. 'They're watching, aren't they? Counter-Terrorism and MI5?'

'Why kill all those people?' Moone asked. 'Teenagers. An old man and woman. Police officers? Our friends.'

Abel shook his head and sighed. 'You don't understand. They're meaningless.'

'Meaningless?' Butler snapped again. 'They're bloody people. You've taken their bloody lives. Don't you feel anything?'

He ignored Butler and kept staring at Moone. 'They're not real. None of this is real.'

'The *Akashic Record*?' Moone said.

Abel smiled and nodded. 'You've looked it up. I knew you would. But you don't understand it.'

'You do?'

'I've studied it a long, long time and I've studied our world, our so-called life. I know this existence isn't real life, it's just a facade. A delicate facade that can be cracked open.'

'You're insane,' Butler said, shaking her head as she sat back. 'You read some conspiracy theory online and now you believe it. Bloody hell.'

Moone looked at the questions. He noticed they didn't want him to ask who he was or what his background was. Because they knew who he was. 'Who else are you working with?'

'No one.' Abel didn't blink. 'This is my mission. Mine alone. Can I ask you something, DCI Moone? Peter?'

He nodded.

Abel leaned forward. 'Have you ever noticed those strange, inexplicable moments when the news says stuff like... it's been ten years since a war started or someone famous died… but you know it's not true. You know in your heart, it was only a year or two ago? Do you have those moments?'

Butler laughed. 'Time flies, gets past us. Jesus.'

'I do,' Moone said. 'So?'

'Time isn't what we think it is. It's not solid. It changes, alters, we just don't realise. Have you heard of the Mandela effect?'

'Yes. Everyone has. People misremember things…'

Abel nodded. 'It's real. It's not misremembered events. How can so many people remember things differently than another million people? It's because time, events, are changing slightly, every so often. But to change time, to alter things, you need a shock wave, you need another event to occur that sends a ripple through everything. Do you understand?'

'No.' Moone sat back, realising how deluded the man before him was.

'9-11, for instance,' Abel said, his voice filling with a kind of excitement. 'That was such a devastating event, a massive moment in our history… it sent massive shock waves through the world, through time itself. I started studying the world after that event and before. The amount of memories that people had after that event compared to before… there were so many news reports and TV shows and... everything that people remembered differently... millions of people recalled completely different versions of history after 9-11. It had changed time, the fabric of time. Or what we perceive as time. But what it is, is the simulation we're in. We're in one big computer program. Every time there's a major event like 9-11, the program glitches, events change, little details.'

Moone looked at the questions again but ignored them. 'Is this what this is about? You're trying to create your own 9-11?'

Abel lost his smile. 'Kind of. I've been experimenting...'

'Oh my God!' Butler huffed. 'Those people you've murdered have been an experiment? You realise how sick you are, don't you?'

The lights in the interview room flickered again. Abel looked up, a strange look on his face, and Moone wasn't sure if it was a smile or excitement, or even fear.

'You feel that?' Abel asked him. 'The bomb I left outside Argyll. It did its job, partly. Things have changed. Have you felt it? I know you've been feeling things aren't right, ever since you visited Joy.'

'How do you know about Joy? About the Drake Inn? Who've you talked to?'

Abel sat back. 'No one. Now, I believe the government, the men watching, want to know the answers to the questions they've kindly written down for you.'

Moone sat back, watched his face, which had now fallen into a strange state of calm. He looked down at the questions and sighed. 'Are there any more bombs planted around the city?'

'No.'

Moone studied his face. He didn't believe him. 'There are no more in Plymouth?'

'That's not what you asked.' Abel leaned forward. 'You asked if there were any more bombs around the city.'

'Don't try and be smart now,' Butler said, hardly holding back her rage. 'We've got you. You're caught. You're going to prison for a long, long time.'

He looked at her, smiling. 'I don't think so.'

'Why not?' Butler asked, glaring at him.

'You'll see.' He turned to Moone. 'I don't think I'll answer any more questions. Not until later.'

'Later?' Moone said.

'Tonight.' Abel gave a strange laugh.

'There you go, laughing again,' Butler said. 'All those people dead. Real people, and you're laughing. Why?'

Abel looked between them, then leaned forward, staring. 'Because I know what's coming.'

The door to the interview room opened

and Agent Fitzgerald stood there and crooked a finger at them. 'You two. Out. Time's up.'

'That was not very helpful,' Fitzgerald said as he slowly paced the smaller incident room, his hands behind his back. Lacroix was standing by the door, arms folded, face stony.

Butler and Moone were standing in the middle of the room. Moone went to the window and looked out at the city. 'There's more bombs out there. There must be.'

'I agree,' Fitzgerald said. 'Probably not many. He might not have had time...'

Moone turned round. 'He's been planning this for ages. You heard him. He's had plenty of time to plant bombs all over the place. This is what this is about. Did you listen to him?'

'I heard,' Fitzgerald said. 'But it was all bravado. I've been well trained to spot when a suspect is telling the truth or lying and when they're just trying to fuck with us. We caught him, and now he's saying whatever he likes to try and get inside our heads. He's got inside your head, Moone. He mentions a place you used to go on holiday when you were a kid and now you're a mess. Pull yourself together.'

Butler huffed. 'Can I ask you something, Fitzgerald?'

'Yes.'

Butler straightened up, staring at him. 'When they trained you, was being a complete cockwomble part of that training?'

'Butler!' Lacroix growled.

'It's fine,' Fitzgerald said. 'I know you have both been through a lot the last few days. You've lost colleagues. I get that. But you have to be professional…'

'There's a memorial service on the Hoe tonight,' Moone said. 'Can you at least make sure there are no bombs around that area?'

Fitzgerald nodded. 'We'll have officers all around there and we'll have sniffer dogs. It'll be one hundred percent safe. Now, I'll need both of you to sign the Official Secrets Act.'

'We'll sort that later,' Lacroix said. 'You two just get out of here. Take some time. We'll let you know if there are any developments.'

Moone nodded and was about to leave the room, but he started thinking about the strange man in the interview room. 'What happens to him now? You interrogate him?'

'Of course,' Fitzgerald said. 'Tomorrow he'll be taken to a special facility.'

'Come on, Moone,' Butler said, holding the door open for him.

As they left the police station through the entrance that led to the car park, Moone said, 'There'll be more bombs. There has to be.'

Butler stopped and faced him. 'There might be, but it's up to their lot now.'

Moone found his cigarettes and took one

out. His hands were trembling as he lit it. 'He's had loads of time to prepare for this. They think he's messing with us, but I don't think so.'

'Then what do we do?'

He shrugged as he took a deep, shaky pull on the cigarette. 'I wish I knew. He gave us that map to mess with us, to spread ourselves thin. What about that photo he had?'

'What photo?'

'The space on the board in the house in Sherford. I mean, did he have it on him when he was arrested?'

Butler sighed and looked at him sadly. 'If he did, then I'm sure they would've examined it by now. Come on, I'll buy you a coffee. Maybe one of those cream cakes you like.'

His stomach rolled over. 'No. I think I'll go home.'

She narrowed her eyes. 'You all right? You don't seem yourself.'

He shrugged again. 'I don't know. I guess…'

He looked at her, the old invisible hand crushing his heart again, a rush of something filling his veins, words wanting to race to his lips. Words she wouldn't want to hear.

'What? Talk to me, you wally.'

He scrambled for something else to say. 'I suppose it's the message on King's back, the Drake Inn. Joy Morten. There's something going on there…'

'Maybe Fitzgerald's right about that. He's a tosser, but maybe he's right that Abel's messing with your head.'

Moone nodded, even though his gut was saying it wasn't just a way to get into his head. It was more, so much more, he just didn't understand yet. 'Maybe.'

'So, I'll see you at the memorial service?' Butler started to take out her keys.

'Wait!' a voice called.

They both looked around and saw a man decked out in black combats coming towards them carrying a mirror on a long stick. He got on the ground next to Butler's car and checked under it for devices. He did the same for Moone's and then gave them the thumbs up.

He watched Butler climb into her car and then drive off with a wave. He let out a shaky breath, his heart thumping, his stomach weighed down with regret as he trudged to his car and climbed in.

Shit.

He put his hands on the wheel, then lowered his head to it, tapping it lightly. Shit. Shit. Shit.

Moone jumped a little when he unlocked the door of his mobile home and saw a figure standing by the oven. It was Kelly, wiping everything over.

'You're a messy sod, Peter Moone,' she

said.

He shut the door, regretting a little that he didn't have any alone time to think. 'I cleaned that... not long ago.'

'Not very well.' She straightened up and folded her arms. 'So, I hear you've got someone for the shootings and bombings?'

'Yes, we have.' Moone loosened his tie and took it off as he sat down on the sofa. 'I've just talked to him.'

'And?'

He shrugged. 'Not much. I think there's more to it. I mean, we just went to this house on the off chance, and there he was and suddenly he's in custody.'

'Well, that's good.' She grabbed his tie and rolled it up.

'It is, but it can't be that simple. It's never that simple.'

'You know what your problem is, Petey? You overthink things. You always have. Even as a kid, you were a worrier. Worrying what everyone thought of you. Worrying what the girls thought of you.'

Moone recalled something, a glint of gold in a pile of shit. 'I got asked out today, I think.'

Kelly's face lit up. 'By Mandy?'

'No. By Dr Jenkins. We went out before and nothing came of it, but she suggested we try again.'

'A doctor, eh? Nice.'

'She's the pathologist.'

'Oh my God, you mean she dissects the bodies? Oh no.'

'She's very nice.'

Kelly stared at him. 'But she's not Mandy Butler. Is she?'

He shook his head. 'No, she's not. But I think she's with someone else, and I tried to tell her how I feel…'

'When?'

'Just after the bomb went off.'

Kelly laughed. 'Sorry, I shouldn't laugh. You daft bugger, she probably couldn't hear you. Probably had ringing in her ears.'

'She heard.'

'Well, even if she did, she was probably in shock. You need to tell her again. Properly. Take her for a drink, then tell her.'

He stared at her and knew she was right. He had to know one way or the other so they could either start seeing each other or lay it to rest once and for all.

He nodded. 'OK. I'll do it.'

'Hurray!' Kelly said. 'Your problem is, you're too slow.'

'Do I faff?'

She pointed at him, her eyes lighting up. 'That's it! That's the perfect word. Faff. You faff, Peter Moone.'

He smiled as his heart rampaged on.

It was several hours later when Moone drove him and Kelly to Mutley where they picked up Alice from Butler's flat. She climbed in and sat in the back.

'Where's Butler?' he asked, looking at her in the rear-view mirror.

'She's out with someone and she's going to meet us there,' Alice said, looking away.

'Someone?' Moone asked, trying to see her eyes.

'Leave the poor girl alone,' Kelly said, digging him in the ribs.

'I was just asking.'

'Well, don't,' she said. 'Now's not the time.'

He could see Alice was staring out the window, looking thoughtful. He decided to be quiet too, to think of Abel's victims. Then his mind raced on, once more trying to comprehend what it had all been about. Now it was over and the city would need time to grieve.

They drove on in silence and parked close to the Hoe. Moone walked alongside Kelly and Alice, as they made their way towards the Hoe. The summer evening was warm, but he felt a weight in the air that had nothing to do with the heat; a heavy silence had settled over the city like a blanket of grief.

Kelly glanced at him. 'Feels different, doesn't it?' she said. 'Like the whole city's holding its breath.'

Moone nodded. The usual hum of Plymouth life, the laughter of families lingering after a day at the waterfront, in West Hoe Park, or around the city centre itself, was muted.

Alice walked a step ahead, her hands stuffed into the pockets of her black jeans. She hadn't said much since they'd left the car. Moone didn't blame her.

She had only lived in Plymouth for the past few years, but in that time, she'd grown up a lot. She'd walked these streets with new friends, finding her place. Now, she was seeing the city in a way she never had before, shadowed by tragedy.

As they climbed the gentle slope towards the Hoe, the golden glow of the setting sun melted across the horizon. Hundreds of people had already gathered near Smeaton's Tower, the red-and-white lighthouse standing tall against the soft hues of the evening sky. The sea stretched beyond, calm and indifferent, unaware of the sorrow unfolding on its shore.

Moone breathed out. The sight was both beautiful and devastating. A large table had been set out which had flowers and the photos of some of the victims upon it. The flames of the candles set all around it wavered in the faint breeze, reflecting in tear-streaked faces. Some held photographs of the victims, others clutched hands, drawing what comfort they could from being together.

Alice stopped walking, her eyes fixed on the scene.

'You all right?' he asked and put a gentle hand on her back.

She shrugged. 'It's awful, Dad. So many have died.'

'I know. But it's over now. We've got him.'

Kelly stepped forward, gently nudging them on. 'Come on, you two,' she said. 'Let's find a spot.'

As they moved through the gathering crowd, Moone spotted familiar faces—officers he'd worked with, paramedics who had been on the scene of the explosion outside Home Park. Their eyes met as silent acknowledgements passed between them. No ranks, no titles tonight. Just people, sharing in the weight of loss.

A man at the front of the gathering began to speak, his voice carrying over the hush. Moone barely registered the words. Instead, he watched Alice as she reached into her pocket, pulled out a small candle, and lit it.

He felt proud of her as her face was illuminated by the tiny flame. She looked solemn but steady. Stronger than she knew she was.

'Don't look now, but here's your Mandy,' Kelly whispered in his ear.

Moone looked round and saw Butler, dressed in a dark trouser suit coming towards them through the crowd of mourners. He let out a sharp breath when he saw she was holding hands with a dark-haired man in his forties. He had that rugged, workmanlike look about him, and tattoos on both of his muscular arms that were hardly covered by his checked short-sleeve shirt.

'Hello,' Butler said, looking them all in the eye. 'This is Chris. Chris, this is Moone, his sister, Kelly, and his daughter, Alice.'

'Hello, Chris!' Kelly said and grabbed him for a hug. Moone watched on as Butler's friend laughed.

'Sorry,' Kelly said, letting him go. 'Probably a bit inappropriate.'

'Not at all, love,' Chris said and laughed.

'Watch yourself with this one,' Butler said to Kelly.

'How did you two meet?' Kelly asked, looking between them. Moone caught Butler's eye and she smiled strangely at him.

'We met at school,' Chris said. 'Back when this one was a tearaway.'

'Me?' Butler pointed a thumb at herself. 'Me? I'm the tearaway? Do you remember getting up and walking out of Mr Davis' Maths class because you were bored?'

Chris shrugged. 'Well, I was. I don't even use maths now, not really. Only to count how many pipes I've got on my van.'

'Hey, you,' a voice said behind Moone.

He turned to see Dr Jenkins coming through the crowd. Her hair was down, her face made-up, looking almost unrecognisable in a blue summery dress and denim jacket. She gave him a brief kiss on the lips, then greeted the others, introducing herself as Dawn. While everyone shook hands and chatted, he looked at Butler and thought he caught a strange expression flutter across her face as she stared at Jenkins. Then Chris put his arm around her, dragging her back into the conversation. He seemed like a good guy, he thought and noted his obvious rugged good looks with a sense of hopelessness. Chris said something to the group while Jenkins lit a candle, and everyone laughed, including Butler. She looked happy.

Alice put her arm through his. 'Are you all right, Dad?'

He smiled. 'Of course. You?'

Alice nodded towards the others. 'He seems nice. Chris, I mean.'

'He does. But he's clearly a serial killer.'

Alice laughed, her eyes jumping to Jenkins. 'Dawn's beautiful.'

'She is. I'm definitely punching above my weight.'

'You are. Don't mess it up.' She let go and walked to the others.

'Well, got to be time for a pint, hasn't

it?' Chris said, rubbing his hands together. 'I'm buying.'

The gang all turned and started walking across the grass towards the pub. Moone let himself get swept up with the others as they walked across the Hoe, the evening breeze rolling in off the water. The pub was only a short stroll away, its lights glowing warmly against the darkening sky. It felt good to be among people, to have Alice beside him, to see Kelly and Butler laughing with Chris and Jenkins. A normal moment, which seemed a rare thing these days.

They had barely made it halfway when a deep, gut-punching boom split the air.

The explosion ripped through the night, rolling over the gathering like thunder. Moone felt the shock wave hit his chest as a car, parked a hundred yards away, erupted into a fireball. Glass and debris shot into the air, silhouetted against the orange glow. Alarms sounded from all the other cars and a cacophony of screams came from the panicking crowds.

Moone grabbed Alice, pulling her close as a shower of tiny fragments rained down. Around him, people were frozen, some ducking, others scrambling back towards the safety of the crowd.

'What the fu...!' Chris yelled, shielding Butler with an arm.

Jenkins had grabbed Kelly's wrist, her face

stark with shock.

Moone's mind snapped into focus. He let go of Alice, checking her over quickly. 'You OK?'

She stared at him, her eyes wide. She was in a state of shock.

'Alice?'

She nodded, wide-eyed, breathless. 'Yeah, Dad, I'm all right.'

'Kelly? Everyone?'

They all replied that they were OK but they were all staring across at the scene of destruction. He turned, scanning the fireball, his gut already twisting. A bomb going off so close to the memorial. It wasn't a coincidence. Abel had planned this. He was making a statement. His mind rewound, running at speed through their interview with him as he sat so calmly, staring back at them.

Later! He'd said he wouldn't answer any more questions until later. Tonight. Oh fucking God.

'Moone!' Butler's voice cut through the chaos. He swung his head around to see her already moving, ID in hand, her detective instincts overriding everything else. Chris stayed close behind, watching helplessly.

'Get everyone back!' Moone shouted towards the crowds, already stepping forward. He could see the shapes of the armed officers rushing towards the fireball.

The flames roared higher, the wreck of the

car spitting heat and smoke into the night. A moment later, the sirens started, getting closer.

Everyone would be here. Distracted. He looked at Butler, her face flickering orange and yellow. 'I need to talk to Abel. Right now.'

CHAPTER 21

'They're not going to let you talk to him,' Butler said as she drove them back to the station. Everyone had been taken home by Chris, and Moone had made sure Alice was OK before he and Butler rushed off.

'Everyone'll be distracted,' Moone said as he watched the lights of the city race by. 'Most of their team will be at the Hoe. He planned this.'

Butler flashed her eyes at him. 'I know. He planted a bloody great big bomb in a car, so how the hell did they miss it?'

'He said he wouldn't answer any more questions until later,' Moone said. 'Not until tonight. This is what he meant. He knew there was a memorial service, so he planted the bomb...'

'So he knew he'd be locked up by now? No

way. That's bloody crazy.'

Moone stared at her as she turned the car towards the car park at Charles Cross. 'Think about it. He kills King and then sits and waits in his house. He knew we'd go there.'

Butler sighed as the gates screeched open and she drove in. She parked up close to the building and turned to him. 'He'll be in the custody suite by now. Tomorrow, they'll take him off to God knows where, some secret government building where they'll torture him until he spills his guts. He'll tell them if there are more bombs, so you don't need to do this.'

'I do need to talk to him now. This has something to do with me, and the Drake Inn, I know it does. He's reached out to me, so if I can use that to find out if there are any more bombs… then I've got to do it. Haven't I?'

Butler looked toward the building as she exhaled. 'They'll have a uniform on guard doing cell watch. Let me go and talk to the custody sergeants, I know most of them. You come in with me and stay quiet.'

Moone nodded, so they headed towards the back entrance. As Butler swiped her ID card, Moone said, 'Chris seems like a nice bloke.'

She didn't look at him as they went in, but said, 'He is. He was always a laugh at school. Cakey as hell.'

Moone smiled as they hurried up the stairwell. 'As long as he makes you happy.'

'He does.' Butler went along the next floor and pushed through the door to the custody suite. As she headed to the tall counter, where the custody sergeants operated, Moone stood just inside the door. He tried to remain unnoticed as he looked towards the line of cells at the far end. He could just make out a uniformed officer sitting on a chair in one of the open cell doorways.

'How're you then, Mand?' a bearded sergeant said, leaning over the counter like he was some kind of police god. That's what they pretty much were in the police station, Moone knew. They took their job very seriously.

'The usual, Matt,' Butler said. 'Just one woman single-handedly cleaning up Plymouth's streets.'

Moone edged along, hands in pockets, watching the uniform on cell watch duty as he read a newspaper.

'Oh, Mand, if you can smell vomit, it's John's shoes. This scrawny smackhead threw up on them earlier.'

'They're new as well, bloody junkie.'

Moone nudged Butler and she turned to him.

'I can try and have a chat with him in his cell,' he whispered.

She nodded, then looked at the sergeants as she said, 'By the way, you've got our mad bomber in the cells, haven't you?'

'Yeah, Mand, we booked him in this afternoon. Didn't say much. Why's that?'

Moone saw her shoot him a look before she said, 'Just hoping to check in on him. Another bomb just went off.'

'Who's that with you?' one of the custody sergeants said. Moone looked around and saw one of them, a fair-haired, bearded man leaning over the counter. 'Oh, didn't see you there, DCI Moone. Everything all right, boss?'

He smiled. 'Yeah, just checking in on our suspect.'

'He's on cell watch,' the bearded sergeant said. 'Not to worry.'

'Is it OK if I check in with him?' Moone asked, pointing a thumb behind him, towards the cells.

The sergeant's eyes jumped to Butler, narrowing, knowing something was up. 'This above board, is it, Mand? I mean, I'm not going to get the brass on my back, am I?'

'I thought you lot were in charge down here?' Butler said. 'What you say goes, doesn't it?'

'It does,' the bearded one said. 'I suppose if DCI Moone was to take over cell watch duties for a bit, it wouldn't hurt.'

Butler turned to Moone and gave him the nod, so he moved towards the corridor of cells. Moone's footsteps echoed off the hard floor as he walked past the cells, his eyes fixed on the last one.

The young PC was sitting in a plastic chair by the open doorway, the Herald spread over his lap. He barely glanced up as Moone approached, only reacting when he noticed the detective looming over him.

'Sir.' The PC stood up and folded the paper away.

Moone nodded at the cell. 'I'll take over for a bit. Why don't you take a break and get a coffee?'

The PC hesitated. 'I was told...'

'I'll take responsibility here,' Moone cut in. 'Go on. It's fine. The custody sergeant said it's fine and you know they reign supreme down here.'

The PC looked awkward and unsure for a moment, so Moone forced a smile he hoped was reassuring. The PC stuffed the newspaper under his arm as he said, 'Cheers, sir. I'll be back in ten minutes.'

He gave one last glance at the prisoner before disappearing down the corridor.

Moone stepped into the doorway, resting a hand on the frame. Abel was sitting on the edge of the thin mattress, hands resting between his knees, fingers twitching slightly. Moone noticed the tattoo on his wrist, the sun with the triangle at the centre.

The prisoner didn't say a word, just stared back at him. Moone felt his eyes, dark and unwavering, tracking his every move.

Moone breathed out slowly, then sat down on the chair and faced him. 'OK, you've got my attention. You obviously want to talk, so let's talk.'

Abel's lips curled into a slow smile, his eyes locked onto Moone's. He leaned forward slightly, elbows on his knees. 'I knew you would come,' he said, his voice calm, almost amused. 'It took you long enough. You must feel it, don't you? That... wrongness. Like the world's just a little off. A second too slow. A shadow where there shouldn't be one.'

Abel's eyes twitched. 'We're trapped, you and me. Stuck in this... thing. This lie. But I can break it. I am breaking it.'

He grinned, eyes glinting with something dark and unreadable. 'You want to know the best part? I think you might be real, Peter. Just like me.'

'Let's pretend I agree with you, that this is all a... simulation? Why me?'

Abel let out a quiet laugh, shaking his head as if he was talking to a slow learner. 'Why you?'

He leaned back against the cold cell wall, tapping his fingers against his knee. 'Because you see things, Moone. Maybe you don't realise it yet, maybe you brush it off as instinct, gut feeling, but it's more than that, isn't it? The way the world doesn't sit right sometimes, the way things repeat, the way people... glitch. That's what they call it.'

He sat forward again, eyes dark and intense. 'I've been watching you, Peter. You don't just follow the rules, you question them. You push, test the edges of this... so-called world. That's what makes you different from the rest of them.' He nodded towards the corridor. 'NPCs. Non-Player Characters. They're just background noise. They don't matter. But you? You matter, Moone. I can feel it.'

Moone kept his disbelief from poisoning his face. 'Where did this all start? You didn't just wake up one day thinking we're all in The Matrix.'

Abel's expression changed, his grin fading into something more thoughtful.

'Nepal,' he said finally, voice quieter now. 'That's where it started. I was out there with my regiment, recruiting Gurkhas. Good lads. Fierce. Loyal. But I was on leave, just blowing off steam, and some locals decided I was fair game. Didn't end well for them. One dead. A couple of them barely made it. And me? I was facing charges.'

He let the words hang in the air for a moment. 'I was stuck. Nowhere to go, no way out. So I started looking... really looking, I mean. I spoke to some of the locals, spiritual types. Not just monks, either, but people who knew things.' He tapped the side of his head.

'They told me about the *Akashic Record*. The blueprint of everything. Past, present, and future, all written down, like a script. A program. That's when it hit me. Life's not real. It's just data, a repeating cycle, playing out over and over. And I saw the patterns, Moone. Same events, same faces, just… rearranged.'

Abel leaned forward again, his voice dropping to a whisper. 'That's when I knew. And once you know, you can't unsee it.'

His lips twisted into a smirk, his eyes all flame. 'So I decided to do something about it.'

'You mean you started making bombs? Killing innocent people? That's what they are, real living, breathing people… not… avatars or whatever you want to call them.'

Abel shook his head. 'You're still thinking small, Peter.' He tapped his forehead. 'Still clinging hopelessly to the illusion.'

He leaned forward. 'They feel real, I get it. They talk, they bleed, they cry. But that's just the program running its course. A well-designed NPC doesn't know it's scripted. It thinks it's alive, just like a character in a video game thinks it's making choices.'

Abel's gaze darkened, his voice lowering. 'I tested it at first. Just small things. Messed with routines, and watched how people reacted. And it was all so… predictable. Like clockwork. So I escalated. A glitch here, a crack there, push the system hard enough, cause enough chaos, and maybe, just maybe, the walls start to break.'

'What if you're wrong?' Moone said, balling his fists, flashes of Harding and all the other casualties surging into his mind.

'If I'm wrong? If they are real?' He shrugged. 'Then I guess I'm a monster. But if I'm right...' He smiled, slow and unsettling. 'Then none of this matters anyway.'

Moone sat back, his mind racing. 'Why did you put a bomb in that car and set it off tonight?'

Abel's smile widened, a flicker of amusement in his eyes. 'See, that's where you're wrong. I didn't put a bomb in the car. It was in the drain under it.' He tilted his head. 'Details matter, Peter. You should understand that.'

Moone didn't react, just watched him and waited for the punchline.

Abel leaned in slightly. 'But the why, that's the real question, isn't it? I needed a distraction. Something big enough to keep everyone running in circles, so you'd end up right here, in this room, with me.' He spread his hands. 'And here we are.'

His expression changed, the smile fading. 'This conversation? It's more important than any of them realise. While they're out there picking through wreckage, chasing shadows, you're here. Listening and thinking, Peter.'

He paused. 'Which means I've already

won.'

Moone decided to change tack. 'Tell me about the Drake Inn.'

Abel's expression changed again as soon as Moone mentioned the Drake Inn. A flicker of recognition passed across his face, like a memory resurfacing that he hadn't planned on revisiting.

'The Drake Inn,' Abel said. 'That place. Funny how memories get twisted, isn't it?' He paused as if savouring the moment. He leaned his head back and closed his eyes. 'I remember that night. I was in the room at the end of the hall. My parents were out, drinking somewhere. They didn't care.' He leaned forward and opened his eyes, his voice lower. 'But you, Peter... You were there too, weren't you? Just a little kid, lost in the halls, scared like the whole place was trying to swallow you up. Calling for Mummy and Daddy.'

Moone's pulse quickened, a knot tightening in his stomach. He'd never been able to shake the feeling that something terrible had happened that night.

Abel's eyes gleamed. 'Rodney Fox. He was there. Big, bad bastard. He'd been eyeing me, you know? Found me in my room, thought he'd take me downstairs. Maybe for a little chat, or something... else. But then there was you. The little kid, standing in the hallway in his pyjamas, looking lost and scared. I didn't know it at the time, but you were just in the right place at the right time.'

Moone's throat tightened. He couldn't breathe for a moment. It was all flooding back, fragments of that night.

Abel continued, his voice wavering. 'Fox tried to take both of us downstairs. He had plans. But I wasn't having any of it.' His fingers twitched. 'So I did what I had to do. Pushed him. Down the stairs. He fell like a sack of shit. Broke his neck.'

Moone's mind reeled. The memory of the screams, the panic, it was all coming together now. His parents waking up, coming down to find him. Did they see Rodney Fox lying dead? Did they know what happened?

'And then the owners,' Abel said. 'They covered it up. Quieted things down. Didn't want anyone poking around, especially not when they had their hands in so many dirty little dealings. Oh, yes, there was some other illegal stuff going on there. They didn't care about us. Just wanted to keep their hotel running smoothly and keep the police away.'

Abel leaned back on the bed, his gaze never leaving Moone. 'Funny how you don't remember all of it, though. Guess you were too young. But I do. And now you're sitting here, wondering why you've always felt lost. Like there's something you can't quite remember.'

Moone didn't know what to say. If it was

true, which he sensed it was, then Abel had saved him. He opened his mouth. 'Thank you for what you did, but you need to realise that what happened back then, and in the army, those things affected you. This whole… simulation thing, it's just a way to… escape what happened.'

Abel's eyes had flickered at the word escape and for a moment, there was something almost human in his gaze, a flicker of emotion. But it passed quickly, replaced by the cold, calculating look Moone had come to expect.

Abel leaned forward again, fingers tapping rhythmically on his leg.

'Escape? You think this is about escaping? No, Peter, this isn't some excuse. This is the truth. Everything I've seen, everything I've done, it all led me here. To this moment.'

He nodded slowly, as if trying to convince Moone of something he already knew. 'I didn't need to escape. I needed to understand, to make sense of what's been happening to me, to all of us. You think the army messed me up? Of course it did. But the real damage, that came when I saw the world for what it truly is.'

Abel's voice grew colder, more intense. 'You think I'm running away from it? That it's some fantasy? No. This is the only reality, Peter. It's the rest of them that are lost.' He leaned back. 'But I get it. You can't see it yet. It's not your fault. You haven't had the time I've had to figure it out. To crack the code.'

He met Moone's eyes, unwavering. 'No, I'm not escaping anything, Peter. I'm just opening your eyes. Whether you want to see the truth or not.'

'So, you're going to break us out of this matrix with bombs? That's your plan? I don't understand. You think if you cause enough destruction and horror, it'll somehow break us out?'

Abel's smile faded into something more serious, almost solemn. He nodded, his gaze fixed on Moone with an unsettling calm. 'Destruction. It's not just about causing chaos for chaos's sake, Peter. It's about breaking the pattern. You're right in one sense, because it's not easy to see how it all fits together from where you're sitting.' He leaned in, his eyes shining. 'But that's the point. The system is built on repetition, on predictability. You think everything that happens is random, that we're all just living out our lives in some twisted, flawed way. But it's all designed. It's all controlled.'

He leaned back, folding his arms, his gaze still locked on Moone. 'The destruction? That's the crack in the foundation. A shift in the frequency. The more I push, the more the system reacts. It's like a pressure point, right? The more you squeeze it, the more the cracks start to show. Like I said earlier, with 9-11, the system, the program started to glitch. Dates, events changed. I keep records. It caused chaos, shocked everyone, sent a ripple through the program. Causing fear, chaos, destruction, that's how it works. You break the cycle by making it impossible to ignore. You wake people up, even if it's with blood. The system tries to fight it, tries to fix its mistakes, but it glitches more, alters more of our history. Eventually, with enough destruction, the program will fail. Error message. The end.'

His voice dropped to a whisper. 'You think I'm just some lunatic blowing things up? No. I'm the one trying to free us all. To break the chains. I'm the only one who can see it.'

'Tell me where the other bombs are. There are more bombs, aren't there?'

Abel smiled. 'I don't think you can be trusted with that information, Peter.'

'Then they'll take you away, to some secret location and they'll torture you until you tell them where the bombs are and there'll be nothing I can do. Listen…'

Moone leaned forward, engaging his empty eyes. 'If all that's true… what happened in the hotel… then you helped me. Let me help you. If you tell me what I need to know to stop all this, then I can help you…'

'No. It's already set in motion.'

'What do you mean?'

Abel looked down at his leg and brushed

something off. 'I mean you can't stop it. Neither can they. They can torture me, but by the time they find out what they want to know, it'll be too late.'

Moone closed his eyes, feeling Abel's walls had already come down. It was useless.

'But I'll give you a little clue.'

His eyes opened to find Abel leaning forward, his eyes digging into him. 'Let's see if I'm right, let's see if you're real. You found me at King's house. Why don't you start there? Maybe there's something in his files that might help.'

Moone heard footsteps coming from down the corridor. He looked and saw the PC coming back. He looked at Abel. 'What does that mean?'

He shrugged. 'Maybe I left a clue for you. You'd better hurry.'

'I'm back, sir,' the uniform said and stood by the open cell, and cast an eye towards the prisoner. Moone was still watching Abel, trying to read his expression.

'Sir?'

Moone blinked and looked up at the PC as he got to his feet. 'Thanks.'

Moone didn't stop for any chat as he hurried on through the corridor of cells, heading to where Butler was waiting, talking to the custody sergeants. His mind raced as he saw her, his heart doing its usual jig, thinking about what he was going to do next. King's house.

He stopped and looked back towards the cells, where the PC was back in position. Then he turned round to face Butler, who was shooting him a questioning look.

'What's happening?' she asked. 'Prisoner OK? All comfy and tucked in?'

'Fine,' Moone said and walked past the desk, thinking everything through. He went out the exit and into the dark of the car park, where he waited for Butler.

She stepped out, staring at him with her eyebrows raised. 'So?'

He was speechless for a moment, but then he realised there was little point hiding it all from her. 'He was there that night. In the Drake Inn.'

She stared at him, eyes narrowed. 'What? What do you mean, he was there?'

'Him and his parents were staying there, or so he says.' Moone searched for his cigarettes, found them and put one in his mouth. As he lit it, his hand was trembling.

'Can you make a very long story short?'

He nodded and blew out some smoke. 'He was left alone in his room. Rodney Fox was staying there too, and apparently he found his way into his room…'

'Jesus. Fox was a…? Bloody hell, now it makes sense. His wife must have found out and told him to sling his hook. Go on.'

'Fox was dragging him off somewhere when a kid appears out of nowhere.' Moone stared at her. 'Me.'

Butler let out a strange sound, not quite a huff.

He took another drag. 'The way Abel tells it, me appearing distracted Fox and he pushed him down the stairs. Broke his neck. The owners covered it up.'

Butler stepped back, shaking her head. 'So, he saved you from a peado? And now what?'

'I think he believes that us, me and him, coming back together like this is proof of something. Don't ask me what.'

'But he didn't tell you where he's planted the bombs?'

'No.'

She let out a sigh and headed to the car and unlocked it. 'Come on, I'll drive you home.'

'I'm not going home.'

She stopped and looked at him. 'That sounds ominous. Where the bloody hell're you going, then?'

'King's house.'

'Why the bloody hell would you be going there at this time?'

He blew the air from his cheeks, dropped his cigarette and stubbed it out. 'I know this sounds crazy, but he said he might've left something there for us.'

'Left us something? What, like a bomb?'

She let out an exhausted laugh.

'I don't think so. There's a connection between him and me. I think, maybe, he's somehow reaching out to me. I think there might be something in King's files, some clue as to where he's planted the bombs.'

Butler stared at him, shaking her head. 'We can't go in there. Not without getting hold of Bomb Disposal and everyone.'

Moone took a breath. 'I don't think we've got time for that. I need to take a look. Now. By myself.'

'Oh no. I'm not letting you go in there alone. You must be nuts. Come on.' Butler walked to her car, climbed in and started the engine. Moone took a shaky breath and followed her into the car.

They pulled up outside King's narrow house, the amber streetlights lending everything a ghostly glow. A breeze pushed the litter up the street, while laughter and music drifted from the pub on the corner. Moone was sitting in the passenger seat, staring at the house, his stomach churned up, his pulse beating fast in his neck.

Butler killed the engine and let out a heavy sigh.

'Are we really going in there?'

'No,' he said, not looking at her. 'You're not. I am. You stay here. I won't be long.' He went to push open his door, but she grabbed his arm.

'We go in together or not at all.' Her eyes burned into his.

He sighed, realising he might as well be arguing with a rock. 'OK. Let's get this over with.'

He climbed out and headed over the street. He took out the key as Butler joined him and kept an eye out. He opened the door to darkness and the waft of stale tobacco. He found the light switch and turned it on. The well-worn carpet and flowery wallpaper stared back at him as he slowly went in. The kitchen was a little untidy, with remnants of the takeaway from the other night still scattered around. Butler had headed into the living room, so Moone caught up and found her stood by the sofa, looking around.

'Not much here,' she said.

'No.' Moone looked towards the door. 'I think he kept his files in the back room. I'll take a look. You stay here. Put the kettle on.'

'Geddon, Moone,' she said and followed him out the door and into a crowded, dusty back room where there were a couple of filing cabinets as well as a pile of plastic boxes in one corner. An ancient-looking PC sat on a desk by the back window that looked onto a small concrete yard.

Moone sighed, looking it all over,

wondering where to start. 'Well, he certainly liked to hoard.'

'Let's get started, then.'

'You take the plastic boxes, I'll take the filing cabinets.'

'Fine.' Butler huffed.

Moone knelt down and pulled out the bottom drawer of the cabinet. There was a clicking noise, then a beep. He looked down and saw numbers glowing up at him. His heart started to pound as he saw wires coming out of the black box that had the numbers on.

'Butler,' Moone said as he noticed a Post-it note attached to the box.

Two words written on the note said, "DON'T MOVE".

'What've you found?'

He could see her blurry face looking his way out the corner of his eye. His hand was shaking, clenched to the filing cabinet. He swallowed, trying to think. He looked at her. Get her out of here, was his first thought. 'Can you get us both... a drink. Go to Mutley.'

Butler narrowed her eyes. 'What? No, go yourself. What are you on about?'

Her eyes jumped to him, then all over the filing cabinet. Her face lost colour.

'What've you got there, Moone?' There was a tremble to her voice.

'I think... I'm pretty sure... it's a bomb, and if I let go, I think it might go off.'

CHAPTER 22

'You need to get out,' Moone said, his voice breaking, his whole body shaking. A cold sweat had broken out and was dripping down his sides. His palms were damp.

'I'm not going anywhere, do you bloody well hear me?' she said, the anger in her voice trying to paper over the cracks. She took out her phone. 'I'm calling Bomb Disposal.'

'It won't do any good.' He closed his eyes.

'What do you mean? Course it will. Shut up, you wally. They'll come and stop it. Right, I'm calling them.'

'What if a phone sets it off?' He turned his head slightly towards her.

'What? Is that a thing? Oh shit.' She lowered her phone. 'Now, listen to me, Peter Moone. I'm going outside to call them, then I'm coming back. Try not to move.'

She headed across the room.

'Don't.'

'What? I've got to go outside and call.'

'No, don't come back. Please. Please, Butler.'

He could feel her eyes on him as she stood in the doorway.

'Please, Mandy.'

He could hear her breathing.

'I'll be back in a minute.' She turned away.

'Mandy?'

She stopped. 'What now?'

'They'll need to evacuate the street.'

She huffed, then he heard the front door open and he lowered his head and let out a deep cry. Fuck. Fuck. He looked at the counter. Fifty-eight minutes. His breath was coming fast, the pounding of blood around his skull and ears. His hands were shaking.

Alice and the rest of his kids flashed into his mind. He'd never see them again. He wondered if it would hurt, or if it would be instantaneous. Jesus fucking Christ.

He coughed and retched. Don't think about it. He tried to control his breathing, took deep breaths and released them slowly. His heart was sprinting.

Abel came to mind, sitting in his comfy cell with a smirk on his face. He knew what he was doing. All along, he knew. He was sending him to his death. The bastard, and he'd walked right into it.

He pushed the smug bastard out of his thoughts and tried to focus on something else. Anything.

Butler. Where was she?

He was going to die and he hadn't told her how he felt. Well, technically he had, but… now she was with Chris. A good-looking and seemingly nice bloke. He shook his head. She wasn't interested in him, they were just work colleagues, friends, and that was all.

He looked down. Fifty-four minutes.

Oh, God. Please. Please don't let this be the end. He looked up, towards the tobacco-stained ceiling, up to heaven if there was such a thing. 'If anyone's listening,' he said, 'please help me. I'll be a better man, or at least I'll try. I'm sorry about all the mistakes I've made. I'm sorry about writing "fuck" on Martin Farah's homework book and then pretending I didn't when he got detention. I'm sorry about my marriage failing because I was always working. I'm just… sorry. And please, let Butler survive this. She hasn't done anything. If you make this all right, and we get through it, I'll leave her alone. I'll let her be happy with Chris. I promise. Scout's honour.'

He heard the front door open, and Butler's footsteps coming back. He saw her coming in, her skin pale, her cheeks red.

'They're on their way,' she said, her voice rigid. 'Stupid question, but are you all right?'

He nodded. 'Tickety-boo. How long? Please say quicker than… fifty minutes.'

'They'll be here soon.'

He smiled at her, holding back his tears. 'Call them back and tell them not to faff.'

She laughed, then stopped. She came over and crouched down, staring into his eyes. 'Listen to me, Peter Moone, everything's going to be OK. Got it?'

'You promise?'

She raised her middle finger with a grin. 'Brownie's promise.'

He laughed.

They both looked around when they heard loud engine sounds coming from outside. Then there were voices, people shouting.

'Sounds like they're here,' she said and gripped his shoulder. 'You'll be out of here soon.'

It was a man who came in and stood in the doorway. He was stocky, decked out in black combats, a thick black vest with several pockets over the top of it all. His sleeves were rolled up. He had a thick grey moustache that matched the grey wad of hair that sat on the top of his square head.

A thin sheen of sweat clung to Moone's forehead, while his heart pounded away.

'Are you going to take a look?' Butler asked in a shaky voice.

The man nodded. 'In good time. I need the room cleared, apart from DCI Peter Moone here, obviously.'

'I'm not going...'

'Butler, you heard him.' He stared up at her. 'Please.'

She stared back at him, flickers of emotion running across her face. 'OK, I'll be just outside.'

The Bomb Disposal officer came over, crouched down and peered inside the open drawer. He seemed calm, his hands steady, Moone noticed. That was good.

His name patch read Kiernan, but Moone barely registered it. The man's blue eyes flicked between the tangled mess of wires and the crude explosive device nestled among a stack of discoloured folders. He gave a low whistle.

'Well... that's creative,' the man said, nodding.

Moone breathed out. 'Is that meant to be reassuring?'

Kiernan gave a grin. 'That depends, Peter. Are you a fan of surprises?' He reached into a pouch on his vest, pulled out a small torch, and angled it inside the cabinet. 'Right, here's what we've got. It looks like a pressure release switch wired to a fairly rudimentary ignition system. If you let go, that spring underneath will snap up, complete the circuit, and… well, boom.'

Moone's grip tightened. 'Yeah, that's what I thought.'

Kiernan nodded, seemingly unfazed. 'The silver lining? The wiring's messy, which means whoever built this wasn't an expert. Downside? That doesn't make it any less lethal.' He shifted slightly, reaching for a tool from his belt. 'I've seen worse, though. Consider yourself lucky. We once had a bloke sit on a pressure plate in his kitchen for six hours.'

Moone gave him a dry look. 'Forgive me, but if I don't feel very lucky right about now.'

Kiernan smirked but kept his focus on the bomb. 'OK, let's keep you that way. I'm going to wedge something under this drawer so you can take your hand off without redecorating the place in high-velocity shrapnel.' He reached into his kit, pulling out a slim metal brace. 'Just stay still a sec…'

Then he froze. The smirk vanished.

He leaned in, squinting at something deeper inside the drawer. His breath came out in a harsh sound. 'Shit.'

Moone's stomach turned to lead. 'That's not a word I wanted to hear right now.'

Kiernan barely moved, his voice a little strained. 'OK. I might have underestimated our bomb maker. He must have made the wiring look messy to fool me, which it almost did. Yes, he's a clever so-and-so. So, a slight adjustment to the plan.'

He exhaled through his nose. 'See that second wire running along the side? That's a dead man's switch. If I wedge this in and relieve the pressure, it'll trigger a second circuit.' He swallowed. 'Which means... you really can't let go.'

Moone felt his pulse hammering in his throat and his ears. 'Great. What now?'

'We have a rethink.' Kiernan sat back on his heels, running a hand over his mouth. Then he let out a breath and shook his head. 'Well, I was getting bored today anyway.'

He reached into his kit, pulling out a scalpel-thin blade and a set of clippers. His expression was still calm, but there was a sharpness in his eyes. 'OK, Moone, change of plan. You and me? We're going to be here a little longer.'

Butler stepped out of the house and into the cold night air, feeling the weight of it press against her. The street was a blur of flashing blue and red, shadows dancing over the old brick houses. She could smell the booze from the pub up the road that was now empty, the door still open.

She ran a shaky hand through her hair, breathing slowly, trying to steady herself. Moone was still inside. That thought alone threatened to knock the breath from her chest, but she pushed it down. Be professional. Stay in control.

Her eyes swept the scene, taking in the Bomb Disposal team clustered by their van, helmets off, chatting among themselves. To one side stood Major Lacroix, standing rigid as always, his broad shoulders squared, his cold eyes on her. Just off to his side, looking as smug and self-important as ever, was Fitzgerald, MI5's man on the ground. He was as watchful as ever, taking it all in, but playing his cards close to his chest. She wondered what he knew and felt like going over and slapping it out of him.

Butler straightened her back, pulling herself together. She would not let him see her shaken. Fuck that.

Fitzgerald turned as she approached, hands tucked into the pockets of his expensive coat. 'Well?' he asked, one eyebrow raised.

Butler kept her voice level. 'The Bomb Disposal guy's in there now. He wouldn't let me stay.'

Lacroix looked at her. 'Of course not. We have to keep casualties at a minimum.'

'Casualties?' she huffed. 'That's Moone in there! He's got a bloody name.'

'I know,' Lacroix said. 'Try and keep calm. They know what they're doing.'

'I bloody well hope so.' She looked around the street. Uniforms were knocking on doors, evacuating the houses. 'Is everyone out yet?'

'Not everyone,' Lacroix said, then pointed to the house next door to where the bomb was.

'A man and wife are still in there, won't come out,' he said.

Butler swept around. 'What? Jesus. I'll get them out.'

'They need to decide what to bring. They might lose their house, DS Butler.'

She looked briefly at Lacroix, then stormed up to the house and rang the bell. A dark-haired inspector answered. She recognised him, and nodded to the interior of the house. 'Are they still in there, Paul?'

'Yes, Mandy.' He looked back into the house. 'They're trying to decide what to take and what not to. I think they're just stalling.'

Butler headed in and found them in the dining room at the back of the house. It was a woman and a man, both around thirty, a form in front of them. The woman had tears in her eyes as she looked up at Butler.

'I'm sorry,' the wife said, her voice breaking. 'It's just... it's hard...what do you take? I mean...'

'It's a house, it's stuff,' Butler said and stood by the table, looking between them. 'Have you got kids?'

'My mum took them,' the husband said.

'Then they're safe. You need to be too. Just get out. My colleague is next door. He can't move. He can't leave. He might...'

'You all right?' the wife asked.

'I'm fine. Anyway, you need to go. Right now. Come on, let's move it.'

The woman started crying but she nodded and got up, the husband coming over and escorting her towards the front door. As they went out into the street, Butler followed. Then her eyes jumped to the King's house. Somebody was coming out. It was the Bomb Disposal guy and he was alone. She stormed over, grabbing his elbow.

'What's happening?' she demanded, her voice strained.

Sergeant Kiernan faced Butler, Lacroix, Fitzgerald, and the rest of the gathered officers. His face was set, jaw tight. 'I could kill for a cigarette and I haven't smoked in years.'

'What the hell's happening?' Butler snapped.

'The device is more complicated than I first thought,' Kiernan said, voice rough with exhaustion. 'We're dealing with a double trigger. A pressure release switch, which we expected, but also a dead man's switch. That means if Moone moves, if he lets go, if we so much as jostle that cabinet the wrong way, it goes off.'

A heavy silence settled over them. The only sound was the distant crackle of radios and seagulls squawking above them on the roofs.

Butler closed her eyes and looked down. Moone. He was still inside. Still holding on. He must be terrified.

'So, what are you saying?' Fitzgerald asked. 'That he's stuck there until you figure this out?'

Kiernan exhaled sharply, rubbing the back of his neck. 'At the moment, yeah. We don't have a way to move him safely. If we try to defuse the bomb while he's holding it, there's too much risk of setting it off. We need more time to assess. But the timer says half an hour left.'

Lacroix frowned. 'If it does detonate?'

Kiernan glanced towards the house, then back at them. 'Then Peter's right at the centre of it.' His voice was tight. 'Best we can do, if it comes to that, is protect him as much as possible.'

Butler's stomach knotted. 'Protect him? From a bloody bomb he's sat right on bloody top of? How?'

Kiernan sighed. 'We can try to shield him. Get ballistic plates, and body armour, and stack whatever we can around him. It won't stop the blast completely, but it might... just might give him a chance.'

Butler clenched her fists, forcing herself to keep her expression neutral. She wouldn't let them see how much the whole situation unnerved her.

Fitzgerald scoffed. 'That's not a solution, that's damage control.'

Kiernan's face hardened. 'That's all we've got for now. And we're running out of time.' He crossed his arms. 'Look, I'll be honest with you. Whoever built this thing knew exactly what they were doing. It's meant to be a death trap.'

Butler's heart pounded. Please God, don't let this happen.

'So, what's the plan?' Lacroix asked.

Kiernan took a breath. 'I'll go back in and assess the device further. If there's a way to disarm it, I'll find it. In the meantime, get me the armour and plating. We need to be ready for the worst.'

His words settled over them like a lead umbrella. No one spoke for a moment.

Then Butler nodded, forcing steel into her voice. 'I'll go and see him.'

She turned away before anyone could stop her and stormed into the house, the sound of the street becoming muffled as she sank into her own head. They were going to put armour around him. The bomb was going to go off. She stopped in the hallway as a sob burst from her lips. She clamped a hand over her mouth as tears trickled down her cheeks. She sniffed, cleared her throat, wiped her eyes and carried on into the back room. There he was, still knelt on the ground, his face pale, bags under his eyes. He was staring up at her, trying to put on a smile. She knelt beside him, moving an open bottle of water.

'How're you doing, Pete?' she asked.

He let out a dry laugh. 'Pete? You never call me Pete. Things must be bad.'

'They're coming up with…'

He lowered his head. 'They're going to try and protect me from the blast. But chances are I'm going to die. I know.'

She gripped his free hand, squeezed it.

'I need to call Alice and the kids,' he said, his voice breaking.

'Not yet you don't,' she said, squeezing his hand tighter. 'We'll think of something.'

'There's another Bomb Disposal person on their way, but he won't get here in time,' Moone said and looked into the cabinet. 'Oh fuck. Half an hour. Thirty minutes left.'

She stared at him, her heart thumping, panic rushing through her veins. She didn't want to lose him. 'I need to say something…'

He looked at her. 'What?'

'You shouldn't be in here,' the Bomb Disposal man said as he came back in. 'You need to go. Now.'

Moone stared up at her as she got to her feet. 'What were you going to say?'

'DS Butler, with me.'

She turned and saw Fitzgerald standing in the doorway. 'Now, Butler.'

She looked at Moone, trying to find the words. 'I'll be back.'

She turned and hurried after Fitzgerald as her tears came. When they stood on the street, the emergency lights flashing everywhere, Fitzgerald stared at her.

'I've got an idea,' he said, his eyes darting up and down the street.

'What?'

'We go and bring Abel here.' He kept staring at her, his eyes travelling all over her face.

'Then what? Make him stop the bomb?' She laughed, a sob almost coming with it.

'He's got less than thirty minutes. So we bring him here, sit him with Moone. He doesn't defuse it, then he dies too.'

Butler absorbed what she was hearing. 'That's not legal. You can't do that.'

'Not legal? Fuck that. I work for MI5, I can pretty much do what I want. You in or not?'

She turned, her heart thumping as she looked at the house lit up by the flashing blue lights. He didn't have long. Shit.

'Butler? We need to move.'

She looked at him. 'All right. Let's get a move on.'

It was Butler who drove them to Charles Cross station at speed and with the blue light blinking on the dashboard. But when they arrived, and she turned off the engine, she realised she had no memory of the journey. Her heart felt wrenched out of her chest knowing Moone was back in the house and she was away from him. What if something happened? What if...?

'DS Butler!'

She flickered out of her dream state as Fitzgerald tapped on her window, glaring at her. 'Hurry up, we've got to move.'

Butler jumped out, hurried to the building and swiped in. She let Fitzgerald in, then hurried to the custody suite with the MI5 agent behind her.

'What about the custody sergeants?' she said over her shoulder.

'What about them?'

'They won't let you take him.'

'They don't have a choice.'

As they got through the main door and reached the counter where the custody sergeants were standing, Fitzgerald barged past her. He took out his warrant card as he said, 'Fitzgerald. MI5. We need to transport the prisoner. Abel.'

The custody sergeant folded his arms, his brow creasing. 'We need authorisation to hand him over into your care. We need the proper paperwork.'

'No, you don't,' Fitzgerald said, an edge to his voice. 'I'm MI5. I'm above you. Far above you. We're taking him to defuse a bomb or a police officer will die. Do you hear me?'

The custody officers looked at each other, then the bearded one faced Butler.

'This true, Mand?'

She nodded. 'Yeah. We need him. We haven't got much time.'

'Then you better move it,' the bearded sergeant said. 'I'll do the paperwork.'

Fitzgerald didn't wait, just rushed down to the cell at the end. Another uniform, an older, grey-haired man was camped out in front of the cell, reading a book.

Fitzgerald showed him his ID as he looked into the cell. 'MI5. We're taking him.'

'It's fine,' Butler said as the older uniform sat up and looked at her for confirmation.

'Righty-oh,' the uniform said, getting up. 'He's all yours.'

Butler stood in the doorway, watching as Fitzgerald took out some cable ties.

Abel was staring up at Butler, his face blank.

'What's this?' Abel said.

'A road trip,' Fitzgerald said. 'Stand up and turn around.'

Abel stood up, turned and faced the wall. The MI5 agent grabbed hold of his hands, put the straps around them and then pulled them tight.

'Come on, move.' Fitzgerald swung him

around and shoved him out of the cell.

'Let me guess,' Abel said as they took him along the corridor of cells. 'Good old Peter Moone is stuck in King's house, holding a filing cabinet drawer open?'

Butler swung round and grabbed him by his top. 'You psycho bastard. You're going to come with us, and you're going to disarm that bomb. Do you hear me?'

Abel smiled into her face. 'Do you think he's really taking me to disarm that bomb?'

'What the hell're you talking about?'

'Let's get moving,' Fitzgerald said, trying to push Abel further on.

Butler raised a hand.

'Wait a minute,' she said. 'What're you saying?'

'I'm saying that he doesn't want that bomb defused. He wants it to go off, and me with it.'

'Don't listen to him,' Fitzgerald said, shaking his head. 'He's trying to get inside your head.'

'He wants rid of me because of what I know.'

Butler looked at Fitzgerald, but he was just staring at her. 'What do you know?'

'He knows nothing. Fuck all. If we don't hurry up, Moone is dead.'

He was right. Time was running out. She took hold of Abel's arm and pulled him out of the custody suite and through the building. 'Come on, you.'

'Where do you think I learnt to make bombs?' Abel asked as they took him out of the back entrance and out into the car park.

Fitzgerald opened the back door of their car. 'Shut the fuck up.'

Abel was pushed into the back seat while Butler got behind the wheel. She started the engine and stared at Abel in the rear-view mirror.

'In the British army,' he said, his lifeless eyes staring deep into her. 'They had us working undercover, making bombs for the IRA. Can you imagine that?'

Fitzgerald climbed in and jerked around to Abel. He had a gun in his hand, now pointed at Abel's face.

'You say another fucking word and you're dead,' he growled. 'I can shoot you dead and say you tried to escape.'

Butler stared at Fitzgerald. 'Is that true?'

Fitzgerald kept staring at Abel. 'Of course it's not true. Conspiracy theory bollocks. Now let's move.'

Butler put the car into first as a dark feeling of unease rose over her body. She turned the car around and headed back to Stonehouse.

The streets of Stonehouse were lit up by the glow of all the police cars and fire engines. The weight of what they were heading towards sat heavy in the car, somehow sucking out all the air. Butler kept her hands steady on the wheel, but her thoughts churned. Fitzgerald was sitting beside her in silence, his MI5 arrogance muted for once. Abel was in the back, his hands strapped behind his back, watching them both with a smirk that never left his face.

As they neared the cordoned-off street, Butler slowed, her eyes scanning the scene. Emergency vehicles clustered around the house like vultures waiting for something to die. The blue lights flashed over the dark figures of armed officers stationed outside.

She parked just outside the cordon, switched off the blues and turned the engine off, then glanced at Fitzgerald.

'What about Lacroix?' she asked, keeping her voice low. 'I can't see him going along with this.'

'You'd better hurry,' Abel said. 'Time's running out.'

Fitzgerald breathed out, shaking his head. 'No, I doubt he would go along with this.' His eyes turned to her. 'But it looks like he's not here. We need to move before he turns up again.'

Butler pushed open her door as she looked at the dashboard clock. There were only fifteen minutes left.

Abel laughed from the back seat.

'Fitzgerald knows it's pointless,' he said, his voice full of amusement. 'None of us are coming out of that house alive.'

Butler stared at Fitzgerald.

'What?' Fitzgerald said. 'Are you going to listen to the man who's been killing innocent people and your colleagues? He's trying to get inside your head, Butler. Are you going to let Moone die?'

Butler ignored the bad feeling and climbed out into the cooler night air. Fitzgerald did the same. Abel was still grinning as they hauled him from the car. The guards at the cordon eyed them warily but let them through once Fitzgerald showed his ID.

'Maybe Lacroix doesn't want to be here when it all goes to shit,' Abel muttered as they walked toward the house. 'I can't say I blame him. You should take note, Butler. Do you think MI5 will let me live?'

She shot him a sharp look but didn't take the bait. Fitzgerald didn't react either, but she saw the look in his eye, the way his hands flinched as they entered the hallway.

Moone was exactly where they'd left him, but now he was wearing a thick, armour-plated vest. He looked at Butler, the worry cut deep into his pale skin.

Across the room, the Bomb Disposal officer was setting out armoured vests, preparing them carefully. Precautionary measures. If things went wrong, they wouldn't stop the blast, just soften the blow.

No one spoke for a moment. Just the sound of seagulls outside.

Abel breathed out slowly, looking between them all. 'Well,' he said, smiling. 'Should we get started?'

The Bomb Disposal guy straightened up, his eyes narrowing. 'Who's this?'

'It doesn't matter,' Fitzgerald said, his voice hollow. 'Get out.'

'Get out?' Kiernan looked between them all. 'Get out? What the hell do you mean, get out?'

'This... man, here is going to stop this bomb, or he'll go up with it,' Fitzgerald said and pushed Abel towards the cabinet.

'Who authorised this?' Kiernan looked at them all.

'I did. Go and talk to your boss about it if you've got a problem.'

The man looked at Butler, then around at everyone before storming towards the door.

'Don't worry, Peter,' Kiernan said, looking back at Moone. 'I'll find someone and I'll be back.'

Fitzgerald closed the front door after he walked out, then came back to the room. A gun was now in his hand. 'Time to get started.'

CHAPTER 23

Fitzgerald stayed at the back of the room, resting his backside on the old dining table that had been shoved in the corner. His gun was resting on his leg as his eyes stayed fixed on Abel. Butler stood by the closed door, flinching every time there was a shout outside or the letterbox rattled.

Moone looked up at Abel as he came and stood by him. He had a calm smile on his lips as if a government agent wasn't holding him at gunpoint.

'Ten minutes,' Fitzgerald said.

'It's impossible to defuse a bomb with my hands tied behind my back,' Abel said, shaking his hands.

Fitzgerald reached into the Bomb Disposal officer's kit and tossed a pair of snips to

Butler. She fumbled them with trembling hands, before hurrying over to cut Abel's ties. He rubbed his wrists and rolled his shoulders, then knelt beside Moone.

'Nine minutes,' Abel said, staring at him.

'Please, hurry up,' Moone said, his arm burning.

'Hang on,' Butler said. 'How do we know he's not going to set it off?'

'Because, my dear Butler,' Fitzgerald said with a smirk. 'He doesn't want to be blown to pieces.'

'But he thinks this isn't real,' she said, pointing a finger at Abel. 'He thinks this is all make-believe. How can we bloody well trust him?'

'He knows this is all real,' Fitzgerald said. 'He doesn't believe that rubbish. It's just an excuse to kill, to wreak havoc. Go on, hurry up. Seven minutes.'

Abel dragged the tool bag toward him and whistled as he rummaged through it. He pulled out a pair of pliers and a screwdriver, then glanced at Moone.

'Why don't you call me by my name?' Abel asked as he started to work. He flicked his eyes up at Moone. 'He knows who I am.'

'I don't know who you are,' Fitzgerald said. 'I know what you are. A psychopath. A narcissist. Just another lunatic who wants to be remembered and revered. But you won't be.'

Abel laughed. 'Don't be so sure.'

'What does that mean?' Butler asked.

Moone looked up at her, saw how pale she looked as she wrapped her arms around herself. He caught her eye but she looked away.

'It means he's got something big and juicy planned,' Fitzgerald said, shaking his head. 'You will tell us exactly where those bombs are. We might have to take you apart, bit by bit, but you'll talk.'

'It'll be too late,' Abel reached deep into the cabinet. A quiet click sounded. He turned to Moone, smiling. 'Now, you can let go.'

Moone looked at his trembling arm, then into the cabinet and back at Abel, too terrified to move.

'It's all right, Peter,' he said, staring at him. 'That night, all those years ago, you saved me. I'm returning the favour. Go on, let go.'

Moone closed his eyes and pulled his numb hand away. Nothing. His breath shuddered out of him as he staggered to his feet, his legs weak beneath him. Butler caught his arm, steadying him and helped him towards the door.

'I'd leave if I was you,' Abel said. 'This will go off in four minutes.'

Fitzgerald stood up. 'Disable it.'

Abel looked around at him. 'Why? None of this is real. This goes off and then all the others I've planted and the simulation ends.'

'If you believe this is all fake,' Butler said, 'then why tell us to get out?'

Fitzgerald rushed over, aiming the gun at Abel's head. 'She's got you there. She's seen right through you.'

Abel shrugged. 'You still believe it's real. I'm just going along with your mindset.'

The MI5 agent pressed the muzzle against his skull. 'Disable the bomb. Now.'

'Let's go, Moone,' Butler said as a thud, then a hard pounding came from the front door.

But Moone was watching Abel as he slowly got to his feet and turned to face Fitzgerald with a calm smile on his face.

'No,' he said.

'We've got to go.' Butler grabbed Moone's arm and tried to drag him out of the room. But Moone wasn't moving. He watched as Abel stepped closer to Fitzgerald.

'You want to play chicken?' Fitzgerald said. 'Two minutes.'

Moone stepped towards the cabinet and stared into it. The timer had stopped.

'He's disabled it,' Moone said.

Fitzgerald's eyes jumped to him. 'What?'

Abel lunged and caught Fitzgerald's wrist, wrenched the gun away, and slammed his forearm into the agent's face. Blood sprayed as Fitzgerald staggered back. In the next heartbeat, Abel raised the gun and pointed it at the dazed agent. Two gunshots reverberated through the house. Moone shuddered.

Abel lowered the gun as the MI5 agent slumped to the ground. He then turned and stared at Moone, his eyes burning into him.

'Don't do this,' Moone said.

'He won't listen,' Butler said. 'He's enjoying this. We'll find you!'

A crash echoed from the hallway as the front door splintered open and shouts filled the house.

Abel grabbed a chair and swung it into the back window, shattering the glass. He cleared the frame, glanced at Moone one last time, then climbed through and vanished into the darkness.

Armed officers flooded the room, MP5s raised, shouting for Moone and Butler to get on the ground as gunshots rang out outside.

Twenty minutes later, Moone and Butler were sitting inside the Counter-Terrorism mobile command unit, which he realised was just a long police van filled with desks and a few computer screens screwed to the walls. A couple of paramedics looked them over, waving torches in their eyes and asking them some basic questions before they hurried out.

Then the door hissed open and Major Lacroix appeared, the rumble of helicopters blustering in with him. He shut the door, came up the steps and stood, arms folded, in front of them both. It was impossible to know what he was thinking beyond those cold, grey eyes, Moone decided. He was also too exhausted to even care.

'So, Fitzgerald is dead,' he said, looking between them.

'Well, Abel shot him twice,' Butler said. 'So, I'm thinking yes, probably.'

Lacroix stared at her briefly with the same unreadable look, then turned to Moone. 'How are you feeling?'

Moone felt like he could easily vomit all night long. 'I'm fine. Arm's killing me, but I'll live.'

'I don't go in for it myself, but there are people you can talk to. You've been through a traumatic experience tonight. But you handled yourself well.'

'High praise,' Butler huffed.

Lacroix turned his eyes on her. 'Whose idea was it to bring Abel here?'

'Well, it wasn't bleeding mine,' she said, then she looked up at him, unwavering. 'But I went along with it. I'm guessing I'm in the shit?'

He stared back at her. 'I get it. You wanted to save Moone, but you could've been blown up with him.'

'I wasn't really thinking about that. Anyway, if you're going to fire me, or drag me across hot coals or whatever, tell me the time and place, and I'll bring along my union rep.'

He nodded. 'I'm not your boss. That's down to your Chief Super.'

'Great. I'll clean my drawers out now,' she said. 'And don't get excited, I meant my desk, not my knickers.'

Moone held in his laugh. It felt good to hear her joke. She flashed him a smile before staring up at Lacroix with her eyebrows raised. 'So?'

'Listen to me, both of you,' Lacroix said, lowering his voice. 'Fitzgerald was out of control. He forced you at gunpoint to get Abel. You had no choice. Understand?'

Butler sat back, looking surprised. 'OK.'

Lacroix nodded.

'Sir,' Moone said. 'I heard shots fired. Is Abel dead?'

'No. He wounded a couple of our people and managed to get away. Helicopters are sweeping the streets trying to find him.'

'He could be miles away by now,' Butler said.

'No.' Moone looked at her. 'No, he's not done yet. He's got bombs planted somewhere.'

'Did he say anything to you?' Lacroix asked him. 'I know you talked to him in his cell. Anything helpful?'

Moone raised his shoulders and let out a harsh breath. 'Not really. But I should probably tell you I sort of know him.'

For a brief moment, the Major's eyes seemed to show a glint of human reaction, a flicker of surprise. 'How do you know him and why the hell didn't you tell us before?'

'I didn't know, not until I talked to him in his cell. It was years ago when we were both kids. We were staying at the Drake Inn Hotel. He claims a man called Rodney Fox tried to molest him. Apparently, I appeared out of nowhere and that gave him the chance to push him down the stairs.'

'So Rodney Fox is dead?'

'I think so. Officially, Rodney Fox disappeared. He was meant to stay at the Drake Inn, but the owners said he never turned up. I think they helped cover it up because they had something else criminal going on at that hotel.'

Lacroix nodded. 'So his story sounds like it could be true. The connection you two share might be useful later on.'

'Connection?' Butler huffed out a laugh. 'He tried to blow him up.'

'But he didn't, did he?' Lacroix said. 'Fitzgerald's gamble paid off.'

'Not for him it didn't.' Butler stood up. 'Can we go home now?'

'Yes, you can. Get some sleep. There'll be statements to write up tomorrow, and you two need to get your stories to match up.'

'Fantastic,' Butler said, opened the door

and left the van.

Moone got up, his whole body feeling strange while his head was spinning slowly.

'What happened to you tonight won't be easy to get over, it'll take time.'

Moone, standing quite close to the Major, saw the faint scars on his jaw and neck. He wanted to ask him about them and how he had dealt with it all, but he could see the steel bars drawn down over his eyes, so he said, 'Thanks.'

Then as he started down the steps, he turned and said, 'Do you know who he really is?'

Lacroix nodded. 'Intelligence came through a day or so ago, but Fitzgerald kept it to himself, because his bosses didn't want the embarrassment. Joe Harper. He was a corporal in the British army. Saw a lot of rough stuff, and fought in wars that none of us will ever know the truth about. His mind must have broken along the way. He tried to make sense of all the horror he'd seen by inventing a pretend world.'

Moone nodded. 'Have you got any leads on his whereabouts?'

'None at all.'

'And all the areas on the map he left have been searched?'

Lacroix nodded. 'They have, but they'll be searched again. Go home and rest and try not to think about all this. We'll find Harper.'

Moone forced a smile as he stepped onto

the street again, the blue and red lights flashing into his eyes. Butler was waiting, leaning against the house opposite.

'That was a close call,' she said when he reached her.

'Tell me about it.' He rolled his eyes. 'He's called Joe Harper. Former soldier.'

'Well, we guessed that already.'

'Thanks, by the way.'

'For what? I didn't do anything.'

'You and Fitzgerald brought him here and got him to stop the bomb. I was nearly a goner.'

'It was nothing. But I don't think he was going to let you get blown up. You've got this connection. I think his plan was always to stop it before it went off.'

'Why?'

'So he had a chance to escape. If Fitzgerald hadn't dragged him there, Abel would have got one of the custody sergeants to contact us. I bet my life on it. The more I think about it, the more I'm convinced this was all set up so he could get away. Which he did.'

Moone shrugged and looked at his shaky hands.

'Have a fag, it might calm you down.'

'What?' He stared at her. 'Are you encouraging me to smoke? What have you done with Mandy Butler?'

She laughed. 'I don't know. I guess you look at things differently when you almost get blown to pieces.'

He took out a cigarette and poked it between his dry lips. He recalled Butler almost saying something, a strange look in her eyes as he'd been stuck holding a bomb. 'What were you going to say before?'

'When?'

'Back in the house. You were going to tell me something.'

'Oh, right.' She looked away, blinking. He thought he saw tears in her eyes.

'You all right?' he asked.

'Yeah, tough as old boots, me.' She turned to him, her eyes looking a little wet. 'Let's just go to mine and we can match up our stories. You can sleep on my sofa.'

'That would be good. Thanks.'

She laughed. 'Don't thank me yet, Moone. It's a bloody uncomfortable sofa.'

Butler hadn't been wrong about it being an uncomfortable sofa. He'd spent most of the night tossing and turning. It had been getting close to dawn before he knew it, the deep blue of it starting to edge up over the buildings of Mutley. He kept staring towards Butler's room, his heart thumping out a beat. Whichever way he turned, he could hear his pulse beating in his ear. He had this longing to get up and knock on her door, but he just didn't have a clue what he would say. She was with Chris. He turned over and tried to close his eyes, but the seagulls started to complain loudly about something outside. Every time he almost fell asleep, he'd have a flash of the room, the bomb still sitting in front of him, the counter counting down.

He sighed, then sat up and rubbed his eyes. It was no good, so he went to the kitchen, made himself a cup of coffee, returned to the living room and stared out the window. How the hell were they going to find Abel? He had a name, he reminded himself. Joe Harper. An ordinary sounding name, for a man who seemed anything but. Fitzgerald had tried to hide his past because undoubtedly he'd been ordered to by someone high above him. They didn't want the embarrassment of one of their own going rogue and killing innocent people. He buried his face in his hands, enclosing himself in darkness as he tried to find an iota of a clue that might lead him to where Harper was.

'Dad?'

Moone looked around and saw Alice. She was wearing pink pyjamas, her hair tangled, blinking at him.

'Morning,' he said, putting on a smile that ached his jaw.

'What're you doing here?' She sat down on the armchair.

'We had a late one,' he said.

'Oh right,' Alice said, then picked up the

remote control and turned on the TV.

'Good morning,' the newsreader said. 'We begin with breaking news from Plymouth, where police and Counter-Terrorism officers surrounded a house in the Stonehouse area of the city late last night. Residents reported seeing several armed officers approach the house at approximately 11:45 p.m., followed by a significant emergency response. Armed officers, Bomb Disposal units, and forensic teams were seen at the scene well into the early hours.

'Authorities have not yet confirmed the nature of the incident, but initial reports suggest an explosive device may have been discovered inside the property. Devon and Cornwall Police have described the situation as "contained" but have yet to provide further details on whether there are any casualties or arrests.

'Counter-Terrorism officers are now thought to be leading the investigation, though officials remain tight-lipped about any potential links to wider threats. Residents have been advised to remain vigilant, but authorities insist there is no immediate danger to the public.

'We will bring you more updates as soon as we have them.'

Moone turned off the TV. Alice was staring at him, shaking her head slightly.

'Don't tell me that was you, Dad?'

'Of course not.' He smiled. 'Where's your Aunt Kelly?'

'At your place, tidying up. She says you're a messy so and so.'

'What a night we had!' Butler said, appearing from her room, wrapped in a pale-blue robe. 'Don't look at me, Moone, I haven't got my slap on,' she said before disappearing into the bathroom.

He looked away, still sensing Alice's disapproval.

'Mandy!' Alice called as she got up. 'Did you have to dispose of a bomb last night?'

Butler's head popped out of the bathroom. 'Not dispose of it. But yeah, there was a bomb…'

She stopped talking as her eyes caught Moone's look.

'But there was no danger to us,' she said, disappearing again. Her voice echoed out of the bathroom, 'The Bomb Disposal team handled all that. We sat and had a cup of tea. Didn't we, Moone?'

He sighed when he saw Alice staring at him. 'It's fine. We're OK.'

'For now you are. Bloody hell. Please stay out of trouble, Dad!'

'I'll try.' He sipped his coffee. 'I'll be happy

when we find him.'

'Well, I won't be.' She stormed off into the kitchen and started making noise with cups and plates, while he stayed where he was, watching the sky getting lighter, trying to figure out what to do next. Then he told himself he should leave it well enough alone and let the Counter-Terrorism group get on with it.

Within the hour, after getting their stories straight about Fitzgerald, Moone and Butler had driven to the station, both of them bleary-eyed and seemingly wrapped in their own thoughts. They parked up, and Moone sat there looking up at the old station, his mind flashing with images of the night before and pretty much all the events of the past few days. He looked at his hands. They were shaking but only a little.

'You all right?' Butler asked. 'No one would blame you if you took some time off.'

'I can't,' he said, feeling a deep craving for a cigarette. Then he looked at her, seeing the worry that had been etched into her eyes the night before. 'What about you? You were in that room too. Do you want any time off?'

'Yeah, right. I want to find this psycho. That's what I want.'

'Me too.'

'Good. But how're we going to find him?

He could be anywhere.'

'He's probably got bombs planted all round the city, waiting to go off.'

'But where?' Butler sat back, letting out a deep, unhappy breath. 'They've checked all the targets on the map, the dockyards, the barracks, anywhere that he might want to blow up.'

Moone pushed open his door and climbed out, feeling like an old man. He reached for his cigarettes, then thought better of it; he just needed to get inside and see what was what. Butler had already climbed out and was heading inside.

He followed her up the stairs and to the incident room, where there was a sudden eruption of clapping and cheers.

They both stopped by the whiteboard as Lacroix, Molly, Jones and a few of the Counter-Terrorism officers applauded them.

'What the hell's all this about?' Butler demanded.

Lacroix stepped forward, his face a steel trap as always. 'You did manage to stop Stonehouse from being blown up. So, that probably warrants some applause. Don't let it go to your heads though. We've got a lot of work to do.'

'Like what?' Butler asked. 'We've got no bloody idea where he is.'

'That's what we need to figure out,'

Lacroix said. 'I've got your lot checking CCTV last night around the area to see if they can pick him up.'

'So, trailing through CCTV footage again?' she sighed and headed to her desk.

Moone was left facing Lacroix, his mind running through it all and ending up with an image of Fitzgerald in his head. 'What happens about Fitzgerald?'

'They'll be an enquiry,' he said. 'There always is. The thing is, someone high up obviously sent him here to make sure none of Joe Harper's past caught up with them. So any enquiry won't come to much. They'll just cover it up.'

'What about his body?'

'Your pathologist, Dr Jenkins has him while we wait for someone to pick him up. It's a sorry state of affairs.'

Moone nodded. 'I just wish I knew where to look for him.'

'All we can do is try and pick up the trail.'

'None of the helicopters saw where he went?'

'No, but he's a pro. He knows how to evade capture.'

'Great.' Moone headed over to his desk, feeling empty and shaky again. He looked up at the map of Plymouth, trying to somehow spot a pattern that had eluded the collective clever minds of the Counter-Terrorism unit. He sat back, empty. All he could think to do, was rewind to the beginning, look at it all again to see if he could spot anything significant.

He sighed and started going through their first statements and crime scene reports. There were the images of Ryan Preston, the plumber who Abel had killed to get hold of his guns. He was lying in the van, several stab wounds to his body. He sighed, looking through the other images of the van. He kept staring at each one, running his eyes over the images in case something had escaped him. It was like playing Spot the Difference.

Nothing. He put them down and buried his face in his hands. Think, Moone, think, he told himself, then got up. He needed a coffee. He was about to ask Butler if she wanted one when his phone started ringing in his pocket. He prayed it wasn't more bad news.

'DCI Moone,' he answered as he stepped out into the corridor.

'My favourite person,' Dr Jenkins said. 'Also the person who hasn't called me since we nearly got blown up on the Hoe.'

'Oh God, I'm sorry. We've had a lot going on here...' He cringed.

'It's OK,' she said with a laugh. 'I figured you had seeing as I've got a dead male on my table who used to be an MI5 agent by all accounts.'

'Fitzgerald. He was shot right in front of

me last night.'

'Oh my God, Pete. Are you OK?'

'Of course. A nervous wreck, but I'll survive.' He laughed, but even he heard the strain in it.

'What're you doing right now?'

'Trying to find some kind of lead that might help me find where Abel is.'

'You need a doctor too, to check you over. No excuses, Peter Moone, meet me in the cafe in Derriford. Half an hour. That's an order.'

He sighed. 'OK. I'll see you then. I'll be the man smoking ten cigarettes.'

She laughed. 'See you soon.'

He put away his phone and turned to tell Butler where he was going to go. He flinched when he saw her already standing in the doorway, eyebrows raised.

'Where're you off to?' she asked.

He hesitated. 'I'm off to see the pathologist. Fitzgerald is on the table. You can tag along if you want?'

'And get between you and Shirley Bassey? No thanks.'

'Shirley Bassey?'

'She was the only Welsh person I could think of. It was either her or Tom Jones. Anyway, go and have a nice time. I'll hold the fort. Go on.'

He smiled, even though his stomach had already reached the bottom floor. He turned and headed down the stairs.

Moone pulled into the hospital car park, his window cracked open to let in the warm morning air. The sky was a cloudless blue, the heat of the day building. He killed the engine and sat there for a moment, rolling his shoulders, trying to ease the tension that had settled somewhere at the centre of his back. His mind wouldn't stop circling the case, especially the whereabouts of Abel. Joe Harper. Whoever the hell he was.

Where the bloody hell was he?

Moone sighed, running a hand over his face before grabbing his jacket. As he stepped out of the car, a wave of warm air rose from the ground, carrying the scent of cut grass and exhaust fumes from the buses that rumbled by the rank of bus stops. The bulk of the hospital lay ahead, its entrance surrounded by the usual crowd of visitors, patients and hospital staff. He walked towards it and headed through the automatic doors into the only slightly cooler main concourse.

As he made his way toward Warren's cafe, moving out of the way of two porters pushing a bed, his thoughts shifted to Butler. That moment in the house, where they nearly got blown to smithereens. She'd almost said something. He could see it now, the way she hesitated, the flicker of doubt in her eyes. But then she had swallowed it down, and whatever it was remained locked up with all the other stuff she never talked about.

What had she been about to tell him?

He walked through the seating area of Warren's, the smell of fresh pasties and strong coffee hitting him immediately, mingling with the chatter of staff and customers. A few tables were occupied, one by a pair of doctors deep in conversation, another by a paramedic scrolling through their phone, an elderly couple picking at a slice of cake.

His focus was still on Butler, on Abel, on the tangled mess of the case. Abel wasn't the type to just disappear. No. He was out there somewhere. Waiting. Planning.

Moone had the awful feeling they were running out of time.

'Hey!'

He looked around and saw Dr Jenkins, in green scrubs, her hair tied back, and her phone on the table in front of her.

'Hi,' he said, putting on a smile, even though he had been so distracted he'd almost forgotten he was meeting her. 'Do you want a coffee?' he asked.

'Please. Three sugars.' She smiled.

'Three?'

She shrugged. 'I'm not sweet enough, I guess.'

'I disagree.' He walked to the long queue,

half congratulating himself on his quick reply. He soon grabbed a couple of coffees, then put one in front of Jenkins and sat down. He sipped his black Americano and smiled at her, digging around for conversation that wasn't work-related.

'You can ask me about Fitzgerald,' she said, picking up her drink.

'Oh, OK.' He leaned forward. 'I don't suppose I have to ask about the cause of death?'

'Gunshot wounds,' she said and sipped her coffee. 'Both entrance wounds were located in the centre of the deceased's chest between the sternum and the left nipple. Very good shooting.'

'The killer's ex-army.'

She nodded. 'Makes sense. And Fitzgerald was MI5. I'm surprised there hasn't been more fuss.'

'I don't think they want the fuss. They knew who he was, or at least suspected.'

'Those spooks and their little games.'

'Their games have cost lives,' Moone said, the acid bubbling away inside him. 'But they won't be held accountable.'

She sighed. 'Have you got any idea where he might strike next?'

'No. Our team and the Counter-Terrorism lot have covered most of Plymouth, searching anywhere that might be an appropriate target for a terrorist, but so far nothing.'

'So what's his aim?'

'Well, he told me he believes we're in a matrix type simulation and he thinks that if he causes enough death and destruction, it'll somehow crack the program open or something. But I'm wondering if all this wasn't about that at all.'

She leaned towards him, resting her head on her hands as she stared at him. 'Then what is it about, Peter Moone?'

He shrugged. 'Death. Chaos. Maybe getting back at his old paymasters. I really don't know.'

Moone looked around and saw the elderly couple shuffling past. The old lady suddenly looked at them both and smiled.

'Don't you two make a lovely couple?' she said.

'What's that?' her husband said, cupping his ear.

'I said they make a lovely couple.'

Moone felt his face burn as the old couple ambled off, leaving him to look into the smiling eyes of Jenkins.

'At least we have the approval of Enid and Fred,' she said.

'Or George and Mable?'

Jenkins crooked her finger. 'Come here.'

He smiled and leaned closer. She kissed him gently on the lips, then sat back.

'I quite like you, Peter Moone.'

'I like you too.'

Then she sat up, her eyes widening. 'I almost forgot...'

He watched as she reached beside her and brought up an evidence bag and handed it to him. Moone took it and let out a sharp breath when he saw a photograph was inside it. He held it up and saw it was an old and battered photo of a building. Two heads had been cut off as if the image had been enlarged. Then he noticed pin holes in each corner, lots of them. The penny dropped and smacked him on the top of his skull. 'Bloody hell. This is it. This is the photo.'

'What photo?'

He looked at Jenkins. 'When we found where Harper, or Abel, our killer, had been staying, he had this notice board on the wall of the garage. There was a collection of pinholes in one area, the size of a photograph. This is the photo, I'm sure of it.'

Jenkins leaned in. 'So what's the significance?'

'This is the Drake Inn Hotel. It's a long story, but we both stayed there when we were kids. This photo must mean something to him. But what?'

'It's just the front of the hotel, isn't it? I can see the sign.'

Moone nodded, staring at it, trying to see why Harper would be so obsessed with that image. He sat back. 'I thought if we found this photo, it might give us a clue to... well, something. But it's just a photo.'

'It must mean...'

They both looked around when they heard sirens blaring. A couple of ambulances roared past. Then came the rumble of a helicopter overhead.

'Looks like something's occurred,' Jenkins said.

Moone looked around, noticing people staring at their phones, looking a little shocked.

'Excuse me,' he said, waving at a couple of teenagers close by. 'Do you know what's happened?'

A young lad shrugged. 'Some fire or something.'

'Nah, there's been an explosion,' an older man said, a couple of tables away.

Jenkins was already looking at her phone. 'Oh God. He's right. There's been an explosion near the Hoe. Says it's a hotel.'

'A hotel? Where?'

She looked up. 'I don't know. Near Citadel Road, I think. Is this him? Your killer?'

Moone got up. 'I think so.'

CHAPTER 24

Moone pulled up at the edge of the cordon, the smoke still hanging in the air. The acrid stench of burning plaster, plastic, and something worse clawed at the back of his throat as he climbed out of the car.

Ahead of him, blue lights flickered against the facades of the surrounding evacuated houses. The firefighters moved in coordinated urgency, shouting to each other. Paramedics worked away inside their ambulances, treating the survivors, while a horde of displaced residents stood behind the cordon, some wrapped in hastily grabbed coats, others still in dressing gowns, staring at the ruin of their street.

At the centre of it all, was the Leigham Hotel, or what was left of it. The ground floor was blackened, its windows blown out, jagged remnants of glass catching the sunlight through the cloud of smoke that curled from the gaping wound where the explosion had ripped through. The place was dead silent, apart from the occasional sound of debris crumbling to the ground.

Moone let out a slow breath. A bomb. Right here, where the Drake Inn used to stand. Harper had wanted to make a statement.

A figure in tactical gear moved towards him, an MP5 submachine gun cradled in his arms, pointed downwards, his visor reflecting the chaos. 'Sir, you can't be here…'

Moone barely glanced at him as he took out his warrant card and showed it to him. 'DCI Peter Moone. How bad is it?'

His own voice sounded strange and detached.

The officer pushed his visor up, then shrugged. 'Five confirmed dead. Two critical, just been pulled out. They're still looking for more.' His tone was flat, professional, but Moone thought he caught a look in his eye, a kind of haunted expression.

'It's bad,' the officer said, then walked back towards the cordon.

Moone let out a harsh breath as he fumbled for his cigarettes, fingers unsteady as he lit one. The first drag burned its way down to his lungs. That's all he needed, to breathe in more smoke, but he didn't care any more.

Behind him, he heard another car pull up. Butler was first out, storming over. She stood beside him, arms folded, looking at the scene. DI Jones followed, slower, her injured leg forcing her to lean on a crutch. She took in the destruction and said, 'Christ on a bike.'

Moone nodded, eyes still on the wreckage, lifting his cigarette to his lips. 'That used to be the Drake Inn.' Moone pointed his fag at the ruins. 'Five dead. Two injured.'

Butler stared at him. 'Jesus Christ. Is this because of…'

He nodded, then took out the evidence bag with the photo inside and handed it to Butler.

'What's this?'

'Remember we thought there was a photo that had been pinned to the board he used in that house in Sherford?'

'Yeah, and this is it?' Butler held it up. 'It's just a photo of the hotel. Two heads have been cut off. So, this bomb is because of what happened that night or something?'

Moone took another drag. 'I think so. I don't know. Why blow it up otherwise? Destroying it serves no other purpose, does it?'

'Search me,' Butler said and handed back the photo. 'I haven't got a bloody clue what's going on in his sick brain. And don't start blaming yourself, Moone. Just because you two met all those years ago, this has got nothing to do with all that.'

'What if it has?' He looked at her.

'What do you mean?'

'He told me that Fox came to his room and was going to take him off for... God only knows. What if it wasn't the first time?'

'You think he was abused?' Jones asked, hobbling closer. 'That would make sense. Now he's acting out, causing mayhem.'

Butler huffed. 'If he was abused, that's horrible, but it's no excuse for all this death.'

Moone took another drag. 'Imagine inventing a fake world just to help you cushion yourself from reality.'

'What do we do now?' Jones asked. 'He could be planning to blow up anywhere.'

Moone dropped his cigarette and stepped on it, realising he had no idea where to start, except the beginning. 'I'm going to retrace our steps.'

'All right,' Butler said. 'We started with the murder of the plumber. So what do we do? Who do we talk to?'

Moone sighed. 'I don't know. I honestly don't know. It's either that or the house where he was staying in Sherford, but they've been over that. Maybe we missed something somewhere.'

Butler huffed again. 'I don't think we've missed something because there's nothing to miss. He's left us nothing to go on.'

'There must be something,' Jones said. 'He can't move around or do all this without leaving something behind. It's impossible.'

'She's right,' Butler said. 'While Counter-Terrorism is examining bomb fragments and crunching numbers, whatever they bleeding do, let's get back to basics.'

'Which is?' Moone asked.

Butler hesitated before she said, 'Let's talk to Ryan Preston's ex, and ask her if there's any other properties he used. For all we know, Harper could be using the place where he stored his plumbing gear.'

Moone nodded. 'That's a good idea. Come on then, let's go.'

'What about me?' Jones said, watching them head to Moone's car.

'Come on, then, Hop-a-long,' Butler said. 'I'll drop you on the way. But no bloody Celine Dion.'

The courtroom was silent, save for the distant hum of traffic beyond the high windows. To DS Molly Chambers, the air seemed thick with everything that had come before, the testimony, the evidence, the cross-examinations. The jurors were sitting upright in their seats, all watching as Simon Bray KC rose from the bench, buttoning his suit jacket with slow, deliberate movements.

He turned to face them, his voice calm but firm.

'Ladies and gentlemen of the jury,' he said, 'this case is, at its heart, about betrayal, about obsession, and ultimately... about murder.'

He let the words hang in the air for a moment, his eyes scanning the room, before pacing the courtroom a little. 'Detective Inspector Maxine Rivers is missing, presumed dead. Presumed murdered. We say that the woman responsible is sitting right there.' He turned slightly, gesturing towards the dock, where Faith Carthew was sitting, a solemn look on her face, a tinge of worry. She was putting on a good act, Chambers thought.

'She is Maxine Rivers' former lover, her former colleague, and she was a woman consumed by resentment and jealousy,' Bray said. 'Why had she come to resent her? Because the accused had spent the last few years trying to climb the ladder of promotion. She had, after a long time, made it to the rank of detective sergeant, whereas her lover, Maxine Rivers had made it to detective inspector after successfully solving a particularly difficult murder investigation. An investigation, I might add, that at one time, the defendant was involved in.'

Bray moved towards the jury, hands clasped lightly in front of him.

'You have heard the evidence. Maxine

Rivers' blood and DNA were found at the flat close to Mutley. The same flat where a witness saw the defendant.' He glanced at the jury, eyes scanning their faces, weighing their reactions. 'And Maxine Rivers' mobile phone was last used in Plymouth before being found in the possession of none other than Faith Carthew, hidden in her car. What does that tell you?'

He let the question settle before continuing. 'The defence will try to argue that Rivers' mobile phone could have ended up in the accused car by accident.' He gave a small, knowing shake of his head. 'An accident? You must ask yourselves how likely that is. Because the reality is, ladies and gentlemen, that Maxine Rivers did not simply vanish. She did not walk away from her life, her career, or her family. She was taken. And the evidence, the clear, undeniable evidence, points to the defendant. The last person known to have seen Maxine Rivers alive. There can be only one outcome. Faith Carthew must be found guilty of murder.'

Bray turned back towards the judge, nodded once, and then returned to his seat.

There was a beat of silence, then Hanna Martin KC, lead counsel for the defence, stood up. As always, Chambers noticed there was a sharpness in her expression, a confidence that cut through the courtroom like a knife.

'Members of the jury,' she began, moving

to stand before them. 'Let's talk about what the prosecution doesn't have.'

She held up one finger as she looked them all over. 'No body. No murder weapon. No forensic evidence that proves beyond doubt that Maxine Rivers is even dead, let alone that my client was responsible.'

She took a step forward. 'The prosecution is asking you to assume guilt. To take a little circumstantial evidence and treat it all as undeniable proof. But let's examine that proof, shall we?'

She began to pace slightly, gesturing as she spoke.

'The blood evidence. The prosecution makes much of it, but let's be clear, this is not a crime scene soaked in Rivers' DNA, only small amounts of it. We have no proof of a struggle, no overwhelming forensic evidence that she was even harmed in that flat. So ask yourselves, is this truly the kind of evidence you would send someone to prison for the rest of their life over?'

Martin left the question in the air for a moment. 'And then, crucially, we have the matter of how my client was arrested in the first place.' Her voice sharpened. Chambers cringed, her heart thumping as the barrister continued.

'The police had no reasonable grounds to arrest Faith Carthew when they did. The search of her car, where, incidentally, no real damning evidence was found, was conducted without proper cause. Reasonable suspicion is required in such circumstances, it says so in PACE, the police handbook, and as you have heard from the arresting officer himself, DCI Peter Moone, he had none.'

She paused, then turned towards the jury, her expression firm.

'Then why did he get a warrant for her arrest and search of her property? Because DCI Moone, the officer in charge, was biased. He had already made up his mind about Faith Carthew's guilt. His own prejudices led him to build a case against her. When he heard that Maxine Rivers was missing, rather than investigate fairly, he built a case around the one person he knew had been in a relationship with the deceased. This was very lazy police work.'

Martin KC let the statement linger, then took a final step back.

'This case is full of assumptions, errors, and gaps. And if you have even the smallest doubt, then you know what you must do.' She glanced towards Carthew then back to the jury. 'You must find the defendant not guilty.'

She returned to her seat.

The judge adjusted his glasses, preparing to deliver his final directions. The courtroom remained still, thick with tension. Chambers let out a breath. Now, it was in the jury's hands.

They returned to the box-like newbuild house in Swilly in time to see Danni James with Daisy, her daughter, in one hand and a couple of bags of shopping in the other. Moone climbed out as he saw her struggling with the shopping, the young girl and her door keys. He hurried over and said, 'Hi, can I help?'

Her head spun around to him, her face tight with apprehension. 'Who are you?'

He took out his ID as Butler appeared at his side. 'DCI Peter Moone. This is DI Mandy Butler. We came and talked to you a while back. Seems like ages ago now. Anyway, we talked to you about Ryan.'

'Daddy's gone to heaven,' the little girl said, her face full of sadness. Moone felt his heart being squeezed and wrung out.

'That's right, Daisy,' her mum said, smiling down at the girl before looking at Moone and then Butler. 'You'd better come in.'

Moone took her bags and followed them into the house. The girl's toys littered the hallway, and most of the house. Moone took the bags into the kitchen and put them on the side, while he watched Butler put the kettle on. They could hear Danni James talking to the girl, telling her to do some drawing or play with her toys.

Then the young woman came into the kitchen and stood in the door for a moment looking wary before she went to the bags and started putting away some frozen food.

'What did you want, then?' she said, her voice sharp.

Moone put his hands behind his back. 'I'm sure you've heard about all the shootings and bombs going off.'

She turned and stared at him. 'Yeah, of course. What's that got to do with me? Is this about Ryan?'

'Sort of. The man who murdered Ryan, took some weapons he was planning to sell. Now that man is shooting innocent people and planting bombs.'

She folded her arms, looking upset. 'So you're saying this is all Ryan's fault?'

'No, we're not,' Butler said, setting out some mugs. 'What my colleague is trying to say, is that we need to know if Ryan had anywhere he stored his plumbing supplies or if he owned or rented any other properties.'

Danni rested her back against the work surface and relaxed her arms. 'Not really. Only his flat and his shed.'

'They've been searched,' Butler said with a heavy sigh. 'So, we're still nowhere.'

'I'm sorry,' Danni said with a shrug. 'I can't think of anywhere else. Sometimes... it sounds awful, but I wished I'd never met him. I don't regret having Daisy, don't get me wrong...'

Butler smiled. 'I get it. Men. Right pain in

the arse. Can't live with them, can't bury them in your garden.'

Danni gave a short laugh. 'It's the plumbing business that's causing me aggro now. All I get is messages and calls complaining.'

'Complaining?' Moone asked, absently. His mind was already out the door, trying to think where Harper could be hiding.

'Yeah,' the young mum said, rolling her eyes. 'His customers keep getting hold of me to complain. I don't have nothing to do with it. Just cause he didn't do the work properly. I was surprised though. He was always so obsessed with doing a good job.'

'Maybe he was too busy selling weapons,' Butler said. 'Sorry.'

Danni sighed. 'It's fine. Weird thing is, one of them was complaining about a job he couldn't have even done.'

Moone looked up at her, his curiosity rising. 'What do you mean?'

'Well, it was a job he'd done for a woman a week ago. Well, he couldn't have done that, could he? Because he was...'

Moone looked at Butler to see if she was on the same page. She was staring at him, her eyebrows raised.

'Do you have a number for this woman?' Moone asked.

'Eh, yeah,' Danni said, throwing him a

look. 'Is it important?'

'I don't know,' Moone said, lying. He was beginning to feel deep in his gut that it was very significant. His heart had started to beat faster as the young woman went off into the house. When she came back, she was carrying a smartphone and looking at the screen.

'Ryan left this phone last time he was here,' she said. 'It's one of the numbers he used to give out. Now all I get is texts and calls from people complaining.'

Moone smiled and took the phone from her. 'Thanks. We'll check it out. No need for you to be bothered by it.'

'Do you think it's something to do with what happened to him?' The young mum looked between them, obviously desperate for some kind of answer.

'I honestly don't know,' Moone said. 'But we'll let you know if we find out anything.'

The courtroom was rigid with tension, a heavy, suffocating feeling that seemed to settle over every occupied seat. The jury had just returned, their expressions blank and unreadable as they filed back into the box. DC Molly Chambers was sitting toward the back of the public gallery, her hands clasped tightly in her lap, knuckles white. It seemed like she had been waiting her whole life for this moment, for justice to be served, for Faith Carthew to finally face the consequences of what she had done.

Carthew was standing upright in the dock, her face drawn, her blonde hair neatly tucked behind her ears. She was staring towards the jury, her hands balled at her sides.

The clerk stood up and said, 'Members of the jury, have you reached a verdict?'

The foreperson rose to her feet. It was a middle-aged woman in a grey blazer. 'Yes, we have.'

Molly sucked in her breath. It had all come down to this moment, all the worry and stress caused by her sociopathic ways. So many dead people lay in her wake. Molly gripped her knees. She can't get off, she thought.

'On the charge of murder...'

There was a long pause, long enough for Molly's stomach to clench.

'...of Maxine Rivers, we find the defendant... not guilty.'

A murmur rippled through the courtroom. Molly's heart sank. She swallowed hard, her pulse hammering.

The judge gave a warning glance to those in attendance before the foreperson continued reading:

'On the charge of conspiracy to murder Lloyd Redrobe, we find the defendant... not guilty.'

Molly exhaled sharply, the disbelief punching her in her chest.

Faith Carthew remained still, seeming to absorb the words, then she turned slightly. Her gaze found Molly's across the courtroom. There it was, that flicker of triumph. A subtle shift in her expression, the slightest tightening at the corners of her mouth, the way her chin lifted ever so slightly. A silent celebration of victory.

Molly felt the heat of anger rise into her chest, while her stomach tied itself in several tight knots. Faith Carthew had got away with murder. She would walk free.

The judge gave his final instructions, the formality of dismissal ringing hollow in Molly's ears. As Carthew was standing there, moving her shoulders and stretching as if she was shrugging off the weight of the last few months, she gave a final glance in Molly's direction. It was not quite a smile, but the message was clear.

You all lost. I won.

'No, there's not a problem, Mrs Marshall,' Butler said as they were sitting in their car outside Danni James' house. 'There's just been... a few reports...' Butler stared at Moone with desperation in her eyes.

Moone mouthed, 'Burglaries.'

'There's been a few burglaries,' she said. 'Can we just pop by? Is that all right, Mrs Marshall? Yes, that's right. Where're you to? Right, OK, we'll be there soon.'

She hung up and stared at Moone. 'He came to look in her loft. She thought there was a pipe leaking or something. She's in Ford. Let's go.'

Butler started the engine and took them out of North Prospect and onto Wolsley Road, where she turned off near Lidl. They ended up in Melville Road, where Butler pulled up in front of a beige, semi-detached house that had a garage and driveway, both sitting beyond a wide, metal garden gate. They both climbed out, and Moone stepped up to the gate, staring up at the average, Plymouth house. Nothing seemed out of the ordinary, but his stomach had already buried itself in his shoes while his heart began to pound. He felt the ache in his shoulder.

He was in King's house, the filing cabinet open in front of him, the timer counting down.

'Are we going in?' Butler asked.

He nodded, opened the gate and headed up the paved path to the house. Before he could ring the bell, the front door opened and a middle-aged woman with frizzy-blonde hair, dressed in a dark pink jumper and long denim skirt, stood looking out at him.

He showed his warrant card and forced a smile to his lips. 'DCI Peter Moone, this DI Mandy Butler. My colleague talked to you on the phone...'

'That's right,' she said, looking between

them, her eyes full of suspicion. 'So you think that plumber was here to rob me?'

'We're not sure,' Moone said, looking over her shoulder and into the house. 'Is it OK if we take a look?'

'I suppose,' she said, stepping back. 'But nothing's been taken, far as I can see. Are your shoes clean? Just had my carpet cleaned.'

Moone wiped his feet, then went in, staring towards the hallway and the stairs to his left, both covered in beige carpet. 'Where was he working? Did you say the loft?'

'That's right,' she said as he started up the stairs, looking up. He saw the loft hatch, then turned to the woman who was behind him. Butler was near the top of the stairs, her face drawn.

'How does it open?' Moone asked and the woman grabbed a long stick from another room. She poked the hatch until there was a click and it started to open, revealing a folded-up ladder. Moone pulled it down, then stood at the bottom of it. His heart was starting to race as he looked at Butler.

'Maybe we should wait?' Butler said.

Moone took a breath and climbed up slowly until he poked his head up in the stifling heat of the dark space. He could only make out grey shapes, so took out his phone and turned on the torch app. He shone the light over the room, seeing the wooden beams, the yellow insulation, pipes... He stopped and went back when he thought he saw a large square shape at the back. There was a light too, a hazy red light. A counter. There were wires too. His heart pounded as he put his torch away, then hurried back down the ladder. The woman wasn't there.

'Where is she?' Moone asked, the panic beating in his chest.

'Gone to make a cup of tea,' Butler said. 'Why? What've you found?'

He opened his mouth, but nothing came out for a moment. 'A bomb. A really big bomb.'

CHAPTER 25

The back passenger door of their car opened and Major Lacroix climbed in. Moone looked at him in the rear-view mirror, noticing he didn't look quite as unaffected as he usually did. They were parked down a street, a little way from the house with the bomb. The owner had been taken to a relative's house.

'Where're Bomb Disposal?' Butler asked.

'Parked up a couple of streets away,' the Major said, his voice strained. 'The problem is getting our people and their equipment in there without making a fuss. We don't want to alert him in case he's watching.'

'No, we don't,' Butler said.

'Moone,' Lacroix said after a pause, leaning forward. 'You never should have gone up there. The hatch could've been booby-trapped. That was bloody irresponsible.'

Moone nodded. 'I wasn't really thinking. I'm sorry, but we need to find out how many other houses he's visited, pretending to be a plumber.'

Lacroix sat back. 'I've given the phone to the team, and they're going through the people who've tried to contact him. It might take a while, and there could be more people who haven't bothered to phone and complain.'

Butler turned in her seat to face Lacroix. 'That's why our lot are going through CCTV and ANPR to see if the bastard shows up. Looks like he cloned Ryan Preston's plumbing van. That's why we hadn't spotted Harper driving round Plymouth on camera because he was in a van with Ryan Preston's firm's name on the side. Bleeding bastard's been bloody clever.'

'But we're on to him now,' Moone said, then watched as a couple of men walked up the street, heading towards the house. They were dressed as workmen, carrying tool bags. He sighed, his chest tight, thinking about the bomb in King's house, how complex it had been. He looked at Lacroix in the rear-view mirror. 'What if they can't disarm it? They didn't manage it last time.'

Lacroix nodded. 'True. But we've got a few more bomb experts from around the country now. Better equipment too. There's not a bomb he's built that we can't disarm.'

'I hope you're right,' Butler said.

Moone was still watching the house when he saw the door open and a figure coming out. It was one of the fake workmen and he hurried to the car and stood by Lacroix's window.

'Is there a problem, Wheeler?' Lacroix asked.

The Bomb Disposal officer, a broad-shouldered man with shaved grey hair, nodded as he let out a heavy breath. His face was taut with tension.

'Yeah, there's a problem,' he said. 'A big one.'

Moone braced himself.

'Go on,' Lacroix said, sighing.

'The device was stable when we got up there. We started working on it, standard procedure, nice and slow, but something tripped the system. Could be a tamper trigger, could be faulty wiring. Either way, the countdown's started.'

Lacroix exhaled sharply. 'How long?'

'Thirty minutes.'

The words hammered into Moone's skull. Thirty minutes. A bomb. In a loft. And now it was live. His hands were trembling. His shoulder started to burn, the open filing cabinet in front of him. The timer ticking down. He could feel a cold sweat breaking out over his back.

'How much explosives are we looking at?'

Lacroix asked.

The bomb tech hesitated for a second. That was never a good sign, Moone had learned.

'Enough to take out a good few houses in this street, and the gas mains along with it.'

Moone glanced up at the house, then at the rows of houses flanking it. Families. Kids. The elderly couple he'd seen earlier peering through their lace curtains as he and Butler drove into the street. 'We need to start evacuating. Now.'

Lacroix climbed out, pulling a phone from his pocket. 'We've got transport ready. I'm calling it in. Let's just pray he doesn't get wind of this operation and start setting off other bombs.'

Moone watched Lacroix as he turned and stormed up the street, his phone to his ear, then turned to Butler. 'We'd better start knocking on doors.'

'OK,' she said and climbed out.

They both hurried towards the houses on either side of the one with the bomb.

'By the way,' Butler said as she opened the gate of one of the houses. 'I've got some more bad news.'

Moone stopped dead. 'What is it?'

A coach rumbled as it turned into the street. There were several armed officers following it, hurrying in their direction.

'She was found not guilty,' Butler said.

Moone stared at her, trying to take in her words. He couldn't think about that now. He nodded and hurried towards the door of the neighbour's house. His mind raced, his stomach sinking in quicksand as he rang the bell.

'Clear!' a shout rang out in the street.

Moone turned to see one of the Bomb Disposal team standing out the front of the house wearing a heavy green EOD suit, his arm in the air, giving a thumbs up.

Moone breathed out, his body still trembling. The door to the house opened and a woman looked out at Moone, eyebrows raised.

'Hello?' she said. 'I hope you're not selling anything.'

He smiled, then shook his head. 'No, sorry. Think I've got the wrong house.'

He turned around and headed back down the path and closed the gate behind him. Butler was waiting for him and they headed back to where Lacroix was leaning against their vehicle, arms folded.

'Has the bomb been disarmed?' Butler asked and stood, hands on hips in front of him.

'It has.' He straightened up. 'I've just received word that a few other devices have been found in homes that had visits from a man who said he worked for Preston Plumbing. The devices vary in size and the amount of explosives, but safe to say if they'd gone off, then it would have been devastating.'

'That's good news,' Butler said. 'But what about all the other homes he might've visited? There could be loads of bombs waiting to go off.'

Lacroix's jaw was grinding as he nodded. 'I'm aware of that, DI Butler. That's why we're thinking of putting out an appeal for anyone who's had work carried out by him.'

'But if he sees that appeal, then he could set off the bombs,' Moone said.

'Have you got a better idea?' Lacroix said, an edge to his voice as his cold grey eyes burned out to Moone. 'Because right now, I'd love to hear it.'

Moone let out a shaky breath. 'No, I don't. But we need to hold off on that.'

'We don't even know when he's set the bombs to go off,' Butler said with a huff as she rested her backside on the car and folded her arms.

'No, we don't,' Lacroix said. 'It could be any date that has relevance to him…'

'Or the *Akashic Record*,' Moone said with a shrug.

'Our people have been through that,' he said. 'We didn't find any relevant dates in it that are coming up. There must be something, some date that had significance to him. Did he mention any dates to you, Moone?'

They were both looking at him, waiting, so he ran it all through his mind, everything he and Abel had talked about. He couldn't come up with any dates. He shook his head. 'No, nothing. Sorry.'

As Lacroix started talking, he wondered what the date had been the night he and Abel, or Harper, met as kids all those years before. He took out his phone to call Kelly to see if she had any idea what the date might have been. He looked at his phone. The date caught his eye. September 10th.

He froze, staring at it, as it dawned on him. Shit.

He looked up. 'Tomorrow. I think he's planning on setting them off tomorrow.'

'Why?' Butler asked.

'Oh fuck,' Lacroix groaned as he took out his phone. 'We've been bloody slow on this one. 911. Jesus Christ.'

Lacroix looked at Moone. 'Did he mention 911 at all?'

Moone stomach knotted. 'He did. He did mention it. He said how he's been studying what happened that day and how he thinks other events in the past altered when it happened. You know, like the Mandela effect? I don't understand it, but he believes that when the Twin Towers came down, it had some kind of catastrophic effect on time or something. I don't know, but, yeah, I'm pretty sure he's planning on setting them off tomorrow.'

'Like I said,' Butler muttered. 'Just another crazy bastard.'

Lacroix looked at his phone again. 'So, if we're assuming he's got the bombs timed for midnight, we've got... ten hours to find the rest of the devices and disarm them.'

'Bloody great,' Butler said and straightened up. 'Ten hours until Plymouth goes through its second blitz and facelift.'

Moone was about to say something, but he heard his phone ringing and took it out of his pocket. It was an unknown number. His heart started to thump in chest, his hands trembling. He looked up at Butler.

'Who's calling?' she said, frowning.

'I don't know.' He answered. 'DCI Peter Moone. Who's this?'

'Hanna Martin,' a well-spoken voice said.

'Hanna Martin KC?' he asked as he turned and walked along the road.

'The very same. And you are DCI Peter Moone. I've heard a lot about you. I'm very sorry I had to tear you to pieces on the witness stand, but you left me with little choice.'

'What is this about? I'm in the middle of something.'

There was a pause on the other end. 'My client would like to talk to you.'

'Tell her I haven't got time.'

'She says that it's very important. Come to

the court, she'll be waiting in the conference room on the second floor. I hope we meet again one day, Peter Moone. No hard feelings.'

The call ended, leaving Moone to walk back to the car. The Major had gone. Butler was already peering at him, her eyes brimming with questions.

'Who was that?' Butler asked. 'I thought I heard you say Hanna Martin.'

He didn't look at her. 'I did.'

Butler let out a laugh that dissolved into a huff. 'Oh, I don't believe the balls on that cow. Is she reaching out to you?'

'She is.' He looked at her, thinking it over, wondering what was so important.

'You're not thinking of talking to her?'

He shrugged. 'She wants to see me at the Crown Court.'

Butler turned away, letting out another empty laugh. 'Bloody hell, Moone.'

'I need to see her anyway,' he said. 'Just to say to her... you know, to stay away.'

Butler faced him again, then pointed a finger at him. 'Then do just that. See her, lay it on the line, then bugger off.'

'I will.'

She kept staring at him, her face softening. Again, he could sense there was something else she wanted to say. Something had a grasp of his heart strings and was swinging on them. 'What is it?' he asked.

'Nothing.' She unlocked the car and climbed in. 'Come on, I'll drop you off.'

Butler pulled up outside the Plymouth Combined Courts building, switched off the engine, and sat for a moment. Moone turned and stared at the grey stone facade.

'Say your piece and get out, Moone,' Butler said. 'Don't let her back into your head.'

'I won't.'

He exhaled through his nose, then grabbed the door handle and stepped out. The air was warm, the street a little damp from an earlier late-summer shower. He adjusted his jacket and tie as he crossed the road, heading towards the entrance. He heard Butler start the car and turned to see it heading up the street towards the Guildhall.

Inside the court building, the security was the usual routine; he emptied his pockets, stepped through the scanner, and got his warrant card checked. The uniformed officer patted him down and gave him a good look over before he waved him through. Security was obviously a lot more rigorous since all the shootings and the bombs going off.

Moone took the stairs to the second floor, his footsteps echoing in the stairwell. He knew where he was going, and he knew, with a huge amount of regret, who was waiting for him.

He found the conference room, pushed

open the door and found Faith Carthew sitting at the table, a white polystyrene cup of tea in her hands. She looked up as he entered, a slow smile spreading across her face. She looked relaxed. At ease. Victorious.

'Wotcha,' she said, raising her cup in a mock toast.

Moone shut the door behind him, making sure he kept any emotions from his face.

'Isn't that how they greet each other in your neck of the woods?' she added, smirking. 'Sit down, Peter. Take the weight off.'

Moone pulled out a chair and sat opposite her. He didn't speak, just waited.

Carthew took another sip of tea, watching him over the rim of the cup. Then, finally, she set it down and leaned forward. 'Let's talk.'

'OK,' he said. 'Let's start with what I'm doing here. What's so important?'

There came the smile again. 'I might have slightly exaggerated the importance of the situation.'

He sighed and got up, the anger beginning to spread through his body. 'I thought so. I'm a bloody police officer, not someone who comes running when you call.'

'Please, sit down, Peter,' she said, her voice softening. 'I know you've been busy. Come on, we need to clear the air.'

He stared at her, then sat back down, arms folded. 'Go on then. Is this the part where you confess?'

'No, Peter. Because I'm innocent. I was just found not guilty, or haven't you heard?'

He laughed. 'Good one. So what happened to Maxine Rivers? Did she just disappear?'

'How am I supposed to know? There's a great deal of mystery surrounding the whole affair.' Carthew leaned in, looking conspiratorial. 'Her mobile phone magically appearing in my car for instance. Bravo, Peter. That was inspired. I never thought you had it in you.'

'I didn't do anything.' He kept his poker face on.

She smiled. 'Of course you didn't. You wouldn't want to get your hands dirty. So you must have had someone else to do it, someone who already had mucky hands. I think people underestimate you. I certainly did. That won't happen again.'

'I hope it won't, because I hope you won't stay in Plymouth.'

She raised her eyebrows. 'Not stay in Plymouth? Why wouldn't I?'

'Because of all this, this thing between us. It's got to end. Otherwise… I don't know what's going to happen, and quite frankly that scares me. So, please, Faith, just go somewhere else. Start a new life.'

She didn't say anything for a while, just looked at him with a smile on her lips. 'But I've got a new business going. I had to, since you got me fired from my last job.'

'You got yourself fired. Not me. Anyway, what new business?'

'That's for me to know. But I'm sure our paths will cross.'

He let out a breath, realising once again that his words had fallen on not only deaf ears, but utterly stubborn and psychopathic ones. Butler had been right as usual, it was a waste of time. 'I better go.'

'Why have you been so busy lately?' she asked, tilting her head to the side. 'Is it all those bombs going off and the shootings?'

He stood up. 'I can't discuss that. You're not a police officer, remember?'

'Oh, I know. But I'm still smarter than all of you. I think I've proved that.'

He stared at her as he stood there, wondering if she might have any insight.

'Go on, try me,' she said. 'I might be able to help.'

He looked towards the door, thinking it over. He sat down again.

'So,' she said, resting her elbows on the desk as she put her hands together. 'Tell me all about it.'

What the hell was he doing? He let out a deep sigh, dragging his mind back through it all. 'Where do I begin?'

'He likes to shoot and blow up his victims,

doesn't he?'

He nodded. 'Yes. We think he's planted several bombs around Plymouth. Probably in people's homes...'

'Why?' She stared at him.

'Why? Why is he doing it? He says he believes we're all living in a simulation, a kind of matrix, like the film.'

'I've seen it. I found it hard to stay awake.' She sat back. 'You realise he doesn't really believe all that, don't you, Peter?'

He raised his shoulders. 'I'm not sure if he does or not...'

'He doesn't. For him it's an excuse, a way to justify his blood lust. Does he have a history of violence?'

'Well, he had some trouble in the army.'

'The army, of course.'

Moone leaned forward. 'But being a former soldier, doesn't make him a cold-blooded killer.'

'No, but you said he had trouble in the army. I take it he injured or killed some innocent people?'

Moone sat back again. 'Yes, he did.'

Her eyes narrowed as she seemed to examine him for a moment. 'There's a note in your voice when you talk about him, as if you kind of feel sorry for him. Why is that?'

Moone forced out a laugh. 'I don't.'

'But there's something, isn't there?

Something between you?'

'We met when we were kids, apparently. My parents used to bring us here when we were kids. Once we stayed in a hotel near the Hoe. He was staying there too and in the middle of the night... well, I somehow ended up out of my room and walked into him at the moment he almost got taken off by a paedophile. Then he says he pushed the man down the stairs and he died. I think the hotel owners at the time covered it up because they had other illegal activities going on that they didn't want the police to know about.'

'Was he abused before that night?'

'I think so. I can't be sure.'

'Let's assume he was. Probably started before that night. If he was born a psychopath or had some kind of personality disorder, then the abuse he suffered as a child might have tipped him over the edge.'

'Jesus. I never thought of that.'

Carthew nodded. 'Of course not. So, he's reached out to you. That's interesting.'

'It is, considering he tried to blow me up not that long ago.'

'But he didn't, obviously, so what happened?'

'It's a long story, but he ended up disarming the bomb...'

'So, he saved you.'

Moone exhaled. 'He put me in danger in

the first place.'

'But then he saved you. You saved him once then he saved you. So, he's using this connection you have to his advantage.'

'Is he? How?'

Carthew smiled. 'It's just psychology. You're in charge of the investigation, you symbolise authority. He obviously hates any kind of authority, so he's trying to break you down, get inside your head.'

It was all starting to sound feasible to him. He leaned forward. 'How can you be so sure?'

She smiled again. 'It's what I would do.'

He nodded. 'OK. So how do I find him?'

'That's the easy part.'

'Is it?'

'Yes.' Then she stared at him, and he could almost feel her digging around in his brain. 'But it's also the most dangerous part.'

'Why?'

'Because he wants you to find him.'

Moone sat back and folded his arms. 'He might well do, but I still don't know how to find him.'

'He will have left you a few breadcrumbs. Do you have anything to go on?'

He looked down at his suit jacket, then looked up at Carthew. Her eyes lowered, staring at his pocket as she said, 'What is it?'

'A photo.' He reached into his pocket and brought out the evidence bag and placed it on the desk. 'It belonged to our killer. He's been carrying it around with him.'

Carthew leaned forward and stared at it, then looked up. 'The hotel where you met, by any chance? I take it you've tried there?'

'He blew it up.'

Carthew's smile stretched wider as she nodded. 'Of course he did. How did you come by this photo?'

'It was in the pocket of an MI5 agent who was sent to help us catch him. We had him in custody, but he escaped.'

'The MI5 agent is now dead, I take it? Killed by your killer?'

'That's right.'

Carthew gave a brief amused sound in her throat.

'What?'

'Well, he knew the MI5 agent had the photo, so he killed him because he knew the photo would then end up in evidence and in front of you. He's clever.'

Moone stared at the photo as he ran what she had said through his mind. It made sense, kind of. He looked up. 'Where do I find him?'

'Silly rabbit.' She sat back, smiling. 'It's all there. It's in the photograph. You can work it out, you're clever.'

He let out a laugh that crumbled. 'Well, obviously, I'm not very clever. So can you just tell me?'

'No. It's there, Peter Moone. You work it out. But I will give you a word of advice. A kind of warning.'

'What?'

She lost any signs of humour and her eyes seemed to grow darker, with more intent. 'I suggest you don't go there.'

'I have to.'

'Then you'll die. He means to kill you. You represent authority to him. He wants to destroy authority. The reason he disarmed that bomb was so you'd be even. Now he plans to kill you.'

'I don't think so. I think you're wrong about that. I think he thinks I'll understand…'

She sighed. 'Trust me, Peter. I understand him better than you. When you realise where he is, call Armed Response, then sit at home and drink a beer or have a coffee. Just sit this one out.'

'That's funny coming from you. I thought you'd be glad if he killed me.'

Carthew put on a look of shock. 'Oh, how could you think such a thing? I think the world is definitely more interesting with you in it. Besides, when I start my new business, you might come in handy.'

'What business?'

'You'll see.'

He shook his head. 'Please, whatever you're thinking of doing, do it somewhere else.

Otherwise... I feel like something bad's going to happen to one of us.'

She stared at him, that faint smile on her lips. 'No, I think I'll stay in Plymouth. I like it here. Now, you run along, take your photograph and go and figure out where he is.'

Moone reached out and dragged the photo back towards him, then gave her a long hard look before pushing himself to his feet. He couldn't bring himself to say any more, he felt all too exhausted suddenly, so he turned, opened the door and went to leave the room.

'Peter,' she called.

He let out another shaky breath, then looked at her, eyebrows raised.

She smiled. 'I'll be seeing you real soon.'

CHAPTER 26

All the way to his mobile home, he racked his brain to try and figure out where Abel, or Harper, or whoever the hell the crazy bastard really was, could be hiding. The photo in the evidence bag was on the passenger seat as he drove. He looked at the clock on the dashboard. They had roughly nine hours left to find all the bombs. *Shit*. He knew the team was going through all the traffic cameras to find out where he might have headed and what homes he visited, but even so, they had little time to find and disarm any bombs.

He drove into the caravan park, his eyes jumping to families that walked past, all smiles, kids holding buckets and spades or bodyboards. He parked up outside his home, then rested his head against the headrest for a moment, feeling like he could sleep for a month.

There was a tap on the window. He jumped and looked up to see Kelly's concerned face staring at him. He dredged up a smile from the murky depths of his soul, grabbed the photo, and then pushed open the door.

She stepped back as she said, 'You all right, Pete?'

'Yep,' he said, loosening his tie. 'You know me, top of the world. You OK?'

She narrowed her eyes at him, watching him as he headed up the steps into the caravan. He took off his jacket and tie then collapsed on the sofa, feeling the stifling warmth of the mobile home closing around him. The windows were open, but only a light breeze fluttered the net curtains.

'You look like death after it's been in the microwave,' she said, filling the kettle up.

'Thanks.'

'You need a nice cup of tea.'

He laughed, but it was dry and empty. 'What I need is a proper drink.'

'Don't get like Dad.' She tutted.

Moone hunched over, burying his face in his hands. His mind flashed back to the night in the Drake Inn – a blurry memory of flowered wallpaper, gaudy patterned carpets, then his parents collecting him from downstairs in the hotel. He looked up at Kelly as she put out two mugs.

'Do you think Mum and Dad knew?' he asked, watching her.

Her brow creased as she looked at him. 'Knew what?'

'That a man died in the Drake Inn all those years ago. Do you think they helped cover it up?'

She faced him, hands on hips, the same look of disappointment Mum used to wear. 'Do you really think Mum and Dad would help cover up something like that?'

'No, honestly, I don't. But I don't really know anything any more.'

She shook her head. 'The answer's no, Petey. Now, drink your tea. There's three sugars in it.'

'Three sugars?' He took the mug, staring at it as if it was on fire. 'Are you trying to rot my teeth?'

'It's good for shock. Go on, drink it.'

'But I'm not in shock.' He sipped it and grimaced. He didn't even like tea that much.

'Well, you're in something. You're shaking and I can practically see right through you, Peter Moone.'

He sighed. 'I'm fine. At least I will be when I figure out where the crazy bastard is.'

She picked up her tea and sat at the kitchen table. 'Aren't your lot tracking him down, or whatever it is they do?'

'Course they are, but we haven't got much to go on. He's like a ghost. All I've got is this old photo.'

He held it up, so Kelly got up, took it from him and sat down as she studied it. 'That's the hotel, isn't it? Where we stayed?'

'Ten points.'

'I take it you've checked there?'

Then he remembered, she didn't know. He took a breath. 'It's gone.'

She looked lost. 'It's gone? What does that mean?'

'He planted a bomb. It went off.'

She was staring at him, her mouth opening, her skin losing a little colour. 'Oh my God. Those people... the people I talked to... are they?'

He nodded. 'I think so. I'm sorry.'

'Why're you sorry? You didn't blow it up.'

He sat back, somehow not convinced it wasn't his fault. 'It started that night. This all began that night. I talked to... I just consulted with someone, and they reckon he might have been abused before that night, and that trauma added to some personality disorder, might have made him into a killer.'

Kelly sipped her tea. 'Well, I don't know about that, but I know you need to rest. Why don't you go and lie down?'

'Because I haven't found him yet.'

Kelly was about to say something else, but

thankfully he was saved by the bell, or at least the muffled ringing of his phone.

It was a number he didn't recognise, and once again his body stiffened as his heart burst into life. He took a breath then answered. 'DCI Peter Moone.'

'Moone, good.' It was Lacroix.

'Everything all right?' He stood up, looking round for his tie in case he needed to head back to work. 'I just popped back home…'

'It's fine. Have some rest. The good news is, we think we've found most of the bombs. We hope. As expected, they were set to go off at midnight…'

'Bloody hell.'

'There's something else.'

'Go on.'

'They've been sifting through the debris of the hotel he blew up. The one that used to be the Drake Inn. They think the bomb was set off in the lobby. Looks like someone entered wearing a bomb vest, then activated it.'

'Jesus. Who was it?'

'Well, it's hard to tell, but there was blood found, and some remains, so they'll be analysed. But they found an arm. There was a tattoo on the wrist. The same tattoo Harper had.'

'So he blew himself up? Why would he do that?'

'Well, wasn't that where it all started? In

that hotel? And think about it, he had all those bombs ready to go. What more did he have left to do? Maybe this was the grand finale for him. Doesn't that make sense?'

Moone walked over to the table and picked up the old, battered image of the Drake Inn. 'I guess it does. OK, thanks for letting me know.'

'That's OK,' Lacroix said. Then there was a pause. 'Thank you, Moone. You've been a great help. Now get some rest.'

The call ended. Moone stood there for a moment, staring at his phone, taking it all in.

'What?' Kelly asked, eyes wide. 'Not more bad news?'

'No. They think they've found most of the bombs. All of them I hope.'

She breathed out. 'Thank God for that.'

'And they found a body in the rubble of the Drake Inn. They think our suspect... he went in wearing a bomb and set it off.'

'So... he's gone?'

Moone shrugged. 'I suppose. Sounds like it.'

'Well, you shouldn't speak ill of the dead and all that, and excuse my bloody French, but thank fuck for that.'

Moone sat down again. The relief tried to flood through him, but his heart was still beating hard, half believing that Lacroix had delivered devastating news. He tried to shake himself out of it.

His phone was ringing again. It was Butler.

'Hello,' he said.

'Have you heard?' she asked, her voice distant, quiet.

'Lacroix just called. I'm finding it hard to believe it might all be over.'

'Me too. But I guess it all makes sense... sort of. I mean if this was the plot of a film or something, I wouldn't believe it.'

'True. But it's not. How are you?'

'Good. Think I might get very drunk tonight.'

'Sounds like a plan. You staying in or...'

'Chris is taking me out.'

He felt his heart being clenched again. The silence dragged on. 'I see. That's nice. I'd better go.'

'Moone... Pete...'

'I'll talk to you at work tomorrow.' He ended the call and sat there for a moment as a wave of sadness and loss washed over him, drenching him inside and out. He closed his eyes, absorbed the knowledge that he had lost her. No. He never had her to lose. She was with Chris. He should've been happy for her. He was happy for her. She deserved happiness and he didn't feel like he was somebody who could make someone else happy. No, it was better like this.

'You all right?' Kelly asked.

'What?'

'You were sitting there staring into space with a really weird look on your face.'

'I'm fine. I might lie down.' He dragged himself to his feet.

'I think that is the wisest decision of your life.' She looked at him, nodding as he headed for his bedroom.

'And Petey!' she called.

He looked at her. 'Yes?'

She tilted her head to one side, the sympathy oozing out of her. 'There's plenty more fish in the sea.'

He sighed. 'That's great.'

'I mean, look where you're living. Right next to the sea!'

As she laughed, he went into his bedroom and shut the door behind him. The room was stifling. He lay on the bed as he listened to the sound of kids laughing and screaming outside, seagulls squawking and hopping over his roof. Someone was cutting grass nearby. He closed his eyes and tried to blot it all out. He breathed deeply, calming his heart. It was over. He let out a breath, then breathed in more deeply. He let out that breath. He felt heavy, relaxed, children's laughter distant and soothing...

His eyes fluttered open and Moone found darkness had flooded his room. He rubbed the sleep from his eyes and sat up, trying to fathom where he was for a moment before he came to his senses. He stood up and stretched, listening to music playing somewhere and raucous voices drifting over the park.

He found his phone on the bed saw it was almost eleven p.m. His heart beat to life as he realised it was only an hour until the bombs were meant to go off. He sat, breathed deeply, telling himself that the Counter Terrorism team had it all in hand. He hoped.

Then his mind flickered with a recent memory, as if a fluorescent light was trying to come on in his skull. He kept seeing flashes of it. He'd been flying, travelling over the city. Not a real memory, but a dream he'd been having. He recalled seeing Smeaton's Tower and the Sound below. Then he was sitting with Butler at Devil's Point, eating ice cream, staring out at the water. He told her he loved her, but she didn't seem to hear him and stood up and started walking along the stony beach where a battered wooden boat was moored. He followed her but she climbed in the boat and started rowing away from him. He kept calling but she didn't look back, just kept rowing, getting closer to the large rocky shape beyond the Sound.

Drake's Island.

Moone's head jerked up, staring through the half-light to his closed door. He jumped up, pulled open the door and turned on the kitchen light. Kelly was snoring in the spare bedroom as he picked up the photograph. Then he saw it, not only the name of the hotel, The Drake Inn, but the shape that had been painted beside it. He'd been stupid. Before he thought it was a blob of paint or a word that had become faded away over time. It was the shape of the island, Drake's Island.

He looked at the time. Just gone eleven. His heart was thudding. He went through his thoughts, tried to make sense of them, put them in order.

What if that was what Abel was trying to tell him? That he'd been hiding out on Drake's Island. As far as he knew, it was abandoned, several businesses having tried to bring it back to life but failed.

What if?

He looked at the time again. Just under an hour until midnight. Could he go and check? How the hell would he get there so late at night? He could call Lacroix, tell him his theory, but somehow he felt the Major wouldn't listen to the fact that it had come to him in a dream. No. He needed to go himself.

He used his phone to Google local boat hire. Loads came up, so he started to ring a few of them. Most of them had answer phone messages, so he hung up. Then one of the numbers answered, a thick West Country voice came through.

'Dylan's boat hire and fishing trips,' the man said, sounding groggy.

'I need someone to take me to Drake's Island,' Moone said.

'There's tours around the island,' he said. 'You can't go on there at the moment. Closed to the public. Call tomorrow...'

'I need to go now. I'm a police officer. DCI Peter Moone.'

'Sure you are mate. Night...'

'Please. This is important. Life and death. I can pay, too.'

'How much?'

Moone scrambled for a monetary figure that might induce him to go along with his crazy plan. Then he remembered the five hundred quid he had bundled up and hidden at the back of the kitchen drawer. 'Five hundred quid?'

'Done. You better not be pulling my leg.'

'I'm not. I'm a police officer...'

'For five hundred quid, you could be Bob The Builder for all I care. I'll meet you down by The Ship pub in half an hour.'

Moone looked at the time. He'd have to break the speed limit, but he could make it. What the hell was he doing? Why didn't he call Butler? Because if Carthew was right and danger was awaiting him, then he didn't want to put her in harm's way. But chances were their killer was dead, blown up with his own bomb.

'I'll see you there,' he said, then ended the call. He hurried to the bathroom, threw water into his face and looked at himself, his tired eyes asking exactly what he thought he was doing. He took a shaky breath and went back out to the kitchen table and quickly left a note for Kelly to say where he was heading. Then he grabbed the wad of cash, his car keys and headed out.

Moone was panting as he ran towards the Barbican after he'd managed to find a parking spot on a grass verge. Some of the pubs were shut, some still had music thumping out of them, stragglers on the street were shouting and laughing. Young women wearing next to nothing tottered on their heels.

He jogged towards The Ship pub, scanning the street and the heated area outside. He had no idea what Dylan looked like, he realised and started moving towards a lad stood outside one of the bars, but a young woman staggered out of the Cider Press and grabbed the lad's hand. Shit. Had he been stood up?

'Hey!' a voice called out behind him, towards the harbour. Moone turned around and spotted a small red, white and blue striped fishing boat bobbing in the water. A young man with a sparse brown beard, dressed in a thick red hoodie, was stood at the wheel. He raised his hand as he shouted, 'You the copper?'

Moone went over to the railings as he took out his warrant card and held it up.

'Hang on,' Dylan said, as he touched the controls and the boat's engine rumbled as it came closer.

'Get on board,' Dylan said, so Moone climbed awkwardly over the railing and then jumped down onto the boat. The lad caught him before he went careering into a pile of nets that stank of fish. Moone steadied himself.

'You really a copper, then?' Dylan asked as he smirked, taking the wheel again and turning the boat around.

Moone showed his warrant card again and the young man gave it a fleeting glance.

'Cash?' he asked. 'Sorry, but fishing isn't paying that well these days.'

Moone brought out the wad of cash and handed it over. Dylan stuffed it in the pocket of his hoodie then steered. 'Right then, midnight at the oasis, it is.'

'What?'

'It's midnight. And you're going to the ball, Cinders.' Dylan laughed.

As the boat chugged and turned around, Moone took out his mobile phone. He stared at the time. It was one minute to midnight. 'Shit.'

'Something wrong, mate?'

'I hope not,' Moone said, staring at his phone as the clock hit midnight.

His heart pounding, Moone looked round at the Barbican and the lights of the city beyond it. 'I can't see any explosions going off, can you?'

'Should there be?'

Moone Googled the local news. Nothing. No bombs or random shootings. 'Thank God. Looks like they did it.'

'Did what?' Dylan asked.

'Never mind. Just head for the island.'

The small fishing boat rocked gently as it cut through the black water, the low rumble of the engine taking them into the vastness of the night. Moone was standing near the bow, a saltwater fret spraying up at him. He looked around and saw the Barbican's lights disappearing behind them, their faint glow now just a memory. Ahead, Plymouth Sound opened up like a fathomless mouth, and beyond it, a thick black shadow against the starlit sky, was Drake's Island, emerging from the horizon.

The warm summer night air was thick and still. The water beneath the hull reflected a little moonlight. But despite the calm, Moone felt the unease creeping in. The closer he got to the island, the heavier the feeling sat in his stomach.

Drake's Island. He'd never been there before, even though he had always meant to visit. Most people hadn't either. A place left to time and the elements, its old fortress walls cracked and weather-beaten. From the shore, it was a curiosity, something tourists admired from a distance. Up close, it was something else entirely. It was ominous, and it seemed to Moone as if it was waiting for him.

The island rose higher, blacker than the sea, the remains of the Victorian battery silhouetted against the night sky. Moone could just make out the dark outline of the tower, the narrow windows like vacant eyes staring at him. For centuries it had guarded the Sound, now it was little more than a husk.

The boat's engine sputtered, breaking the silence. Moone clenched and unclenched his hands at his sides. He didn't like any of it. Didn't like the way the night seemed to breathe around him, the air heavy with the smell of salt and seaweed. He had a bad feeling, that lingering sense of déjà vu.

'Almost there, mate,' Dylan called out. He was little more than a shadow beneath the dim navigation lights, his hands steady on the wheel.

Moone didn't respond. His eyes stayed fixed on the island. There were no lights, no signs of life, only the dark, jagged edges of stone and tangled brush. He thought about what waited for him out there.

'Take us in slow,' Moone said, his voice low.

Dylan gave him a look but just shrugged and obeyed. The rumble of the motor became a little quieter. The boat nudged forward, the current tugging gently. Moone's eyes never left the shoreline. The bad feeling was growing now, spreading out from his gut and curling around the base of his spine. He told himself it was just the isolation, the darkness, but something else gnawed at him.

A seagull cried in the distance, its call lost to the inky dark night. Moone's jaw tightened, his fists clenching. He couldn't shake the thought that whatever was waiting on that island, it had been waiting a long time for something or someone. *Was it him?*

'Best hold on to the rail,' Dylan said, as the boat chugged closer to the rocks.

Moone gripped the rail as Dylan steered them gently towards a jetty, the boat bumping gently against the tyres tied to the jetty's side, the dull thud echoing in the night. He cut the engine, leaving only the soft slap of water against the hull. The silence came closing in.

Dylan moved quickly, grabbing a rope from the deck and leaping onto the jetty. He looped the rope around a rusted mooring ring, yanking it tight.

Moone watched him from the bow.

'You sure about this, mate?' Dylan called, his voice cutting through the night, while his eyes drifted up to the dark outline of the island.

'Not many people come out here after dark. The place gives me the creeps.'

Moone didn't know how to answer the question as he wasn't sure at all. It was a warm night but still his body trembled and his teeth chattered a little as he climbed onto the jetty. It seemed much cooler on the island, a breeze rising from somewhere. He looked at Dylan. 'I'll be as quick as I can.'

Dylan snorted. 'No such thing on this island, mate. Time moves different out here.' He glanced up at the looming silhouette of the old fortress. 'You ask me, there's a reason no one wants it.'

Moone said nothing. He didn't believe in ghost stories, but still, the strange feeling in his chest and stomach hadn't eased off.

The island stood silent, the remains of its stone walls jutting out like jagged teeth. Ivy strangled the towers, the ruins hollow and blackened by time. Somewhere deep within, tunnels twisted through the bedrock, dark, endless, and empty. Or at least, they should be empty, Moone told himself as he stood there, listening out. Only the water lapping at the boat and the shore found his ears, and the occasional cry of a seagull.

Dylan finished tying off a second rope and stepped back, his eyes lingering on Moone. 'You've got my number if you need me. Although there's hardly any signal here.'

'It's all right, I'll be OK.' He paused, thinking it all over. 'If you hear anything... just go.'

'Like what?' The fisherman stared at him through the gloom.

'Gunshots. Anything really. Any signs of trouble. Just go.'

Dylan spat over the side. 'If you're not here in an hour, mate, I'm gone.'

Moone didn't bother arguing and just nodded. He couldn't blame the young man for not wanting to wait around in a place like this; he didn't want to be there himself.

He took out his phone and turned on the torch app, the beam cutting a narrow path through the dark. He climbed down from the short jetty and onto the stony ground. The rocks beneath his feet were slippery, the sea lapping lazily up at them. The boat shifted behind him, the ropes groaning. Dylan lingered just long enough to watch him go, then turned away, lighting a cigarette with cupped hands.

Moone moved forward, ignoring the urge to find his fags. Each step brought him closer to the fortress, its crumbling facade towering above him, black against the deep blue night sky. The air was thick with the pungent stench of the sea and the deep scent of damp earth. He shone his torchlight over the rocky ground and up at stone buildings in front of him. It was quiet, far too quiet for him. He could feel himself trembling as he followed a crumbling path around the island, his torchlight bouncing over the ground and up at the buildings, dispersing the shadows briefly.

He saw one of the larger stone buildings, its doors open, and headed for it. He jumped a little, his heart racing when a screeching seagull appeared above. He took a breath and continued to the building. He stood in the open doorway, feeling a breeze twisting through from the broken windows high above. There was a cracked concrete floor beneath his shoes, grass and weeds sprouting through. Cobwebs covered most of the corners. Then his eyes fell on the old, battered table at one end and the tarpaulin draped over it. He looked around into the shadows as he moved, taking short steps towards the table and what looked like a large metal cupboard on the other side. He swept the torchlight over the room again, making sure no one was hiding in the dark, then pulled back the tarpaulin.

Before him, lying on the table was a large collection of metal tubes, wires and pieces of electronic equipment. He was no expert, but to him they seemed like parts of a bomb. He shone the torch over to the metal cupboard. There was a small bolt on the door, so he went over and pulled it across. It screamed into the night, making him shudder. The doors creaked open and he looked into the almost empty space.

There were pieces of paper and an ID. He picked it up and saw, as a harsh breath escaped his lips, a photo of Harper staring up at him. The name said Adam Morten. A fake ID. Then it dawned on him. It was an ID for CabTV, a local internet and cable TV company.

Shit. Not only had he been into people's homes pretending to be a plumber, he'd also masqueraded as an internet repair man. Oh shit. There could be more bombs out there. He turned off the torch, leaving the darkness to swallow him again, then brought up the station's number. He tried to ring, but nothing happened. No signal.

'You won't get a signal in this place.'

The voice echoed around the stone room. Moone almost dropped his phone.

'Who's there?' he said. 'Dylan?'

There were footsteps. He turned the phone round and hurried to turn on the torch light. He shone it over the broken flooring, the weeds, until he saw two heavy boots and camouflage trousers. He raised the light up the man's body as he started to shake, knowing who was standing there but not wanting it to be true.

CHAPTER 27

Abel blinked into the light as he held an assault rifle, cradled in his arms, the muzzle pointed to the floor.

'It's OK, Peter,' he said, holding up one hand to the light. 'I'm not a ghost.'

Moone lowered the torchlight a little, his chest tight and his pulse throbbing in his ears. 'They found your body in the wreckage of the Drake Inn.'

He stepped closer. 'No. They found the body of a homeless man, the same kind of build as me. I paid him to let me tattoo his wrist. I put a vest stuffed full of explosives on him, as well as a few packs of my blood I'd stored up. It was enough to fool them for a while. And you.'

'They've found the bombs you planted when you pretended to be Ryan Preston.'

He smiled. 'Of course. All timed to go off at midnight.'

'911,' Moone said, his eyes scanning the ground for anything he could use as a weapon.

'That's right. Took you all long enough to work it out.'

'What about the other ID? Adam Morten?'

Abel's eyes jumped to the cupboard and back to Moone. 'That's how I got into the other homes, where I planted the bombs you've yet to find.'

'If there are other bombs, why didn't they go off?' Moone gripped his phone tighter, his brain scrabbling around for a solution.

'911 didn't happen until 13:46, our time. The other bombs were just a distraction.'

Jesus Christ. 'Why? You must know this isn't a simulation. This is real and thousands of people could die...'

'Will die. And we'll watch it happen from here. We've got a perfect view.' He took out a mobile phone and held it up. 'No timer this time, just a good old phone signal.'

Moone didn't know what to say as the crazy, deranged eyes of Abel stared back at him. He tried to delve into his brain to drag back some kind of psychological... something to help. 'Why me? I know about that night, how we met, but why do I get to watch this with you?'

'Because the program brought us back

together.'

'No, you did that. When you took Adam Morten's identity.'

He laughed, the sound of it reverberating around the stone walls. 'You think I planned that?'

'You didn't?'

'No. I randomly picked that place, that old people's home to find someone like Joy, someone who had what they call dementia. Dementia isn't real. What it really is, is a glitch. I wanted to see what she remembered before and after 911. I tested her. She remembered things how it used to be before the towers came down. It was proof that I was right… but imagine my surprise when she talked about the hotel. The Drake Inn. And about the two boys and the man who died, pushed down the stairs. The murder she helped cover up.'

Moone shook his head. 'It's just coincidence. Plymouth is a small place.'

Abel lifted the gun. 'I know you don't believe, so I'll prove it to you.'

'Prove what?'

'That you and I are outside the matrix. It doesn't have control of us, and we're not affected by its idea of life and death.'

Moone stepped back when Abel drew out a revolver from his jacket. He held it up so Moone could see, then opened up the chamber and slipped one bullet into it. Then he spun it, smiling as he said, 'Don't be afraid.'

'What the hell're you doing with that?'

Abel turned the pistol in his hand, holding the butt out to Moone. 'Russian roulette. You know how to play. You put the gun to your temple and pull the trigger. There's only one bullet.'

Moone nearly threw up. 'I'm not going to do that. That's crazy. It's suicide. No, actually… it'll be murder.'

'Take the gun or I'll just prove my point by trying to shoot you.'

Moone stared at the silver gun being held out to him. He didn't have much choice, he decided, as he raced to come up with a way to escape. With a trembling hand, Moone put his fingers around the gun, then brought it back towards him. It felt heavy. He looked down at it, then up at Abel as he shook all over. The room had grown cold, his teeth chattering.

'Now, you put it to your temple,' Abel said, nodding, egging him on with his wild eyes.

Moone didn't move, his arm refused to lift it.

Abel shook his head and lifted his assault rifle and pointed it at Moone. 'Shall I test my theory?'

Moone took a deep shaky breath. His heart beat like mad as he lifted the gun. He felt tears threatening to come to his eyes. He had to say something, anything. He grasped hold of the first thing that came to him.

'It wasn't the first time, was it?' he said. 'That night, in the hotel.'

'Put it to your temple.'

Moone put the cold muzzle against his head. 'It wasn't the first time someone did something like that to you, was it? They abused you before, didn't they?'

Abel stared at him, seeming to lose his look of supreme confidence in what he was doing. 'You can't play games with me, Peter. Now, squeeze the trigger.'

'I can get you help.'

'I don't need help. I need you to pull the trigger or I pull mine. My rifle is full of ammunition. Your gun has one bullet. The odds are in your favour. Don't be afraid. I promise you, you'll be OK.'

'No, I won't! I'll die!' Moone shouted as the gun trembled.

Abel came closer, his wide eyes burning into Moone's. 'You won't die! Look at me! Keep looking into my eyes. Squeeze the trigger… slowly.'

Moone fought to keep the tears from his eyes as the thump of his pulse deafened him to everything else. He put his finger around the trigger, staring into the mad eyes that watched him like a child watching a magic show.

'Do it!' Abel growled, pointing his gun at him.

'Oh God, oh God, please...' His body trembled as he squeezed the trigger tighter. He let out a howl through gritted teeth as he pulled it harder.

Alice.
Butler.
Butler...
Click.

He let out a pant, a harsh and heavy breath as his entire body shuddered. *Oh God. Oh fuck.* He bent over, the gun hanging at his side as he panted.

'See? How easy was that?'

Moone raised his eyes, the relief washing away, leaving the thud and burn of anger. 'Easy? I'm sorry, but you're crazy. That was luck. Pure luck.'

Abel laughed. 'Oh, Peter. You don't understand. You still don't get it. Well, maybe the next go will convince you. Let's go again.'

Moone looked up at him. 'I'm not doing that again... I can't. Please don't make me do that again.'

The rifle was pointed at him again. 'Come on, Peter. You're tougher than this. You can do it.'

'Please. I have a daughter. A son. A toddler...'

'They're not real. Put the gun to your temple.'

Moone didn't move.

'Now!' Abel screamed.

Moone flinched. He raised the gun, the cold barrel finding his head. This time a tear escaped his eye and travelled down his face.

'Crying?' Abel said. 'Really? When will you realise? Now, pull the trigger. Go on, Peter, be brave.'

'Why're you making me do this?'

'Just do it!' The assault rifle was aimed at his head.

He closed his eyes. Please help me. Someone. He squeezed the trigger.

Click.

He blew out a shaky breath as the tears came. 'Oh, Jesus. Oh God… please, no more. I can't… I can't…'

Abel grasped the gun and yanked it from his hand. Moone staggered backwards, hitting the metal cupboard, banging his back on it as he saw the gun being turned on him. Abel was lifting it, pointing it at his head.

'Don't, please,' Moone begged. 'I know what you believe, but if you keep pulling that trigger, I'll die!'

Moone flinched, raising his hands to his face as he saw Abel's finger squeezing.

Click.

'Fuck!' Moone yelled, lifting his head to the dark ceiling. He realised that this was where he was going to die. They would find him, shot, lying in some tumbledown building. He shook his head.

'Are you getting it now?' Abel said, shaking the gun. 'Three down. Three to go.'

Moone looked at him and sniffed. 'That's enough.'

'No, it's not!' he shouted. 'It's not enough. It'll never be enough until you understand. We're special, you and I.'

The gun lifted, the dark barrel pointed at his head. This was it, his luck couldn't hold out any longer.

Click.

Moone stared at the gun, his chest beating. If the bullet didn't kill him, a heart attack would.

The gun was pointed again. Moone closed his eyes and saw Butler.

Click.

He opened them. One chamber left.

Moone shook his head as he saw the gun rising, wavering as it aimed. He focused on the wild, white eyes beyond it.

'Don't kill me! Please.'

Abel smiled. 'I won't. I'm about to break you out of the matrix.'

Click.

Moone stared at the gun, then looked at Abel. But then he felt his stomach lurch and he turned and threw up on the floor. He wiped his mouth and stared at the man still holding the gun.

'There were no bullets in that gun, were there?' Moone asked, his hands becoming fists. 'You put me through that as some kind of… sick joke.'

Abel closed his eyes for a moment and shook his head. 'Oh, Peter. Poor little Peter. In a lot of ways, you're still that scared and lost little boy, aren't you?'

Moone felt a pulse of anger beating through his chest. He was going to die here, he was sure of it. What did it matter any more? He stared at Abel. 'What about you?'

Abel raised his eyebrows. 'What about me?'

Moone straightened up, wiping his mouth again. 'If I'm still that little lost kid, then you're still…'

Moone stopped talking when Abel's eyes blazed, becoming wilder than ever as he pointed the assault rifle at him.

'What?' Abel demanded, a darker edge to his voice. 'Go on, what were you going to say?'

'Nothing.'

'No, go on.' He laughed, but it was an empty, dead sound. 'You were going to say I'm still that little boy being led away by an evil paedophile.'

'Evil? Do you believe in evil? If this is a simulation, some computer program, then how can he be evil? He doesn't even exist.'

'He doesn't!' he snapped. Then he stepped

closer. 'You don't remember the rest of that night, do you? When the parents put us in a room to play together, while they... you were crying, so I talked to you, and I asked you if you ever got that feeling that you're the only real person in the world, that everyone else is just... robots or something and they no longer exist when you can't see them...'

'Everyone thinks that at some point.'

Abel's dead eyes stared into him, rummaging around. 'You said you did. You said you thought nothing was real. It was all pretend. And that you and me, we were the only two that were real. Do you remember?'

Moone shook his head. 'I was just a scared kid. It didn't mean...'

'It did. It stayed with me. You started all this, that night.'

'Please tell me you didn't do all this because of something I said when I was a child. Please tell me that you're making this shit up.'

But Abel didn't say anything as he slung the rifle over his shoulder and lifted the revolver.

'Now what?' Moone asked, his heart pounding as he watched him open up the cylinder. He took out more bullets and slipped them into the gun's chambers, then closed it.

'Don't worry,' he said, smiling at Moone. 'We're not playing Russian roulette again.'

'Good. Thank fuck.'

Abel turned the gun round and held out the handle to him. 'Here. Take it.'

'Why?'

'There are six bullets in that gun. Six shots.'

Moone stepped back as the gun was being held out to him. This had to be some kind of trick.

'Take it,' Abel said again, shaking it. 'It won't explode. It's not one of my bombs. If you have it, then you can use it.'

'I'm not going to shoot anyone.'

'No, not anyone.' The mad eyes dug into him again. 'Me.'

Moone opened his mouth but nothing came out for a moment. He cleared his throat. 'I'm not going to shoot you either. Listen, it's not too late. You can give yourself up. Tell me where the bombs are.'

Abel pushed the gun closer to him. 'Take it. Now!'

Moone took another shaky breath and reached out his hand. He closed it around the handle and then lowered it down by his side. 'Now what?'

'You shoot me.'

'I'm not going to kill you.'

Abel rubbed his face as he shook his head. 'How many times, Peter? I'm not going to die. Those are real bullets. Six of them. Shoot me and you'll see.'

'No.' Moone thought he heard something outside. He looked out towards the doorway.

'Shoot me, or I shoot you.'

'But you said I won't die.'

Abel smiled. 'You won't. But you believe you will. I'm just trying to break you out of your closed-off mindset. There's no red or blue pill here. Only life and death.'

'Hello!' the voice echoed out to them both. Moone's heart raced even more. Dylan. He'd come looking for him.

'Oh, it's your boatman,' Abel said. 'I'd better get rid of him.'

'What do you mean?'

'Shoot him. What else?'

'No.' Moone raised the gun. It was trembling in his hand. He swallowed. 'Don't.'

'That's more like it. So, that's what it takes to turn Peter into a killer. Just threaten someone, a so-called innocent person and there he is, ready to take another person's life.'

'Hello?' Dylan's voice called. 'Are you there? Detective?'

Abel smiled, then turned his head a little as he called, 'We're in here!'

Moone took his chance and lurched forward, throwing his weight at Abel and knocking him sideways. He stumbled as Moone started running towards the open doorway. He could see a silhouette of someone coming towards him. Dylan. 'Run!'

'Where are you going?' Abel called out. 'There's nowhere to go.'

Dylan was now heading towards the jetty.

'Not that way!' Moone shouted and realised he still had the gun in his hand. 'He'll shoot us before we can get away.'

Dylan stopped running, frozen for a second, his eyes jumping between Moone and the boat.

'This way. Hurry,' Moone said and started running down the crumbling path that curved around the island. There was another longer and larger building on the other side. The barracks, he recalled reading. He started to run faster, glancing back to see Dylan hot on his heels. In the distance was the silhouette of Abel, the rifle in his hands as he stood watching them.

'It's an island, Peter!' he called out. 'There's nowhere to run to.'

Moone took another path that seemed to lead towards the barracks.

'Wait!' Dylan called so Moone turned to him, panting.

'You've got a gun!' Dylan said, pointing at it, his breath coming fast.

'I can't shoot someone,' he said.

'Give it to me. It's him or us. Who is he?'

'A killer. Is there anywhere we can hide?'

Dylan looked around, then pointed further along the darkened path. 'Down there.

There's some tunnels.'

Moone started heading into darkness, his chest heaving, the pounding of blood in his skull. Dylan was behind him in the dark, his breath harsh.

'Maybe we can somehow circle back round to the boat,' Dylan said as Moone turned to his left. He could make out another set of doors and headed to them. He tried to open them but they were heavy and refused to move.

'Don't be afraid to use that gun!' Abel called into the night. A seagull cried out as it flew over their heads.

Dylan grabbed hold of the door too and they scraped it towards them, the screech of it echoing into the night. Inside there was a long but narrow corridor, with rooms on either side.

'Down there somewhere,' Dylan said, pointing at the darker end of the corridor. 'There's a hatch, I think.'

Moone turned when he heard Abel's footsteps behind them, his mind changing course, veering away from his own safety to the people, the families back on the mainland. Abel had a phone in his pocket, ready to set off the devices.

Moone stopped, making Dylan bump into him in the dark.

'Keep moving!' the fisherman whispered, his voice tense. 'He's coming.'

'He's got a mobile phone, he's going to use

it to set off the bombs.'

'So? Let's hide. I want to live through this.'

'There's no phone signal. How's he going to set it off if there's no signal?'

'There is.'

'What?' Moone stared up at the dark, charcoal shape of Dylan's face.

'On the other side of the island, you have to climb up on top of one of these old pill boxes. I managed to get a signal there anyway.'

Moone heard the footsteps coming, his heart racing. He looked at the shape of Dylan's face again. 'You hide. I need to do something.'

'What? Don't be stupid.'

'Just go down there, he'll follow me. Go!' Moone jogged back towards the sound of the footsteps, bringing up the gun and aiming it at anything that moved in the dark.

'Oh there you are, Peter,' the voice called, drifting from somewhere. 'Where's your friend?'

Moone saw the blurry lights of Plymouth across the Sound.

'Go on then, shoot me, Peter.'

He scanned the darkness. His eyes jumped to a shape emerging from the shadows.

Moone turned and started running again, his vision bouncing, his breath panting out of him as he followed the crumbling path around the island. The dark shapes of the building loomed overhead. He couldn't see the pill box anywhere. Where the hell was it?

'Where are you going, Peter?'

Moone stopped moving, his chest squeezing around his heart as his breath pounded into the night. He looked up and saw the stars in the sky. The footsteps were coming closer. He looked around, scanning the terrain. There it was, the rectangular block shape of it. He started running for it, looking for a way to climb up to the top.

'What are you up to now?' Abel called out, now closer.

As Moone rushed around the back of the pillbox, he saw that some of the concrete had crumbled away from the corners, leaving several clumps of stone jutting out, forming a crude set of steps. After he rested the gun on the ledge above him, he grasped hold of the stone, found a foothold and pushed himself up. His leg slipped, the concrete crumbling away.

He found another foot and handhold, gritted his teeth and pushed himself up. He managed to get the top half of him up onto the ledge. He was breathing hard, almost ready to give up. No. He took a deep breath and scrambled, pushing with his other leg until he was scraping his knees and fingernails to get purchase. He did it. He lay on his front, panting, wanting to cry.

'What do you think you're going to do up there, Peter?'

Moone rolled over, searching for the gun in the dark, scratching around, blindly. His hand fell on the cold metal. He grasped it, clambered to his feet, and pointed the gun at the silhouette of Abel. The lights of Plymouth shone bright, reflected in the Sound. It looked so quiet and picturesque.

The gun trembled in his hand as he took out his mobile.

'I see,' Abel said, a touch of laughter in his voice. 'You've found the place to get a signal. Well done, Peter.'

There was a signal. Barely a couple of bars, but he would able to send a text or make a call. He called the station.

'Charles Cross Police…'

'Listen to me,' he said, the words tumbling out of his mouth.

'It's no good, Peter. I have my phone here. I can just set them off now.'

Moone was now able to make out his darkened face, the arm that came out holding his mobile.

Shit. Was there a signal down there?

'Hello?' the voice said on the other end. 'If this is an emergency…'

'This is DCI Peter Moone. There are more bombs planted around Plymouth. I'm on Drake's Island. Tell Major Lacroix. Abel's here with me…'

'Shall I set them off now, Peter? Or do you

want to end that call?' The green glow of the phone lit up his face.

Moone lowered the phone to the floor, leaving the connection open, then straightened up again, pointing the revolver at him. He was breathing hard, ragged breaths. 'You don't have any signal. You need to come up here to be able to make that call.'

'Do I? Are you sure?' The green face stared up at him. 'Come down and I won't have to set them off now.'

'You're bluffing.'

'Am I? Why don't you try and shoot me?'

Moone's gun hand was shaking as he raised it, aiming a little way from him. He started to squeeze the trigger, half convinced that the gun still wouldn't work. He had done something to it, some technical detail that meant he couldn't have shot himself. He closed his eyes.

He staggered back as his arm vibrated, the gunshot booming.

'It's got a lot of recoil, hasn't it?' Abel said, sounding amused.

Moone's ears were ringing, every sound around him muffled. His pulse was beating in his skull. 'The next one will hit you.'

'Will it? I don't think you've ever fired a gun before, and a revolver with that much recoil is hard to control. I'd use both hands if I were you, Peter.'

Moone put his other hand on the gun, gripping it, steadying the weapon as he aimed it closer to Abel. 'I don't want to kill you…'

'Don't worry, you won't.'

Moone looked up, a rumbling sound reaching his ringing ears. It was distant, echoing around the Sound.

'A helicopter,' Abel said. 'Did you tell someone you were coming here?'

He saw the chopper's lights and the dark shape coming closer.

'Well, looks like I've got no choice but to set them off,' Abel said, looking down at his phone. 'Maybe you'll understand after this.'

'Don't!' Moone aimed, half closing his eyes as he squeezed the trigger. The gunshot barked.

Abel was still standing, looking at the ground a couple of feet away. 'You're getting better, Peter. But you're not a killer. Time for Plymouth to fall and for us to be free.'

'No!' Moone shouted.

There came a growl or shout from the darkness, then a human shape flying towards Abel. They merged into the darkness, tumbling, shouting, limbs flying. Moone was trying to make out what was going on. Then he saw the phone glowing on the ground as the bodies rolled over the ground. Moone clambered down, racing towards the phone. He saw Abel on top of Dylan, drawing back his fists and hammering punches at him.

'I've got it!' Moone shouted.

Abel stopped and stared at him. The helicopter rumbled loudly overhead, the wind whipping the sea into a frenzy, the island alive with dust clouds.

'Give me that, Peter.' Abel climbed off Dylan and held out his hand. 'We can be free. Me and you.'

Moone stepped back, holding the phone in one hand, the gun raised in the other.

'Give me that phone, Peter.'

A voice called out across the water from a speaker, commanding anyone to drop their weapons. Two police boats were cutting through the water.

'Peter,' Abel said, stepping closer. 'It's not too late. Give me that phone and we can be free. Please.'

Moone edged closer to the sea, bringing his arm back.

'No!' Abel screamed, rushing forward.

Moone threw the phone and it fell, flipping over and over until it made a small splash.

Abel watched it, then spun round to him, grasping him by his shirt. 'What have you done?! We could've been free!'

Moone numbly watched as a sobbing Abel dropped to his knees.

One of the boats reached the island and armed officers jumped to the shore. They shouted commands, screaming for Moone to drop the gun. To kneel. He did it, throwing the gun behind him, and waited. The officers came in and grabbed all three of them, securing their hands behind their backs.

'Not him,' a familiar voice called out.

There she was, standing on the jetty, arms folded, shaking her head. Butler sighed as she said, 'He, believe it or not, is a copper. Let him go.'

One of the officers released him, so he went over to her and joined her on the jetty, watching the armed officers transport Abel off the island.

'Well, Moone,' she said, 'looks like you saved the day.'

'Not me. Dylan.'

'Who the bloody hell's Dylan?'

Moone pointed to the slender lad being put on the boat. 'He's a fisherman, brought me over.'

'You should've said. Oi, take the cuffs off the lad. He's not involved.'

The boat turned and roared off towards Plymouth, leaving them staring out at the lights of the city.

'Now what?' Butler asked.

'We go home. Go back to work. I lose my job.'

'Oh shit, I forgot about that. What will I do without you?'

He looked at her and saw her smiling at him. 'I keep meaning to tell you something…'

'It can wait until we get back, come on.'

Butler started heading towards the second police boat waiting for them. He watched her traipsing off. Maybe it wasn't the right time, he told himself. He was alive, and that meant he'd have another chance to tell her how he felt.

'Come on, stop faffing!' Butler shouted from the boat.

CHAPTER 28

The corridor was quiet, the hum of distant office chatter barely reaching Moone. Fluorescent lights buzzed overhead, casting a dull, clinical glow over the narrow corridor. He was leaning against the wall, hands stuffed into his pockets. His palms were damp. His fingers twitched, the last tremors of adrenaline refusing to let go of him. He kept seeing it all, playing over and over.

The hearing had gone exactly how he'd expected. They had nodded, frowned, scribbled notes. Their questions had been savage, their judgment in their disapproving eyes. It wasn't like he'd walked in there thinking he'd get a slap on the wrist, a brief telling off. But still, hearing it all, the not-so-polite, bureaucratic dissection of everything he'd done wrong…

well, it had hit harder than he'd thought it would. The sack was inevitable, he knew that, and had almost accepted it. He could almost feel the weight lifting, knowing it was all over. No more reports. No more politics. No more waking up in cold sweats, Abel's face burning behind his eyelids. No more drinking a bottle of vodka to get back to sleep. No more wondering if the next decision he made would end someone's life.

He'd survived, but the damage had been done. His hands trembled thinking about it all, how close he and thousands of people in Plymouth had come to dying.

But he was still here, still waiting. What the hell was he waiting for? Maybe for some faint sliver of hope. Perhaps just because he wasn't ready to face what came next, the search for another job and a new life. One thing was for sure, he wouldn't leave Plymouth.

He rubbed at the back of his neck, trying to massage some calm into himself, while the craving for a cigarette clawed its way into his throat. Christ, he needed a fag. He hadn't even managed to tell Butler how he felt. He'd stood next to her on that bloody island, the sea wind in his face, his heart pounding, and he'd said... sweet F.A. Coward. But next time he saw her, he'd say it. No excuses. No more faffing.

The squeak of shoes on the polished floor broke his thoughts. Major Lacroix strode down the corridor, all stiff-backed and composed, his uniform sharp and spotless. Moone straightened instinctively, the old reflex kicking in. Lacroix didn't slow until he was standing in front of him.

'Moone,' Lacroix said, extending his hand. 'Good to see you.'

'Major,' Moone replied, his voice coming out louder than he'd intended. He shook the man's hand, feeling his firm grip.

Lacroix gave a small nod. 'I wanted to congratulate you. What you did, what you stopped… it won't be forgotten. Not by me or my people.'

Moone said nothing. He didn't feel like a hero, only a man who'd been in the wrong place at the wrong time, doing what he could to keep the pieces from falling apart.

'And Dylan,' Lacroix said, his tone softening. 'The fisherman. Brave man. He'll get a medal for what he did.'

'He deserves it,' Moone said quietly.

Lacroix held his gaze a moment longer, then nodded. 'Good luck, Moone.'

Without another word, the Major turned and entered the hearing room, the heavy door clicking shut behind him. Moone stayed where he was, the emptiness of the corridor swallowing him up. The minutes dragged on, waiting for their judgement. He tried not to think, but it was impossible. He saw Abel's eyes, heard the crack of gunfire, felt the biting wind from the water. It was all still there.

When the door finally opened again, Lacroix stepped out. The rigid formality had eased from his shoulders. He paused, then walked straight up to Moone.

'I had a word,' Lacroix said.

Moone blinked. 'What? What do you mean?'

'You're a good officer, Moone. A damn good one.' Lacroix's voice was low. 'Sometimes the people in there forget what that means. I reminded them. Told them about the lives you saved.'

The words hit him, heavy and unexpected. 'What about my job?'

'You're still a police officer,' he said.

'Really? Thanks. I don't know what to say.'

'One thing though.'

'OK?'

Lacroix took a breath. 'They still wanted their pound of flesh. They wanted you gone, but they settled for a demotion.'

'Demotion?'

'You'll be back to plain old DI Moone, I'm afraid. You'll just have to fight a little harder to get back up there.'

Moone really didn't know what to say. The man before him, the man he took to be an unthinking... robot programmed to follow orders... had saved him. He felt like hugging him, but the cold grey eyes stared back at him.

'Thank you,' Moone said. 'Thank you so much.'

Lacroix gave a curt nod, then disappeared down the corridor.

Moone stayed rooted to the spot, his pulse thudding. Maybe it wasn't over. Not yet.

Moone grabbed a Get Well Soon card from WH Smiths in the hospital and a bottle of Lucozade, then headed for the ward where Keith Harding was being looked after. He was out of the woods, sitting up in bed and joking, or so he had been told by Chambers over the phone. He was relieved and loosened his tie as he climbed into the lift, squeezing himself against the wall as two porters brought a bed in.

He got out of the lift and headed to the ward and buzzed the entrance. When the doors clicked open, he stepped into the busy ward, the beeps of machines and the chatter of staff and patients filling his ears. There was a private room just off to the right, he'd been told.

As he got closer, he saw Chris was sitting on a chair outside, staring at his phone. Moone stood in front of him until he looked up. He smiled.

'Hey, it's the bloody hero,' Chris said, getting to his feet and shaking his hand.

'Not me, the real hero is a fisherman called Dylan. Where's Butler?'

Chris sat back down and nodded to the door opposite. 'Mand's in there. We've got to wait until people leave.'

Moone nodded and sat down next to him. 'It's nice she lets you call her Mand. If I did, she'd rip my balls off.'

Chris laughed. 'She's always been Mand to me. Even at school, all those years ago. She was really... you know, cool back then.'

Moone stared at him. 'Really?'

'Yeah, she didn't take any shit off anyone.'

Moone laughed. 'Nothing's changed, then.'

'I liked her back then, but I always bottled out of telling her. Then when I saw her on Facebook. I thought, why not?'

Moone tried to smile.

Chris sat back. 'I really like her. I haven't liked anyone seriously since... well, since my marriage went tits up. But Mand's different.'

'She's definitely different.'

Chris nodded. 'I wouldn't want to be without her now.'

Moone stared at him as he went back to scrolling through his phone, feeling like all his organs were melting through the floor.

The door to the bay opened and Butler came out. Her eyes jumped to Moone, widening. 'So? What happened?'

'I'm still a detective.' He shrugged.

'See? What did I say? You were worrying

over nothing. You should've heard him, Chris.'

'But it means a demotion.'

Butler gasped. 'A demotion? Really?'

'DI.'

Her eyebrows rose, almost off her head. 'No! Oh God. That means three of us will be detective inspectors on the team. Shit. They won't want that. They'll move one of us!'

Moone stood up. 'Let's deal with that later. At least we're all in one piece and they found all the bombs.'

'How did they find them?' Chris asked, standing up.

'They managed to find the van he used,' Butler said. 'They were able to track his movements and locate the bombs. If they'd gone off... well, would've been the blitz all over again.'

'It was a close call,' Moone said with a sigh.

'Oh, by the way,' Butler said. 'I just got word that Jim Loughty, the prison guard was found on Dartmoor. Shot. Execution-style. Looks like the cow has struck again.'

'Bloody hell...'

'You coming in?' Chambers said, poking her head around the door.

Moone nodded and headed into the private room, trying not to think about Carthew and what she might have planned.

The next day, Moone and Butler were sitting

in the car park at Jenny Cliff, with the cafe on their right. It was busy as usual. The seagulls were riding the thermals, squawking about something. The sun was bright and warm, giving one last burn of energy before the autumn arrived for its shift.

Moone took the top off his coffee and blew on it.

As Butler copied him, she said, 'Do you ever wonder if he was right?'

Moone looked at her, confused. 'Who?'

'Abel… Harper, whatever he's really called. What if this is all a simulation or something? Every time I look online, some scientist is going on about how we could be part of a computer program. Makes my head ache.'

'Nah.' Moone sipped his coffee. 'This isn't a simulation. A computer couldn't come up with all this.'

She nodded. 'True. And I don't think a computer would make a man who faffs quite as much as you.'

He stared at her. 'I saved the day! Well, Dylan did, anyway. But I ran on that island, ran like the wind…'

'Yeah, yeah. I'd like to have seen that.' She leaned forward. 'Let's have some music on.'

The radio crackled to life.

'This is BBC Radio Plymouth, and this is Majesty with Gypsy Reverie…'

'I love this song,' Butler said. 'It's a shame

Teddie Neptune died so young.'

The song started playing:

'Is this the world I know, or just a waking dream? Lost in a facsimile, no way back to reality...'

They stared at each other. Butler turned off the radio, then sat back. 'That doesn't mean anything.'

'No.' He sipped his coffee, then they both laughed. 'I suppose we'd better get back to work.'

Butler nodded, set her coffee in the holder, and started the engine. She glanced at him and smiled.

His chest burned inside. He thought about trying to say how he felt again, but Chris' voice came back to him, how happy he'd sounded.

It was enough to be near her, he decided, as she eased the car into reverse.

He had survived. That meant time, more of it... for the two of them.

He turned his face to the window, watching the road slip by.

Then Carthew's words came back to him. *I'll be seeing you soon.*

A thinly veiled threat. Let her come, then. He wasn't going to run and hide. Whatever happened next, Butler, or Plymouth for that matter, wouldn't be rid of him.

He wasn't going anywhere.

GET TWO FREE AND EXCLUSIVE CRIME THRILLERS

I think building a relationship with the readers of my books is something very important, and makes the writing process even more fulfilling. Sign up to my mailing list and you'll receive two exclusive crime thrillers for FREE! Get SOMETHING DEAD- an Edmonton Police Station novella, and BITER- a standalone serial killer thriller.

Just visit markyarwood.co.uk

or you can find me here:

https://www.bookbub.com/authors/mark-yarwood

facebook.com/MarkYarwoodcrimewriter/

@MarkYarwood72

DID YOU ENJOY THIS BOOK?
YOU COULD MAKE A DIFFERENCE.

Because reviews are critical to the success of an author's career, if you have enjoyed reading this novel, please do me a massive favour by leaving one on Amazon.

THANK YOU

Reviews increase visibility. Your help in leaving one would make a massive difference to this author. Thank you for taking the time to read my work.

ACKNOWLEDGMENTS

My heartfelt thanks to Inspector Paul Laity for his invaluable advice on police matters.

Thank you to Edie Yarwood. I am also deeply grateful to the Plymouth Mariners baseball team for the great honour of letting me pitch the first ball of the season.

Finally, my love and thanks to my family, my wife, my daughter, Mittens, and my mum, dad, and brother.

Printed in Dunstable, United Kingdom